CASTLE
IN THE
MOUNTAINS

Mission 2 of the Castle of Spies Series

TD COCHRAN

Castle in the Mountains

by TD Cochran

Missoula/Billings, Montana USA

© 2018

This paperback/e-book is an original work solely by the author.

References to other works of fiction, TV shows and movies are respectfully used to create the mood of this story and are covered under Fair Use Copyright Laws.

Library of Congress: 2018903200

ISBN: 978-0692089378

"AN ENTERTAINING RIDE! T.D. COCHRAN PUTS THE CHEEKY FUN BACK INTO THE SPY GENRE!"
- JAMES SVED, HERALD DE PARIS

CASTLE IN THE MOUNTAINS

is

MISSION TWO

of The Castle of Spies Series

~ ~ ~

MISSION ONE:

is

CASTLE ON THE ISLAND

and is available on:

Amazon.com

For …

My Mom, My Dad & My Sister
My Best Friends, Tara, Meghan and Stephanie
My Spy Story & Spy Flight Friends

With Admiration and Gratitude to the Authors & Producers who
came before …

Ian Fleming, John LaCarré, Len Deighton,
Harry Saltzman, The Broccoli Family, Bruce Geller and Veronica
Roth

… also …

The Amazing Musicians who help create the 'mood'.

And with Respect to…

The real world spies and analysts who work day after day, but don't
get to have as much fun as Léa & Tara.

T.D. Cochran
Billings, Montana USA - 2018

CONTENTS

PROLOGUE—Best Friends   1

PART 1: BACK TO THE CASTLE

1   Riding Home in the Rain   4

2   First Morning Back   9

3   The Range   13

4   Ale at the Pit   17

5   A Total Waste of Time   22

6   Another Waste of Time   28

7   Top of The Castle   33

8   Some Movies Can Help   37

9   Any More of That Ale?   41

10   The Next Morning   47

11   Late For Lunch   51

12   Hacking the Bad Guys   61

13   Closing the Dungeon   70

14   Off to The Pub   75

15   High Tech Trouble   77

16   A Ping   82

PART 2: 1991, MISSION TO MOSCOW

17   Janet and Helena's 1st Three Weeks   85

18   Scavenger Hunt   91

19   It's Called The Internet   99

20   Playing to Win   108

21   The Last Clue   112

22 August 19, 1991   119

23 The Lubyanka   127

24 Cell 313   135

25 Escape From Moscow   142

PART 3: THE COLD TRAIL

26 That Ping   150

27 Movie Night   155

28 Gear Up   162

29 The Maze   165

30 Main Street at The Castle   173

31 The Control Room by the Hill   181

32 The 757   184

33 Hard Lessons   195

34 Out in the Cold   202

35 Another Ping   204

PART 4: CASTLE IN AUSTRIA

36 Stuck on a Train   208

37 Werfen   211

38 Out the Window   218

39 False Trail   223

PART 5: A LODGE IN MONTANA

40 First Priority, Pizza   228

41 On The Run   233

42 Hopping The "L"   240

43 The Train West   246

44 Coffee at the Spyhouse   253

45 Dinner and Drinks   256

46 Glacier Ghosts   261

47 Ripped Apart   265

48 Just a Little Screwed   271

49 Movie Files   275

    EXTRA: Tara's Playlist   281

    EXTRA: Léa's Links   282

    EPILOGUE: An Unusual Meeting   283

PROLOGUE—BEST FRIENDS

Edinburgh Waverley to London Train
(Ten Years After Our Story Begins)

"How did we get talked into this?" said Léa Taylor to herself.

She looked up to see the train was just coming to a stop at London's famous King's Cross Station. Léa and her best friend Tara Wells would soon take a 16 minute ride on the Tube to Leicester Square station. From there, it was only a six minute walk to Trafalgar Square and a bomb.

A nuclear bomb.

Léa looked over at Tara who was looking down at her computer. Leaning next to Tara's shoulder, Léa saw Tara was researching nuclear bomb design.

"How did we get talked into this?" said Léa softly.

"We didn't. We were ordered here," said Tara dryly.

"Oh. Yeah," said Léa.

The train coasted to a stop. Tara snapped her laptop closed and stood up. Léa looked up at her best friend and sighed.

"When we pull this off, I want another two weeks in Mykonos," said Léa.

She stood, slipped on her backpack and looked at Tara.

"They're paying," she said simply.

"Deal," said Tara with a slight smile.

The two women quickly left the train, walked down the platform and turned to the stairs leading down to the tube station. A lone police officer stood in their way.

"And just where do you girls think you're going?" he said.

Tara gave him her best 'don't fuck with me' look. Léa watched as the officer started walking toward Tara. She looked up, took a deep breath and smiled at the officer.

"It's okay officer. We're expected," said Léa.

The officer stopped a few steps away from Tara, looking her over. As usual, she was dressed in black from head to toe. Black boots, black commando pants and a black leather jacket. By contrast, Léa was dressed in blue jeans, running shoes and a colorful sweater.

"You are huh?" said the officer.

"We're from The Castle," said Tara.

"No. You?" said the officer genuinely shocked.

"That would be us," smiled Léa.

The officer looked the two young women over for a few moments, then cleared his throat.

"Don't you have something to show me?" he asked.

Tara and Léa looked at each other briefly, then stretched out their right arms. Tugging on their jacket sleeves revealed a small brass bracelet with a single word stamped into the metal. Tara's said:

GOTH

Léa's said:

STRIPPER

The officer pulled out his note pad and flipped a few pages. Looking back down at the bracelets, he shook his head and looked up.

"Okay then," he said.

The officer stepped aside and motioned for the two women to pass. His face had turned ash gray.

Léa glanced back at the officer over her shoulder as they passed. After they started down the stairs, she looked at Tara.

"He didn't seem all that confident in our bomb defusing skills," she said.

"He didn't say much about our new jewelry either," said Tara.

"Maybe he would have liked them if they had some numeric code or something," smiled Léa.

Tara shrugged as she took off on a run and jumped over the fare collection barriers. She quickly spun around on one heel, then flipped the bird to the nearest security camera. Léa cleared the turn-style with a running jump too. She smiled as she landed by Tara.

"I have always wanted to do that," said Léa.

"And the best part is, we'll get away with it too," said Tara with her slightly sarcastic smile.

The two women turned and started walking toward the platform. An empty train was waiting for them and quickly departed once Léa and Tara were aboard. Looking straight ahead, Tara broke the silence.

"Nervous?" she said.

Léa shook her head slowly and took a deep breath. She looked at Tara.

"Trying not to think about it," she said.

"I think we'll be okay," said Tara.

"Glad you're more confident than the Bobby back there," said Léa.

"Fuck him," said Tara as she lifted the lid on her laptop and pointed to the screen. "This is the basic design of any bomb. Chances are this one has a few land mines. But if we're careful, we should be okay."

Léa looked over the diagrams displayed on Tara's computer. After a few moments she reached over Tara's arm and scrolled the screen down a bit.

"Do we have any pictures of what's actually there?" asked Léa.

Tara tapped a few buttons and a montage of pictures appeared. There was a wide shot of Trafalgar Square with one of the lions circled in red. The next shot was of a lion sitting on it's pedestal, the dedication plaque laying on the ground and the hole in the pedestal. The last few pictures were of a black travel suitcase hidden in the pedestal. Finally there was one picture of what was in the suitcase.

"I guess we'll be okay if we go slow," said Léa.

Tara snapped the lid of her laptop closed as the train slid quietly into the station. The doors quietly opened and Léa and Tara stepped out on the deserted platform.

"Let's go," said Tara.

As the two women emerged from the station, they started down the sidewalk that would take them to Trafalgar Square. The street, the shops, everything was deserted.

"How did they clear everyone out without creating a panic?" asked Léa.

"Said it was an annual emergency response exercise," said Tara.

As they continued walking down the sidewalk, Léa glanced through the window of one of the shops. She suddenly stopped and pointed to the window.

"I have always wanted one of those," said Léa.

"We're about to go defuse a bomb and you want to go shopping?" said Tara.

"Priorities," smiled Léa as she walked on.

Soon, they emerged from the street and a deserted Trafalgar Square lay before them. Tara reached into her pocket, pulled out her iPhone and snapped a picture.

"I don't think we'll ever see it like this again," said Tara.

The normally crowded square was completely deserted. Except for all the birds, of course. Tara pointed to one of the lions perched on it's stone pedestal.

"That's our kitty," said Tara.

The two women walked up to the lion, unslung their backpacks and knelt down in front of the hole. Both took a deep breath, then looked at each other.

"Ready?" asked Léa.

"Ready. You?" said Tara.

Light rain began to fall from the gray clouds hanging over the square.

"Yeah, let's get this done. I need some Aegean sunshine," said Léa.

PART 1: BACK TO THE CASTLE

1 RIDING HOME IN THE RAIN

Stromness, Orkney
(Ten Years Earlier)

~ ~ ~

PLAYLIST:
"Waking UP" - Oblivion - M83

~ ~ ~

A lone, black motorcycle sped down the narrow two lane road leading north out of the town of Stromness on the Scottish Island of Orkney. Clouds hung low on the horizon as a light rain began to fall. Water began collecting on the road. But the motorcycle continued to accelerate. Tara's graphite-black motorcycle was built for speed and she never missed a chance to run it wide open.

Léa inched up just enough to look over Tara's shoulder and down at the motorcycle's speedometer. The number surprised her as Léa did some quick calculations in her head.

The Castle was 13 miles north of Stromness on the A967. The speedometer read 191 km/h. That was 118 mph which meant they'd be at The Castle in 6 minutes and 36 seconds.

Léa looked down at the wet road, then back up at the speedometer. Tara was accelerating. But Léa also noticed Tara's thumb hovering over the slick roads button on the left handlebar grip. She quickly pressed it once as the motorcycle's speed increased.

As Léa inched back down on her seat, her black helmet pressed up against Tara's helmet. As the helmets made contact, Léa could hear Tara's music pulsing. Even if Léa wanted to tell Tara to slow down, the music and wind noise were just too loud.

Looking off to side, Léa watched the passing countryside speed by. Just beyond the hills, she saw the perpetually stormy north Atlantic through her helmet's rain-streaked visor. After spending the past two weeks on the sunny Greek island of Mykonos, the chilly rain of Orkney was a bit of a shock. But it was home and Léa was happy to be back.

This stormy little island was the only home Léa had ever known. She grew up here. Went to school here. Suffered her first broken heart here. No matter where she may go, there was something special about returning home.

Tara slowed the motorcycle as they passed Léa's family home. The lights were still on and Léa had wanted to stop. She had dozens of questions for her Mum and Dad.

Growing up, Léa knew both she and her best friend Tara had been adopted. Later, she learned most of the kids she grew up with had been adopted. Whenever she asked her parents why they didn't have kids of their own, they always gave her the same answer.

"You turned out to be more than we could handle," her Mum said with a smile.

The next day, Léa told her best friend Tara what her Mum said. Tara laughed and said her parents told her the same thing.

"But we're such little angles," said Léa with a smile.

"Maybe you are. I'm not so lucky,"said Tara with a sly smile.

"What did you do now?" asked Léa.

"Remember that old army telephone switchboard my Dad gave me?" said Tara.

"Yeah," said Léa.

"I wanted to see if it would work with the main home system," said Tara.

After a few moments of silence, Léa shook her head sadly. She knew what was coming.

"And," said Léa simply.

"And. It worked a little too well. The next day, the local phone repair crew stopped by and gave my Dad quite a talking to," said Tara.

"And then you got quite a talking to?" asked Léa.

"Mum was furious. Dad kept looking away and laughing," said Tara.

It was the same way at Léa's house. She'd get into trouble about as much as Tara, but her parents never seemed all that upset.

And that was Léa and Tara's life growing up in Stromness. They were the only straight A students who were regularly in trouble with their teacher, the local constable or their parents. Sometimes with all three.

But somehow, Léa never felt the trouble she was in was all that bad and that always puzzled her. It was one of the many things in Léa's life that didn't make sense.

On one hand, she was the smartest kid in school. On the other hand, she was always in some kind of trouble. Then there was the day her Dad called her down to the basement of their family home. It was the day after her 12th birthday.

"Dad?" Léa said peering down the stairs leading to the basement.

"Come on down, Sweetie," yelled her Dad up the stairs.

Léa slowly walked down the stairs. Normally, she wasn't allowed in the basement. Her Dad told her it was because he had dangerous power tools and he didn't want his little girl getting hurt. Even though Léa's curiosity got the better of her most of the time, she never wanted to violate her father's trust. This was the first time in her life she walked down those stairs.

"It's okay Léa. Come on down," said her Dad.

When Léa stepped off the last step, she peered around the corner and saw a her Dad standing by a small work bench. The basement was a very long room. There was a small table in front of a long tunnel dug into the ground surrounding her house. Looking down the tunnel, Léa saw what looked like a target.

"How you doing Léa?" her Dad asked.

"Fine," said said.

"You're not afraid are you?" he asked.

Léa thought about that a few moments. She was never afraid of her Dad. It was an odd question that took her completely by surprise.

"No. Should I be?" she asked.

"Not at all," said her Dad.

Léa looked at her Dad, then down at the black box on the work bench. It was made of hard plastic and had gray latches and a large handle. Two big letters, S & W, were stamped into the box.

"What's in the box?" Léa asked.

"It's something I want to give to you," said her Dad.

"It's not a new computer is it?" asked Léa.

Her Dad laughed out loud.

"You've already got a new computer. This is something much more serious," said her Dad.

"Serious?" said Léa.

"Yes," said her Dad.

He walked over to a small stool and sat down. Looking up at Léa, he pointed to an identical stool.

"Come and sit down Léa," he said.

Léa looked at the empty stool, the black box and then back at her Dad. She knew she wasn't in trouble, but this wasn't going to be fun and games. She looked back at the black box. After a few moments, Léa looked down, took a deep breath and sat down on the stool. She looked up at her Dad and smiled.

"I understand," she said.

Her Dad had seen this look before and was amazed at how grown up his little girl could be. Then again, he wasn't all that surprised. It's how he and his wife had raised her. He smiled kindly.

"You know you're safe here at home, but it's not such a safe world out there, right?" he said.

"Yes," said Léa.

"You also know your Mum and I love you very much and want to make sure you have everything you need to not just be safe, but also have wonderful adventures," he said.

"Yes," said Léa.

Her Dad nodded toward the black box.

"Your Mum and I think it's time that you begin learning about something new," he said.

Léa looked over at the black box, then back up at her Dad. At that moment, she knew her life was about to change. But she wasn't afraid.

Twenty-five years later, as the motorcycle sped down the wet narrow road, Léa remembered the day her Dad gave her the small gun hidden in her backpack. She remembered the hours she spent down in the basement honing her shooting skills.

It was just a small, but important part of a larger plan to make her into the woman she was today.

Tara slowed the motorcycle as it neared the top of a hill. Looking up, Léa saw the old castle through the mist, low clouds and rain. The plan for her life started there. At that dirty old castle with the scary ghost stories she feared as a small child.

Léa fidgeted on her seat and held onto Tara tighter as the motorcycle began to pick up speed. As they got closer, the old castle got bigger. Léa thought back to the day all the loose ends of her life came together. It happened just about a month ago in a dimly lit office deep in the cliffs, under The Castle.

Léa remembered looking up into the kind eyes of the old man who had done so much to shape her life. It happened so fast ...

In an instant, her past, present and future came into instant focus.

"My Mum, my Dad and you. You've all been training me to be an assassin my whole life," said Léa.

"Not just an assassin," said Alan Dennis.

For just a moment, Léa felt sad that her life had been so completely planned out. But just as soon as the sadness hit, she quickly brushed it away as wrong. She wasn't sad at all because there wasn't a thing she wanted to change.

She had the best friend anyone could ever have. She had mental and physical skills unmatched by anyone she knew. Both she and her best friend had a purpose in life. And they had the support of what Léa had just begin to realize was an amazing group of people.

The rain began to pick up as the motorcycle sped by The Castle. Léa looked down at the speedometer and saw Tara wasn't slowing down.

Confusion began to creep into Léa's mind for a brief moment before she shoved it away. Tara had passed the turn off to The Castle.

"Weren't they going home?" Léa briefly though.

She shoved the confusion and doubt away as Léa reminded herself that Tara was driving and there was nothing to worry about. It took less than a minute for Léa's confidence to be reaffirmed.

About a mile down the road, Tara slowed the motorcycle to a stop. They were at the top of another hill. Tara looked straight ahead, then behind her long enough to make sure they were alone on the road.

Then she released one of the handlebar grips and put her hand on Léa's hands. She gave Léa's hands some tight squeezes, then grabbed the handlebar and the motorcycle took off down a narrow path that lead back to the castle. Tara's message was clear.

Hold on tight!

As Tara continued accelerating down the bumpy path, the motorcycle began flying from the top of one bump to the next. Léa gripped her best friend tighter to keep from flying off.

The tall, gray castle wall was coming up fast. A moment before they would crash, Tara made a sudden turn and they were riding parallel to the wall. Léa looked ahead and saw the edge of the cliff and the stormy sea below was coming up fast.

She felt her heart began to race as Tara showed no sign of slowing down. Léa held on even tighter as the edge of the cliff loomed closer and closer.

Suddenly, Tara brought the motorcycle to a screeching stop. Planting her left black boot firmly in the dirt, Tara gunned the motor and spun the motorcycle around to face the wall.

A small hole was cleverly hidden in the brush and behind a small hill. Tara patted Léa's hand again as the motorcycle disappeared into the hole in the castle's wall.

2 FIRST MORNING BACK

The Castle - Léa's Dorm Room

Léa reached over and lightly ran her fingers over the backpack sitting on her desk. Her half empty coffee cup hung loosely from the fingers of her other hand. Her hair was still wet from the morning shower. A wet towel was on the floor in front of the chair. Her feet rested on her still unmade bed.

Léa looked around her room at The Castle. It was bigger than her dorm room back at college. Big enough for her to easily get around the new, queen sized bed. Big enough for her to roll out her blue mat and complete her morning workout with room to spare.

A new LCD TV hung on the wall. Two large Bose speakers hung on either side of the TV. Two more speakers hung on the wall behind her bed completing the home theater sound system. It was a very comfortable, modern room. But it was also kinda chilly.

A more than gentle breeze blew across Léa's still wet body sending a shiver down her spine. The room had been carved out of solid rock in a steep cliff below The Castle. An industrial strength ventilation system was always blowing fresh, cool air through every room. Léa looked down at her flat stomach and saw a few small goose bumps had begun to appear.

Looking up, Léa's eyes ran over the bare, stone walls of her room. To make the room a little more like home, recessed lighting ran along the floor and ceiling. The lights were modern LEDs and Léa could choose whatever color she wanted.

The lights, like everything in her room, were controlled by the iPad next to her bed. Once she found the room control app, she set the lights to a soft gold during the day and soft blue at night.

The iPad beeped a few times, then a soft voice reminded her that she needed to be at breakfast in fifteen minutes. Léa sighed loudly and looked down at her half empty coffee cup. Normally, Léa started her morning with coffee and a small shot of Bailey's Irish Cream. But not this morning.

Things that annoyed most people never bothered Léa. She always felt letting things annoy her was a waste of energy. Letting things make her mad was an even worse waste of energy. But this morning, Léa was not only annoyed, but close to genuine anger.

Her bad mood started the night before as Léa and Tara walked down the long, stone hallway in the dormitory section of The Castle complex. More LED lights ran along the ceiling and along the floor. They changed intensity to match the time of day. Fresh, cool air constantly blew from the many vents that lined the stone walls.

After the long flight, train, ferry and motorcycle rides, Léa and Tara had finally arrived back at The Castle from their first mission together. Both were feeling fairly good after their their first time out. But as Léa approached her door, her mood instantly changed.

Taped up on the wall next to the door were two targets. One had a bull's eye sketched over a silhouette of a person. The other had two bull's eyes sketched over a silhouette of a car.

There were over twenty notes of congratulations scratched along the sides of each piece of paper. Notes like: Well Done, Nice Shooting and Way to Go Stripper.

"What the fuck is this?" said Léa angrily.

Tara looked at her friend with genuine surprise. Léa never got angry and hardly ever used the "f" word.

In one swift motion, Léa angrily swiped all the paper off the wall, tore up the bigger sheets and threw it all on the ground. Looking straight ahead, Léa steadied her breathing. She closed her eyes for a few moments, then slowly turned to Tara.

"Sorry about that," she said quietly.

Tara smiled at her friend and gave her a gentle hug.

"No need to apologize," said Tara.

"It's just," began Léa.

"No need to explain," said Tara.

Tara looked down at the torn up pieces of paper on the floor. Léa looked down too.

"I'm no expert, but I don't think spies should dance on graves. Even the graves of your enemy. That was really bad and whoever did that should get their ass kicked," said Tara.

Léa reached out and took Tara's hand.

"I'm so lucky to have you as my best friend," said Léa.

"Me too," said Tara.

The two friends continued to stare at the torn up pieces of paper on the ground. They were back from their first mission together and after two weeks on an island in the Aegean, they were generally feeling good about their work. But at least three people had died and both Léa and Tara had mixed emotions. They were also exhausted.

Strangely, there was no debriefing when they arrived at The Castle. Commander Alan Dennis met them outside the long hallway that lead to Léa and Tara's rooms. He simply welcomed them home, told them how happy he was that they came back safe and that they'd talk in a few days.

"Think you can sleep?" asked Tara.

"I hope so," said Léa.

She turned and gave her friend a long hug, then looked her in the eye.

"You call me if you can't sleep," said Léa.

"Same to you," said Tara.

Léa nodded once, then turned and pressed the button that silently slid open the door to her room. As Tara turned and began walking down to her room, she saw Léa glance one more time at the torn up paper on the ground.

"Fuckers," said Tara under her breath.

Tara had no problem with the 'f' word and enjoyed using it frequently.

The next morning, Léa looked down at her nearly empty coffee cup, then back over at her backpack. The guns she had to use to save her and Tara's lives were still securely snapped in their holsters in the pack's hidden pockets. The guns still had six bullets missing from the magazines. They were the six bullets Léa had to shoot, or both she and her best friend would be dead.

Léa wasn't annoyed and angry because she had to shoot. She wasn't feeling the least bit guilty about the lives she had taken either. After all, one of the people she killed had a gun to her best friend's head.

Léa's mind wandered back to the alley behind the Foreign Language building at the University of Uppsala in Sweden. She remembered how her mind quickly formulated a plan and then how quickly she executed that plan. It took two shots. One to create a diversion, the other to save Tara's life.

There had been no margin for error. Her target was the head of the man holding a gun to Tara's head. The man was shorter than Tara and was using her best friend as a shield. Léa remembered the instant she fired the second shot. Her target leaned out from behind Tara just enough to give Léa a clear shot. If Léa had been off by no more than an inch, Tara would be dead.

For most, it was an impossible situation. But Léa never doubted she could make the shot. It was an amazing display of her skill.

But someone died. That someone was threatening to kill her best friend and there wasn't a trace of guilt in Léa. Even though it was an amazing shot, Léa felt no pride either. Someone died.

In one movement, Léa pushed her toes off the side of the bed, slid one foot under the towel at her feet and kicked it up to her empty hand. As she stood, she drained the last drops of her morning coffee and started for her bathroom.

Pausing to look at herself in the mirror beside the LCD TV, Léa ran her eyes up her still damp body until they came to a stop at her face. The woman looking back at Léa was still annoyed and angry and that was no good.

Léa closed her eyes. After a few moments, she quickly snapped her head once to each side and opened her eyes. The annoyed, angry woman was gone. The reflection Léa saw was what she wanted. Confident, determined and ready for anything.

Today, Léa was determined to put a stop the any more unsportsmanlike celebration of the lives she had to take.

This wasn't a game.

3 THE RANGE

The Castle - Later That Morning

An hour after breakfast, Léa slowly walked alone down the stone hallway. She was not looking forward to her next destination. After being congratulated one too many times for something she took no pride in, she was heading to The Castle's combat training range to have her shooting evaluated, dissected and probably congratulated some more. Léa stopped just outside the door. She knew she was late, but just couldn't go another step. Tara suddenly appeared as Léa stared at the door.

"Hey," said Léa.

"Hey," said Tara.

"What have you been up to?" asked Léa.

"Checking in with Janet," said Tara. "You ready for this shit?"

"Not really," said Léa quietly.

"Well. Come on. Let's get it over with and then we can take the rest of the day off," said Tara.

Léa looked at her best friend and smiled.

"I'm going to need some of my favorite wine later tonight," she said.

"Got you covered," smiled Tara.

After a few more moments of looking at each other, the two friends slowly walked through the door to the shooting range.

The room was packed. People Léa had never seen before lined the walls. Alan Dennis stood in one corner with David McNally and Thomas Austin. Dick Boxx was standing in the center of the room.

A series of three special targets had been set up. Each represented the shots Léa fired on the Uppsala mission. The quiet conversations quickly stopped as Léa and Tara entered the room. Janet Austin slid in just as the door closed and walked over to Alan Dennis. She whispered something in his ear as Dick Boxx began talking.

"Good afternoon Ladies and Gentlemen. We're here for a demonstration of some amazing shooting," said Dick.

"Excuse me a moment Sargent-Major, may I interrupt?" said Alan Dennis.

"Of course Commander," said Dick Boxx.

"We need to keep the congratulatory part of this demonstration to an absolute minimum. Just the facts if you please. Go ahead Sargent-Major," said Alan quietly.

"Well you have to admit Sir, this was and extraordinary piece of marksmanship," said Dick.

Alan held up his hand and shook his head.

"Just the facts please Dick," said Janet.

"Of course, Sir," said Dick and he walked over to the first target.

Léa looked at Tara with a confused look in her eyes. Tara's half smile appeared as she nodded toward Janet Austin. It didn't take a genius to figure out what happened. Tara let Janet know that Léa didn't appreciate all the unsportsmanlike celebration. Janet was able to get Alan to put a stop to it. Léa smiled at Tara, then looked at Janet.

"Thank you," said Léa silently.

Janet smiled back as Dick Boxx began explaining the set up.

"This scenario represents the first shot in the alleyway. The target was shielding himself behind a hostage. From the surveillance camera, we estimated the distance of the shot," said Dick.

He looked over at Léa and Tara.

"Does the distance look right to you?" he asked.

Léa and Tara looked at each other for a moment, then turned back to Dick.

"Yeah," said Léa simply.

"Miss Taylor also used a trashcan off to the side of the alley as a diversion. It was just behind the target and I believe I saw a cat in the video too," said Dick.

He looked at Léa and Tara for confirmation. After a few moments, Léa said, "Yeah, there was a cat,"

"Excellent. Would you care to demonstrate?" asked Dick.

Léa looked at Tara. Tara looked at Léa and nodded. She turned to Dick.

"Why don't you explain all the scenarios first, then Léa will demonstrate," said Tara.

Dick appeared annoyed and looked over at Alan Dennis who nodded. So Dick continued his discussion of the other two scenarios. The second scenario, he explained, was from a moving bicycle going about 10 miles per hour when Tara interrupted him.

"It was more like 15 miles per hour," said Tara.

Léa looked at Tara.

"Really?" said Léa.

"Yeah. We were going at least 15 miles per hour," said Tara.

Léa continued to look at Tara. Some silent communication only possible between the best of friends happened for a few moments. Then Léa spoke up.

"Okay. Closer to 15," she said.

Dick corrected the speed and described the four shots Léa fired from her moving bicycle. Then he went on to explain the last two shots were fired from the engineer's hatch of a moving, electric train. The target was a cable on the power rack on the rear locomotive.

Referring to his notes, Dick said the train had five cars and two engines. He said each train car measured around 75 feet and according to his calculations, the shot Léa fired was over 5 hundred feet.

Dick pointed to a small target way down at the end of the longest shooting bay and reminded everyone that the shot was made from a moving train, in the rain, at night.

Dick then informed everyone that Léa was using The Castle's standard issue 9MM Smith & Wesson semi auto when Léa interrupted him.

"Actually, I used my smaller gun for the first five shots and the bigger gun for the last two shots," said Léa.

"You didn't use the gun we issued you?" asked Dick.

"No. I told you I would be more accurate with my smaller gun and I was," said Léa.

"Then why did you use the larger gun for the last two shots?" asked Dick.

"It was at night and I don't have glow in the dark sights on the smaller gun," said Léa.

"I see," said Dick as he started moving away from the targets. Once he was out of the firing line, he looked at Alan Dennis.

"With your permission Commander?" said Dick a bit pompously.

Alan looked tiredly up at Dick.

"Yes of course," said Alan.

"Any time you are ready Miss Taylor," said Dick.

Léa looked at Dick, then at the people who lined the walls of the range. She looked at the targets, then her friend.

"Do I have to do this?" she whispered to Tara.

"Just get it done and we'll get out of here," said Tara quietly.

"I feel like a performing seal," said Léa.

She unslung her backpack and handed it to Tara. Reaching up with both hands, she unzipped the hidden compartments and pulled out the two guns.

Stuffing the smaller gun between her belt and right hip, Léa quickly examined the bullets in the larger gun's magazine, then quickly racked the slide chambering a bullet and stuffed the gun in her jeans behind her back.

Then she pulled out the smaller gun and dropped the nearly empty clip. Tara had fished a loaded clip out of Léa's backpack. After examining the gun, Léa slapped the full clip into the grip, then racked the slide to chamber a bullet. Snapping off the safety she looked up at Tara.

"I changed my mind. I'm gonna want some very good beer tonight," said Léa quietly.

Tara smiled at her friend as Léa walked up to the first target. She looked down at her shoes for a while. Then she shook her head from side to side not able to believe what she was expected to do.

"Any time your ready," said Dick impatiently.

Léa shot him an angry glance, then looked at the target. She was a blur of motion. Anyone who blinked missed the whole thing.

Léa quickly fired the first two shots with her small gun, then took three steps to the next scenario. There she quickly fired four shots. As she took the three steps to the last scenario, she quickly stuffed the smaller gun in the waist of her jeans, drew the larger gun and fired the last two shots.

She stood on the line just long enough to stuff the larger gun back where it came from, then turned and walked toward Tara. After taking a few breaths, she gently placed the guns back into her back pack. As she zipped up the hidden zippers, Léa looked at her friend.

"I hope they're happy," she said quietly.

Then Léa turned and walked out of the room.

Dick Boxx quickly walked up and examined all the targets. For the last one, he pulled a small spotter's scope out of his pocket and checked the last target far down the range. He slowly turned to Alan Dennis.

"Bull's eyes. Every one," he said.

"It's what you all brought her up to be. So what the fuck were you expecting?" said Tara as she left to follow her friend.

4 ALE AT THE PIT

The Castle - Residential Level

Léa and Tara slowly walked down the long, stone hallway lined with doors. As Léa stopped by the door to her room, Tara gently grabbed her best friend's arm and kept walking.

"No. Not here," said Tara.

"What's wrong with my place?" asked Léa.

"It's pretty bare," said Tara.

"I've only lived there four nights," said Léa.

"I've been here a year. It's time you saw The Pit," said Tara.

"The Pit?" said Léa.

"My world," said Tara.

Léa looked at her friend as they slowly walked down the hall. How much could her friend's life have changed for her to call her room: The Pit?

They kept walking, passing door after door. Then more doors. As they came to the end of the hall, Tara stopped at the last one.

It was just like all the other doors along the hallway. It had a number and a keypad on the wall. But Tara's door had a small black and white circle painted on the door itself. The graphic depicted flames. Léa looked at the logo, then at Tara.

"I didn't realize you lived so far away," said Léa.

"I like my privacy," said Tara.

"What are the flames on your door," asked Léa.

"A warning," said Tara simply.

"Wait a minute. I've seen those flames before," said Léa.

Tara looked at the ground. Léa thought a few moments, then snapped her fingers.

"I remember. Those are the same flames you have tattooed on your left shoulder," said Léa.

Tara smiled. Nothing ever got past Léa.

"Nothing wrong with your memory," said Tara.

Léa nodded toward the door.

"So who are those flames a warning for?" asked Léa.

"For everyone but you," said Tara dryly.

The answer surprised Léa as she watched Tara enter a long string of numbers on the keypad. The door slid silently open. Tara stood aside and held her hand out inviting Léa into her world. The room was very dark. Léa peered inside, looked at Tara, then walked in.

As Léa entered the room, a dark, gray light began emerging from along the ceiling and floor. Once Léa's eyes adjusted to the darkness, she saw a black weight bench along one wall. An unmade bed was shoved up against the other wall, It was about twice as high off the ground as a normal bed and rested on several rows of heavy duty, black plastic bins.

Just like Léa's room, a large LCD TV was bolted to the wall. Eight surround sound speakers were attached to each wall. The walls, the floor and the ceiling were all painted dull black.

Tara walked over to the desk. Another black weight bench sat where the desk chair should have been. Tara sat down and turned to a small, black refrigerator next to the desk. A coffee maker with a black mug and a bag of chips sat on top of the refrigerator. Tara opened the refrigerator and a bright, white light blasted out illuminating part of the room.

Léa had to shield her eyes from the light for a moment. She blinked a few times, then looked into the refrigerator. There were a few half eaten sandwiches, some bags of salad, two of Léa's favorite bottles of wine, a bottle of Bailey's and four large, unlabeled brown bottles.

"What's in those?" asked Léa.

"Those are growlers from Deep in the Cliffs," said Tara.

She pulled one out, then shoved the others aside. Reaching deep into the back of the refrigerator, Tara pulled out two beer glasses.

"I've been saving these till you got here," said Tara.

She cracked open the growler and poured two glasses of what looked like a dark, amber ale. Tara handed one to Léa, then held her's up for a toast.

"I was really proud of you today," said Tara simply.

Léa looked at her friend and smiled. Holding up her glass, Léa lightly touched Tara's glass and took a sip.

"Not bad," said Léa.

"Something new they imported from The States," said Tara as she sipped from her own glass.

Léa pulled her face away from glass, tilted her head slightly to one side and looked at Tara.

"You mean from THE States. Like the U.S.?" she asked scrunching up her nose.

"Took them over 200 years, but they're finally figuring out how to make some good brew," said Tara dryly.

Léa laughed once through her nose and took another sip.

"Okay. Not bad. You're right. As always," smiled Léa.

Tara took a sip and nodded to her room. The message was clear. She wanted her best friend to check out her world.

As Léa's eyes became more adjusted to the light, they wandered around the room. She was quickly realizing that a lot had happened in the last year of Tara's life.

The TV was on. The logo Léa saw on Tara's door was also displayed in the center of the screen. Léa took a closer look and saw the flames on the LCD were moving.

"Animated gif?" asked Léa.

"Yeah," said Tara.

Léa nodded and continued to sip her beer and walk around the room. Just like Léa, Tara had a work out mat and some dumbbells.

Like everything else in the room, they were black.

Hanging next to the TV were some blood stained handcuffs and leg shackles. They were just like the ones Léa kept from her dungeon test.

"You kept yours too?" asked Léa.

"Not for the same reasons you kept yours," said Tara.

Léa nodded and kept walking around the room.

There were two framed posters hanging on the walls. One showed a young woman who looked a little like Tara sitting in front of a fireplace. She wore a black leather jacket and pants. After a few moments, Léa recognized it as the poster from the Swedish version of The Girl with the Dragon Tattoo movie.

"Friend of yours?" asked Léa.

Tara just shrugged and took a sip of her ale. After a few moments Tara looked up at Léa.

"The girl was fucking brilliant with computers," she said.

Léa nodded and continued walking around the room. Another poster hung over Tara's bed. This one was of a guy with closely cut black hair. He was standing with his back to the camera, but his head was turned so you could only see half of his face. His back was covered with black tattoos.

There were five circles down the man's spine. Each had a different picture. One had an eye, another showed one hand helping another hand. The middle showed someone holding two scales of justice. A tree was in the fourth circle. The top one had flames. Just like the flames on Tara's door. Just like the animated flames on Tara's TV. And just like the flames tattooed on Tara's left shoulder.

The only text on the poster was a single word: Four.

"New boyfriend?" smiled Léa playfully.

Tara looked down at the glass of ale in her hand. She was clearly thinking about her answer. After a few moments, she spoke up.

"It's more than that. He is ... " Tara's voice trailed off.

Léa looked back at the poster. Then back at her friend. Tara was still looking at her glass of ale.

"Beautiful? A hunk? Awesome?" asked Léa with a smile.

"I wouldn't throw him out of my bed," said Tara.

She looked up at Léa.

"But it's more than just a beefcake thing for me," Tara added.

"Really?" said Léa.

"Yeah," said Tara.

Léa looked at her friend. Tara didn't say anything. Finally, Léa broke the silence.

"I don't know. All this. It's certainly not the girl I grew up with. But it's clearly who you are today," said Léa.

Tara shrugged and looked around the room. After a few moments, she looked down at her ale glass, then up at Léa.

"Yeah. It's who I am now," said Tara.

Léa looked at her friend.

"So what happened to you?" asked Léa.

"Life. This place," said Tara.

Léa nodded toward the handcuffs and shackles.

"Was it the dungeon test?" she asked.

Tara half laughed, half huffed in disgust.

"That was part of it. Going through Spy School alone was another. But being away from you was so hard," she said.

Léa walked over and sat down on the weight bench next to Tara. She turned and looked directly at her best friend.

"So tell me what happened. Help me understand all this and the new you," she said.

Tara looked down at her hands. Her fingers were laced together, but her hands weren't still. Her fingers were opening and closing, tightly gripping and un-gripping each other.

"I'm scared to," said Tara.

Léa reached out and touched her friend's face. She gently pressed up under Tara's chin so she was able to see her eyes.

"Don't be," said Léa.

"I'm just not sure you'll like me anymore," said Tara nervously.

Léa put her hand on Tara's.

"Hey. It's me. Your best friend. Nothing is going to change that. Ever," said Léa.

"Promise?" said Tara.

"Promise," said Léa.

She took another big drink of her ale, then jumped on Tara's bed. Leaning up against the wall, she nodded to the other end of the bed.

"Come on. Just like when we were kids at home," said Léa.

Tara smiled.

She reached down and began unlacing her black boots. Once Tara kicked them off, she hitched up her right pant leg and unzipped the Velcro strap holding a black knife against her ankle. She tossed the knife on the desk, grabbed a full growler from the small refrigerator and jumped up on the bed.

"More?" said Tara holding up the growler.

Léa emptied her glass, nodded and held it out. As Tara filled the glass, Léa took another look around the room. Once Tara filled her glass, Léa held hers out.

"Best friends," said Léa.

"Best friends," said Tara.

The glasses clinked together. Drinks were enjoyed. Then they leaned back against the wall, staring at the small animated flame on Tara's TV. After another drink from the nearly full glasses, Léa sat up and slid around so she was looking directly at Tara.

"So tell me everything. What happened last year?" said Léa.

Tara took a big drink of her ale. After staring out into space for a few moments, she looked over at Léa.

"I guess it all really started on my last day at school," said Tara.

5 A TOTAL WASTE OF TIME

U of M College Lecture Hall - A Year Earlier

Tara sat in the back of the classroom at the University of Manchester. It was her fourth year and Tara was disgusted. She was one semester away from picking up her degree in Computer Science, but felt the only thing she had learned was her student I.D. number and how to drink.

Maybe not so good with the drinking part.

Tara was badly hung over. Worse, she was irritated at having to waste more time in a class she'd already aced. But the instructor insisted on 100% attendance to his stodgy lectures.

Tara reached her hand under her notebook and thumbed the home button on the her iPhone. The teacher had a strict rule about mobile phones. They were not allowed in his classroom. So, like all the other students, Tara kept her's hidden. She quickly glanced down. Twenty more minutes before she could make her escape. Twenty more minutes.

The old professor droned on and on.

Tara yawned.

Looking around the room, Tara was comforted to see she clearly wasn't the only student in pain. She thumbed the home button again. Nineteen minutes to go.

Suddenly, the door to the old lecture hall opened and a student quietly walked in and laid a note on the lectern. The cranky, old professor gave the delivery boy an annoyed look, adjusted his broken reading glasses and looked at the note. After reading it a few times, he looked up over his glasses.

"Miss Wells, you are wanted in Professor Anderson's office immediately," he said.

Tara looked around the room like she'd been caught stealing something. Everyone was looking at her as she nervously got up and started walking down to the front of the room and the door. Along the way, her iPhone dropped out of the notebook and clattered down the steps. It landed in front of the old instructor.

"You know my rules about those infernal devices in my classroom," he said.

"Sorry," muttered Tara as she picked it up and stuffed the rest of her junk into her battered backpack.

"That'll cost you a letter grade for the class," said the old professor.

"Seems only fair since no one learns anything in this stupid class anyway," said Tara sarcastically.

"Two letter grades Miss Wells. Please leave now before you make it a third," said the professor.

Tara was about to fire off another sarcastic comment. But she looked away from the cranky professor and continued to walk to the door. She paused, turned and looked back at the other students. They were all watching her closely. Looking around the room, Tara tossed them her best "whatever" look and left the room.

Out in the hall, Tara looked for the student who delivered the note, but he was long gone. Looking over her shoulder, Tara saw a woman standing next to the closed door. She had long black hair, was about 50'ish and appeared to be in very good shape. She was smiling at Tara.

"What?" said Tara with a little attitude.

The woman nodded back toward the classroom with an amused smile.

"That was quite the crash and burn. Two letter grades in less than two seconds. That's gotta be some kind of record," said the woman.

"What do you care?" said Tara as she turned to leave.

A few seconds later, Tara heard a cellphone ring behind her. She turned and saw the woman answer it. After a few seconds, the woman held out the phone.

"It's for you," she said simply.

Tara looked at her, then at the phone.

"It's okay. And it won't cost you any more letter grades," said the woman with a smirk.

Tara shot the woman some hatchet eyes, then looked down at the phone. She didn't move. The woman held the phone closer to Tara and tiled her head impatiently to one side.

"Today would be nice," she said.

Tara looked back down at the phone. After a few more seconds, she took a few steps forward and took the phone.

"Hello?" said Tara quietly.

"Honey, it's Dad," said her father.

"Dad?" said Tara.

"Everything is okay Tara. I want you meet a friend of mine. Her name is Janet Austin. She's got something to talk to you about," said her father.

"Okay," said Tara slowly.

"I'll call you right back," said her father and he hung up.

Tara handed the phone back to the woman. The two women stood there a few moments, then Tara's iPhone rang. It was stuffed deep in her backpack and it took a while for her to fish it out. It rang several more times before Tara was able to silence the ringer. As she held the phone up to her ear, the door to the classroom opened.

"Miss Wells. I should have known. Your continual interruptions of my class will cost you another letter grade. Please leave now before you completely flunk out," said the cranky old professor.

Janet looked down and smiled again. Tara shot the closing door of the classroom the international sign of angry disapproval, then looked down at the floor.

"What?" said Tara impatiently.

"Honey, it's me again," said her father.

"Dad?" said Tara.

"I just wanted to call you on your own phone and assure you that it really was me on the other phone and that Janet is okay," said her father.

A look of disbelief washed over Tara's face. She looked up at Janet, then down at the floor.

"Really? You called again to make sure that I knew it really was you and that this woman is okay?" said Tara.

"Yep. Remember what we talked about last summer? About how your classes were a waste of time? Well, Janet is going to help you change all that," said her father.

"Okay," said Tara slowly.

"Go with her Tara. Everything will be okay," said her father.

"Go with her?" repeated Tara.

"If you're still worried, ask her about her family," said her father.

Tara started to say something, but her father had hung up. She looked down at her phone, then up at Janet. After a few moments, Tara shook her head.

"I had a message to go see Professor Anderson," she said.

"You mean old Red Nose Anderson really is still alive and kicking?" said Janet.

"Yeah," said Tara.

"He was a wasted drunk back when I was here," said Janet.

She reached out her hand. Tara stared at it.

"Like your Dad said, I'm Janet Austin. There's a coffee shop a few blocks away. My husband is there and we'll fill you in on what's going on," said Janet.

Tara looked at Janet's outstretched hand.

"You knew Red Nose Anderson?" she asked.

Janet kept her hand out and laughed.

"Yep. Slept through three of his classes. Got an 'A' every time," said Janet.

Tara looked at the outstretched hand, then up at Janet.

"I don't trust a lot of people," she said.

"I know. I'm kind of the same way," said Janet.

Tara looked down at the outstretched hand again. After a few moments, she took a step forward and took her hand.

"Tara Wells," said Tara.

"Janet Austin," said Janet.

"I'm supposed to ask you about your family," said Tara.

"Yeah," said Janet. "We're related."

"Related?" repeated Tara.

"Your Grandpa was my adopted father," said Janet.

"So you're Aunt Janet?" asked Tara.

"Oh please, no. Never. Just Janet. But yeah. We're all part of the big, happy Wells family," said Janet.

The two began slowly walking down the hall. Tara looked straight ahead. Janet glanced at Tara once, then began quietly talking.

"Your world is about to completely change Tara. Just like mine changed almost twenty years ago. You're going to face some scary things, but you will be okay and it'll all be worth it. I promise," said Janet.

"Scary things?" said Tara.

Janet looked down at the scars ringing her wrists. She rubbed them, then put her hand on Tara's shoulder.

Tara didn't like anyone touching her and wanted to shrug Janet's hand off her shoulder. But she resisted the urge and kept walking.

"If I could handle it, you can handle it," said Janet.

24 hours later, Tara groggily woke up in one of the The Castle's dirty dungeon cells. She'd been stripped, handcuffed and shackled. It was her time to take the infamous initiation by fire that nearly every Castle recruit had to endure.

It was exactly what would happen to her best friend Léa the next year. But it would take Léa less than two days to figure out how to escape from The Castle's dungeon test. It took Tara almost a week to make her escape.

That wasn't the only difference. Tara's best friend would not only escape in record time, but Léa would later confess to Tara that she really enjoyed the test. Tara however, did not enjoy the test. She emerged from the dungeon filthy dirty with cuts from the handcuffs and shackles. Tara was hungry, tired, badly bruised and very, very angry.

Despite being weak and physically hurt from her six day ordeal, Tara violently attacked the man who released her from her handcuffs. She shattered David McNally's knee and was halfway across Alan Dennis' desk before she'd be subdued by two other guards.

A few days later, Tara woke up in The Castle's hospital with a concussion and three cracked ribs. She was also very groggy from the pain drugs. As her eyes focused, she saw Janet Austin's smiling face staring down at her.

"Welcome back," said Janet.

Tara tried to talk, but her voice wasn't working so well. She tried to lift her head, but that was impossible. Then Tara tried to move her hands, but they were secured to the bed with hospital restraints. She looked up at Janet. Even though her eyes were still fuzzy with pain drugs, Janet could tell Tara was still very angry.

"We knew you had a temper, but I had no idea you could get that outta control," said Janet.

Tara looked away from Janet.

"You're not the first recruit to come out of the dungeon swinging. But you are the first to put David McNally and two of his goons in the hospital," smiled Janet.

Tara looked back at Janet.

"Good," croaked Tara.

"You're just lucky you didn't get your hands on Alan," said Janet seriously.

"Alan?" asked Tara.

"The old man," said Janet.

"Next time," said Tara as she looked away.

"You won't get a next time," said Janet.

Tara continued to look away from Janet. After a few minutes, Janet reached out and turned Tara's face toward her. When Tara tried to turn away, Janet gripped her chin and held it tightly.

"I get it that you're angry. A lot of people don't like that fucking test. I'm one of them. But you better get a grip on that temper of yours and damn fast. I can help make this a lot easier on you. But not until I can trust you not to try to kill a 90 year old man," said Janet.

Janet released Tara's head and turned to walk away. Tara lifted her head and watched as Janet reached for the hospital room door. As it opened, Tara let her head fall back on the pillow. She tugged on the hospital restraints holding her wrists to the bed rails. Then she closed her eyes, shook her head a few times and cleared her throat.

"Don't go," she said quietly.

Janet turned and smiled at Tara. But she didn't let go of the hospital door. Tara looked up at Janet who didn't move. Tara looked down at her restrained hands, then up at the IV drip plugged into her arm. She looked back at Janet.

The ice cracked.

Tears welled up in Tara's eyes as she looked at Janet.

"I'm really scared," said Tara simply.

Janet closed the door and walked over to the bed. She sat down beside Tara's restrained hand and looked at her. Tara blinked away the tears. But Janet didn't say a word.

"Please help me," she repeated.

Janet nodded once and smiled at Tara. She took her hand and looked deep into Tara's eyes.

"Okay. One condition. Don't you dare betray my trust. Ever. If you do, there won't be a second chance," said Janet.

Letting go of Tara's hand, she slowly unbuckled the wrist and leg restraints. Sitting back down on the bed, Janet took Tara's hand again.

"Better?" she said.

"Yes," said Tara.

"Okay then. You're pretty badly torn up. But everything should heal and you'll be okay," said Janet.

Tara tried to sit up, but the cracked ribs quickly put a stop to that. Her head fell back on the pillow. Looking up at the ceiling, Tara slowly shook her head from side to side.

"I've never been so scared in my life," said Tara.

"I know. So was I," said Janet.

"Why then? What did it prove?" said Tara.

Janet smiled down at Tara. She looked down at the scars that circled her wrists and remembered her own experience in that awful dungeon.

"That's a question more and more of us are asking," said Janet.

"But," began Tara.

"No. Not now. You're still too groggy from the pain meds. We'll have plenty of time to hash it all out when you start Spy School," said Janet.

Tara looked up at Janet with surprise in her eyes. It was hard for her to focus. The pain medication kept her brain foggy and she was exhausted. But Tara's curiosity couldn't wait.

"Spy School?" she asked.

"Sleep," smiled Janet. "You'll have plenty of time to figure it all out soon."

Tara tried to talk again.

"Sleep," Janet repeated.

Tara looked up and smiled as her heavy eyes closed.

6 ANOTHER WASTE OF TIME

The Castle - Spy School Classroom

The next few weeks were like a blur. Once Tara was out of the hospital, she found herself running from one class to the next. It was like an entire university had been created just for her.

Janet was at her side all the way. When Tara asked why she'd taken such a special interest in her, Janet's answer surprised her.

"Because we never allow anyone to go through the Dungeon Test or Spy School alone. But there's a serious crisis here at The Castle and we need you up to speed fast," said Janet.

"But why are you being so nice to me?" asked Tara.

Janet looked down. She thought a few moments, then looked up at Tara.

"You're a good kid. I guess I see a little of what I once was in you and I want to see you succeed," said Janet.

"Oh," was all Tara could say.

"And a few other reasons," said Janet.

"Family reasons?" asked Tara.

"Sure. That's a good reason," said Janet.

"Still feels a little scary," said Tara.

"I'm not going to sugarcoat it. You're in for a rough ten weeks Tara. You'll do well in some of your classes. But more than a few will kick your ass. I'm here to help you any way I can," said Janet.

And that's exactly what happened. Tara found some of her classes interesting and challenging. But just as Janet promised, she was struggling with a few classes. The physical and combat training was daunting, but Tara was determined to ace them.

Then there was this one class. Just one that was totally kicking her ass. And it wasn't physical at all.

Tara looked down at her schedule for the day. She was only in her third week of Spy School. She was beat up, lonely and afraid. The Castle's Spy School is a combination of intense class work, coupled with intense physical training. The one word you could use to describe Spy School was: intense.

It's where you learn how to watch someone without them knowing they're being watched.

It's where you learn how to slip past guards into a secure military base to photograph plans of a new weapons system.

It's where you learn how to hack any computer from anywhere on the planet. (Not that Tara needed a class in that.)

It was also where you learn how to protect yourself in some of the most dangerous and frightening situations imaginable.

Just as Janet predicted, some of the classes were not going well for Tara. Specifically, the self defense classes. She was small and skinny and was getting thrown around by trainers three times her size. But it was this one class called: Verbal Manipulation that was driving Tara crazy.

Just like the advanced programming class back at the University of Manchester, Tara decided that Verbal Manipulation was a complete waste of her time. Like that awful class back at the "U", Tara had nothing in common with her near 70 year old teacher at The Castle. Plus, she was the only one in the class and couldn't hid in the back row. But the worst part was, the ancient teacher was also the most annoying person at The Castle.

"Perhaps we should spend a little time working on developing some of your womanly charms," said Pattie McNally condescendingly.

That comment brought a loud, sarcastic snort of laughter through Tara's nose. She was trying to learn the subtle art of getting people to do whatever she needed them to do. She looked up at Pattie with her best hatchet eyes. Tara was failing literally everything she was expected to do in that class.

Part of the problem was generational. Tara and Patty came from totally different times and worlds. Tara was twenty-four and Pattie was pushing seventy. Pattie was old school, very old school. Tara was 100 percent high-tech, Millennial with no illusions about life and consequently, little to no capacity for pointless bullshit.

Tara didn't like failing at anything, regardless of the reasons. But this class was clearly a lost cause. After staring at Pattie for a few moments, Tara made a decision. It was an easy one.

She calmly stuffed her iPad into her backpack and got up. Walking wasn't easy because of the growing number of injuries from self defense class. But she was not going to limp in front of this wretched excuse for a teacher and tried to walk like nothing hurt.

"Sit down young lady. We're not finished for today," said Pattie.

Tara calmly walked to the classroom door and opened it. Stepping out into the hallway, she turned and looked at Pattie. Tara took a deep breath. Her last words to Pattie were quiet and final.

"Yes we are finished. And not just for today, but everyday," said Tara.

"Get back in here right now," said Pattie.

Tara gave her one more look. Her eyes were like daggers. Then she turned and walked away.

Pattie stood in the middle of the classroom with her hands on her hips and huffed a few times. Kids these days were so irritating and that one was the worst. She picked up her overstuffed bag and left the room. On her way to her office, Pattie spotted Janet Austin.

When Janet saw Pattie, she looked down and smiled. Janet knew Tara was supposed to be in Pattie's class. Seeing Pattie in the hall at this time lead to only one conclusion. Verbal Manipulation wasn't going so well.

Pattie walked right up to Janet, stopping her in the hallway. Janet continued looking down. Pattie was clearly upset and was about to vent some frustration. Janet was Pattie's perfect target because Janet was Tara's sponsor in The Castle. Basically, Janet was responsible for anything and everything concerning Tara.

Taking a deep breath, Janet bit her cheek and wondered how she was going to get through the coming confrontation. She wasn't afraid of Pattie. And she wasn't worried that Tara had done something awful. No, Janet was worried that she'd start laughing at Pattie the moment she opened her mouth.

"If you don't hammer some respect into that foul mouthed, skinny little Romanian brat, I swear, I will find a way to beat some into her myself," said Pattie angrily.

Janet could't help herself. She tried, honestly. But she just couldn't take Pattie seriously. Still looking down, a combination snort and laugh erupted from Janet's nose.

"Actually, I believe it was you who processed that little Romanian brat's citizenship into the U.K. So let's at least get her nationality right," said Janet.

Pattie shook her head once and quickly fired back at Janet.

"Don't play your word games with me. That girl is your responsibility. Both she and you are failing miserably," snapped Pattie.

"I wouldn't call bombing one class, your class by the way, and acing all of her other classes failing miserably," said Janet with a smile.

"She is not 'acing' all of her other classes. Just because she's clever with computers doesn't qualify her as class valedictorian," said Pattie.

"Actually, she's the only one in her class, so I guess she'll automatically be valedictorian," smirked Janet.

Pattie closed her eyes and took a deep breath. Thinking for a few moments, she started to say something else. But Janet cut her off.

"Look, I know Tara is rough around the edges by your old school standards. But it's a different world out there from days when you were dodging Nazis. Hell, it's a different world from the days I was kicking the shit out of Boris," said Janet.

Pattie started to say something else. But Janet cut her off again.

"Nobody has a smooth ride through Spy School and Tara is no different from any of the hundred or so other newbies we've run through this cave. Like everyone she'll have her strengths and her weaknesses. Clearly, Tara won't be getting an 'A' in your class in spy deportment," said Janet.

Pattie's eyes narrowed when Janet referred to her class using the stodgy, old school and obsolete title of: deportment. As she was about to say something, Janet cut her off a third time.

"So go yell at someone else if you need to vent. I'll go visit with Tara and we'll see if we can find a way for us all to move forward," said Janet.

As she started to walk away, Pattie called after her.

"Commander Dennis will be hearing about both of your bad attitudes," said Pattie.

Janet just shook her head as she turned the corner.

The topic of Janet and Pattie's conversation was just arriving at at huge, circular ten story atrium. There were eight levels in The Castle Complex. Each had four or five long hallways branching out from a central area that had been affectionately named: Central Park.

It had taken years of blasting to carve out the round room that covered the eight levels of The Castle Complex. The two lower levels were larger than the rest and were covered with tractors, cranes and other construction gear. At the very bottom of Central Park was a large pool of water, big enough for The Castle's fleet of submarines.

There were stairways leading to every level. But the centerpiece seemed to be an old fashioned lift. It wasn't just your basic elevator. Tara had seen one before on a school trip to Berlin. She searched her memory to remember what it was called. After a few moments, the name popped into her head.

It was a Paternoster lift, basically a continuous chain of open compartments that moved slowly in a loop up and down without stopping. Passengers can step on or off at any floor they like.

As Tara emerged from the classroom hallway into Central Park, she had a decision to make. She could head back to her room and blast the shit out of her speakers or ... or ... what?

Normally, Tara would turn to her large collection of music when she was angry, frustrated or hurt. Depending on her mood, the music could be anything. Lately, with her frustration factor growing, her choice in music was trending toward very heavy metal.

Standing at the rail looking at the large underground atrium, Tara watched the Paternoster lift go up and down. A hundred or so people moved on and off the lift and around the atrium going to their various destinations. These were not bad people. In fact, Tara was growing to not only respect, but even like a few of them.

As she watched people getting on and off the Paternoster, she remembered there were a lot of accidents and the public lifts were being shut down. Basically, most people weren't coordinated enough to step on and off a slow moving lift without tripping. But everyone here seemed to handle the lift without a problem.

Looking down a level, she thought again about heading to her room and loosing herself in her music. No, that wouldn't help. As Tara looked up, she decided it was time for a change.

A couple of technicians walked behind Tara. She tried not to look at them. They were holding hands and laughing. Clearly they were happy. Something Tara desperately wished for.

Sneaking a look as the technicians rounded the atrium and disappeared down one of the many long, stone hallways, Tara decided heading down to her room to sulk was not a good idea.

Looking up again, Tara started climbing stairs. She didn't have a final destination in mind. Tara was just following her nose hoping fate would take her someplace where she could clear her mind and figure out a way to survive Spy School.

7 TOP OF THE CASTLE

The Castle - Sea Side Turret

When Janet finally found Tara, she had to stop and catch her breath. Even though she was in good shape, climbing from the dormitory level all the way to the top of the sea-side castle turret was a lot of work. Janet figured she had just climbed the equivalent of a ten to fifteen story building.

It had been almost an hour since Janet left Pattie standing in the hallway and started searching for Tara.

She looked in Tara's room. Nothing.

She went to the main cafeteria. Nothing.

She stopped by the library and computer lab. Nothing.

Then she checked with Pattie's husband who was cleaning tap lines at Deep in the Cliffs Pub. Nothing.

Janet went back to her office and decided it was time to save herself a few steps. Picking up the phone, she called Central Control. The security people knew where everyone in The Castle was and quickly told Janet she had a lot more stairs to climb.

After taking a few more breaths, Janet slowly walked up to the small young woman sitting on the edge of The Castle's turret. Her feat dangled over the side.

She wasn't worried that she'd startle Tara. As Janet emerged onto the top of The Castle's turret, she saw Tara's head slightly turn back her way. It wasn't much of a turn, just enough for Janet to know Tara knew she wasn't alone.

"*It takes most people months, if not years to be as sensitive to their environment as she already is,*" thought Janet as she sat down.

Janet wasn't afraid of heights. But sitting so close to the edge, with nothing between her feet and the stormy ocean far below, made Janet's heart beat just a little bit faster.

It was chilly up on the top of The Castle. Seemed like it was always a little wet up there too. Rain or sea spray was always falling. Janet had planned ahead and brought something warm and semi-rain proof. Tara was wearing her typical black warm-up jacket, black jeans and black sneakers. A small chill went through Janet as she zipped her jacket up a little higher. Tara glanced at her.

"You don't have to stay if you're too cold," said Tara.

Janet smiled. Despite Tara's rough exterior, she really was nice and considerate.

"I'm okay. How about you?" she asked.

"Full of happiness and joy," said Tara bitterly.

There was defeat and fatigue in Tara's voice. Janet looked down and smiled. It was exactly how she felt after her encounter with Pattie.

"Let me guess. You've have had way too much of Pattie McNally for today," said Janet.

"I've had enough of Pattie McNally to last a lifetime. How does someone like that even end up at a place like this?" said Tara.

"Actually, she was once what you'd call a total badass," smiled Janet.

Tara looked down at let a single huff out through her nose.

"Yeah right," said Tara under her breath.

"It's the truth. About fifty years ago, she was you," said Janet.

Tara closed her eyes and shook her head slowly.

"Hardly," she said quietly.

"No. Seriously. You should check her out sometime. But I'm not here to talk about how annoying Pattie McNally has become in her old age. I'm here for you. What can I do?" said Janet.

Tara looked down and just shook her head. After a few moments Janet nudged her.

"No really. Anything at all. Short of killing someone, of course," smiled Janet.

Tara looked up at Janet, saw her smiling and gave her a small smile back.

"We can't kill her, huh?" said Tara.

"Afraid not," said Janet.

Tara looked out at the stormy sea. She thought a little more. As Janet was about to speak up, Tara started talking.

"I get a lot of what's going on here. I understand why I'm here and why you need me. I know computers and I know the 'net. I know I can give this place what it needs. I just don't know why I need to be in fight class, gun class and Pattie McNally's how to fuck with people class," said Tara.

Janet smiled and nodded her head a few times.

"I don't think anyone has come up with a better name for Verbal Manipulation than you," she said.

"Well seriously. I was brought in to bring your computer security up to speed. Why are you trying to turn me into a field agent?" asked Tara.

"Because a lot of people here think you have the potential to be an extraordinary field agent," said Janet.

"Really? Why?" said Tara.

Janet thought a moment. Should she answer Tara's question completely? There was a lot she didn't know about her past and the future The Castle had been training her for since she was a baby. Some thought it would be best if Tara didn't learn about her past until she finished Spy School.

"I know you're tired of hearing this, but it's a long story and we'd rather you be able to concentrate on the here and now for a little bit longer," said Janet.

"I just don't fit into a lot of this spy shit," said Tara.

Janet and Tara looked at each other.

"Actually, I never felt like I fit in anywhere," said Tara quietly.

Janet put her arm around Tara. At first, Tara tried to pull away. But she stopped as Janet started talking.

"Me too," began Janet. "But it's gonna be okay. You're here in a strange, sometimes dangerous place. You don't have your family near you and I know how much you miss your friend Léa. I'm here for you with anything you need to make it all work out."

She felt Tara tense when she mentioned Léa's name. Janet knew Tara and Léa had been the best of friends since they were five years old. It had been planned that way. They had formed a tight bond over the years and the fact that they weren't in Spy School together was a big problem.

Janet thought back to her own best friend. She had her friend by her side when she went through Spy School. Her best friend was there during The Castle's sadistic dungeon initiation test too. Janet looked away sadly as she remembered the best friend who wasn't there anymore.

Tara looked up at Janet.

"You looked a hundred miles away," said Tara.

"Just remembering someone," said Janet.

"Someone like Léa?" asked Tara.

The question bored deep into Janet's soul. Her body shuddered just once as Tara saw what looked like a tear form in the corner of Janet's left eye. Tara sat up and looked at Janet.

"I'm sorry if I brought up a bad memory," she said.

Janet smiled and blinked her eyes a few times. She reached out and touched Tara's face.

"Best friends are never bad memories," said Janet.

"It just hurts when they're gone," said Tara.

That brought another shudder deep inside Janet to the surface. She shook her head a few times as she smiled at Tara.

"It hurts like a bitch," said Janet.

"Do you want to talk about it?" asked Tara.

Janet quietly laughed and smiled at Tara.

"You really are someone very, very special you know. And yes, someday I'd like to tell you all about Helena," said Janet.

She let herself savor the moment when she got to say her best friend's name. It was so long ago. Janet liked being able to say her best friend's name. Getting to say her name made it feel like she was still there.

Janet let go of Tara's face and reached for her iPhone. She tapped out a quick message and hit send. Then she looked up and smiled.

"But not today. You just said you felt like you didn't fit in anywhere. You may be surprised to know that's just how I felt and sometimes still do," said Janet.

"Really? You're not just saying that?" said Tara.

"No. I'm not just saying that," said Janet.

"Welcome to the island of misfit toys," said Tara.

Janet was about to say something when her phone buzzed once. Janet looked down, read the message and smiled.

"There are quite a few misfit toys on this island for sure. But you and I don't qualify. Come on. Let's go to the movies," said Janet.

"I'm guessing it won't be some stodgy lesson in spy deportment from the Pattie McNally stash," said Tara with a smile.

Remembering the conversation she had with Pattie a little over an hour ago, Janet laughed out loud.

"Not even close," she said.

Tara looked at Janet, saw she was laughing and smiled herself. But it wasn't Tara's half, slightly sarcastic smile. It was full and genuine.

"Don't take this the wrong way, but you have a devastatingly beautiful smile," said Janet.

Tara nervously looked away. She knew Janet wasn't trying to hit on her. Tara just wasn't used to getting complements.

"I don't usually feel beautiful," said Tara.

Janet looked down.

"Not many of us do," said Janet.

She edged back from the side of the turret and slowly stood up. Looking down at Tara, she held out her hand.

"Come on. My man has a movie set up just for us," said Janet.

Tara looked up at Janet, then down at her outstretched hand. It only took a moment for her to make her decision. She carefully edged back from the side of the turret, turned and took Janet's hand. As she stood up, Tara asked one more question.

"What kind of movie is this?" she said.

"It's a movie for people like us. It's for people who don't fit in," smiled Janet.

8 SOME MOVIES CAN HELP

The Pit - Later That Night

~ ~ ~

PLAYLIST:
"Choosing Dauntless" - Divergent - Junkie XL (feat. Ellie Goulding)
~ ~ ~

Music from Junkie XL blasted from the eight speakers surrounding Tara's room. She sat on her bed with her legs crossed in front of her Mac. Tara was wearing her favorite black t'shirt and shorts. The movie she just saw was silently playing on the flat screen TV bolted to the wall.

Looking up, Tara saw her favorite scene from the movie was about to begin. She tapped a few buttons on her Mac and the music blaring from the speakers quickly shut off. Reaching for the remote, she cranked the volume on the TV.

M83's 'I Need You' began softly playing as Tris and the other winners of the Dauntless capture the flag game arrived on the roof of the Hancock Building in downtown Chicago. A few moments later, Tris was strapped into the harness attached to a 1.5 mile zip-line running from the top of the Hancock building back to Dauntless headquarters.

Tara was blown away by not only the movie, but watching Tris zip line off a 100 story building. It was the fourth time she played that scene. As the zip line came to a stop, Tara looked down at herself. Her heart was racing. Her palms were sweaty.

All this from a movie!

Reaching down for her Mac, Tara re-started the movie soundtrack she'd been playing. She lowered the volume a bit as she tried to figure out how a movie could make her heart race. No movie ever had before.

The first track on the soundtrack started out soft and sad. Not Tara's typical taste in music. But she knew she'd play that soundtrack hundreds of times before she'd get tired of it.

Tara slumped back against the wall her bed was shoved up against. As she leaned back, her healing ribs reminded her they were recently broken as a sharp pain shot up and down her side.

After the pain subsided, she gently stretched her legs out on the bed.

Looking down at them, Tara was surprised to see how badly bruised they were. Even her arms were bruised.

Reaching for the growler of ale she brought back from Deep in the Cliffs Pub, Tara opened her mouth for a drink and pain shot through her jaw. Earlier that day, she'd taken a punch from her martial arts instructor because she failed to protect her face.

There was no escaping the conclusion Tara came up with. She was a wreck and things hadn't been getting better. Then she saw the movie. Maybe that's why the movie resonated so deeply with her.

Tara reached for the TV's remote and rewound the movie to another favorite scene. Knives began flying as Tara watched in amazement at how deadly accurate they were thrown.

"Badass," she thought to herself.

Of course, Tara was smart enough to know it was just a movie and the knife that drew just a drop of fake blood from Shailene Woodley's ear was a carefully rehearsed stunt. Reaching for her Mac, Tara looked for some YouTube videos to see if you really could throw a knife with that kind of deadly accuracy.

It took about five minutes for her to hack through all the on-line clutter and finally see what she was looking for. As it turned out, it really was possible to develop some amazing knife throwing skills.

She rewound the movie on her TV back to the beginning of the knife scene. Watching it again, then looking down at the video playing on her Mac, Tara decided that was something she could probably pick up.

Back on-line, she was able to determine they used Hibben Throwing Knives in the movie. She was about to order a set, when she decided to see if any were already at The Castle. A quick check of the internal weapon inventory showed they had about a hundred of those very same knives and several people were listed as qualified instructors. One of those instructors was Janet Austin.

Tara reached for her iPhone and tapped out a quick text. The answer that came back a minute or so later make Tara smile. Not only would Janet be delighted to teach Tara the art of knife throwing and combat, but she would also be able to substitute the new class for Verbal Manipulation.

"Yes!" said Tara loudly.

At the same time, she sat up on her bed as both her arms shot straight up in victory. Almost immediately, pain shot through her side, down her back and up her arms.

"Fuck me," said Tara.

She slumped back against the pillows she'd leaned up against the wall. She started massaging her sore arms, but she still smiled. Knowing that she was done with Pattie McNally's class was a big relief.

Looking up at the screen, Tara returned to the question she was trying to figure out before. How could a movie make her feel the way she was feeling? Tara felt so connected to the story. She looked back down at her badly bruised legs, then up at her messy desk.

Of course, part of the reason was the state of current events in Tara's world. While she was doing well with most of her classes, her body was in bad shape and not getting better. It was a relief that she had been able to scheme her way out of Verbal Manipulation. But there was a constant hole in her world as long as her best friend remained hundreds of miles away and essentially out of her life. In short, Tara was a train wreck.

"Wait a minute," Tara slowly said out loud.

She reached for the remote and restarted the movie from the beginning. The opening narration was a who's who of the movie's world. It ran through the factions and introduced a few things that were about to happen. The last few lines of the narration punched through Tara's thoughts ...

It all works.

Everyone knows where they belong.

Except for me.

Tara sat back up. Ignoring the pain in her side, back and legs, she played those last few lines again. Just to make sure, she played it a third time.

"There it is," said Tara out loud.

It all came together. A big smile appeared on Tara's face. It made sense now. The movie was all about someone like her. Someone who didn't fit in, learning how to do new, scary, badass shit.

As the movie played for the fifth or perhaps the sixth time that night, Tara knew it would be something she could use to get through Spy School. If she had to go through it all without her best friend, she'd pick a few things out of the movie and make them her own. What was it Janet's husband Thomas said?

"Actually, we can learn a lot from movies," he said during Tara's first Movie Night.

So Tara would do just that. She looked up at the screen and watched as the male lead welcomed the initiates into the Dauntless faction. The guy playing Four caught Tara's eye immediately. The first thing she did when she got back to her room was order a few posters of him.

Looking around her room, then back down at her bruised body, Tara decided she could now meet each challenge Spy School threw her way head on. She would master as many self defense techniques as she could. She briefly thought she might even give Verbal Manipulation another chance. But only briefly.

"Fuck that shit," she said out loud.

Tara's new attitude clearly would help here along with 90 percent of Spy School, but Verbal Manipulation a lost cause. There was developing a new, can-do attitude. Then there was doing a Wile E. Coyote off a cliff. Verbal Manipulation was a complete waste of her time and effort.

Most important, she'd take a concept from the movie and create her own Fear Landscape. There were things ahead for Tara that she knew would be terrifying. So she would carefully examine the things she was afraid of. She would study them, then face them down so they would not longer control her.

She would face her fears the way the characters in the story did.

She decided the Dauntless logo was badass and she had already made it her Mac's wall paper.

Maybe she wasn't what her stodgy old computer science professor or that bitch Pattie McNally thought she should be. But Janet Austin seemed to think differently and that was good enough for Tara. It was okay that Tara didn't fit in with most people's image of what she should become.

About twenty doors down from Tara, Janet's iPhone beeped. A new text message was coming in. Janet was just dozing off, so the intrusion wasn't very welcome.

Brushing her black hair out of her eyes, she looked over at her sleeping husband, then reached for her phone and read the message. As she read, a satisfied smile began to appear on her face.

Thank you for the movie ...

I can make this work ...

Janet fell back on her pillow and smiled. She knew she was right about Tara and the world would be learning what she knew very quickly. Tara still had some big challenges ahead of her, but Janet knew she would meet them head on and win.

Her phone beeped one more time. Janet thumbed her phone.

Thank you for being my friend.

Janet tapped out her reply and hit send.

It's so nice to make a great friend like you.

9 ANY MORE OF THAT ALE?

The Pit - Present Day

Léa and Tara were laying on Tara's bed like they did when they were young girls up talking through the night. It was as if the years had melted away. But this time, Tara was doing most of the talking.

Léa was laying on her side listening as her best friend talked. Both had nearly empty ale glasses as Tara finished up the story of her first year at The Castle. She held up her glass.

"More?" asked Tara.

Léa chugged her glass dry and handed it to Tara who jumped off the bed and refilled the glasses. After she handed Léa her full glass, she walked over to the dresser in her closet.

Tara had kicked off her black boots hours ago, but was still wearing her heavy black commando pants, black t'shirt and vest. Léa watched as Tara emptied her pockets and whipped the black web belt from the loops. Léa took a drink of her ale as a question popped into her head.

"So how did the knife throwing class turn out?" she asked.

Tara looked over her shoulder and smiled at Léa. It wasn't her typical 'smirky smile' either. It was genuine and there was a twinkle in her eyes. Léa could see she asked something Tara liked talking about.

"I learned a lot," said Tara.

"Like what?" asked Léa.

"There's basically trick throwing and combat. Both take a lot of practice. The thing about trick throwing is, it only works in certain situations. Mostly, it's just fun," said Tara.

"Are you any good?" smiled Léa.

Léa already knew the answer to that question. Anything Tara did, she did very well. Léa just wanted to see her friend doing something she enjoyed doing.

"Wanna see?" smiled Tara.

"Yeah," smiled Léa back.

Tara turned back to the dresser and quickly tossed aside her work clothes and slipped on her favorite black shorts. Before Tara could pull her her favorite t'shirt over her head, Léa caught sight of the tattoo on Tara's left shoulder.

She saw it first in the bathroom in the Foreign Language building at the University of Uppsala, then again at the pool in Mykonos. Léa didn't know what it was then, but after hearing Tara's story, she knew exactly what those flames were.

"I know what your tattoo is. Those are Dauntless flames," said Léa.

Just before Tara pulled on her t'shirt, she looked down at her shoulder, then over at Léa.

"That movie really means a lot to you," said Léa.

"It was about someone who felt like she didn't belong anywhere she went. It was about her facing challenges like I was facing. So yeah, it was just what I needed, just when I needed it. But that was then and this is now," said Tara.

As she turned around, she pulled on her favorite t'shirt. Like everything Tara wore, it was completely black except for the bold white letters on the front. Léa's eyes opened wide as she read the five faded words.

"Okay," exclaimed Léa. "Tell us how you really feel."

Tara looked down at the shirt, then up at Léa and shrugged.

"It's how I feel about a lot of people." said Tara.

"I've seen it somewhere before." said Léa.

"It's Lisbeth Salander's t'shirt from Dragon Tattoo." said Tara.

"Fuck you, you fucking fuck," said Léa reading the bold, white letters on the shirt.

Hearing Léa use the 'f' word brought a smile to Tara's face.

"I'm guessing you get the standard lecture about profanity when you wear that." said Léa.

"Yeah, but I got tired of their shit so I mostly wear it at home or under stuff now." said Tara.

"You need to get me one of those." smiled Léa.

"Really?" said Tara.

"Just because I don't regularly use what Mr. Spock called: 'colorful metaphors' doesn't mean I'm afraid of them." said Léa.

"Mr. Spock?" said Tara.

"Star Trek four, the whale movie. What kind of sci-fi girl are you?" smiled Léa.

"That's like a thirty year old movie." said Tara.

"Just because it's thirty years old doesn't mean it's a bad movie." said Léa.

"Yeah, whatever." said Tara.

She turned around, opened a drawer and pulled out a t'shirt. After giving it a quick sniff, she tossed it to Léa.

"You have extras?" said Léa holding up the shirt.

"About four or five." said Tara.

Turning back to the dresser, she picked up a small, black sheath loaded with three silver knives. Tara unsnapped the sheath and slid out all three knives. Two knives went into her left hand. She was casually flipping the remaining knife in her right hand, testing the balance. She smiled up at Léa.

"See that black board next to my boyfriend on the wall," said Tara.

Léa looked over her shoulder. The poster hung on the wall over Tara's bed. A small black patch of plywood hung next to the poster. Looking closer, Léa could see the board had been a frequent target. Most of the little knife divots were grouped fairly close together. She sat back on the bed and looked at Tara.

"Yes," said Léa.

Tara smiled. Her eyes were still twinkling with energy.

"Trust me?" asked Tara.

"With my life," said Léa seriously.

Tara looked down at the knife she was tossing in her right hand. Without moving her head, she looked up at Léa through the stands of black hair that had fallen in her face. She looked from Léa to the small black board then down to the knife she was tossing in her right hand. Tara shuffled her right foot back and her left foot forward, looked up, then quickly shook the hair out of her eyes.

Tara took a deep breath, then looked up at Léa.

"Say when," said Tara.

Léa looked at Tara, then at the target. Her head was less than a foot away. But there was never a question in Léa's mind about Tara's skill. She took a drink of her ale and smiled at her best friend.

"When," said Léa.

Three knives.

Three seconds.

Three dead center hits.

Léa didn't even have to look at the board to see where the knives went. She was watching her friend closely. Tara's eye's were focused like lasers on the target. Her hands were lightning fast.

But what surprised Léa was the power that Tara was able to put into each knife throw. Looking over her shoulder, Léa could see each knife was deeply embedded in the wood. She looked back at her friend.

"I think the official word for that is, badass," said Léa.

Tara looked down and smiled.

Léa shook her head and looked around the room again. After a few moments, she looked at Tara.

"Okay, I get it. A lot of this makes sense. What I don't understand why you're so angry all the time," she said.

Tara picked up her half-full glass of ale, then looked down as she walked over to the weight bench by her desk. On the way, she paused and ran her hands over the handcuffs and leg shackles hanging next to the TV. Once she sat down, she finished off the ale, then looked at Léa.

"I guess it started in college," began Tara.

She reached for her iPhone and punched a few buttons. Music from her favorite movie began playing softly on the eight speakers surrounding the room.

She poured another glass of ale and held the growler out. Léa quickly slugged down what was in her glass and held it out. Her hand and the glass seemed a bit unsteady. Tara looked up at her friend.

"You okay," she asked.

"I don't know. The last year was hard on both of us. I missed you more than life and have wondered what was going on for a long time. Now here we are and, like you, I'm a little scared of what the answers might be," said Léa.

Tara took the empty glass from Léa, filled it, then set it down on the weight bench. She stood and hopped up on the bed next to Léa.

"Of all the people who should be scared, it should be me. I'm the one who changed," said Tara.

"Then again, maybe we're making this a bit bigger than it is," said Léa. "Time goes by. Things happen. People change. But best friends stay best friends."

"I guess," said Tara.

Léa slowly looked around the room. Her eyes finally came to a rest on Tara's face. She smiled hesitantly.

"I think I might understand," she said.

"What?" asked Tara.

"Why you're so angry," said Léa.

Tara looked at her friend. Her head tilted off to one side and she smiled. Léa was the smartest person she'd ever met. Tara was always amazed at how quickly her best friend could figure things out.

She reached out for Léa's glass of ale and took a big drink. Handing the glass back, she smiled again.

"Okay. What have you figured out?" she asked.

"You just said you got angry in college, but I'm guessing you were just annoyed with all the bullshit that comes with a college degree. I think the real reason you're so angry is because of what they did to us," said Léa.

"What was that?" asked Tara.

"They kept us apart," said Léa.

Tara looked up at the ceiling and closed her eyes. Her body shook once as the emotions of the past year bubbled up in her. Trying to keep herself under control, Tara took a deep breath and looked down.

"Leave it to you to figure it out in about ten seconds, then wrap it up even sooner," said Tara.

Léa took a drink of her ale.

"These people clearly set us on the path to become the friends we are today and for that, I'll be forever grateful. But it was wrong of them to separate us this past year. Especially during that nasty initiation test of theirs," said Léa.

"I thought you enjoyed your time in the dungeon," said Tara.

Léa nodded.

"I did. But that must be my kinky side, because no one else did. In fact, that test appears to have hurt a lot of people," said Léa.

"It did. And a lot of people in this cave want to shut it down for good," said Tara.

"Why don't they?" asked Léa.

"They say they need some kind of initial trial by fire. They say they want you afraid and very vulnerable so they can see if you can get beyond all that and think your way out," said Tara.

Léa took another drink of her ale, then handed the glass to Tara. Looking down, Léa saw the two friends were holding each other's hands tightly.

"In your case, it was a great test. But not many people are like you," said Tara.

"What, that I like to get naked and apparently have a thing for handcuffs," smiled Léa.

"Partly," said Tara seriously.

"Partly? What else?" said Léa.

"Maybe it's something from that movie I saw last year. For most people, fear is almost always something that shuts them down. But you're different. Like one of the characters, fear doesn't shut you down. It wakes you up," said Tara.

Léa thought about that for a moment and slowly shook her head.

"No. That's a great movie line, but it's not reality. I really was afraid at first. But then as the pieces of the puzzle started fitting together, I decided I wasn't in any real danger. Then I wasn't afraid," said Léa.

This time Tara paused to think for a moment. Then she too began slowly shaking her head.

"Yeah. You were afraid. But you get it under control so much faster than anyone else ever does. Then you used that realization as energy to quickly move beyond it," said Tara.

"Maybe," said Léa.

Tara took a drink of ale and handed the glass back to Léa.

"Finish it. I'll get the other glass," said Tara.

She started to get up. But Léa held on to Tara's hand tighter.

"Don't go just yet," she said.

Tara looked back at her friend. Léa smiled at her best friend for a few moments, then released her hand.

"On second thought, pass me that full glass of ale," she said with a smile.

Tara got up and handed the glass she left on the weight bench to Léa. Then she pulled a new, full growler from the refrigerator and climbed back on the bed.

Léa held up the glass toward Tara who held up the full growler. She clinked the glass against the growler and took a big drink. Tara cracked open the growler and took a big drink too.

"Wanna hear my thinking on this?" asked Léa.

"Always," said Tara.

"They say what doesn't kill you only makes you stronger," said Léa.

"I'll go along with that," said Tara.

"The last year was," Léa's voice tailed off.

"Extremely fucked up," suggested Tara.

"Indeed," said Léa.

They both took another drink of ale. By now, the ale was taking control as they both started stumbling over a few words and loosing track of what they were saying. After a brief pause, Léa tied to finish her thought. Tara looked at Léa and finally broke the silence.

"You were saying," said Tara.

"What?" said Léa.

Tara smiled. Léa appeared to be officially drunk. It didn't happen often, but it was always funny to see.

"You were saying something like what doesn't kill you only makes you stronger," said Tara.

"Oh yeah," said Léa.

She took another big drink of her ale, then looked at the moving flames on Tara's TV. Léa took a deep breath. She looked back at the TV screen, then Tara.

"So I was saying what doesn't kill you only makes you stronger. The last year didn't kill us, it just made us so much stronger," said Léa.

"I'll go along with that," said Tara.

Léa looked over Tara's shoulder at the flame graphic flickering on the TV. She looked back at Tara and smiled.

"That's it. We're stronger," she said.

"Stronger than ever," agreed Tara.

They both took a few more drinks of ale in silence. Then Tara looked at her best friend and smiled. Léa smiled warmly back at Tara. But her smile changed from genuine to slyly wicked.

"What?" said Tara.

"They didn't kill us, but they did make our lives a bit miserable," said Léa.

"Definitely miserable," said Tara.

"I think it's time for a little payback," smiled Léa.

"What did you have in mind?" asked Tara.

"Same thing we did when we were kids. It's time for us to start causing some trouble," said Léa.

10 THE NEXT MORNING

The Castle, Tara's Dorm Room

The next morning, the two iPhones on Tara's desk both started buzzing loudly. A few seconds later, backpacks started buzzing. The buzzing lasted about a minute.

Then silence.

But the silence only lasted three minutes before the buzzing began again. It lasted about a minute, then stopped.

The night before, and soon after Léa suggested that she and Tara start causing some trouble, the effects of the amber ale they were drinking took complete control. In less than fifteen minutes, both Léa and Tara passed out.

The two best friends easily slept through the first round of buzzing from their phones and digital pads. They even slept through the second round. But they weren't so lucky when the iPhones and iPads started buzzing a third time. That third alarm wouldn't stop until someone got up and silenced it.

Tara was the first to open her eyes as the buzzing continued. Those eyes were bloodshot and her head was pounding.

"Oh fuck me," she said.

"Me too," mumbled Léa weakly.

As the phones and pads continued buzzing, the intensity of the hangovers continued building. Léa slowly rolled over on her back. Tara weakly pushed herself up on her elbows and tried to reach her phone. But it was over on the desk. So was Léa's.

Someone was going to have to actually get off the bed and walk to the desk to silence the alarms.

Léa held her head as a slow, painful groan slowly emerged from her half open mouth. Resting on her elbows, Tara held her throbbing head in her hands. With her eyes barely open, Tara slowly looked around her dark room. Her eyes finally stopped on the buzzing iPhones and backpacks on the desk.

"Somebody kill those damn things, now," moaned Tara.

"Why did I let you get me so drunk last night?" moaned Léa.

Tara closed her eyes and huffed in disgust.

"What? I got you drunk? I don't remember anyone holding a gun to your head," said Tara.

Léa put her hands over her ears.

"If I had my gun right now I'd shoot those damn phones," said Léa.

"Yeah sure. You couldn't even hit the wall in your present condition," said Tara.

Léa moaned in pain then tried to roll herself off the bed. It took several tries, but once she succeeded she wished she'd just stayed still. Instead of landing on her feet as she'd hoped, Lea forgot Tara's bed was about twice as high off the ground as a normal bed.

She basically did a face plant on Tara's floor.

Tara saw the whole thing and tried hard not to laugh. But when it looked like Léa had actually bounced once, Tara couldn't help herself.

Of course, once she started laughing, the hangover kicked her in the head and she quickly stopped. Léa looked up just as Tara started laughing and quickly stopped.

"Serves you right. Laughing at your best friend," moaned Léa.

Tara looked down at her friend and smiled as best someone with a massive hangover could smile.

"Sorry. But you bounced when you hit the ground," said Tara.

"And you thought that was funny? Nice," said Léa.

"Sorry. But it really was kinda funny," said Tara.

The phones and backpacks continued to buzz.

Léa closed her eyes in pain as she covered her ears with her hands.

"Someone please kill those," said Léa desperately.

"You're closer," said Tara.

Léa opened her eyes and looked up. Tara was staring down at her from the bed.

"You look just like I feel," said Léa.

"Could be worse. Back in college, I had some massive hangovers from stuff a lot stronger than this," said Tara.

"Tequila was my worst hangover," said Léa.

"Jack," said Tara.

Looking away from Tara, Léa spotted one of the beer glasses from the party last night. It had fallen from the bed when the two friends passed out. She timidly reached out, picked up the glass and set it up near the bed.

The phones and backpacks continue to buzz.

Léa stretched her body once from head to toe, then rubbed her eyes. Looking up at Tara, she held out her hand.

"Help me up," said Léa.

Tara shuffled closer to the edge of her bed, then reached down for Léa's hand. As Léa started pulling, Tara started slipping off the bed.

"No! Stop!" said Tara.

But it was too late.

Léa kept pulling and Tara kept slipping. As Léa pulled herself up enough to sit up, Tara slid off the bed. Then, as Tara fell, she landed squarely on Léa knocking her flat on her back again.

Léa looked at Tara.

Tara looked at Léa.

"So we're supposed to be the next generation of super spies?" said Léa.

"We are so totally fucked," said Tara.

Léa and Tara started laughing at the same time. Even though their heads were pounding, the laughing continued. As the laugh faded, Léa spotted the beer glass she'd set up. Tara's fall knocked it over again. Léa picked it up, looked up at her friend and showed her the glass.

"Thank you so much for last night," said Léa.

"We needed it," said Tara.

Léa dropped the glass and wrapped her arms around Tara. Holding her tight, she whispered in her ear.

"Of all the people in the world who could be my best friend, I'm so glad it's you," said Léa.

"We're lucky. Some people go their whole lives without having a best friend," whispered Tara.

"We're lucky," agreed Léa.

The phones and backpacks continued to buzz.

Tara rolled off Léa and stared at the ceiling.

"We'd be luckier if someone would shut those fucking things off," said Tara.

Léa rolled over, then pushed herself up on her hands and knees. That took some effort and Léa needed to take a few deep breaths. Looking up at the desk, she crawled over to the weight bench Tara used for a desk chair.

"I like your desk chair," said Léa.

"Helps keep me from slouching," said Tara.

Léa nodded as she used the bench to push herself up on her feet. As she stood, the effects of the hangover gave her a massive head rush and she wobbled a bit before quickly sitting down on the bench. Then, the toxic waste dump in her stomach sent a wave of nausea through her body. Léa had to lean over so she could rest her head in her hands as she balanced her elbows on her knees.

"This is a wicked hangover," moaned Léa.

Tara nodded as she looked up at Léa through her long, black hair. She put her hands over her ears.

"Kill those damn phones so we can go back to sleep," said Tara.

Léa looked around toward the desk until she saw the phones. All she had to do was hit the home button on each phone and all the racket from the buzzing would stop. She took a deep breath, sat up and turned toward the desk.

Reaching out, her first attempt to hit the button on a phone completely missed. She tried again. Success! A phone and a backpack stopped buzzing. Léa looked at the other phone, aimed her finger at the button and hit it the first time. Wonderful silence descended over the room.

"That's better," said Tara.

"Finally," said Léa.

After a few moments, Tara looked up at Léa.

"What time is it?" she asked.

"Gimme a minute," said Léa.

She took another few breaths, then a deep breath as she reached for a phone. She punched the home button and the screen lit up.

"10:45," said Léa.

"Wow! I guess we missed breakfast," said Tara.

When Léa didn't say anything, Tara looked up at her. A single ripple of panic flooded over Tara as she saw the expression on her friend's face.

"What?" said Tara.

A look of utter disbelief washed over Léa's face as she looked up from the phone. Looking down at Tara, she shook her head slowly.

"I do not believe this," she said.

"What?" repeated Tara.

"Of all the mornings," said Léa.

"What?" said Tara a third time.

"We have to be at lunch with Commander Dennis and Janet Austin at 11:30," said Léa.

"Are you fucking kidding me?" said Tara.

"See for yourself," said Léa.

She tossed the phone down to Tara. Normally Tara would be able to catch a phone tossed to her. But the hangover was just too much.

The phone bounced off her nose.

A single snort type laugh erupted from Léa's nose as a thin, liquid stream emerged and stretched to the ground. Once Tara got over being hit in the face with a phone, she looked up at Léa. The thin liquid stream hanging from Léa's nose was getting longer. Tara started laughing hysterically. Léa looked down, wiped her nose and started laughing too.

After a few moments of laughing, Léa slid off the weight bench and lay down next to Tara. Keeping her head propped up on her arm, she smiled down at her friend.

"Super spies. That's what we are," said Léa.

"Pretty fucking pathetic," said Tara.

The phone that had landed on Tara's nose began buzzing again. Léa picked it up, read the message then looked up at Tara.

"We have forty five minutes before we need to meet Alan Dennis for lunch," said Léa.

Tara looked up at the ceiling and closed her eyes.

"We are so screwed," said Tara.

11 LATE FOR LUNCH

The Castle, Deep In The Cliffs Pub

Alan Dennis and Janet Austin sat alone in a booth at The Castle's Deep in the Cliff's Pub. It was early afternoon and the place was completely deserted. Most of the HD monitors in the room were dark except for the view of the North Atlantic from a webcam hidden in the ocean-side castle turret. Alan pulled out his battered old pocket watch. He wound it a few times, adjusted his reading glasses and looked at the time.

Janet caught a quick glance at the watch and looked over at Alan. Her boss was a pretty easy going guy. But he was just over 90 years old and some things made him cranky. Things like people being late to meetings. Alan slipped the watch back into his vest pocket.

Janet looked away and tried to stifle a smile. After nearly twenty yeas as a field agent and one of The Castle's top assassins, Janet found herself looking back on her life on the run with anger and bitterness. As she adjusted to her new role as a top level administrator, Janet decided she didn't want that anger and bitterness to rule the rest of her life.

It wasn't easy, and it took years of soul searching. But Janet finally realized the past was unchangeable and the present and the future was what truly mattered. Only the memories of her sister and best friend Helena caused Janet pain. The rest of her memories had been neatly filed away into the dust bin of a past Janet learned to care less about. Consequently, Janet didn't take anything too seriously.

Alan pulled his watch out again and looked at it. Janet loved Alan like a father, but when he got cranky, she started laughing. He tapped the watch, checked the time again then looked at Janet.

"We did say 11:30 at Deep in the Cliffs, didn't we?" groused Alan.

"I'm sure they got the message and will be here any minute," said Janet.

Alan huffed as he took a sip of his tea, then started twirling the tea cup in circle on the saucer. After a few circles, he pulled his watch out and checked the time again. Janet couldn't help herself as a slight snicker popped out through her mouth and nose. She gently patted Alan's hand.

"Sorry. You know my twisted sense of humor," said Janet.

Alan put his watch back in the vest pocket and smiled over at Janet.

"It's that twisted sense of humor that makes you uniquely you," he said.

"If only others appreciated it like you do," said Janet.

"My dear, if I were a hundred years younger, that husband of yours would still be single," said the old man.

Janet smiled.

"Sorry. I'm afraid Thomas stole my heart for good," she said warmly.

"He was there for you during the worst days of your life," said Alan.

"He was and always will be. And he gets my twisted sense of humor. Not many do," said Janet.

"He was the only one who got just how deeply Helena's loss meant to you," said Alan.

Janet looked down and didn't say anything. Looking away she felt the familiar lump rising in her heart, past her lungs and into her throat. Like clockwork, whenever anyone mentioned Helena, Janet would barely be able to hold it together. Anyone but Tara that is. Somehow, Janet could talk about Helena with Tara and not break down into a puddle of tears.

Janet guessed it was because Tara had a friend just like she did. And Helena was so much more than just her best friend. Like Léa and Tara, Janet and Helena bonded at an early age. They were together right up to the moment Helena died in Janet's arms.

Over the past year, Janet had often found herself desperately wanting Helena around for just one more day so she could meet Tara and Léa. They were all birds of a feather and Janet often thought they'd have the most wonderful time.

Janet took a deep breath and tried to bring herself back to the present. Not many people understood why Janet didn't take much seriously. If they understood what it was like to loose a friend like Helena, they'd understand why not much mattered to Janet anymore.

She felt the old man put his hand on hers.

"I'm sorry if I brought back painful memories," said Alan.

Janet gulped down the lump in her throat, turned and smiled at the old man.

"It's been over twenty years and it still hurts like I lost her yesterday," said Janet.

"The idiot who came up with 'time heals all wounds' probably never lost anyone they really cared about," said Alan.

"You lost someone important to you too didn't you?" asked Janet.

"Well, that was a long time ago," said Alan.

He looked around the little pub carved deep in the cliffs under the old castle. It took years to blast the complex they now called home into the cliffs looking over the stormy Atlantic. It was the dream of his mentor and friend Sir. Richard. A dream he would never live to see. Alan smiled at Janet.

"Sir Richard was more of a mentor than a best friend like Helena," said Alan.

"No person's loss is greater than another's," said Janet.

"For someone with a wicked sense of humor and the ability to take literally nothing seriously, you're really quite smart," said Alan.

"I call it stealth wisdom. The more people view me as the class clown, the less I get volunteered for," said Janet.

"Nice strategy, but I think your secret is blown," said Alan.

"I'm sure you'll keep my secret," smiled Janet.

"Why should I do that?" smiled Alan.

"Because I know a few secrets about you," said Janet slyly.

Alan smiled.

"My past is pure as the driven snow," he said.

"Yeah, except for those years in East Berlin," said Janet.

"And your third trip to Moscow," said Alan.

"So we've both got the goods on each other," said Janet.

""Louis, I think this is the beginning of a beautiful friendship," said Alan.

"Casablanca. Right?" said Janet.

"One of my favorites," said Alan.

The table got quiet for a few moments before Alan pulled his battered pocket watch from his vest. Looking at it, he looked up at the empty door to the pub and huffed.

"I understand being ten minutes late, but it's almost noon," said Alan.

Janet continued looking at the old man and smiled.

"Something must have happened. I'm sure they're not being rude," said Janet.

As she looked at Alan, Janet watched his expression go from mild irritation to a mix of disbelief, then humor.

"Oh I'd say something's definitely happened," said Alan.

Janet looked over at the door. Her small, wicked smile appeared on one corner of her mouth. She looked down.

"So, those two are who you think will be the best spies ever?" smirked Janet.

"Shut up," said Alan.

Tara and Léa stood in the doorway of Deep in the Cliff's Pub. Tara was wearing her usual black pants, boots and t'shirt. Léa's clothes were rumpled, like she'd slept in them. Both were wearing ball caps. Both were pale with red, puffy eyes.

"I'd say the next generation of super spies here at The Castle are a little hung over," smirked Janet.

"I'd say a lot hung over," said Alan.

Janet looked at Alan and saw he was smiling. She was relieved because it appeared that Tara and Léa were in enough pain and didn't need suffer the wrath, or worse, a lecture from the Old Man.

Alan waved Léa and Tara over to the table, then waved toward the bar and David McNally. He pointed to the two young women slowly walking toward his table and smiled. David looked at Alan, pointed to his head and stomach. Alan nodded as David disappeared into the room behind the bar.

Léa and Tara arrived at the table looking like they were in excruciating hangover pain. Alan looked up and smiled.

"Good afternoon," he said a little too loudly.

It had the desired effect. Both Léa and Tara closed their eyes in pain. Their eyebrows compressed and their lips tightened. They were clearly not doing well.

"Hi girls," said Janet quietly.

"Hey," said Tara softly to Janet.

Léa sat down next to Tara and tried to smile. Tara looked from Janet to Alan, trying to figure out how much trouble she and Léa were in. They were both smiling, so Tara guessed they weren't that busted.

"I guess I should apologize for our condition," said Léa quietly.

Alan smiled. He looked at Janet, then at Léa and Tara.

"As you may have heard, I was once a world class drunk. Just looking into your eyes reminds me of the past I'm happy I left behind," said Alan.

"So you gave it up?" asked Léa.

"No. I just cut way back," said Alan.

David McNally suddenly appeared at the table with a tray full of food and some green bottles. Tara looked up at the tray with dread in her eyes. Léa looked straight ahead clearly steeling herself for whatever nauseating food was on the tray.

Janet looked at both Tara and Léa and thanked her lucky stars that she didn't feel as bad as they appeared. Like Alan, she went through her 'drinking stage' of life long ago and while she still liked a nice buzz, she'd grown out of getting plowed.

"So what happened to you two?" asked Alan.

Léa and Tara looked at each other. Janet watched as a few moments of non-verbal communication only possible between the best of friends took place.

"We went back to my place last night," said Tara.

Janet looked at Léa.

"How did you like The Pit?" asked Janet.

Léa looked up at Janet, surprised that anyone knew enough about Tara to know she called her room The Pit. Then she remembered Tara's story and that Janet was a more than just a friend.

"Uniquely Tara," said Léa.

"Can't wait to see what you do with your room," said Janet.

Léa looked over at Tara, then back at Janet.

"I'm not as creative as Tara. So don't expect much," said Léa.

"As I recall, you didn't do much with your room either," said Alan.

"Home is pretty much wherever I'm sleeping at night," said Janet.

Léa looked at Janet, then down at her hands which were folded on the table. She thought about that a while and nodded.

"Yeah. Sounds about right," said Léa as she looked at Tara. "As long as you're somewhere close."

Tara looked over at Léa and managed a weak smile.

Alan looked up at David McNally who was waiting patiently by the table with a tray full of food.

"What have you got there David?" asked Alan.

"The perfect cure for a hangover," said David a little too loudly.

He looked down at Tara and Léa and saw his booming voice had the desired effect. They both cringed as he talked. Now that he'd had his fun, it was time to be nice.

"First things first," said David as he gently placed a bottle of Tylenol on the table between Tara and Léa.

Léa made a grab for the bottle, but Tara was quicker. Léa tried to snatch the bottle out of Tara's hands, but Tara hung on tight. Léa didn't give up though. She made another grab for the bottle which Tara held out of her reach.

Janet sat watching the two friends battle for the bottle and started laughing out loud. Even Alan was smiling. As Léa kept reaching for the bottle, Tara gently pushed her away.

Even hung over and in pain, there was something special about these two.

"Okay. Enough. Didn't your parents teach you two to share?" laughed Janet.

Léa and Tara stopped struggling and looked over at Janet and Alan. Their guilty expressions were what you'd expect if you'd caught two kids trying to steal cookies from a cookie jar.

"Sorry," said Tara simply.

"Probably not the best way to behave in front of the boss of an international spy ring," said Léa.

"That's okay. As you might remember we're not opposed to fun around here," smiled Alan.

"And we know you two were brutally separated for a year. I can understand what that meant to you and how good it must feel to be back together," said Janet.

Léa looked at Tara, then back at Janet.

"Tara told me a little about her year here. I know a bit about what happened to you and that you were there for Tara. So thank you," said Léa.

Tara looked down at the Tylenol bottle in her hand, then up at Janet. She nodded once and smiled.

Alan looked around the table, then up at David McNally. He was still standing at the table with his tray full of hangover goodies.

"What else do you have up there David?" asked Alan.

David deposited two big bottles of Pellegrino Sparkling Water in front of Tara and Léa.

"Use that to wash down those pills. The bubbles will help wash the beer and acid out of your stomachs. A good burp will probably feel good about now," said David.

Léa and Tara looked at each other. Tara unscrewed the bottle and shook two pills out into Léa's hand. Léa opened both bottles and chugged some water along with the Tylenol. They drained half the bottles before looking up at David.

The Pellegrino worked fast. Very fast. Léa looked up as a loud belch rumbled up from her very nauseated stomach. Tara's belch was surprisingly loud for such a small woman.

"Sorry," said Léa apologetically.

"That's okay," smiled Janet.

"Been there. Done that," smiled the old man.

Everyone looked up at David who was shuffling a few things around on the tray. He looked down at the table.

"Ready for the next course?" he asked.

"Bring it on," said Tara.

David smiled and deftly placed two steaming plates in front of Tara and Léa. Each plate had a big omelet, some links of sausage and toast. Tara and Léa looked at each other, then up at David.

"Dive in. That's one of the best hangover breakfasts I've ever found," she said.

Léa and Tara looked at each other again. A moment of non-verbal communication passed between them, then they turned and attacked the breakfast.

Alan looked up at David.

"Anything else?" asked Alan.

David placed a pot of coffee and a third plate of eggs, sausage and toast on the table. He tossed the tray on a nearby table, limped over to grab a chair and sat down.

Léa watched him out of the corner of her eye. She remembered Tara telling her how she attacked David the moment her handcuffs were removed at the end of her dungeon test. David was a big man and Tara was a small, skinny girl. As he limped back to the table, Léa tried to imagine Tara shattering his knee.

Looking back at her own plate, she stole a glance at Tara's small, skinny arms and never realized her friend was so strong. Taking a quick break from eating, she reached out and gave her friend a hug and a smile.

"What's that for?" asked Tara.

"You're amazing," said Léa as she returned to her hangover breakfast.

They ate in silence.

Once the plates were empty, Alan began pouring coffee for everyone. As he poured, he watched as everyone began leaning back and relaxing. Janet smiled at Léa.

"What? No Bailey's this morning?" she said wickedly.

Léa closed her eyes, then quickly and slightly shook her head once from side to side. Janet smiled. Tara had told her about Léa's habit of clearing the cobwebs. Some found it annoying, but Tara called it one of Léa's endearing qualities.

"So predictable," said Tara quietly.

Léa looked toward the ceiling and shook her head slowly.

"Yeah. Whatever," she said quietly.

Then she looked at Janet and saw she was smiling. Léa decided the older woman was okay and smiled back.

"I'll pass on the Bailey's this morning," said Léa.

"Maybe tomorrow morning too," suggested Tara.

Léa looked down at her empty plate, then up at David McNally.

"I think we'll be fine after that great breakfast. How did you know that was the perfect cure?" said Léa.

"Years of experience," said David.

Alan looked around the table. These were moments he savored. Watching people working together, supporting each other, being nice to each other. In the fifty years of his life building his mentor's dream, there was one thing he insisted on. The people working for him could be anything, do anything, except be nasty and cruel. The world was cruel enough, he would say.

Alan smiled.

"Everyone doing okay? Got enough coffee?" he asked.

Léa and Tara nodded. Janet held her cup out for more. David nodded that he was fine.

"Well then. We've got some talking to do about your last mission," said Alan.

Tara and Léa looked at each other. Janet picked up on their look immediately. She remembered one day long ago when she and Helena sat down to talk about a mission with Alan. It was in this very same booth in The Castle's pub over breakfast. Janet and Helena thought they were in trouble too.

"Relax. You're not in trouble. We're just here to figure out what's next," smiled Janet.

That was all it took. Immediate relief washed over Léa and Tara's faces. Janet remembered how relieved she and Helena were when they figured out they weren't in trouble either.

"We've reconstructed everything that happened and it's pretty obvious that Perry Drilling is still out there causing trouble and we've got to do something about it," said David.

"We got the message you sent over that One Time Pad scheme you and

Thomas concocted. The Castle's computer system is completely locked down," said Alan.

"Brilliant using old and new technology to keep your message off the servers," smiled Janet.

Tara and Janet's husband Thomas resurrected an old World War II method of secret communication. They wired up an old printer to a modern iPhone in Thomas' office. So when the message came in, it wouldn't appear anywhere on The Castle's computer network.

"We confirmed that millions of packets of data were going out that we couldn't account for. That was what you told us to look for and that's just what we found," said David.

Tara nodded.

"I figure Perry Drilling has complete access to the network," said Tara.

"Thomas told us you suggested that we continue to keep the data rolling around the building, but keep the critical information off the network. We weren't sure why," said Alan.

"If you shut everything down, Drilling would have figured out that we were on to him. We want him to continue reading our traffic so we can send stuff his way to help us find him" said Tara.

"Just like during the war. We had to keep Jerry from finding out that we'd cracked Enigma, so we had to come up with a cover story for every piece of intelligence we acted on," said Alan.

"Did you figure out a way to keep the stuff about Drilling off the net and still get things done?" asked Tara.

"Easy. There are now two computers on every desk. One that's only connected to a printer. The one that's connected to the net has a red keyboard. We are killing a lot of trees," said Janet.

We were able to revive the old pneumatic message transport system for all the off-net stuff. It's slowed us down, but we're keeping up," said David.

"I remember when those tubes were considered state of the art," smiled Alan.

"Tubes?" asked Léa.

"An old pneumatic system. The pipes go all over the building. You put your paper message in a carrier, stick it in the correct tube and it blows the carrier to it's destination. They still work, but it's noisy as hell," said Janet.

"We kept the network active like you said. But I'm still not sure how that helps us," said David.

"Are millions of unaccounted for packets still going out of the pipe?" asked Tara.

"Yes," said Janet.

"Good. That means Perry Drilling is still reading our data. Now we're going to turn the tables on him and send him a little present," said Tara.

Léa looked at her friend. She smiled and prepared herself to be impressed.

"What kind of present did you have in mind Miss Wells?" asked Alan.

Tara smiled at the old man, then at Janet.

"Actually, it was a movie your husband turned me on to that gave me the idea," said Tara.

"Not that Dauntless crap again," sighed David.

Tara's eyes flashed in anger for a split second. But the flash faded quickly.

"Sorry, not this time," she said.

She turned and looked at Janet.

"This was one of Thomas' first movie nights I ever experienced. The movie was Girl with the Dragon Tattoo," said Tara.

Janet nodded and thought back to the movie that had become one of Tara's favorites. But she didn't know how it would help them track down Perry Drilling.

"What did you figure out?" asked Janet.

"Remember the little app Lisbeth Salander used to hack into people's computers?" asked Tara.

Everyone at the table looked down and tried to remember. Most moviegoers don't remember small details like apps in movies. But it was those little details that rarely escaped Tara. She looked around the table, saw no one had figured it out and smiled.

"She called it Asphyxia. It basically let her read anything on anyone's computer," said Tara.

"You have that?" asked David.

"That's a bit obvious. I'll guess it's how she was able to read all those things you got so upset about during the Uppsala Op meeting," said Léa.

"The next step is to to get my real world version of Asphyxia onto Perry Drilling's computer," she said.

"And how do we do that?" asked Alan.

"Easier said than done. First, we have to find him. Then we have to hack his password," said Tara.

"What do you need to make it happen?" asked Janet.

Tara looked at Léa and smiled. Léa smiled back. Her best friend was about to impress people. Léa felt so proud of Tara.

"I've been playing around with this for a while now. I just have a few last details to figure out," said Tara.

"But when can you deploy this Asphyxia?" asked Alan.

Tara thought a few moments.

"If you can spare Thomas Austin, that kid who helps him out and Léa, I might be able to deploy in a few days. Maybe even by tonight if we're lucky," said Tara.

Alan looked at Janet who nodded. He looked at David who nodded too. Alan pulled out his pocket watch, checked the time and looked back at Léa and Tara.

"Then go get yourselves cleaned up and get to work. I'm afraid I'm late for my next meeting," he said.

Tara smiled, looked at Léa and stood up. Léa quickly followed. Tara looked at Alan.

"We'll get it done," she said.

Tara looked at David.

"Thanks for the breakfast," she said.

Then Tara looked at Janet. All she did was smile and nod as she and Léa turned to leave.

"Try to lay off that American ale till you get it done," said David.

Tara and Léa stopped walking for a moment. They didn't even have to look at each for their magic non-verbal communication to work. After a moment, they just kept walking, but they didn't walk far.

"Oh fuck. Not her," growled Tara.

"Not this morning," said Léa.

Cindy Martin suddenly appeared in the door to the pub. As she started walking toward Janet and Alan, her eyes ran up and down Léa and Tara.

"It's not fair. Having this bad of a hangover and having to deal with her in the same day," said Léa.

"If she even opens her fucking mouth, I swear I'll put her in the hospital," said Tara.

As Cindy got closer, Léa and Tara saw a smile growing on her face. Clearly Cindy was trying to come up with something clever to say. But all she could do was smile and shake her head.

The three passed in silence.

12 HACKING THE BAD GUYS

The Castle, Léa's Dorm Room

After breakfast, Léa and Tara headed back to their rooms on the living quarters level. Once Léa arrived, she longingly eyed her bed for just a moment before she quickly walked into the bathroom. As much as she wanted a nap, there was no time for sleep now. Along the way, she quickly peeled away the clothes she had been wearing way too long. It felt so good to just get them off.

The amazing shower in her bathroom made her feel better from the moment she turned on the water. Léa started with the powerful massage jets blasting her body from each corner of the cut stone shower. She slowly moved around in the jets for fifteen minutes before she pushed the lever switching to the gentle overhead shower mode and reached for the shampoo.

After she was finished with the soap, Léa switched back to massage mode and let the powerful jets pound the rest of the hangover out of her system. After a half an hour in the shower, she began to feel human.

Of course, David McNally's excellent 'day after drinking too much' breakfast helped a lot too.

So did the pain killers.

Shutting off the shower, Léa grabbed a towel as she walked back into her room. Standing in the middle of the room, one hand was using the towel to dry off while the other was checking her iPad for messages. There weren't any.

As Léa dried off, her nose began picking up a strange smell. She kept working with the towel while trying to figure out what it was. After drying off, she tossed the towel into a clothes basket and scooped up the clothes she'd left on the floor. One sniff was all it took. The evil smell was coming from her clothes.

Not only did she show up for breakfast with the boss hungover, but she smelled like a brewery too. Léa closed her eyes and huffed once in disgust.

"*Great*," thought Léa to herself.

She quickly cleared the cobwebs and tossed the clothes into the dirty clothes basket. As she turned toward the closet, Léa caught sight of herself in the large, floor to ceiling mirror by the door.

She'd only retuned to The Castle a day ago, but her Aegean tan was already fading. Léa decided long ago that she didn't want a case of skin cancer and didn't spend much time laying out. But it was impossible to hang around the Aegean Island of Mykonos and not get a little sun.

Looking at her back, then up and down the front, Léa was glad the tan was quickly fading. Even though Léa wasn't into tanning, she hated tan lines.

As Léa walked over to the closet for clean clothes, her iPhone buzzed. Stepping back a few steps from the closet, she reached for the phone on her bed, tapped the home button and a message popped up. It was from Tara.

You about ready?

Léa tapped out her reply and tossed her phone back on the bed.

Five minutes.

Less than five minutes later, she opened the door to her room, set the dirty clothes basket out in the hall and waited for Tara.

Almost immediately, Tara emerged from her room at the end of the long hall. As she walked through her door, Tara kicked her own dirty clothes basket into the hall too.

Once Tara was close enough, Léa looked at her friend then back down the hallway toward Tara's room.

"Did your clothes smell as bad as mine?" she asked.

"Yep," said Tara.

"Kinda embarrassing that we went to breakfast smelling that way," said Léa,

"Oh well," said Tara.

The two friends walked down the long hallway toward Central Park. As they emerged from the hallway into the huge underground atrium, they were quickly absorbed into the hundreds of people running around The Castle complex.

At the main stairway, Tara started heading up. Léa and Tara's rooms were on the sixth floor of the eight level complex. When they arrived at the third level, Tara stepped off the stairway and started heading down another long hallway.

"How you tell which hallway is which?" asked Léa.

"Afraid you have to rely on your memory. They don't label floors and hallways in case some bad guy gets loose," said Tara.

"How long did it take for you to learn your way around?" asked Léa.

"Not long. There are eight levels. Each door has a number. The hallways are laid out about the same. So just remember the level, the hall and number and you'll be fine," said Tara.

As they walked down the hallway, Léa noticed the only thing on the doors was a number and a entry keypad. Nothing else. All the hallways were neatly carved out of the rock in the cliffs. The hallway walls were a brownish-white. The only difference Léa could see was the hallways on living quarters levels had a nice carpet.

"So how did you get permission to paint the Dauntless flames on your door?" asked Léa.

"Didn't ask," said Tara dryly.

"Of course," said Léa.

As they walked down the hall, Léa suddenly tugged at her friends shirt.

"Hey. Remember last night when we said we needed to start causing a little trouble?" said Léa.

"Yep," said Tara.

"Well. Any ideas?" said Léa.

Tara smiled at Léa.

"Got it covered," said Tara.

Léa looked at Tara hoping to learn more. Growing up, perpetrating minor schemes of mischief was a little hobby for Léa and Tara. The goal was to cause just enough trouble to get noticed, but not enough to get into serious trouble.

"So what's the plan?" asked Léa.

Tara gave Léa her sideways half smile, kept walking and didn't say anything.

"Fine. Be mysterious," said Léa.

"It's a little something I've been plotting for a while. You'll like it," said Tara.

"We'll see," said Léa.

About halfway down the long hallway, Tara finally turned and stopped in front of door number 237. She tapped out a long code on the keypad and the door slid silently open. Just like the night before, Tara stood aside and held out her hand, inviting Léa into her world.

"So if you call your room The Pit, what do you call this?" asked Léa.

"The Furnace," said Tara.

"The Furnace?" repeated Léa.

"Out of the frying pan, into the fire," said Tara.

"Charming," said Léa as she walked in.

"Appropriate," said Tara.

Just like their rooms, the lights in Tara's 'Furnace' slowly brightened when the room sensed movement. It was about twice as big as Léa's room. One wall was lined with racks of computers, blinking lights and some big screen LCDs.

A workbench with various projects scattered over them ran along another wall. One project took up half of the bench. It was a model of The Castle's atrium.

"Okay. What's this?" asked Léa.

Tara looked over at Léa, then at the model she constructed. A big smile appeared on her face.

"That's a little idea for some fun I've come up with," said Tara.

Léa walked up to the bench and looked it over closely. Tara had constructed a fairly accurate model of the atrium right down to the benches, the heavy duty railing, stairway and even the old Paternoster lift. Scattered around the model were different kinds of rope ladders, heavy padding and multi level scaffolding. Several rope ladders and what looked like more pads were scattered by the side of the model.

"I know what this is. It's a very big obstacle course," she said excitedly.

Tara smiled. There wasn't much Léa couldn't quickly figure out.

Léa looked back at the model, then up at Tara.

"This thing is going to be tough," said Léa.

"There are some very tough people here who spend a lot of time in the gym keeping in shape. We have some smaller obstacle courses that are pretty good, but nothing like this," said Tara.

"They're not going to let you actually build that are they?" asked Léa.

"I've been working out the details for about six months. We've been collecting materials and the boss says go for it," smiled Tara.

"I can't wait to try it," smiled Léa.

Tara smiled too. She'd been waiting months to show her idea to her best friend.

"That's gotta cost a lot," said Léa.

"You need to forget about money around here. They're loaded and won't run out in our lifetime," said Tara.

"How?" asked Léa.

"These people have literally saved the world more than a few times. It's something they're happy to do, but they also get some pretty big checks from grateful governments," said Tara.

"Why would governments pay us?" asked Léa.

"Because we can do things governments could never do," said Tara.

Léa thought about that a few moments and slowly nodded her head a few times. But before Léa could ask any more questions, the door opened and Thomas Austin and a skinny kid entered the room. Léa thought she recognized the kid, but couldn't remember where she'd seen him. But she knew she'd seen him before.

Tara walked over to a single computer sitting on a desk and sat down. After powering up the monitor, she turned back to her best friend.

"I'd love to talk about the my jungle gym more, but we need to focus on some serious shit for a while," said Tara.

She pointed to a chair and then to a spot next to her at the desk. Léa hooked the chair with her foot and rolled it over next to Tara. Sitting down, she watched as Tara pulled out her phone and started some music playing quietly on the speakers scattered around the room.

"Grab a seat you two and let me show you what I've come up with so far. We need to overcome a few last snags to get it working," said Tara to the newcomers.

Léa looked at the kid and smiled.

"I'm Léa Taylor. I know we've met, but I don't remember your name," she said.

The kid looked down at the floor and turned beet red. Léa looked over at Tara.

"Did I say something wrong?" asked Léa.

Tara's half smile, half smirk appeared on her face. She looked over at Thomas, then at the kid.

"This is Toby Barnes. He's my assistant in the media department," said Thomas.

Toby continued to look down at the floor.

"Hello?" said Léa hesitantly.

She looked back at Tara. After a few moments of non-verbal, best friend communication, Tara started explaining.

"Remember your second night here? I stopped by your room with a bottle of wine," said Tara.

"Sure," said Léa.

She thought back to her first week at The Castle. It was a whirlwind of activity. She searched her memory, but couldn't remember who the kid was. She slowly shook her head.

"No. Sorry. Don't remember," said Léa.

Tara looked down and smiled.

"You're gonna love this. Remember when you opened your door to let me in?" said Tara.

"Yeah," said Léa.

"You opened the door, dressed in your favorite outfit, right about the time this guy walked by," said Tara.

Léa shook her head not remembering. She looked at the kid, then back at Tara. She shook her head a few more times, then stopped. She looked back up at the kid.

He was still looking down. His face was still red. Léa's head tilted off to one side as she tried to figure out what this kid's problem was. She thought back to what Tara said. Then it clicked, Tara said she was wearing her favorite outfit. Léa's favorite outfit was no outfit at all. The kid walked by just as she opened the door for Tara.

Léa sighed. It wasn't the first time her comfort with nudity had caused uncomfortable moments. But it wasn't like she was running around town naked. When she was at home, she just liked tossing off her clothes and being comfortable. Léa looked down, took a breath, then looked up at the kid.

"Nice to meet you. Sorry if I made you uncomfortable," said Léa.

"Nice to meet you too," said Toby.

He still wouldn't look at Léa.

"I should probably apologize to you. I'm basically a geek that no girl would ever be interested in. And you're just so amazingly .. Well .. You know ... You're ..," stammered Toby.

"Thanks. But we've probably got to move things along," said Léa.

She looked up at Tara, nodded to the kid with a pleading look in her eyes. It was more of that special non-verbal, best friends communication. Then again, probably anyone could figure out what Léa was trying to tell Tara.

"Please put an end to this. NOW," was her silent message.

Tara smiled at Léa and decided it was time to take pity on her best friend.

"Okay. Yeah. Great. We do indeed need to move this along," said Tara.

"Thank you," said Léa.

Tara let the conversation fall off for a few moments. Once the room quieted down, the music Tara had turned on became easier to hear. As always, Tara had picked the perfect music. It was a movie soundtrack. Tara nodded toward the speakers.

"I think you all know me well enough to know some of my favorite movies. The music you're hearing is from the Dragon Tattoo movies," said Tara.

She looked at Léa.

"As I told you last night, the girl was fucking brilliant with computers. One thing was a little app she created called: Asphyxia," said Tara.

She looked around the room hoping everyone was following her. Only Thomas Austin seemed to be following her. Tara wasn't surprised. He knew every movie ever made. Every book ever written. And, Thomas knew every detail about every movie, book and TV show he'd ever seen. Tara looked at Toby, then at Léa.

Léa.

Tara felt a ripple of joy wash over her. She was just so happy that Léa was finally with her at The Castle. But Tara didn't dare enjoy the happy feelings too long. She'd learned that happiness was like a beer buzz. It felt so good, but eventually wore off. Tara had learned that she had a weakness for happy feelings that needed to be controlled.

But still.

Léa was finally here with her!

Tara let the ripple of joy wash over her again. She closed her eyes and quickly shook her head from side to side. Then she laughed at herself. She just cleared the cobwebs like Léa always did. She looked at her best friend who was looking at her.

Léa knew one of her personality tics was what Tara long ago named: clearing the cobwebs. So it was surprising for her to see her best friend doing what she did all the time. Léa's brain kicked in and before she knew what she was doing she heard herself quietly saying something to Tara.

"So predictable," said Léa.

Tara looked at Léa. Her best friend just threw a line that she'd been tossing at Léa for years. It was probably the only time Tara had pulled a Léa and cleared the cobwebs. Léa picked up on it and with lightning speed, threw it back at her. Of all the best friends in the world, Tara had the best. She started laughing.

"You've been waiting years to say that haven't you?" said Tara.

Léa smiled.

The other two people in the room looked at the best friends and realized something special was happening. They knew it was something only possible between the best of friends and wished they had a friend like Léa and Tara.

Best friends are special.

Even though only a few seconds had gone by, Tara looked around the room and decided she needed to get the meeting going again.

"So back to what I was saying. The app Lisbeth Salander came up with, allowed her to connect to any computer on the planet and read everything on that computer," said Tara.

"Even if they had security set up?" asked Thomas.

"Well, Lisbeth's system was fictional. But I assumed it would be able to get around conventional security fairly easily. After all, the only thing most people do is put a lame password on their system and leave it for years," said Tara.

"Which I'll bet you can get by with a simple password cracker," said Léa.

"Pretty much," said Tara.

"About six months ago, I decided to try to engineer a real version of Asphyxia," said Tara.

She pointed to the screen she was sitting in front of. Everyone looked at Tara, then crowded around the computer.

"It's pretty simple. You start by figuring out the i.p. address of the computer you want to hack, then start the app from the command line console," said Tara.

She tapped on the keyboard, clicked the mouse and a black window popped up. Reaching for her phone, she looked up an i.p. address, and tapped it into the computer. A few moments later, another window opened showing what looked like the desktop of another computer. Someone was tapping out a memo.

Everyone looked at the screen for a while, then at Tara who was watching the memo appear. It was a private message to Alan Dennis from David McNally expressing his concerns about a meeting that was about to be called that evening.

"You've hacked David McNally's computer?" asked Thomas.

"His was the first one," said Tara.

"I'm going to have to tell him to change his password," said Thomas.

"Won't do any good," said Tara.

"Why?" asked Léa,

"Because once my app sets up a link, it'll keep track of any security changes so you always have access," said Tara.

Thomas Austin looked down and shook his head.

"It's a damn good thing you're on our side," he said.

"Just don't piss me off," said Tara dryly.

Léa was watching the memo appear on the computer. As Tara and Thomas talked about the app, Léa kept reading until she rolled her eyes and broke into the conversation.

"Great," said Léa.

"What?" asked Tara.

Léa nodded to the screen.

"Apparently they've decided to start a committee looking into ending the Dungeon Initiation Test," said Léa.

"About fucking time," said Tara.

Léa nodded at the computer again.

"Don't cheer too loudly. They've put Cindy in charge and the first thing she did was appoint us to the committee," said Léa.

"Ha, ha," said Thomas quietly.

Léa looked at him and smiled sympathetically.

"Don't laugh so soon. You're on the committee too," said Léa.

"Wonderful," moaned Thomas. "Another committee."

"What the fuck are we supposed to do on a committee," said Tara.

"According to David McNally's memo, you're on the committee because of that little brawl you staged after they took the handcuffs off. How bad was it?" said Léa.

Tara shrugged and didn't say anything.

Léa looked from Tara to Thomas. He looked down and smiled.

"Most people aren't too pleased when they come out of the dungeon and learn it was all a test. Some are so angry that they start a fight. Let's just say the fight this one started was one for the record books," said Thomas.

Léa nodded and smiled at Tara.

"Way to go," said Léa.

Tara shrugged again and looked down at the computer.

"You're being appointed because, apparently, you're the only person who ever enjoyed it," said Tara.

"And figured it out in record time," added Thomas.

Léa looked at him and smiled.

"Thanks," said Léa.

Tara looked away from the group. She focused on her obstacle course model and thought it over. She hated that test and felt it did more damage than good. So she was glad someone was going to do something about it. But why did it have to be Cindy?

She looked back at the group.

"Yeah. Okay. Fine. We'll worry about that later. Right now we have this problem to figure out," said Tara.

"What's the problem? Looks like you've got it working just fine," asked Thomas.

"My app leaves a little nugget of code on the hacked computer. It's very small, but it keeps us updated on password and other security changes. It also logs the computer's location," said Tara.

"So what's the problem?" asked Thomas.

"Perry Drilling has very high level security set up. Once you try to crack his password, the computer shuts down your access before the nugget can install," said Tara.

"How big it is?" asked Toby.

"Only about 36 kilobytes," said Tara.

"What if we break it into three or four, smaller chunks, then try multiple attacks at the same time?" said Toby.

Léa looked from the kid to Tara.

"How will that help?" she said.

"Smaller bits of data might just make it through between the time you hack the password and the computer shuts down," said Toby.

Tara started tapping away on her computer. After a few moments, she looked up.

"Okay. If I break it up, I have to add some code to have it re-assemble itself once it arrives at it's destination. That'll increase the size to about 43 kilobytes Best thing to do is break it into five parts. We'll have to wait a few hours between attacks so nothing looks suspicious," said Tara.

"How long will it take to break the nugget up?" asked Thomas.

"I've already got that done. I just have to set up five separate attacks and schedule them for the next four hours," said Tara.

Léa thumbed the home button on her iPhone and checked the time. She rolled her eyes and looked up at Tara.

"That means it'll be done a few hours after Cindy's committee meeting is scheduled to end," smiled Léa.

"Wonderful," scowled Tara as she continued tapping away on her computer.

13 CLOSING THE DUNGEON

The Castle, Main Auditorium

"Everyone ready to have a little fun with dungeons and handcuffs?" said Cindy nervously.

Tara slouched in her chair next to Léa and whispered under her breath.

"Great. Now's she's a comedian. It's not fair to have the leftovers of brutal hangover and have to listen to her all in the same day," Tara scowled.

"Let's give her a chance. This could be better than we think," said Léa.

Cindy glanced at Tara and Léa, then looked at the twenty people scattered around the stage. They were in The Castle's large auditorium. A long table and chairs had been set up on the stage.

Léa and Tara sat together at the end of the table. Alan Dennis sat next to Pattie and David McNally at the other end. Janet and Thomas Austin sat by themselves in the first row of theater seats. A few more people sat a few rows back and more were arriving by the minute.

Looking around the room, Léa realized she only knew a few of the people there. But more than a few were whispering to each other while looking at nodding toward Léa. Everyone clearly knew her.

"It's a little creepy that everyone knows me," whispered Léa.

"The field agents are the rock stars here. So we've already got some pretty big reputations," said Tara.

"We do?" said Léa.

"Well, you more than me," said Tara.

"Great," said Léa.

She looked toward the center of the table on the stage. Cindy was looking through her notes. Every now and then, she'd glance up as the number of people in the auditorium continued to grow. Cindy looked down and fidgeted with her notes again.

She hated public speaking and was still angry about the brutal way she and all of the new recruits were brought into The Castle. Commander Dennis told her that her anger made her perfect to head up an effort to eliminate The Castle's infamous Dungeon Initiation Test.

"*Why am I doing this again?*" Cindy thought to herself

Cindy's troubles began that morning at a lunch meeting with Alan Dennis and Janet Austin when she was told her first big assignment was to

70

come up with an alternative to the widely hated test. After lunch, Cindy decided to head back to her room. Like so many before her, she stopped to gaze out into Central Park's huge atrium. Hundreds of people always seemed to be scurrying around.

Cindy was on the second level of the huge underground complex. It was just after midday, and the L.E.D. lighting made it look like it was a warm, sunny afternoon. Even though they were deep underground, the ventilation system constantly kept fresh air circulating through the complex.

Peering over the sturdy safety rail, Cindy peered down the the bottom of the atrium. Central Park was located over a deep underground pool of water fed by a natural underground tunnel that lead to the sea. As Cindy looked down, one of The Castle's three submarines was just emerging from the tunnel. She watched as it smoothly pulled up to dock.

Watching as the shore crew tied the sub to the dock, Cindy shook her head in amazement. The mere size of The Castle's operation was mind-boggling. Thousands of people scattered around the world worked for The Castle. They had a fleet of airplanes and submarines. They had safe houses in every capital of every nation.

And now, Cindy Martin had just been asked to take charge of getting rid of something nearly everyone she'd met hated, but was a central part of The Castle's operations. She slowly turned around and walked to one of the many stone benches that lined the circular wall of Central Park.

As she sat, Cindy slung her backpack off her shoulder and let it gently fall next to her feet. Leaning back in the chair, Cindy looked up and closed her eyes. How the hell was she supposed get this done. As she sat with her eyes closed, Cindy felt someone sit down next to her. She slowly opened her eyes, turned her head and saw it was Janet Austin.

"You're always appearing when I've got my eyes closed," said Cindy.

She met Janet her first night at The Castle's unusual watering hole, Deep in the Cliff's Pub. She got pretty drunk that night, but remembered that first meeting.

She'd just taken her first drink from her pint of ale, when she closed her eyes to shut out the chaos around her. It was Cindy's first night after being welcomed into what she called "The Den of Thieves" and life was a bit overwhelming.

Just like right now, Janet sat down while Cindy was overwhelmed and she had her eyes closed to shut out the chaos.

"I try to be there at the exact moment when people need me the most," smiled Janet.

"Is that your job? Being there when people need you?" asked Cindy.

Janet looked away from Cindy and nodded a few times.

"I'd say that's my perfect job description," said Janet.

"Well, your advice was spot on the first time. What words of wisdom do you have to get me out of this fix?" asked Cindy.

Cindy wasn't looking at Janet. She was looking down at the backpack she tossed on the ground by her feet.

Janet looked at Cindy with with her strange mix of amusement and her usual, 'I could care less' look. She laughed once, then looked back out into the huge, stone atrium.

"Well, you're not getting out of anything. So, you'd better start coming up with your plan to make it happen," said Janet.

"Great. Any advice on the best way to make it happen?" asked Cindy.

Janet stood up, looked down at Cindy and smiled. Cindy continued to look down at her feet.

"First, realize that no one and I mean no one in this cave likes meetings. So get right to the point. Don't waste any time on speeches or laying out some grand plan of yours. Second, just because you're in charge, doesn't mean you have to come up with all the answers. I suspect a lot of people will show up, so throw the responsibility to solve the problem at them. Simple as that," said Janet.

Cindy looked up. Janet was still smiling down at her. Thinking it over, Cindy nodded a few times. She looked to the right, then to the left. A moment later, she smiled up and Janet.

"Actually, that sound perfect. Thanks," said Cindy quietly.

"Any time," said Janet over her shoulder.

After a few minutes alone, Cindy reached for her backpack, pulled out her headphones and laptop. She worked best with music. She liked classical when she was working on a project. Her favorite working music was Shostakovich.

As soon as the Mac powered up, she started the music, opened a new note and started typing. Cindy started by writing down Janet's two pieces of advice ...

Get To The Point

Make Them Do the Work

Then Cindy wrote out the goal of the meeting. It took her several tries to trim the sentence to as few words as possible. Once she had her goal clearly defined, Cindy started two columns. One was titled: Reasons Why. The second was: Reasons Why Not.

As the music played, Cindy paused to think. Every now and then, she'd tap out a few words under the Reasons Why column. After about half an hour, she looked down at her list. She had ten good reasons why they should ditch the stupid initiation test. The column under Reasons Why Not had just one entry ...

They needed a test

Looking out into the atrium, she saw Alan Dennis slowly walking toward the lift. Cindy quickly snapped her Mac closed, stuffed it into her backpack and ran to catch up to the man who just gave her a big job.

As she approached the old man, she slowed down and eased up beside him. Alan Dennis was over 90 years old and she didn't want to startle him.

"Mr. Dennis, may I ask you a few questions?" said Cindy quietly.

"Of course. But you must promise me something," said Alan.

"What's that?" asked Cindy.

"Don't ever call me Mister or Commander again. My name is Alan," said the Commander of The Castle.

"That seems a bit awkward. You're the boss," said Cindy.

"Not half as awkward as being called Commander or Mister Dennis. I've never liked those titles and we've gotten along without them for the past 40 years," smiled Alan.

Cindy looked down and smiled. Despite her anger at the foul initiation, she was growing to like the old man.

"Okay, I'll try," she said.

"What's your question?" asked Alan.

"Why did you guys start that test in the first place?" asked Cindy.

Alan sighed.

"It's a long story. But basically, we needed some way to test the abilities of recruits to solve problems while under extreme stress," said Alan.

Cindy looked down as they slowly walked to the lift. After a few steps, she looked up as hundreds of people scurried from one place to the other in the huge underground atrium.

"Did everyone who works here go through the test?" asked Cindy.

"At first, yes. But now we only use it for people who we plan to put out in the field," said Alan.

That answer surprised Cindy. She was never all that athletic and she never felt she was clever enough for the kind of quick thinking a field agent needed. Yet they had her go through the test.

"Okay," said Cindy slowly.

They arrived at the lift. Alan turned and smiled at Cindy. He knew what she was thinking.

"Don't try to figure too much out right now. Just concentrate on your meeting tonight," said Alan.

He pulled his battered pocket watch out, quickly checked the time and slipped it back into his vest pocket.

"Remember your meeting starts at 7 o'clock and I'm expecting big things from you," he smiled.

Cindy looked up as the old man turned and walked onto the lift. As Alan turned he nodded toward the headphones Cindy had hanging around her neck. She hadn't stopped the music playing when she ran to catch up with Alan.

"Isn't Shostakovich a little heavy for someone as young as you?" he asked.

"It's just my work zone. Helps keep me focused," said Cindy.

"Well, if it has to be Shostakovich, try The Gadfly Suite. It's a bit more lighthearted and they used it as the theme from one of my favorite spy shows," said Alan.

Cindy looked down, closed her eyes and smiled. These people and their spy shows.

"Of course," she smiled.

As the lift started descending, Alan looked up and smiled at Cindy.

"Remember, we like to keep things fun here," said Alan.

Five hours later, Cindy stood up and took a deep breath. She looked up and down the table on the stage, then out at the near one hundred people scattered around the auditorium. She cleared her throat and started talking.

14 OFF TO THE PUB

The Castle, Outside The Pub

An hour or so later, Léa and Tara approached the pub with the hundred or so people who attended Cindy's meeting. Cindy, her brother Charlie and Janet Austin were all a few steps behind. Everyone was smiling and Cindy's expression was both pleased and relieved.

Léa glanced over her shoulder as everyone walked through Central Park down to Deep in the Cliffs Pub. Cindy's meeting had just wrapped up and everyone seemed happy. Turned out that Cindy had a natural talent for running meetings and getting things done.

"I can't tell if Cindy is relieved or happy," said Léa quietly.

"She did okay," said Tara.

She looked at her friend as they stepped off the steps two levels below the high tech auditorium. She smiled at Léa.

"You were a ton of surprises," said Tara.

"What do you mean?" asked Léa.

"I figured you'd want to keep the initiation just the way it was," said Tara.

"Just because I passed the test faster than anyone and had a good time doesn't mean we shouldn't find a better way to test people's problem solving skills," said Léa.

"I just figured you'd be the one person to stick up for it," said Tara.

"Apparently, I'm the only one here who likes getting naked and waking up in handcuffs," said Léa playfully.

Tara was about to say something, when Léa cut her off.

"But the big reason I said we should get rid of it, is because it hurt my best friend and a lot of other people around here," said Léa.

"Yeah. But it did help me start building my kick-ass reputation first week on the job," said Tara with her sarcastic, half smile.

"You should be ashamed of yourself. Beating the crap out of some guy twice your age," said Léa.

"And three times my size," said Tara.

Léa shook her head and smiled. As they got closer to the entrance to the pub, Tara picked up her walking speed just a bit.

"Will you slow down?" said Léa.

"Sorry," smiled Tara

She slowed down a bit, but not much.

"I'm not so sure I'm ready for more brew the night after our nasty hangover," said Léa.

"You'll want some tonight," said Tara.

Léa looked at Tara. It only took a glance for Léa to know her best friend was stoked about something. She wasn't sure what, but it was great to see Tara so happy.

Lately, Tara's personality had taken a darker turn. It was just last night that Léa learned why Tara's personality had changed so much. So seeing Tara clearly happy made Léa happy.

"What's got you so jazzed?" asked Léa.

Tara looked at her best friend and smiled. It wasn't her smirky, sarcastic smile either. It was genuine.

"Remember last night when we said we needed to start causing some trouble?" said Tara.

"Yeah," smiled Léa.

"Tonight's the night," smiled Tara.

"Oh yeah," said Léa.

"I'm going to try something I've been planning for a few months now," said Tara.

"Really?" said Léa.

"Really," said Tara.

A few moments later, they arrived at the entrance to The Castle's Deep in the Cliffs Pub. It was the only door in the massive complex that had double old world doors and no security lock. Tara pushed one of the doors open and stood aside for Léa.

"Enjoy the show," said Tara.

Léa smiled at Tara and paused before she walked in.

"What are you up to?" asked Léa.

Tara smiled slyly.

"Enjoy the show," she repeated.

Léa's head tiled down and slightly off to the side as she smiled at Tara. After a few moments, she walked through the doors and into the pub.

"I can't wait," said Léa as she passed Tara.

15 HIGH TECH TROUBLE

The Castle, Deep in the Cliffs Pub

Deep in the Cliffs Pub was one of the The Castle's amazing places. The walls were lined with big screen HD monitors. Most played sports channels. There were a few news channels and even the American Weather Channel. But unless there was a game on, no one paid much attention to the outside broadcasts.

Four of the biggest monitors were in one corner of the pub. Together, they showed an amazing panorama from a camera hidden in the stones on the highest turret of the ancient castle. The camera was pointed out toward the North Atlantic. A large rock jutting out from the ocean dominated the right side of the panorama.

David McNally edged past Tara and Léa as they stood near the entrance to the pub. He was the bartender at Deep in the Cliffs since the day it opened over 40 years ago.

"Excuse me Ladies," he said as he limped past Léa and Tara.

As David limped by, he made sure he made eye contact with Tara and smiled.

"Captain McNally," said Tara.

She looked at David and gave him a genuine smile.

Léa watched as David walked behind his bar and started lining up pint glasses. She looked back at her best friend.

"You two seem surprisingly cordial," said Léa.

"He's not a bad guy. In fact, he helped us on our first trip out," said Tara.

"Really?" said Léa

The two friends walked across to one of the booths that lined one of the walls of the pub. As they sat down, Tara smiled at her friend.

"He helped with the mission briefing for our trip to Uppsala. He had some surprising insight into what actually happened," said Tara.

"Really?" said Léa.

"You know, for the smartest girl in town, you might want to come up with something more to say than just, really," said Tara.

"Really," said Léa.

"Funny," said Tara.

Tara looked over at the bar as the pub began filling up. A few people were at the bar and David was getting busy pouring beer.

"We'd better get some brew before it get's too busy," said Tara.

"What was that stuff we had last night?" asked Léa.

"It's called Cold Smoke from a little brewery in Montana," said Tara.

"Amazing that something that good could come from the Colonies," said Léa.

"So, a pint of Cold Smoke for you?" asked Tara as she got up.

"Please," said Léa.

Tara returned a few minutes later with two full pints and a bowl full of pop corn. She held out her glass and smiled at Léa.

"Cheers," smiled Tara.

Léa held out her glass and smiled back.

"Cheers," said Léa.

The glasses clinked together.

Léa and Tara took sips of their ale and looked around the pub. The big room was slowly filling up. David was pouring beer at a furious pace. Léa looked at one monitor showing football. Just as Léa looked at the screen, a rare goal was kicked from the corner of the pitch. The crowd went wild and an explosion of 'goal' graphics wiped over the screen.

The two friends took a few more sips of their ale in silence. The room was fulling up fast. David McNally was pouring beer as fast as ever. The noise level in the room was growing too. A few minutes later, Alan Dennis arrived in the room. He nodded toward David and slowly walked to the table where Janet and Thomas Austin were sitting.

Tara looked at Léa and smiled.

"Time for Operation Earthquake to get under way," she said.

Léa looked up and smiled.

"Operation Earthquake?" she said.

"Here we go," said Tara.

Tara got up and walked to the corner of the pub where the monitors showed the panorama from the ocean-side turret. As she walked, she innocently pulled her iPhone from a side pocket in her black tactical pants, checked the time and let it slide back into the pocket. Once she arrived at the wall, she watched the monitors for a few moments, then turned around.

"Excuse me," she said loudly.

A few people looked up at her, but most everyone else kept talking and drinking. Tara looked at Léa, shrugged and tried it again.

"Excuse me," she yelled at the top of her lungs.

For a small woman, Tara could get quite loud when she needed to. Her second attempt to get everyone's attention was successful. The room quickly quieted down as Tara held out her glass of ale.

"Two things. First of all, cheers to Cindy Martin for taking the first steps in changing something I think we all agree has outlived it's usefulness," said Tara seriously.

Tara looked at Cindy and held her glass high.

"Cheers," said Tara.

Alan Dennis was sitting in a booth along one wall with Janet and Thomas Austin. He lightly tapped his glass on the table, then held it high too.

"Agreed," smiled Alan.

Janet looked at her husband, smiled and held her glass high as well.

"Absolutely," said Janet.

Most everyone in the room echoed Alan and Janet's call as a chorus echoed around the room. Tara watched as everyone joined in her toast. She turned slightly, checked the time on her phone and looked back at the room. As the cheers subsided, Tara spoke up again.

"While we're all here, I thought it might be a good time to bring you up to date on a little project I was given when I first got here. With your permission Sir," said Tara.

Alan smiled and held up his nearly empty glass of ale.

"*Gotcha,*" said Tara to herself.

She smiled at the room.

Sitting near the back of the room, Léa looked down at her half full glass of ale and smiled. She knew Tara's plot to cause some trouble was about to begin. Her best friend would never smile at a room full of strangers unless she had to, let along give a speech. Léa knew the smile was to put everyone off their guard. She looked up as her friend began talking.

"As pretty much everyone knows, I was asked up come up with a new, more modern obstacle course," began Tara.

She looked down.

"The current obstacle courses are okay. But they're all buried in some large rooms down at the lower level. They're small, never change and aren't very real world," said Tara.

She turned and walked to the monitor off to the left, made a show of pulling her iPhone out of her pocket and punched a few buttons. The main atrium of The Castle appeared. Tara pointed to the various levels as a computer animation drew her plan for a multi level training course. After talking for a few minutes, she looked back at everyone in the room.

"We've been able to scrounge all the parts we'll need and you'll all be happy to learn that we start construction Saturday," said Tara.

The room erupted in more than polite applause and a few nice comments. As everyone celebrated, Tara glanced at the time on her iPhone one last time. Out of the corner of her eye, she saw all the monitors in the room flicker just once. She looked down and smiled. The scheme was underway. Looking up, she held out her hands and the room quieted down.

"We're estimating that it'll take about three weeks to build, so first runs could start by the end of next month," said Tara.

A few more polite cheers filled the room. After a few moments, the lights flickered a few times, but remained burning brightly. That was enough to stop all the cheers. Lights in The Castle never flickered like this. Tara looked around the room, then smiled back at everyone.

"Last I heard, Little D ... I mean Sergeant-Major Boxx was coming up with some teams and brackets for a first time ever Deep in the Cliffs Competition," said Tara.

There was polite applause, but much quieter than before. The modern, LED lights never flickered in The Castle. As Tara smiled at everyone, the lights did it again, only longer. A slight rumbling sound briefly grew from deep in the mountain, then stopped.

Tara turned and looked back at Sentinel Rock on the outside monitors. As she turned, a huge chunk of the rock broke off and slid into the sea. The lights flickered again and the strange rumbling sound began again.

As the lights continued to flicker, the room seemed to begin shaking. Then one of the monitors exploded in a shower of sparks. A few people screamed as the rumble grew. A few more chunks of Sentinel Rock broke off and slid into the sea. The room appeared to shake even more.

"Earthquake!" yelled someone.

Then a beer tap behind the bar exploded shooting beer into the middle of the room. A few more people screamed as a few lights appeared to blow out.

Tara quietly walked from the corner of the room back to the booth where Léa was sitting. Once she arrived at the table, she took Léa's hand and pulled her to her feet.

"Time to go," smiled Tara.

As they left the room, Léa and Tara briefly turned and looked at the growing chaos. They both smiled, turned and left the room.

The corridor outside Deep in the Cliff's Pub wasn't shaking at all. The lights burned brightly as always.

"How did you make the room shake like that?" asked Léa.

"I didn't. It's solid stone like everything else in this cave. So I dimmed the lights and set the programming on the monitors around the room in sort of a synchronized shake mode. I also added some sound effects with a lot of bass. The exploding beer taps were small squibs that completed the effect," said Tara.

Léa looked back over her shoulder. She heard a few screams coming from the pub, but no one had left the room yet.

"How much longer will the show go on?" asked Léa.

"Only about another ten seconds. Just long enough for us to make our getaway," said Tara.

Léa looked over her shoulder again.

"Hope they're not too pissed off," she said.

"So what if they are," said Tara.

As the two friends walked toward Central Park, the screams suddenly stopped. There were a few angry shouts, but mostly laughter and applause erupted from the pub.

"I think they got the joke," said Tara.

"Most of them," agreed Léa.

"I feel like a movie," said Tara.

"Your favorite?" asked Léa.

"Naw. Too serious. I'm thinking Pirates of the Caribbean," said Tara.

"Perfect," said Léa.

16 A PING

The Castle, The Pit

"And thirdly, the code is more what you'd call 'guidelines' than actual rules. Welcome aboard the Black Pearl, Miss Turner," said Captain Barbossa.

Léa looked down at her half empty pint of ale, shook her head and laughed. Tara looked over at her friend and smiled.

"Guidelines," laughed Léa. "Good call on the movie."

The best friends were sitting on Tara's bed. Half a dozen pillows were smashed up against the wall as they watched the movie.

Léa chugged down the rest of her brew and held the empty glass out. Tara leaned off the bed, opened the mini fridge's door and snagged a full growler of ale and a jar of salsa. Before sitting up, she grabbed a bag of chips.

"Let's not get too plowed tonight. I have a feeling we could be busy tomorrow," said Tara.

"You think your version of Asphyxia will score a connection?" asked Léa.

"Yeah. I already know that fucker is reading our traffic. All I need to do is plant a lousy 43 k-bs on his system and I own his ass," said Tara.

"So what happens when we own his ass?" asked Léa.

Tara smiled. It was always entertaining when Léa spiced up her language. She always did it on purpose and it was always to make people laugh.

"I'll be able to get an exact location on him whenever he signs on the 'net. Then we can go pick him up," said Tara.

Léa opened the jar of salsa and dipped a chip. Tara opened the tub of guacamole. The two friends continued watching the rest of the movie in silence. Actually, they tried to watch the rest of the movie.

"Now bring me that horizon ... and really bad eggs ... drink up me 'earties. Yo ho. " said Captain Jack Sparrow.

But Tara and Léa never heard Johnny Depp deliver the movie's last line. They fell asleep about fifteen minutes after Tara opened the bag of chips. Just before she nodded off, Tara gently put the top on the jar of salsa. She'd fallen asleep with a full jar of salsa on her bed before.

As the movie's credits finished rolling up the screen, Tara's TV went back to playing the animated gif of flames. After a few moments, the room sensed no movement and the lights began to dim.

At the opposite end of the residence hall from Tara's room, Janet and Thomas Austin appeared from around the corner. They were heading to their room when one of their iPhones began buzzing.

"Yours or mine?" sighed Janet.

"Mine," said Thomas as he pulled his phone out of his pocket.

Janet reached around Thomas' waist and held him closer as they slowly walked down the hall.

"It's been too long of a day. Leave it till tomorrow," she said tiredly.

Thomas thumbed his home button and a brief text message appeared on the screen. He looked at Janet and smiled. She looked at Thomas, then down at the phone. It was just a four word message ...

WE GOT A PING!

"I think our day just got a little bit longer," said Thomas.

"Yeah. Okay. That's worth staying up for," said Janet.

"Wanna go wake up Stripper and Goth," smirked Thomas.

"You like those code names don't you?" smiled Janet.

"Yeah. But our's are better," said Thomas.

Janet stopped in the middle of the hallway and looked over her shoulder. She nodded three doors back.

"Why don't you get Léa. I'd better be the one to wake up Tara," said Janet.

"Absolutely, better you than me," said Thomas.

"She's nicer now that Léa is here," said Janet.

Thomas laughed once as he turned and headed toward Léa's door. Just before he hit the buzzer, his hand stopped in mid-air and he called out to Janet.

"Maybe you should get Léa," he said.

"Why?" said Janet over her shoulder.

"You know, her, uh, preference for sleeping attire," said Thomas.

"Oh grow up. She doesn't care and neither should you," sighed Janet.

As Thomas pressed the door buzzer, Janet stopped and turned around. It might be amusing to see her husband's reaction when Léa opened her door.

But nothing happened.

Thomas buzzed again.

Still nothing.

He looked down at Janet.

"Go ahead and use my override code," said Janet.

Thomas punched in the long string of numbers and the door to Léa's room slid silently open. He peered inside.

"Léa. Miss Taylor," he said quietly.

Janet looked down at her shoes, shook her head and laughed her sarcastic laugh.

"Oh just go wake her up," she said.

Thomas walked into the room and the door slid silently shut. But it opened a few moments later and Thomas walked out.

"Nobody's home," he said.

Janet looked off to the side, closed her eyes, nodded a few times and smiled.

"Of course not. Come on. They're probably both down at The Pit," said Janet.

Thomas hurried to catch up with Janet. As he fell into step beside his wife, he looked at her with a smile.

"You like that name, The Pit, don't you?" he said.

"Totally fits her personality," smiled Janet.

"Stripper, Goth and The Pit. Could be my next blockbuster movie," said Thomas.

"Or your introduction into the porn industry," smirked Janet.

Once they got to the end of the hall, Instead of pushing the door buzzer, Janet punched in her override code and the door slid open.

"Aren't we going to knock first?" asked Thomas.

"Wouldn't do any good. Tara disabled the doorbell about two weeks after she got here," said Janet.

She looked up at Thomas, then into the dark room.

"Let's go wake them up," she said as she walked in.

As Thomas walked in, the lights were slowly rising. Janet had stopped in the middle of the room. Thomas walked up beside her and immediately put his arm around his wife. He felt her muscles tense as a single convulsion of pain shook her body.

"Damn it," she said as she wiped away a tear.

Léa and Tara hadn't moved since they fell asleep halfway through the movie. They lay on the bed side by side. Léa was still holding a half full beer glass. A pile of chips was on the bed near Tara's hand.

Janet wiped away another tear. Thomas held his wife even closer and quietly whispered in her ear.

"Time machine Jan?" he said quietly.

"Yeah," said Janet quietly.

"Yeah," said Thomas.

Remembering back, the two best friends laying on the bed weren't Léa and Tara. 20 years ago. The best friends were Janet Akira and Helena Wells.

PART 2: 1991, MISSION TO MOSCOW

17 JANET AND HELENA'S 1ST THREE WEEKS

The Castle

~ ~ ~

PLAYLIST:
"Science" - Miracles - Two Steps From Hell

~ ~ ~

Helena Wells opened her eyes and looked around her new room at The Castle. Her deep, blue eyes stopped on the long desk built into the wall near the door. Her black messenger bag rested next to her best friend's backpack. As Helena sleepily looked around the room, she suddenly felt an elbow in the middle of her back.

"Sorry about that," mumbled Janet Akira.

Helena looked over her shoulder as Janet slowly woke up. She stretched once, then her her fingers immediately disappeared under the bandages that circled her wrists.

"Stop scratching or they'll never heal," said Helena.

"I can't help it," said Janet.

But she kept scratching.

Helena rolled over and pulled Janet's hands apart.

"I said stop scratching now. It's been three weeks. If you'd left them alone, they'd be healed by now," said Helena.

Janet sat up and deliberately put her hands on her knees. She flexed her hands and rolled her wrists.

"You're right. I know. It's just so irritating," said Janet.

Helena got up and walked over to the desk. She switched on the coffee pot, turned and sat on the edge of the desk. As she turned, she caught one of Janet's fingers reaching for the bandage on her other wrist.

"Don't!" said Helena.

Janet's hand stopped mid-air, then she rested it back on her knee. She closed her eyes.

"Sorry. I'm trying," she said.

Helena smiled at her friend. The coffee machine was slowly sputtering to life. As they waited for the coffee to brew, Janet only reached for the bandages one more time, but she stopped herself.

Janet smiled up at Helena as coffee continued to brew.

"Thanks for letting me camp out with you so long," said Janet.

The coffee pot sputtered and stopped. Helena turned and poured two big mugs of coffee, then sat back down on the bed.

"I'm glad to have the company," said Helena.

"You must think I'm an awful scaredy cat," said Janet as she sipped her coffee.

"Not at all. It's been a scary three weeks for the both of us," said Helena.

Janet and Helena's scary three weeks began innocently enough. The two young women were heading home to Stromness for a quick visit before the fall semester began. They hadn't even stepped off the ferry boat when they spotted their parents standing on the dock waiting for them.

"I don't remember Mum and Dad ever meeting the boat before, do you?" asked Helena.

"Never," said Janet.

They waved at their parents as they picked up their bags and joined the other passengers waiting to get off the boat. As they walked along the railing, Janet looked over at her parents and felt a shiver run down her spine.

"Is it just me or do they look nervous to you?" asked Janet.

Helena quickly looked over Janet's shoulder then straight ahead.

"Definitely nervous," said Helena.

The two young women walked slowly with the other passengers, lost in thought about why their parents were meeting them at the dock and why they seemed nervous.

"They were like that when Grandpa Wells died. Maybe some long lost family member has kicked the bucket," speculated Helena.

"I don't know. It's not like we've been surrounded by aunts, uncles and cousins," said Janet.

Helena stopped in her tracks and grabbed Janet's elbow. She pulled her out of the line of passengers and into the boat's small pub.

"I know what's going on. I'll bet we're going to hear about our natural families today," said Helena.

Janet nodded a few times and smiled up at Helena.

"That's gotta be it," she said.

"Hey you two! The pub's closed till we cast off," barked the barman.

Janet shot the barman an annoyed glance. Helena smiled as she guided her sister out the door and back into the line of passengers. They looked at their parents again.

"If today's the day we find out about where we came from, I don't see why they'd be so nervous," said Janet.

"Maybe there's some deep, dark secret in our pasts," speculated Helena.

The Wells girls had known they were adopted since they were very young. Helena was tall, slim, had dark eyes, dark hair and her skin would turn deep brown in the sun. Janet was just as tall as Helena, but she was part Asian with some unknown European ancestors. Their parents were short and round with light hair and even lighter skin.

As Janet and Helena slowly walked along with the other passengers, they were both lost in thought. Every now and then, one of them would look up at their parents who were watching them closely from the dock. Janet looked down at the deck.

"I don't like this," she said quietly.

"Me too." whispered Helena.

Growing up, Janet and Helena always seemed to know when something was about to happen. Good or bad, they always knew when something was up. It was like a built in radar that was always switched on. It made it tough on their parents when they wanted to surprise their daughters.

Once, when the girls were eleven, their parents had cooked up a surprise trip to London. But at breakfast, Helena and Janet immediately knew something was up when their parents asked them if they had any special plans for the day.

Janet and Helena looked at each other, but they didn't say a word. In the blink of an eye, they decided they weren't in trouble and something fun was about to happen. At the same time, they turned to their parents and smiled.

"Where are we going?" asked Helena.

That wouldn't be the only time that weekend that Janet and Helena's radar would ping. The next morning, the family was walking through Trafalgar Square when Janet tugged on Helena's arm and pointed to a group of guys following a couple walking slowly. Helena took one look, nodded at Janet, then tugged on her father's arm.

"Daddy, something bad is about to happen over there," she said quietly.

Her parents looked at each other, then at their girls. Janet looked up and nodded. The two grownups quickly eyed the scene, then looked at each other and nodded.

"You girls stay with your father," said their mum.

The two girls watched as their mother slipped her shoulder bag over her head and started walking toward the men following the couple.

"Got your back, Kim," said their father slowly.

Kim looked over her shoulder and smiled. She looked at her daughters and winked.

"Meet you at that pub we passed in about twenty minutes, she said.

Janet and Helena looked up at their father.

"Daddy?" said Janet nervously.

"It'll be okay. Your mum is very smart," smiled their father.

What happened next was a moment the two girls would never forget.

Suddenly, their mum changed direction and walked up to a middle aged man dressed in a dark suit. He wore an old school bowler hat and carried an umbrella. It was the standard uniform of London. As their mum passed the man, she appeared to say something as she grabbed his umbrella and started running toward the five guys.

As the two girls watched in amazement, they didn't notice their father had reached behind his back and pulled out three long, shiny throwing knives.

Kim reached into her shoulder bag and pulled out a police whistle. As she got close to the first guy, she flipped the umbrella and used the handle to hook his leg and send him sprawling to the ground. As he fell, a handgun bounced on the ground.

With the police whistle in her mouth, Kim flipped the umbrella again and jabbed one of the other guys in the side. As he fell, another gun fell to the ground.

Kim began blowing on the police whistle as she used the umbrella to knock a third gun out of another one of the bad guy's hands. Without breaking stride, Kim dropped the umbrella and took off into the crowd. As she ran, one of the men left standing aimed a gun at her back. A second later, a shiny knife was sticking out of the man's hand as he dropped the gun.

The two girls looked up at their father. He had a second knife in his throwing hand as he watched to see if anyone else planned to point a gun at his wife. As police began arriving at the pile of men laying in the middle of the square, he quickly hid his remaining two knives and looked at his girls.

"Come on kids. Time to go," he said.

Half an hour later, the family was sitting around a small table. Two large icy cokes sat untouched in front of Janet and Helena. Their parents were sipping from frosty mugs full of Guinness. Janet and Helena looked at each other, then at their parents. After a few more minutes of silence, Helena spoke up.

"You know, most of the other kid's parents would have just told one of the cops about those bad guys," she said.

"But you two took them on and kicked their ass," said Janet.

"Language dear," smiled Kim.

Helena and Janet looked at each other briefly.

"Don't try to change the subject. I actually choose that word to make a point. You totally kicked their asses," said Janet.

"Again, not what most other kid's parents would do," repeated Helena.

"It's time for you two to begin learning how to protect yourselves. It's something we both learned a long time ago. Also, we believe that people with the ability to make a difference should use those abilities," said Kim.

"I'll bet a month of doing the dishes that none of the other kids parents back home have the abilities you two just showed us," said Helena.

Janet and Helena watched as their parent's looked at each other and smiled. Looking back at their kids, the grownups laughed.

"That's a bet you'd loose," said their dad.

Janet and Helena looked at each other, then back at their parents.

"Prove it," said Janet.

The two grownups laughed again.

"Not going to happen. At least not for a few more years," said their mum.

"Until then, I guess you two will still be on dirty dish duty," smiled their dad.

"Not fair," said Janet looking down at her hands.

She looked up at her mum who was smiling at her.

"Just wait until after your twenty-fifth birthdays," she said.

It was a conversation Janet and Helena would never forget. Walking down the gangplank, Janet grabbed her sister's arm.

"I know exactly what's going on," she said.

The two sisters looked at each other.

"It's the twenty fifth birthday talk," they said at the same time.

As they continued walking down to the dock, a shiver of fear ran up and down Janet's spine. She reached for her sister's hand and held on for dear life.

"This is going to be bad," whispered Janet.

"I know," said Janet.

A few hours after the boat docked, the two adopted sisters woke up in The Castle's notorious dungeon. They were part of an incoming class of seven new recruits.

The Class of '91 would end up like most other classes of spies at The Castle. It would take about a week before the seven recruits would figure out how to break out of the dungeon and begin Spy School.

There was always one recruit who would lead the way out. This time, it would be Helena who would rally the other members of the class to work together on their escape.

But Janet almost didn't make it. Like some recruits, she panicked moment she woke up. Waking up alone, stripped, handcuffed and shackled in medieval dungeon was just too much. As she struggled violently against the hardened steel of the old, heavy handcuffs, she quickly tore the skin from her wrists and nearly severed nerves, ligaments and blood vessels. The calming voice of her sister in the next cell was the only thing that prevented Janet from doing permanent damage.

Three weeks later, the skin around Janet's wrists was only barely beginning to heal when the printer on Helena's desk quickly spit out the daily class schedule.

Still sitting at her desk and sipping her coffee, Helena reached her free hand around and plucked a schedule from the printer. She looked over the day's classes, then held up the paper and looked up at her sister.

"Thrilling. Another two hours in lock picking class," said Helena.

"What else," said Janet as she reached for the bandages around her wrists.

Helena rolled up the schedule and used it to slap Janet's hands away from the bandages.

"It says you get to spend an extra hour on handcuff lock picking," said Helena.

"Funny," said Janet.

She snatched the rolled up schedule from Helena and looked it over. Helena sipped her coffee and looked at her sister.

"What's tonight's movie?" she asked.

"Something called The Ipcress File," said Janet.

Helena drained her coffee and stood up.

"Whatever. I've got dibs on the shower," she said.

"You were first yesterday," protested Janet.

"It's my shower," said Helena.

18 SCAVENGER HUNT

The Castle - Spy School Classroom

~ ~ ~

PLAYLIST:
"Sun Gazer" - Miracles - Two Steps From Hell

~ ~ ~

Four small, wooden boxes sat on the student's desks. The boxes weren't very big. A shiny, gold lock held the top firmly in place. Except for the four boxes, the student's desks were bare.

Spy School had started just three weeks ago for Helena, Janet and five other recruits. They'd been through the basics of surveillance, how to get lost in a crowd and a lot of physical training. They went to the shooting range every day for target practice and even got a ride on one of The Castle's submarines.

Lock picking class had started three days ago. The student spies quickly learned that picking locks required lots of patience and a delicate touch.

As the students gathered around the four boxes, Helena whispered to her sister.

"Looks like standard five pin door lock," she said.

"Ugh," said Janet. "I'm only up to three pins. After that I'm dead in the water."

"What do you think we're doing today?" asked Helena.

Before her sister could answer, their instructor burst through the classroom door. He was clearly out of breath as he walked to the front of the class and rapped his knuckles on the desk.

"Sorry I'm late. Today's lesson took a little longer to set up," he said.

Thomas Austin had just celebrated his 28th birthday. In a month, he'd celebrate his first year at The Castle. Hired on for his expertise at creating amazing special effects for the movies, Thomas' main job was to scour the cinema, TV shows, books and magazines looking for anything and everything the spies and technicians could use at The Castle.

He also helped out teaching some of the more not-so-exciting classes during Spy School. Classes like lock picking. For years, the student spies spent hour after hour in front of the world's largest collection of locks.

There was no other word for it. Lock picking class was boring. Deadly boring.

When Thomas was assigned the class, he quickly remembered his own experience as a bored out of his mind student and decided to do something about it. Thomas looked over his class and smiled. He could tell everyone in the room was ready for something new. Today was the first day lock picking classes would stop being boring and become the most fun you could have in Spy School.

"Okay, welcome to day four of the most exciting thing you can learn in Spy School," he said.

The students smiled up at Thomas. At least they appreciated his attempt to lighten the mood. Thomas took a breath and began the lesson.

"Those boxes in front of you contain an object that will give you a clue about where you'll find your next box. Today's lesson is simple. Pick the lock, then figure out where the next box is. The team that finds all their boxes and makes it to the finish first, get's a week off physical training," said Thomas.

Most of the students were looking at their boxes with a little concern in their eyes. All except one.

"It's a scavenger hunt!" exclaimed Helena.

"Exactly," smiled Thomas.

Helena looked at Janet.

"This is going to be fun," she smiled.

"If you say so," said Janet.

"Just a few rules," began Thomas. "All of the boxes are located in The Castle. So don't leave the grounds. Also, none of the boxes are behind any door with a security marking of four or higher."

No one moved a muscle. All the students were still looking at their boxes with a serious look in their eyes. All of them except for Helena. She was fully charged up and ready for an adventure.

"All right then. What are your waiting for?" asked Thomas. "Get going."

Helena reached into her backpack and pulled out her twelve piece lock picking set. As she went to work on their first lock, she motioned to Janet to move closer.

"So, I'm good at picking, you're good at deduction. As soon as I get this open, be ready to figure out where we're going next," said Helena.

"Okay," said Janet.

Helena inserted the small tension tool into the base of the lock and was slowly raking the pins up and down with her pick. It took almost two minutes of gently working the lock before the pins lined up and the top of the box popped open. Almost as soon as Helena's lock opened one of the other boxes popped open.

Janet reached into the box and pulled out an old leather glove. After giving the glove a quick look she motioned to Helena and picked up her bag and started for the door.

"So where are we going?" asked Helena as she stuffed her lock pick set into her backpack and stood up.

"Not here," said Janet quietly as she made for the door.

"Why not?" asked Helena as she arrived at the door.

"Don't want anyone else to hear?" ventured Janet.

"Good call," said Helena.

As she walked through the door, Janet looked back to see Thomas looking at her. He smiled at her. She nervously smiled back as she left the room. Helena looked from Janet to Thomas and back to Janet. As the door closed, Helena smiled at her sister.

"Do you have a 'thing' for our teacher?" she asked playfully.

"No. Absolutely not. No way," said Janet.

"Yeah. You really convinced me there," teased Helena.

"Can we concentrate on, you know, the assignment?" said Janet.

"Janet and her teacher sitting in a tree, k i s s i n g," sang Helena.

"Would your grow up? Don't you want to know where we're going next?" said Janet.

"Okay. But don't think you're getting off the hook about your new boyfriend that easily," smiled Helena.

Janet held out the leather glove.

"Just an old leather glove, but look at what's stamped on it," said Janet.

"Holy shit. That's a swastika!" exclaimed Helena.

"Language dear," smiled Janet.

Helena looked back and smiled too.

"I think we both know exactly where that glove came from," she said.

"The U-Boat!" smiled Janet.

As the two sisters took off down the stone corridor, two more students emerged from the classroom. Just before they turned for the slowly moving Paternoster lift, Janet looked over her shoulder.

"Looks like Little Miss Stuck Up and her puppy dog have figured something out," commented Janet.

Helena quickly looked over her shoulder. She laughed once through her nose as she looked at her sister.

"You always come up with the best names for people," she said.

"Not all that hard with those two," said Janet.

Janet and Helena quickly boarded the same, slowly moving lift car and began descending down to the lowest level of The Castle complex. It was a tight fit in the small car. As Janet shuffled her feet, she bumped a wooden box just like the one they just opened in the classroom. She nudged her sister.

"Well, well. What do we have here?" said Helena.

She began reaching for the box when her sister nudged her again.

"Not our box. Remember, our box is in the submarine," said Janet.

Helena stood up.

"Good point," said Helena.

"But there's a chance that it might be our next box," suggested Janet.

Helena looked at the small brass plaque in the back of the car. She had to rub a few times before she could read the faded number etched in the brass.

"Car 43," she said.

"We may have just caught a big break," said Janet.

"If that's our box, then we'll know which car to jump on for the trip back," said Helena.

"Now if only we knew where to find our first box," said Janet.

"Maybe we can catch another break. Lemme see that glove," said Helena.

Janet pulled the old leather glove out of her jeans pocket and handed it to Helena who began closely examining it. She tuned it over a few times. The only marking was the faded swastika. After a few moments, she handed it to Janet.

"Hmmm," she said. "Just a dirty old leather glove."

Janet looked up at Helena and smiled.

"That's the clue right there. It's dirty," said Janet.

"So it was probably used in the engine room," speculated Helena.

The old lift bumped and creaked as it neared the lowest level of The Castle. Janet and Helena jumped off while the car was still two feet from the landing and took off running toward The Castle's vintage World War II U-Boat.

It was the same submarine that brought The Castle's commander, Alan Dennis, up from Ireland back in the Sixties. Since that fateful trip, the sub had undergone a complete makeover. Every flake of rust had been scraped off the hull. Every inch of the submarine had been lovingly restored to it's original condition.

Then, modern communications and a state of the art navigation system were added to the U-Boat's control room. A few modern conveniences were added to the galley. And a plaque marking the death of The Castle's founder was placed at the spot where he was killed thirty years before.

As Janet and Helena approached the dock, they noticed one of The Castle's more modern submarines was just leaving. The older sub was so much smaller than the modern nuclear sub. But in it's day, the old U-Boat was a most deadly predator.

As dock-lines were released, the newer sub gave a short blast from it's horn signaling it was getting underway. Everyone's attention was on the big submarine, so Janet and Helena were able to slip aboard the old U-Boat and down the ladder unnoticed. They found themselves in the aft torpedo room.

"Come on," said Janet.

She started heading forward through the small watertight hatch. Helena quickly followed. Two large electric motors dominated the room.

"Well, here we are," said Janet.

"It's all metal in here, so any wooden box should stick out," said Helena.

Janet took one side of the room, Helena took the other. But after a quick, but complete search of the compartment, the next locked box was nowhere to be found.

"I was sure we were right about this," said Helena.

"So was I," said Janet.

She took the glove out again and started turning it over in her hands. Helena watched as the glove flipped over a few more times. Janet began slowly shaking her head.

"We're missing something," said Helena.

"We sure are," agreed Janet.

As Janet kept rotating the old glove in her hands, Helena noticed it was covered with oil spots. She looked up at the big electric engines. They clearly had some grease on them, but nothing like the dark spots of black oil on the glove.

"We're in the wrong room," said Helena.

"This is the engine room," said Janet.

"More specifically, it's the electric motor room," said Helena.

"What else is there?" asked Janet.

"The diesel engine room," said Helena.

She started walking toward the next watertight hatch. When Janet joined her, they stood in front of the submarine's twin diesel electric motors. Unlike the electric motor room, the diesel room was a bit dirtier. Grime had built up on a few seals of the big engines. It was the same color as the stains on the old glove.

"This is where our glove came from," said Helena.

Janet was looking forward, when she spotted something. She walked to the front of the room, picked it up, turned to Helena and smiled.

"I think we've found our second box," she said.

Helena pulled her picks out of her backpack and went to work on the shiny, gold lock. This time it took less than a minute before the box sprang open. Janet started to reach into the box when Helena grabbed her hand.

"Not so fast," she said.

"Why?" asked Janet.

"I just think now might be a good time for us to start being a bit more careful about where we stick our hands," said Helena.

Janet looked down at the box, then up at Helena. It took only a few moments for her to figure out what her sister was trying to say.

"You're right. Someday, things are going to get dangerous. Now is the perfect time to start being just a bit more cautious," agreed Janet.

They both peered into the box, then looked at each other and nodded.

Janet stuffed the old glove into her jeans pocket and reached into the box. When her hand emerged, it was holding a hunk of heavy rubber. Half was painted black, the other half was painted yellow. She smiled at Helena.

"We were right about that box in the lift," said Janet.

"That's a piece of the rubber edge of a lift's floor," agreed Helena.

"What was the car number again. 43?" asked Janet.

"43," repeated Helena.

It took less than a minute for Janet and Helena to climb out of the old sub. As they walked down the gangplank, one of the dock guards blocked their way. Even though his rifle remained slung over his shoulder, his right hand rested on the pistol holstered on his belt.

"Just what do you two think you're doing?" asked the guard.

Janet started to pull the glove out of her pocket and opened her mouth to answer, but Helena stepped in front of her and smiled sweetly.

"We took an early lunch to come look around. We've never seen the U-Boat before," she said innocently.

"Didn't you see the restricted area signs on the dock?" asked the guard.

"We hoped you wouldn't mind. We were just so very curious," said Helena sweetly.

Super sweetly if you asked Janet. She stood behind her sister wondering if she banged her head on something in the sub. Helena never talked to anyone like this. It was almost like she was flirting with the guard. Janet looked up at the guard who seemed to be buying Helena's performance.

"Curiosity killed the cat and can get you in serious trouble here on the docks. Next time you want to see something, ask your boss. Okay?" said the guard.

"Right-o," smiled Helena.

The guard looked over Helena's shoulder at Janet.

"Understand?" said the guard to Janet.

"Yeah. Sure," said Janet insincerely.

"Right then. I'll just see you two to the lift," said the guard.

The guard stood aside and walked Janet and Helena to the lumbering old lift. Just before they stepped onto one of the rising cars, the guard cleared his throat. He was standing next to the restricted area sign.

"Next time you see a sign like this one, make damn sure you have permission to be here," said the guard.

"Right-o", smiled Helena enthusiastically.

The guard turned to Janet, waiting.

Helena looked over her shoulder at Janet was looking at the ground. Janet looked up as her sister nudged her and nodded to the guard. Janet clearly didn't like the idea of playing the guard's game, but looked over at him with a half smile.

"Got it," she said.

"Okay then you two. Scram," said the guard.

As Helena turned toward the lift, the guard took a few steps forward and whispered in her ear.

"That one needs to work on her manners," said the guard helpfully.

"She's been cranky like that for years," said Helena.

As the old lift carried Janet and Helena away from the dock, the guard had one more parting comment.

"Pretty girl like you will get a lot further if you learn to smile just a bit," he said.

Once the lift cleared the dock, Janet turned to Helena and started to speak. But Helena cut her off.

"What the hell was that all about?" said said.

Helena was genuinely irritated.

"What do you mean?" asked Janet.

"What if we'd been out in the real world? On a real mission? Your snippy little attitude with guys like that might be all it takes to get us in serious trouble", said Helena.

"I'm not going to flirt with some guard in this nasty old cave", said Janet rubbing her wrists.

Helena slapped Janet's hands away from her wrists, then turned her back on her sister. As the lift started to emerge on the first level above the dock, Helena shook her head once and reached for Janet's hand. Once the lift cleared the landing, she stepped off and pulled her sister over to the railing overlooking the submarine docks. After a few minutes to think, she walked to a nearby bench and sat down. Helena took a deep breath, patted the spot on the bench next to her and waited for Janet to sit down.

"You've got to let all of that anger go, right now. And I mean immediately," said Helena.

Janet looked down at her hands and bandaged wrists. But Helena grabbed her sister's face and gently pushed it up so she could look directly into Janet's eyes. After a few moments, Helena nodded down to the dock.

"In the real world. On a real mission. That could have been fatal you know," she said seriously.

"But it's just a class assignment," protested Janet.

"Not anymore," said Helena.

Helena paused to think a few more moments. Then she gently took her sister's hands in hers. When she spoke, her voice was gentle, but resolved.

"Like it or not, we're in the spy world now. It's a dangerous life, but it's path that was chosen for us when were were babies. From here on out, we've got to stop reaching into boxes without looking inside first. And we've got to say and do things so people like that guard won't know what we're really up to," said Helena.

Janet looked down at the dock. The guard was back at his stand near the old German sub. He looked up, saw Janet and waved. Janet looked at her sister only a moment before she smiled and waved back at the guard.

"Okay. I get it," said Janet.

"Good," said Helena.

She patted her sister's hands and stood up. Looking down at Janet, she nodded toward the old lift.

"Car 43. Let's go," said Helena.

Janet took one more look down at the guard on the dock. He waved up at her again. She gave him another smile and waved back. Looking down at her bandaged wrists, she realized her sister was right. Janet looked from side to side, then down at her hands again.

"I can do this," she said to herself.

Janet nodded once, then stood up and joined her sister watching the old lift cars slowly creak by.

19 IT'S CALLED THE INTERNET

The Castle - New Mission Ops Center

"Looks like your girl is on the move again," said Alan Dennis.

Thomas Austin stopped stirring the cream and sugar into his coffee for only a second. But he suspected it was just long enough for the old man to notice. Thomas shook his head once and continued to stir his coffee. He could feel several pairs of eyes on his back as he picked up the cup and saucer.

"About damn time," groused David McNally.

"Language," said Alan.

A small laugh rose through Thomas' nose as he sipped his coffee. With his coffee just the way he liked it and without looking at the other people in the room, Thomas quickly walked back to the mission controller's desk in The Castle's new Operations Theater.

The room was just one of Thomas' new ideas. Today was the day it was getting it's first practical try out in front of the bosses. Soon after his arrival at The Castle, Thomas presented the first of several ideas that would bring The Castle into the coming new millennium.

The Operations Theater was a semi-circular room. A floor to ceiling map of the world and several banks of video monitors dominated the room's flat wall. The circular part of the room had three levels of chairs and desks facing the map and monitors.

A long table with desktop computers and telephones took up the first level. The second level was lined with leather lounge chairs. Each chair had a side table with several phones and a pitcher of ice water. More desks with computers and phones made up the upper level.

Two large desks were placed on one side of the stage. The first desk had a complex video switcher and audio control panel. Two big computers and a bank of five phones covered the second desk. A well stocked coffee and snack trolly stood at the other end of the stage near the entrance to the room.

Thomas Austin took another sip of his coffee as he sat at the second desk on the stage. He had only been at The Castle six months when he presented the idea that lead to the creation of this new mission command center.

The huge map on the wall was blank. The monitors showed various security cameras located around The Castle. Most of the monitors were small. Two large screens were centered on top of the map. A video technician would occasionally switch the feed from a small monitor into one of the larger monitors.

Thomas tapped a few keys on one of the large desktop computers in front of him and sipped his coffee. This first test of his Operations Theater was going fairly well. As he sipped his coffee, Thomas stole a glance up at the three people seated in the leather chairs on the second level. Two of them were fidgeting in their seats. The last one was seated comfortably and seemed to be enjoying the show. Finally, one of the fidgeters spoke up.

"This is a nice movie room, but I don't see how this will help us in the real world," said David McNally.

"Why do you say that?" asked Alan.

"It's all very nice that we can wire in The Castle's video cameras during Mr. Austin's scavenger hunt. But what happens when we have to send agents into, say Moscow. We can't just wire their security cameras into this room," said David.

Alan nodded his head sadly. He knew he was getting older. So was everyone else at The Castle. It was why Alan insisted they bring someone like Thomas Austin in to help them jump into the high tech world of tomorrow. Alan looked down toward Thomas and waved him up to the empty chair next to him. Alan climbed the steps three at a time.

"What's up?" he asked as he sat down.

"David, it seems, is still concerned about whether all this will actually do anything," said Alan.

"Still wondering how we're going to get video feeds in from say, Moscow?" asked Thomas.

"Not to put too fine point on it. But yes. Exactly," said David.

Alan sat back and looked at Thomas as he thought about his answer. He could almost see the wheels turning in Thomas' head. Thomas was obviously looking for another way to explain it all to David. Clearly the direct answer wasn't working. It didn't take long for Thomas to decide what he wanted to do.

"How long did it take to blast a hole in this rock big enough for you to build that nice pub of yours?" asked Thomas.

"It took about an hour of blasting, but about six months of precision carving," answered David.

"And that big atrium out there? It must have taken months to turn that solid hunk of rock into what we have today," said Thomas.

"Not months. Years," said David.

"And if you hadn't started all those years ago, none of this would be here," said Thomas.

"Correct," said Alan.

Thomas pointed at the map and monitors that filled the wall behind the stage. As he thought about what he would say next, a small smile appeared on his face.

"Think of all those monitors as the rocks you blasted out of this cliff. But instead of creating space for offices, labs, housing and your pub, we're creating space for information," said Thomas.

David started to say something, but Thomas politely smiled and gently cut him off.

"Just one more thought please, so I can tie it all up for you," said Thomas.

David looked away, clearly irritated. But he nodded and impatiently waited.

"Thank you. Sir," said Thomas respectfully.

Alan watched the exchange and was clearly a very happy man. Normally, only he was able to cut off David McNally like that. Of course, that was only because Alan was the boss. Thomas had been at The Castle a year, but quickly learned how to get things done and not create any friction or needless drama.

"It took you six months to carve out your new pub. You were then able to set up your beer lines, CO2 and taps for all that great brew you serve. And now you're open for business," said Thomas.

He paused a second to see if that registered with David. It apparently did, because David was now looking directly at Thomas.

"The technology for your pub has been around for, well, forever. But the technology for my pub is still being developed. That technology is what we're all learning to call the internet. It's emerging technology that one day, will allow you to look at any security camera in the world," said Thomas.

"How do you know?" asked David.

"I guess it's the confluence of my past job and my new job," said Thomas.

Alan smiled. This was exactly the reason he wanted someone like Thomas at The Castle.

"Working down at Pinewood, I had to imagine all sorts of amazing things that didn't exist. Of course, that was fiction and things are far from fiction here at The Castle," said Thomas.

"That still doesn't answer how you know I'll be able to look at any security camera in the world from this room and why you've turned a simple lock picking class into some kind of silly game," said David.

"Fair enough," nodded Thomas.

He stood up and started for the exit. David looked at Alan, then back at Thomas as he reached for the door handle. As he walked out the door, Thomas abruptly turned around.

"Be right back," said Thomas.

He bumped into the side of the door as he spun around and left the room. Alan looked down, shook his head and smiled.

David looked up at the monitor wall for a few moments, shook his head, reached for his coffee and emptied the mug. Once Thomas left the room, David's harsh expression changed dramatically. He looked around the room with curiosity and wonder. After years of working in old school intelligence, David was clearly intrigued by the new Operations Center. He just couldn't show it while the new kid was around because he was under orders from the old man.

"Okay, I understand what you see in him. And I don't think he's being deliberately dis-respectful. But someone who just bolts out of the room in the middle of a conversation is more than just a bit eccentric," said David.

"True, but he's already bringing fresh ways of looking at things to what has become an old and tired way of doing business," said Alan.

"In the end, it might be just what we need to give us the edge on whoever or whatever the next threat is," said David.

Alan turned to David and smiled.

"I know he's not your idea of the perfect recruit and I suspect you find him a bit irritating. But just keep prodding him in the right direction," said Alan.

"He's not that bad. And it's crystal clear how important someone like that is to an organization like ours," said David.

"Unconventional for sure," said Alan.

"But maybe it's just what Sir Richard would have approved of?" speculated David.

Alan looked over at David and smiled. It had been thirty years since he had been tapped to lead his mentor's idea for an international intelligence and action organization. At that time, bringing in a guy like Alan Dennis as the head of The Castle was about as unconventional as Alan bringing in a movie studio special effects technician.

"Do you really think so?" asked Alan.

"Well, we got lucky with you," said David.

Alan reached for his own coffee cup and took a few sips. He thought back to the dinner meeting all those years ago when Sir Richard introduced him to his idea for an international spy ring and the people chosen to build it.

That night, it was clear that David didn't like the idea of putting a washed up, mostly drunk newspaper reporter in charge of what would become The Castle. Now, thirty years later, Alan knew the call Sir Richard made had been the right one. The spies, technicians and staff at The Castle had prevented numerous catastrophes around the world. Sir Richard's scheme had literally saved the world more than once.

Alan took another sip of his coffee.

As he though back over the years, he wished Sir Richard could have known just how well his plans had come together. He wished Sir Richard could have heard David's indirect agreement that putting Alan in charge was the right thing to do. Alan looked at David.

"The old man was right about you. And I think you're right about that kid from the movie studio," said David.

Alan kept looking at David. It was surprising to hear him talk like this. David was old school. Very old school. But he also knew the business of espionage and knew it had to change with the times.

"I just wish his attention span was a bit longer," said David.

Alan laughed.

Suddenly, the door burst open. Thomas wheeled in a stainless steel cart. A small, tan computer sat on the top shelf of the cart. Thomas pulled a long orange electrical cord from the bottom shelf and plugged the small computer in.

He flipped the computer's on switch and tapped on the keyboard for a few minutes. Without looking away from the screen he pointed up at Alan and David. After snapping his fingers once, he motioned for them to join him by the computer.

Almost immediately after snapping his fingers and waving his hand, Thomas stopped typing with the other hand. He stood up, turned and smiled at Alan and David.

"That was a bit rude. Sorry. But I really think you're going to like this," said Thomas.

Alan laughed as he stood up.

As he stood, David leaned close to Alan's ear.

"Okay. At least he's trying to learn some manners," he said.

"Progress," said Alan.

Thomas turned back to the small computer and began typing again. Once Alan and David arrived at the small computer, Thomas stopped tapping and stood up. He looked at David.

"This is the newest thing from across the pond. It's called a Macintosh computer and it's graphics will, one day, change the world. Being a movie guy, I think a picture is worth a thousand words. So maybe this will help you understand what's going to happen in the next ten years," said Thomas.

Thomas hit a button on the keyboard and the small, black and white monitor sprang to life. A small computer icon appeared on the screen. A few seconds later, a second small computer icon appeared, then a third. After that, a line appeared between the first two computers. The line had arrows going between the computers. Then a line appeared between the third computer.

"This is what we have now. Computers here at The Castle beginning to talk to each other. We can exchange messages, pictures and documents," explained Thomas.

He punched another button on the keyboard. The small computers moved up into the corner and a map of the world drew itself onto the screen. Then more computers appeared with animated lines linking them together.

"But it's not just computers here in The Castle that are talking to each other. Computers around the world are joining in the conversation too. It's what we're calling the world wide web because, as you can see, it's beginning to resemble a spider's web," said Thomas.

He punched the keyboard a third time. The map and all the computers pushed off to one side and a small TV camera appeared. Then another. Then another. They too were connected to the web with animated lines.

"Soon, even your basic closed circuit TV camera will become more like a computer than a camera. It'll be sending it's picture to the web and we'll be able to tap into it here," said Thomas.

"Doesn't that mean someone outside The Castle might be able to tap into our cameras?" asked David.

"Absolutely. It's why I think one of the biggest industries of the next century will be web security," said Thomas.

"It had better be one of our biggest industries here at The Castle too," said Alan.

"It's as important as proper maintenance on that nuclear reactor in your newest submarine," said Thomas.

"So this little scavenger hunt of yours is a test of this new operations center. What you movie people would call a coming attraction?" asked David.

"Partly," said Thomas.

"What else?" asked David.

Thomas stood up and looked at the wall of monitors. They showed the teams of Spy School students continuing to make their way around The Castle picking locks and discovering clues. Thomas scanned the monitors until he found the one he was looking for.

"Number six," he said to the technician at the video switcher.

A second later, the security camera focused on the Paternoster Lift just above the submarine docks popped up on one of the larger monitors. Two of the students were patiently waiting as car after car went by. Alan looked over at Thomas as he studied the two young Spy School students. Alan thought he saw a small smile appear on Thomas's face.

But out of the corner of his eye, Thomas saw Alan looking at him. He shook his head once and started talking.

"You guys have been testing and training spies here for thirty years. There's no doubt that what you needed was tough, disciplined and capable people to go out into a rough and dangerous world to do the dirty jobs that needed to be done. But the world is changing and you need something more than rough, tough and disciplined," said Thomas.

"What's missing?" asked David.

"Creativity," said Thomas.

"Creativity," repeated David.

"Yeah," said Thomas.

His eyes focused once more on the monitor and the two young women waiting for the car with the next clue to arrive. More specifically, he couldn't take his eyes off the young woman on the right. The one with bandages on her wrists.

Now both David and Alan were closely watching Thomas. Both recognized the expression on the younger man's face. Thomas stole a glance at the older men, looked down once then back up at the monitor.

"You know, those are probably the two smartest, most capable young women I've ever met," began Thomas.

He stopped talking as one of the two women quickly stepped aboard the lift, snatched a box off the floor and stepped off. The other one pulled a leather pouch from her pocket and went to work on the lock. The first one looked down once, then turned around to keep watch. Thomas walked over to the camera control desk and began zooming in the picture.

"Look at that," said Thomas.

Alan and David looked up as the monitor focused on Janet's face. They looked back at Thomas. Alan smiled, but David was irritated.

"Okay, so she's pretty and it's clear that you have a thing for her. But what are they learning from playing some game?" said David.

Thomas turned toward David with fire in his eyes. He'd been caught. But as quickly as the fire appeared in his eyes, he got ahold of himself and tried to focus on the bigger picture. Ignoring David's comment about his 'thing' for Janet, Thomas nodded toward the screen.

"I get why you do that nasty dungeon test. But it really messed her up. Right now, you all have doubts that she'll even complete Spy School. But look what she's doing. She's keeping watch while the other member of the team picks the lock. She's only in basic field tactics and that's in the more advanced class. Despite the trauma of the Dungeon Test, she's showing growing, natural talent" said Thomas.

"So you concocted this game to help your girlfriend get over getting her hair messed up in the dungeon?" asked David.

Thomas sighed.

"Okay, you caught me. I confess. I like her. A lot. But I didn't just concoct this treasure hunt to help her get over getting her hair messed up. Which by the way is a really nasty thing to say and worse, a ugly way to think," said Thomas.

Alan and David turned toward the monitors. Thomas turned to the monitors in time to see Janet looked back as Helena stood up. She'd made quick work of picking her lock and she held up a gray rock. They talked about it for a few more moments, then took off running for the stairs.

Thomas looked at the monitor with pride. He knew they'd figured out the next stop in their scavenger hunt. In the past few minutes, they had all witnessed a major transformation as Janet went from being a victim of the dungeon back to being the sharp, capable and intelligent woman that had caught his eye.

"Mission accomplished," he said quietly.

"You don't really think your little game had anything to do with her pulling herself out of that pool of self pity she's been wallowing in?" asked David.

Thomas quietly turned and faced David.

"I think my little game has accomplished just that and a hell of lot more," he said confidently.

David didn't say anything. Alan didn't say anything. Thomas turned back to the screen.

"You've been using 'game' like it was a dirty word. But it's not. War games have always been an important part of military training. So why not Spy Games?" said Thomas.

"Instead of sitting in a classroom, you learn by doing? Is that what you're saying?"asked Alan.

"Partly. Classroom learning is good. Basic physical training is good too. But you've been missing some of the best kind of training there is," said Thomas.

"Learning by doing?" said David.

"Learning by having fun," said Thomas.

"Excuse me? Fun?" said David.

"Exactly," said Thomas.

He turned back to Alan and David.

"Think back to all the lessons you've learned in life. I'll bet the easiest lessons you learned were things you picked up while you were having fun. Sure, you can knock someone on the side of the head to try to teach them a lesson. But you get where you want to go a lot quicker when you give people a chance to learn like this," said Thomas.

"How about a few specifics?" asked David.

Thomas looked at all the monitors. He watched as Helena and Janet kept running up stairs, but eventually tore his eyes away to focus on the other students.

"Number 12," he said quietly.

The second large monitor switched to another two students working a lock in hidden under a table in The Castle's shooting range.

"Take those two. Shay and Theo. When it comes to picking locks, those two basically suck. But they're on their second lock and picking up speed. I could have held them hostage in the classroom for days before they'd pick up this kind of speed. Give people a fun challenge like this and there's no telling what they can accomplish," said Thomas.

"So you're saying we need to change Spy School into fun and games?" asked David.

"No way. We're still teaching skills for a dangerous and dirty occupation. But you can't live dangerous and dirty 24-7," said Thomas.

Alan and David looked at the screen as the teams made their way around The Castle, finding clues and picking locks.

"And one more thing. This kind of training gives you something you'll never get from a classroom or being shouted at by a drill instructor. It's teaching creativity," said Thomas pointing at the monitors. "It's simple guys. They're learning to think on their feet."

Alan looked at David who was looking at the monitors. David looked at Alan and smiled.

"Sold," he said simply.

Alan looked over at Thomas and smiled.

"Well done young man," he said.

Thomas looked back at the top monitor. Helena and Janet were only about halfway up the castle's countless steps, but they were still going strong.

"Well then. May I ask a favor?" said Thomas.

"Depends," said David.

"Don't tell anyone. You know. About her. And me. And, you know," stammered Thomas.

Alan and David looked at each other and smiled.

"Secret's safe," said Alan.

David walked over to one of the technicians seated at one of the desks on the level below the soft, leather seats. He was sitting at a lone computer carefully watching the monitors.

"Gravlee, right?" asked David.

"Yes Sir. Sam Gravlee," said the technician.

"What are you doing?" asked David.

Sam looked down at his computer. He has a small spread sheet open. A string of numbers from one to five ran along the top, the names of the student teams ran down the left side of the screen. There were a few x's under the numbers.

"I'm basically keeping score," said Sam.

"Who's winning?" asked Alan.

"Akira and Wells," said Sam.

"By how much?" asked David.

"They're on their way to number three. The next team, Woodley and James just found number two. The rest are on still on their first," said Sam.

"Why do you think those two are doing so well?" asked Alan.

"Simple," said Thomas. "They're playing to win."

20 PLAYING TO WIN

The Castle, Main Atrium

~ ~ ~

PLAYLIST:
"Rain" - Reach for Glory - Blackmill
~ ~ ~

"Explain to me again why we're running up all these stairs?" huffed Janet.

"Two reasons," Helena huffed back.

As they turned a corner in the main staircase of The Castle's atrium, Helena pointed to one of the small, gray closed circuit TV cameras that seemed to be everywhere.

"First, we've probably been on camera since we left the classroom. It's a sure bet that our teachers and bosses are keeping a very close eye on our progress. I want us to look good," said Helena.

"And the second reason?" asked Janet.

"I don't just want to look good. I want to win this thing," said Helena.

"And running up the stairs is going to help us win?" huffed Janet.

"Little Miss Stuck Up and her puppy dog were watching us on the lift," said Helena.

"So we're running to throw them off," said Janet.

Janet and Helena turned another corner and found themselves at a heavy, wooden door. After pushing it open, they found themselves outside in The Castle's center courtyard. Janet pointed to another doorway at the base of a turret.

"I think that's the fastest way to the sea-side turret," she said.

Helena was bent over. Her hands were just above her knees as she continued to breath heavily.

"Great. But let's catch our breath first," said Helena.

"Excellent," said Janet.

She took a few steps back and leaned against the door they had just come through. After a few moments, their breathing started to return to normal. A gentle rain began to fall.

Janet looked up at the sky for a few moments. Looking up, she closed her eyes and let the light rain wash the sweat from her face. Janet took a deep breath, wiped her face and started walking toward The Castle's seaside turret.

"Yeah, lets win this thing," she said over her shoulder.

A few minutes later, Janet and Helena emerged at the top of The Castle. The wind was much stronger at the top of the turret. A blast of rain and sea-spray hit Janet and Helena as they emerged from the stair-well.

Janet walked to the edge and let the wind, rain and sea-spray wash over her face. After a few moments, she licked her lips, tasting the salty water. Without opening her eyes, Janet pushed up the sleeves of her wind breaker, then slowly unwound the bandages around her wrists. She let the wind carry the bandages away and held her wrists in the rain and salty sea-spray.

"What are you doing?" asked Helena.

"Letting the salt water wash these things off," said Janet.

"That's gotta sting," observed Helena.

"Not so bad," said Janet simply.

After a few minutes, Janet wiped the water from her eyes, let her arms fall to her side and began looking around the turret for their next clue. As Helena joined in the search, she put her hand on her sister's shoulder.

"This has been a big day for you," said Helena.

"I'm going to be okay, Thanks to you," said Janet.

"No me. All you. And I always knew you would be," said Helena.

"Sorry it took so long," said Janet.

"Nonsense," said Helena.

After that, Janet and Helena searched in silence. They slowly walked around the turret, but didn't find their next clue. After looping around the turret three times, they stopped in the center.

"There's the pile of rocks I remembered was up here. Just like the clue. I was sure this would be the place," said Janet.

Helena pulled their third clue from her jacket pocket. It was a small, square stone. The rock was gray like the rest of the stones in the turret. It even had what appeared to be spots from the salt in the sea-spray.

Helena tossed the rock up and down in her hand a few times. Then she looked at Janet. Something wasn't right about that rock. Helena smiled and tossed the rock at her.

"What's wrong with that rock?" asked Helena.

Janet examined it closely. She tossed it up in the air a few times. Then she sniffed it, rubbed a few of the salt water spots, then tasted the rock. She looked up at Helena.

"It's not salty at all," said Janet.

"It also seems a bit light for a rock this big," said Helena.

Janet walked over to a small pile of rocks that had been swept into a corner by the stairs. She picked up a rock like the one she had in her hand and compared the weight.

"Definitely lighter," said Janet.

"Lemme see that again," said Helena.

Janet tossed the rock at Helena who tossed it into the air a few times and even gave it her own taste test. She looked up at Janet and walked over to the pile of rocks. Kneeling down, Helena placed the rock on the stone floor of the turret. She quickly picked up another rock, raised it above her head, then quickly smashed it down on their clue. It disintegrated after only one blow.

"Not a real rock," observed Janet.

Helena sifted through what was left of their clue. Among the small bits of heavy cardboard was a small plastic tube. Helena gently picked it up and showed it to Janet.

"I think we just found our next clue," said Helena.

"Great. So we didn't have to run all the way up here after all," groused Janet.

"Your new boyfriend tricked us," smiled Helena.

"Yeah. Whatever. Lemme see that," said Janet

Helena stood up, then tossed the small plastic tube over to Janet. She walked over to the sea-side edge and looked down at the waves crashing against the base of the cliff. After a few moments of enjoying the view, Helena turned, leaned up against turret edge and looked at Janet.

"What have you figured out about our next clue?" she asked

Janet rolled the tube in her fingers a few times, then held it under her nose. Next, she held the clear, plastic tube up to her eye like a spy glass to look through it at Helena.

When she saw Helena standing so close to the edge of the turret, Janet let the hand holding the tube drop away from her eye. Looking away, she huffed once.

"Do you have to stand so close to the edge?" she asked nervously.

"You still don't like heights do you?" smiled Helena.

"You know I don't," said Janet still looking away.

Helena smiled and walked over to Janet.

"Better?" asked Helena.

Janet took a deep breath, then looked at Helena.

"Yes, thanks," she said.

Helena reached for small plastic tube. As she tried to take it, Janet's fingers closed tightly around their next clue. Helena tried to pry the plastic from her sister's fingers, but they were tightly closed around the plastic tube. Helena looked up at Janet.

"Lemme see it," said Helena.

Janet's face was a cocktail of emotions. She was smiling defiantly, but her eyes seemed more amused than defiant. Janet held the plastic tube up in her clenched fist and shook her head. No.

"Come on," said Helena.

Janet shook her head. No.

"Please?" said Helena.

"Not until you promise to stay away from the edge of the steepest cliff on the island," said Janet.

"Okay," said Helena.

"Okay. What?" smiled Janet.

Helena rolled her eyes skyward.

"Okay, I promise not to walk so close to cliffs," said Helena.

"You better," said Janet.

Janet held her hand out offering the empty tube to Helena. But as Helena reached for the clue, Janet suddenly closed her hand and held it back up by her face.

The move surprised Helena. But when she looked up at Janet, she was surprised to see her sister smiling.

"You're feeling better," said Helena.

"I sure am," smiled Janet.

"This little scavenger hunt has made a whole new woman out of you," observed Helena.

Janet only nodded as she looked down at the small, clear plastic tube. It was about two inches long. The inside of the tube was slightly discolored. Tilting her head slightly to one side, Janet held out the tube.

"What do you suppose was running through this that would have started to turn it brown?" asked Janet.

Helena rolled the tube over a few times before holding it up to her eye. She peered through tube at Janet.

"Not a very good telescope," said Helena.

A gust of wind blew a fresh wave of rain and sea-spray over the top of the turret. The wave hit Helena in the back, but caught Janet head on. She wiped the water from her eyes and shook her long, black, wet hair.

"Come on, It's cold up here. I'm a hot, sweaty mess about to be a cold, sweaty mess. Let's go clean up while we try to figure this clue out," said Janet.

21 THE LAST CLUE

The Castle, Helena's Dorm Room

Helena was just stepping out of her shower when she heard a knock on her door. For the first time in weeks, she had her dorm room to herself. On their way back to their rooms from the top of The Castle, Janet stopped at the door to her room and punched in her code.

Ever since the two sisters emerged from The Castle's dungeon initiation, Janet couldn't stand to be alone. But she seemed to make a major breakthrough halfway through the scavenger hunt.

Drying off as she walked toward the door, Helena looked at the unmade bed and knew she wouldn't have to share it any more. The thought made her a bit sad. As she reached for the button that would open the door, whoever was on the other side knocked again.

Helena punched the button and the door slid open. Janet was waiting impatiently. As Helena continued drying her long black hair, Janet pushed her way into the room.

"Come in," said Helena.

She punched the button to close the door and turned around. Before she could finish drying her hair, Janet shoved their latest clue under Helena's nose.

"Here. Smell this," said Janet excitedly.

Helena scrunched up her nose and pulled her head away from her sister's outstretched hand.

"Um. No thank you," said Helena.

"Come on. Help out here. We can win this," said Janet impatiently.

Helena shook her wet hair over her shoulders and smiled at Janet. She reached for the clear plastic tube in her sister's hand. Looking at Janet, Helena gently brought the plastic tube under her nose. After a moment, she closed her eyes and sniffed the clue.

"I know what that is. I just can't place it," said Janet.

It was a sour, yeasty scent. With her eyes still closed, Helena took another sniff. She let the hand holding the tube fall away from her face as she tilted her head back. It was like she was looking at the ceiling, but her eyes were still closed. Her nose twitched once as Helena's head slowly shook from side to side.

Opening her eyes, she looked down at Janet. She handed the tube back and walked over to the bed and finished drying off.

"You're right. I know that scent too. But I just can't place it," said Helena.

As she finished drying off, she was looking at the various objects around the room. The un-made bed. Her dresser. A set of heavy, glass tumblers next to a hotel style ice bucket. She looked over her shoulder at her books on the desk. The coffee machine. She looked down at her knees. There were still some water drops on her legs and feet. Pulling one foot up on the side of the bed she finished drying her toes.

Janet watched as Helena dried off. As Helena looked around the room, Janet followed her gaze. The coffee machine. The books. The water glasses. The dresser.

As Helena finished drying one foot and pulled the other one up on the side of the bed, she looked back at the water glasses. Janet looked at the water glasses at the same time. Then they looked at each other.

"The pub," they said at the same time.

"That's a beer line from a keg to the taps," said Janet.

Helena rushed over to the dresser and pulled some running shorts and a t'shirt on. Janet had the door open as Helena sat down to pull on her socks and running shoes.

"Put those on when we get there," said Janet.

Helena nodded, stood up and grabbed a hoodie jacket as she sprinted for the door. But before the door closed, she rushed back in, snatched the black messenger bag with all the clues and rushed out again.

Janet and Helena ran up three levels of stairs to get to The Castle's pub. As they turned down the corridor that lead to the pub's wooden doors, Janet stopped running. Helena looked back.

"Come on. Why are your stopping?" she asked.

"I have a feeling this is our last stop," said Janet.

"So?" said Helena.

Janet stopped. She took a deep breath, the smiled at Helena.

"Come on. Catch your breath, put your shoes on," said Janet.

Taking a few deep breaths, Helena walked back to Janet, dropped one of her shoes and dusted off the bottom of one foot. As she slipped on the shoe and looked down to tie the laces, Helena glanced up at Janet through her long, black hair.

"So what if this is our last stop?" asked Helena.

"If it is, I'm guessing there might be a welcoming party. If there is, I just think we should walk in looking like something other than two school girls rushing around out of breath," said Janet.

As Helena went to work on her second shoe, she once again glanced up at Janet through her hair. This time, she smiled.

"Maintaining appearances. Just what a good spy needs to do," said

Helena.

Before she stood up, Helena lowered her head even more so her long hair hung straight down. She shook her head a few times, then stood up suddenly. Her hair fell neatly behind her shoulders.

"How's that?" asked Helena.

"Perfect. Me?" said Janet.

Helena smoothed some tangles along one side of Janet's hair, then brushed some dust off the sleeve of her pull over shirt. She gave Janet a quick up and down glance and smiled.

"Perfect," said Helena.

"Righty-ho then. Let's go impress some people," said Janet.

"Righty-ho?" said Helena slowly.

"I'm working on my new, can-do attitude," said Janet.

It took less than a minute for Janet and Helena to arrive at the swinging wooden doors of The Castle's pub. As Helena reached out to push the door open, she stood aside and smiled at Janet.

"Righty-ho, in you go," said Helena a bit sarcastically.

As Janet walked through the door, she gave Helena a brief smile.

"Now you're just mocking me," said Janet as she walked by.

Helena followed Janet into the pub. It took only a second for the new spies to realize they had won scavenger hunt race. The pub was packed with people. Alan Dennis and the McNallys were there. A few of the medical doctors were there, along with the guard who stopped them on the submarine dock. Everyone was clapping and cheering.

Helena patted Janet on the back and leaned over to whisper in her ear.

"You were so right," smiled Helena.

Janet looked back.

"We're going to be good at this," said Janet.

A large table sat off to the side of the room. It was covered with food. Janet started walking toward the table, but Helena quickly caught up and steered her toward Alan Dennis.

"I'm hungry," protested Janet.

"Righty-ho then. Let's go be polite to the boss first," smiled Helena.

"You're not going to let that go are you?" said Janet.

"Oh no. Not for a very long time," smiled Helena.

"Very nicely done you two," smiled Alan Dennis.

As he reached for their hands, Alan looked around the room. Standing near the back was the man he was looking for.

"Thomas," said Alan above all the other conversations in the room.

"Thomas! Come over here," he said.

Thomas Austin looked over at Janet, then quickly looked down as he started meandering through the groups of people. He glanced at Janet once again as he arrived next to Alan.

"Thomas, it would seem that I owe you a fiver," smiled Alan.

That made Janet look up with a little surprise in her eyes. Helena just looked down and smiled.

"A fiver?' repeated Janet.

"Just a friendly wager on who'd arrive here first," smiled Alan.

"Was there any doubt?" asked Helena.

"Not really," said Thomas.

"You know Thomas, this scavenger hunt lesson of yours has really turned out to be a good thing all around," said Alan.

"I'm not so sure the other teams would agree with you," said Helena.

"Any updates on their progress?" asked Alan.

"They're making slower progress, but they'll all be in soon," said Thomas.

Alan was still smiling. He was clearly pleased with Janet and Helena. But there was something more.

"You seem really happy about all this," observed Janet.

"I am. It was a great Spy School exercise for you students. But it was also good for everyone here at The Castle," said Alan.

"How so?" asked Janet.

Alan thought about it a moment. Normally he wouldn't talk about Castle business with a student. But there was something special about Janet. Somehow, Alan knew he could trust her.

"As I'm sure you can imagine, things can get a bit dull around here," said Alan.

He nodded toward Thomas.

"Thomas' idea got everyone in this dusty old cave helping out with planning today's little scheme. Put a bounce in everyone's step, because everyone has so much fun," smiled Alan.

"Everyone knows that learning while you're having fun is the best kind of learning," said Janet.

Thomas looked up at Janet and smiled.

"Exactly," said Thomas.

"You learn faster, retain more and can't wait for more," explained Janet.

"I didn't realize you were an expert in learning," said Alan.

"I'm not. Just seems like common sense to me," said Janet.

She looked at Helena. All this chit-chat was nice, but Janet was hungry and a table full of food was just on the other side of the room. Janet nodded toward the table.

Everyone in the group watched as a few moments of non-verbal communication took place between Janet and Helena. Helena looked back at Alan and smiled.

"We've been running up and down a lot of stairs today and that food table looks amazing. Mind if we migrate over there?" she said.

Before Alan could say anything, Janet started walking toward the table. Thomas quickly brushed past Alan and Helena. He caught up to Janet just as she arrived at the table and was reaching for a plate.

"Mind if I make a suggestion?" asked Thomas.

Janet was already chewing a small sandwich and was reaching for another one. She looked up at Thomas.

"Sure," she said through a mouth full of sandwich.

Helena and Alan arrived at the table and reached for plates. Helena grabbed a few sandwiches. Alan reached for a spoon and deposited a generous scoop of guacamole on Janet's plate.

"This is the best stuff they make here and it goes fast," smiled Thomas.

"Actually, they don't make it here. Thomas makes it for us," said Alan.

Janet looked at the guacamole on her plate, then up at Thomas. She looked at Helena as she dropped a few chips on her plate. Helena smiled as she scooped some guac on her plate too.

Thomas looked from Janet to Helena and back to Janet. Clearly, some more non-verbal communication was going on. Thomas tried to figure out what Janet and Helena were 'talking' about. He slowly followed Janet around the table as she loaded up her plate.

"You should also try the salsa and grab one of those peanut butter, chocolate chip cookies," suggested Thomas.

"You're taking extra good care of me," observed Janet.

She watched as a mix of emotions flashed across Thomas' face. First, it was surprise, quickly followed by guilt and then what looked like sadness. Janet looked down and smiled. Those three emotions that showed up so clearly on Thomas' face made it clear that he liked her. It took less time for Janet to realize that she liked him too. Still smiling, she looked up and leaned closer to him.

"It's okay. I don't mind you taking extra good care of me," said Janet.

A look of hope, then confusion quickly washed over Thomas' face. Janet closed her eyes and slightly shook her head from side to side. She smiled.

"Men," she said quietly.

She opened her eyes.

"I like you too," she said slowly.

Thomas still looked confused. So Janet leaned even closer. She looked around to see if anyone was watching, then gave him a quick kiss on the cheek. Janet turned, walked to the nearest table and sat down to eat. Thomas didn't move. His mind was still buzzing.

"Who's holding up the line?" asked Alan.

Thomas still didn't move. Then he felt a sharp poke in his back.

"Let's go sport," laughed Helena.

She began pushing him out of the food line. That was all it took for Thomas' brain to catch up to current events. He looked down at his full plate of food, then up at Janet. The confusion on his face was washed away by a relieved and very satisfied smile.

"If you ever happen to end up in a game of poker, I do hope you'll allow me to sit in," said Helena.

Still smiling, Thomas began walked toward Janet's table. Helena walked beside him. They never looked at each other.

"Why is that?" asked Thomas.

"Because with a poker face like yours, I'd be winning all of your money," said Helena.

"Don't count on it," said Thomas.

He sat down next to Janet. Helena sat across from Janet. Even Alan took a seat at the table. Janet and Thomas ate in silence. Helena made small talk with Alan until the food was gone. She tossed her napkin on the empty plate, stood up and looked at Alan.

"I know it's a bit early in the afternoon, but how about taking me over to the bar and buying me pint," said Helena.

Alan looked up at Helena. Then back at Janet and Thomas. As he looked back up at Helena, she nodded toward the bar.

"Excellent," smiled Alan.

As Helena and Alan walked toward the bar, Helena looked over her shoulder and winked at Janet.

Janet smiled back.

After a few moments of silence, Janet took a drink of her water, then looked up at Thomas.

"I think we may be in trouble," said Janet quietly.

"But it's the good kind of trouble. Right?" asked Thomas.

Janet looked down and thought about it for a few moments. She smiled as she looked back up.

"Absolutely. Yes. It's the good kind," she said.

Thomas reached over and covered Janet's hand with his. He looked down a moment, then looked back into her eyes.

"Thank you," he said quietly.

"For what?" asked Janet.

"For the gift of you," said Thomas quietly.

Janet looked down and smiled. After a few moments, she felt Thomas give her hand a slight tug.

"Come on," he said.

As they stood up, Janet picked the last cucumber off her plate, finished off her water and smiled at Thomas.

"Where are we going?" she asked.

"To see if it's still raining topside," he said.

"It's always raining topside," said Janet.

"That's not the point," said Thomas.

As they started walking away from the table, Janet reached back for the cookie, broke it in two and handed half to Thomas.

They left the pub in silence and slowly climbed the stairs that lead to

The Castle's sea-side turret. About half-way up the stairs, their hands slowly came together. When they arrived at the top of The Castle, their fingers were tightly interlaced.

A steady rain was falling and the wind was slowly building. It was also getting colder. But Janet and Thomas barely noticed. This was their moment. As they looked into each other's eyes, they both knew they wouldn't be going through life alone.

Thomas thought back earlier in the day when he noticed Janet and Helena taking without saying a word. He wondered how it worked. Now all he had to do was look into Janet's eyes and he understood.

A strong gust of wind whipped across the top of the castle nearly knocking Janet and Thomas off their feet. They had only been out in the rain and wind for a minute or so, but their clothes, shoes and hair were soaked. They looked away from each other for just a moment as another strong gust of wind whipped cold rain across their soaked faces.

Looking back into each other's eyes, Janet and Thomas knew it was time. They had been holding each other's hands tightly since they arrived at the top of The Castle. Thomas released one of Janet's hands and gently wiped some of the rain out of her beautiful black eyes.

Janet smiled, but quickly reached up and took Thomas' free hand.

It was time.

As Janet and Thomas looked into each other's eyes, they both realized that of all the faces in the world, they were lucky enough to find the one that was perfect for each other.

It was time for the first kiss of a love that would last a lifetime.

22 AUGUST 19, 1991

The Castle, Thomas Austin's Dorm Room

The pain that shot through Janet's leg muscles was enough to make her cry out. A second later, Thomas' face appeared in the bathroom's doorway. It was half lathered up. He held a dripping razor in one hand.

"Are you all right?" he asked.

"Fine," said Janet.

She slowly inched out of the bed propping her head and shoulders against the wall. The expression on her face was a mix of happiness and pain.

"You didn't sound fine," said Thomas.

Janet continued inching out of bed until she was sitting with her back against the cold wall. She reached for a pillow, leaned forward and dropped it between her back and the wall. Another look of pain flashed across her face as she pulled her knees up. Thomas smiled as the last bit of blanket slipped away and Janet began rubbing her legs.

"Sore?" asked Thomas.

Janet looked up and saw Thomas smiling at her.

"Either from the running or the sex," smiled Janet.

"Probably both," said Thomas.

He disappeared back into the bathroom. It took less than a minute for him to finish shaving. Janet looked up from her sore legs just as Thomas walked back into the room and over to the dresser. As he dressed, he looked at Janet in the dresser mirror.

They both caught each other's gaze in the mirror at the same time. Thomas finished pulling on a knit shirt and turned to look at Janet. Smiles of contented happiness appeared on their faces. After a few moments, Thomas turned and finished dressing. Without looking at Janet, he reached for his shoes, sat on the bed and started talking.

"Last night was amazing and there's nothing more I'd rather do than spend the day in bed with you. But something big is happening and I've got to be in Alan's office in about three minutes," said Thomas.

"What's happening?" asked Janet.

"World changing," said Thomas.

He finished tying his shoes and looked up at Janet.

"Almost as world changing as what we've found together. And I hate to run, but I've really got to get going," said Thomas.

As he walked to the door, Thomas snagged a heavy black leather briefcase. He punched the button and it silently slid open. Then Thomas turned and looked back at Janet.

"The last thing I want to do is leave you now," he said.

"It's okay. I don't think you'd be leaving if it weren't really important," said Janet.

"I don't have time to say everything I want to say right now. But," said Thomas.

"But what?" smiled Janet.

"I saw the most amazing transformation yesterday. Of everyone I've met in my life, you are simply the most amazing," said Thomas.

Thomas' voice trailed off. He feel pressure building up in his brain. Thomas had to be in the bosses office, basically now. But he couldn't tear himself away from Janet. He forced himself to look down at the floor.

"You should get up, go find Helena and head to the pub for breakfast. It's probably all over the news by now," said Thomas.

He looked up and gave Janet one more smile.

"Love you," he said.

"Love you," said Janet.

The door closed.

Less than three minutes later, the door to Alan's office slid open and Thomas burst into the room. He was out of breath from running up three flights of stairs. Between breaths, he croaked out a few words.

"Is ... it ... happening?" he huffed.

Alan looked up and smiled. The five other people in the room looked at Thomas with varying degrees of contempt.

The six people in the room made up the department heads of The Castle. They were old school intelligence and military and had little to no sense of humor. Of the five department heads, only David McNally didn't regard Thomas with open contempt.

Alan could feel the mood of the room shift and he didn't like it. He brought Thomas Austin in to help prepare The Castle for the coming new millennium. As Alan looked at the scowls on the faces of his most trusted and senior staff, he set his coffee cup down hard on his desk.

"If you could see the expressions on your faces," began Alan. "You'd understand why I brought someone like Mr. Austin in to help breath some life into this stale old cave."

The five department heads looked at each other, then at Thomas, then back at Alan. Clearly, the message didn't sink in. As Thomas caught his breath, he stood up straight and asked his question again.

"Is is happening?" he repeated a bit impatiently.

"It is," said Alan.

Thomas slowly walked over to one of the leather couches the lined Alan's office and sat down. His mind was going about a hundred miles an hour. Alan looked over at David and nodded toward Thomas. David smiled.

"They're saying Gorbachev is too sick to lead and they're just 'temporarily' taking control until he get's well," said David.

Alan looked at his watch.

"Temporarily? Sounds like a coup to me," said Alan.

Thomas' head was spinning. A coup with hard-liners in charge could only mean an escalation of the Cold War.

"So much for Gorbachev's perestroika and glasnost," said Thomas quietly.

"Too bad," said one of the five department heads.

Commodore Wells ran The Castle's fleet of submarines. His father commanded the ferry boat that whisked the first wave of Castle operatives away from that foggy dock back in the sixties.

"They still have the second most powerful navy in the world. The KGB is still fully operational around the world. And there's all those nukes," said the old Commodore.

The conversation went on from there. But when Commodore Wells mentioned the KGB, Thomas grabbed his briefcase and began shuffling through papers. The conversation strayed in several different directions before Alan decided to re-focus the room.

"The main question here is, we have a major coup in Russia. What do we do about it?" he asked.

"We don't do shit," said David McNally.

"It's their fucking problem," agreed Commodore Wells.

"Language," smiled Alan.

Several of the old school department heads rolled their eyes. Alan had decided long ago to keep Sir Richard's policy about clean language. Clearly, some of the old guys in the room never liked that policy.

The conversation continued to examine what, if anything the spies at The Castle should do. Most everyone agreed, there really wasn't anything to do. A coup in the Soviet Union was a big news story, but everyone agreed that life for the rest of the world would go on like normal. Then Thomas broke into the conversation.

"What about Yuri Nikolov?" he asked.

Thomas looked down at one of the folders he pulled out of his briefcase. He leafed through a few pages.

"He's been held by the KGB for the past three years," he said.

"Yeah. So what?" asked David.

"Maybe in all the confusion, now would be a good time to go in and get him out?" ventured Thomas.

"Are you fucking bonkers?" asked one of the quieter department heads.

Alan shot the department head a nasty look, then turned back to Thomas. He thought things over for a few moments. Then Alan looked around the silent room at the stone faced old men.

"Do you really think there is enough confusion to stage a prison break?" asked Alan.

"It's not a guarantee, but I think we might figure something out," said Thomas.

"Why bother?" asked one of the other old department heads.

"Excuse me?" said Thomas incredulously.

"You heard me you impertinent little shit. Nikolov is a professional. He knew the risks of being a sleeper agent in the Soviet Union. Staging a prison break is a needlessly risky waste of agents, time and money," said the grumpy old man.

The other grumpy old men in the room nodded in agreement. Alan looked around the room, over at David, then back at Thomas. He walked behind his desk and sat down.

Alan had been up most of the night monitoring what was going on in Moscow. He rubbed his eyes, then looked up at the portrait of the man who started it all. Sir Richard smiled down at the room. When Alan asked for the portrait, he asked the artist to paint his former boss and mentor with a smile. If there was one thing Alan remembered about Sir Richard, it was that he was always smiling.

Alan looked up at the grumpy old men in the room. It was hard for him to contain his utter disgust with what he'd just heard. Alan made up his mind and it was the easiest decision he had ever made.

"We never leave our comrades behind. Ever," said Alan. "Let's go get him."

He looked up at the other old men in the room and could tell not one of them agreed with his decision. But they all remained silent. Over the years, they learned that when the old man sat behind his desk and made a call, it was a done deal.

Alan looked at Thomas.

"What did you have in mind?" he asked.

"First thoughts? You're not going to like it. Neither do I," said Thomas.

"What?" asked Alan.

"Send in the winners of our scavenger hunt posing as college students on a school trip," said Thomas.

A few of the old men in the room laughed out loud. But David McNally didn't laugh. He slowly walked over to the couch and sat down next to Thomas. He nodded slowly a few times.

"No spy agency would ever consider doing something like this. So no one would suspect them. But it's a hell of a risk," said David.

"They haven't even completed half of Spy School," protested Commodore Wells. "They're also my granddaughters."

"Adopted granddaughters, Adopted for the purpose of being agents for this organization," said Thomas.

"Just because they're adopted, doesn't make them any less precious," said Wells.

Thomas looked up and nodded.

"Of course," he said.

Alan was slowly spinning around in the leather chair. His elbows were resting on the chair's padded arms. His chin rested in his clasped hands. His head slowly nodded a few times.

"Suppose we could get them to Moscow in, say, the next twelve hours. What then?" asked Alan.

Thomas thought a moment. His eyes roamed the room until they fell on a bank of eight television monitors. They were all tuned to the world's news channels. Most showed either talking heads or a static shot of Red Square. But one was focused on the protests outside KGB headquarters. The infamous Lubyanka Prison.

"Well," said Thomas.

He got up and walked over to the TV monitors. Looking carefully at the scene playing out in front of The Lubyanka, a smile began appearing on one half of his face. The other half was dead serious.

Thomas was both exhilarated and terrified. He was forming a plan of action that, if successful, would result in freedom for an imprisoned Castle spy. But that same plan called for sending the woman he'd just fallen in love with into one of the most dangerous places on earth. As frightening as that was, Thomas knew Janet and Helena were just the spies to pull it off.

The camera showing The Lubyanka pulled back to show the square in front of the prison. Since 1926, it had been called Dzerzhinsk Square, named after the feared father of Soviet Intelligence. The name changed back to Lubyanka Square just last year.

The live picture from Moscow zoomed into the protestors at the base of what was known as the Iron Felix statue. The 15-ton statue had stood guard in front of KGB headquarters since 1958.

Up until now, no one would have ever dared protest at the foot of Iron Felix. But today, they weren't just protesting, they were spray painting the base of the statue with slogans that in Dzerzhinsk's day would have resulted in mass arrests and executions.

Thomas nodded a few more times. Still looking at the monitor, he re-traced his steps back across Alan's office to his briefcase. Pulling out a few more files, he assembled a few pictures. After one last look at the monitor, he gently placed the pictures on Alan's desk.

"Those protests and the graffiti at the foot of old Felix there are only going to escalate. So we goose it along a bit and use those protests as our diversion," said Thomas.

"It looks like that's going to erupt into street violence right now. You sure you want to put those two kids in the middle of it?" asked David.

"It won't be comfortable, but I think they can get around the protesters," said Thomas.

"Okay, so you've got your diversion and my granddaughters are inside. What next?" asked Commodore Wells.

Thomas looked at Wells. The old sea dog was looking for anything he could find to kill the plan. Part of Thomas was secretly hoping old Commodore Wells succeeded.

"We spend the 12 hours they're traveling coming up with the exact location of our guy in that building. We draw up a turn by turn plan to get them to Nikolov's cell, then back out on the street," said Thomas.

He looked over at David.

"I know we have a few operatives there who could probably transmit the cell number to us without compromising their cover," said Thomas.

David nodded.

"What next?" asked Alan.

"Once we get our team outside the prison, all we have to do is walk a few blocks to a waiting car that takes them to one of the many airfields scattered around Moscow. With all the chaos over there, I'm guessing more than a few airplanes will slip in and out of Russian airspace in the next few days," said Thomas.

"And how do you 'goose up' the crowd to create more chaos?" asked Commodore Wells.

Thomas pulled a picture from the stack of paper he laid on Alan's desk. Spinning it around, he pointed to what looked like a pile of grey snowballs.

"I call these Psychedelics. It's sort of a mash-up of a small bit of explosive, fireworks and very bright paint. It comes in two separate containers. It looks a lot like the child's toy PlayDoh, You mush the two parts together, then throw it like a snowball. It sticks to the side of a wall or in this case, to that iron statue. You can time your explosion depending on how you mix it. The final product is a very pretty explosion but not much damage," said Thomas.

"How much time do you have before the explosion?" asked Commodore Wells.

"That depends on how you mix it up. Use a little more from package 'A' and you get a longer fuse. More from 'B' is a shorter fuse. In tests, I've gotten anywhere from five minutes to 40 minutes." said Thomas.

"So, on their way in, our team mixes two sets of Psychedelics. One to cover their entry, the other to cover their exit. How do they get them on the target?" asked David.

Thomas shuffled through a few more papers and pulled out another picture. He looked up at Alan and smiled.

"A child's toy will work for that. I've been playing with this sling-shot. It delivers small and medium sized Psychedelics perfectly on target," said

Thomas.

"Great. So now we're sending half trained agents in with child's toys. What happens if they get to our guy's cell and it's locked? What if they run into a few guards who could care less about the chaos outside. What then?" protested Commodore Wells.

Thomas stood up and looked directly at the old Commodore. He looked down at the picture of the sling shot and the Psychedelics. Looking up, he smiled.

"Then they have to use adult toys. Helena is great at picking locks and Janet is a much better than average shot," said Thomas.

Everyone looked down at Alan with stern, serious expressions. Everyone except David and Thomas. Those two were almost smiling. Alan slowly spun around in his chair one more time. When he faced the room again, he said only one word.

"Go." said Alan.

David walked to the door, opened it and called out to his wife.

"Nancy, please have Akira and Wells come to Commander Dennis' office right now," said David.

A few minutes later, Janet and Helena arrived. It only took a moment for them to know something big was up and they would be right in the middle of it.

"What?" said Janet.

It took just five minutes for Thomas to explain what was going on. As the story unfolded, Helena eyes grew wide with excitement and anticipation. Janet's expression never changed from the moment she entered the room. She was all business.

As soon as Thomas finished explaining what they would be doing, Janet and Helena looked at each other. Once again, Thomas wondered what the two sisters were saying during this moment of non-verbal communication. Whatever it was, they didn't take long. After only a few moments, they looked over at Alan.

"Count us in," said Helena.

Everyone looked at Janet. She looked at Thomas.

"Yes. Both of us," said Janet.

Everyone in the room stood up. Alan cleared his throat.

"Okay then. We need to get these two on a plane. David, you go with them as far as Helsinki. You'll need to brief them on our Numbers Station and how to use it. Then you coordinate the flight out," said Alan.

"Yes Sir," said David.

He turned and started walking to the door. Without looking back, he made a few suggestions.

"Mr. Austin, I'll need to see all three of you in your office in fifteen minutes. Commodore, may I suggest you move your ice-cap patrol closer to Archangel in case we need another extraction point? Captain Tucker, I suggest you have that new armor chief, what's his name, Boxx, prepare five standard field weapons bags," said David.

The door closed behind him. Everyone turned back to Alan. He got up and walked over to Janet and Helena. Alan smiled at them for a moment, then put his hand on their shoulders and steered them to the door. He talked to them very quietly.

"Listen here you two. This is going to get rough. You're going into a very dangerous part of the world. So I'm going to give you two pieces of advice I give to everyone I send out of this office," he said.

Janet and Helena looked at each other, then back at Alan.

"What's that?" asked Helena.

"First, no part of this mission is worth either one of you getting killed. So I want you both to be very, very careful," said Alan.

"What's the second piece of advice?" asked Helena.

"It's more of a request," said the old man.

"Anything," said Helena.

"Come back alive," he said.

As the reached the door, Alan snapped his fingers and walked back to his desk. He opened one of the drawers, grabbed a small, black leather pouch and tossed it to Helena. She quickly unzipped the pouch and shook out a new Minox spy camera. It was so small, it could fit in the palm of her hand. She looked up.

"You are going to be snooping around KGB Headquarters. So hang onto that in case you see anything worth taking a picture of," smiled Alan.

Helena and Janet stood in the open door looking at Alan. He smiled once, then nodded.

"Off you go," he said.

23 THE LUBYANKA

Moscow

~ ~ ~

PLAYLIST:
"Blizzard" - Skyworld - Two Steps From Hell

~ ~ ~

Twenty-four hours later, the coup was over. The hardliners had lost and Gorbachev was back in power. That only brought more Muscovites out of their homes and on the streets to celebrate the downfall of the attempt to turn the clock back to darker days.

Helena and Janet walked for several hours before they finally arrived at Dzerzhinsk Square. They weren't able to get a cab at the airport, so they walked. It was nearly midnight and the temperature had been dropping all evening. Walking was the only thing that was keeping them warm against the cold, Moscow air.

The streets were jammed with people celebrating the end of the coup. While there was some violence, most of the people Janet and Helena ran into completely ignored them.

After making a few twists and turns from Red Square, they turned a corner and the first thing they saw was the iron statue they learned about in the mission briefing. It was surrounded by hundreds of people.

Helena and Janet looked at each other and nodded. Janet unslung her backpack and pulled out a large tube of toothpaste and an aluminum sling shot. Helena pulled a similar tube of toothpaste out of her backpack. Both tubes of toothpaste looked identical, but one was printed in green ink, the other was blue. Helena looked around, then pointed to a grey, stone apartment building.

"That stairway to the basement should give us some cover while we mash this stuff up," said Helena.

"We'll probably only need a few short ones to get inside. I think I'd rather have most of them go off to cover our escape," said Janet.

"Maybe a few in the middle, then some big ones for the end," suggested Helena.

It took just a few minutes before Helena and Janet had a small pile of small, medium and large balls of Thomas Austin's magical Psychedelics.

Janet took off her jacket and rolled up two layers of shirt sleeves keeping her left arm warm. She shivered from the cold as she reached for the sling shot. After flexing her hands and arms a few times, Janet pulled the leather pocket back, stretching the elastic as far as it could go. She held it for a few moments before releasing the pocket. As it snapped forward, it sprang back slapping Janet's arm a few times. Helena looked down just as Janet looked up in surprise.

A single, snort-type laugh erupted from Helena's nose.

"Really? You're laughing at me?" asked Janet.

Helena thought about it a moment, then smiled sweetly.

"Yeah. Sure am," she confessed.

"Nice," said Janet.

She looked down and started gently placing the Psychedelics on the top step of the stairwell they were hiding in. After the small, clay balls were neatly arranged, she stretched out the sling shot again. When she released the leather pocket a second time, it shot forward but didn't smack Janet's arm.

"Better," smiled Helena.

"Are we about ready?" asked Janet.

"Just about. Let's see if there are any last minute updates," said Helena.

Helena pulled out a Sony Walkman, shuffled through some cassettes in her backpack and slid one into the player. After gently placing the headphones over her ears, she pulled out a black notebook. Helena checked her watch and opened the notebook.

Times and shortwave radio frequencies filled the first few pages. Helena pulled a pen out of her backpack, After unscrewing the top, she pulled out a small screwdriver. Checking her watch and the list of frequencies again, Helena slowly turned one of the screws on the cassette. After a few moments of making small adjustments, she put the screwdriver back in it's hiding place, flipped to a blank page in the notebook and began writing down numbers.

Watching her sister, Janet was amazed at how they were able to receive last minute information from The Castle. What looked like a popular Walkman cassette player was actually a shortwave radio receiver. But the station Helena was listening to wasn't playing music. It was The Castle's very own Numbers Station.

Helena pressed one of the headphones closer to her ear. There was a lot of static, but through the noise, she was able to hear the calm, confident voice from The Castle reading numbers. Lots of numbers. Nothing but numbers.

"42. 28. 6. 77. 95," said the voice.

They were always in groups of five. The voice repeated each string of numbers three times before moving on to the next.

"88. 16. 32. 2. 9," said the voice.

As Helena jotted down numbers, every now and then, she'd scratch out one and replace it. Then she stopped writing. But her pen slowly moved over each of the numbers on the page. The voice was repeating them again.

Once Helena was sure they were right, she slipped the headphones down around her neck and flipped the Walkman off. Still holding the pen in her fingers, she flipped to the back of the notebook. The last twenty pages were filled with more numbers. Checking her watch again, she found a page with the correct date and time and ripped it out of the book. Flipping back to the first page of numbers, Helena began copying numbers from the ripped page under the numbers she just wrote down.

Janet continued to watch as Helena decoded the message. She remembered back to her first week in Spy School as the instructor explained one of the oldest secret codes ever invented. If the instructor told her she would be in Moscow, using a One Time Pad to decode a message from The Castle's Numbers Station two weeks later, Janet would have laughed in his face.

But there they were. Hiding in a freezing stairwell less than a block away from the headquarters of the feared Soviet KGB. It was a bit mind boggling, but there they were.

"Almost done," said Helena.

Janet nodded and slowly pushed herself up so just her eyes appeared over the cold stone steps. She looked up and down the street. People were everywhere, but no one seemed to be paying attention to Janet and Helena. Everyone was heading toward the iron statue in the square.

"Success!" said Helena quietly.

Janet crouched back down in the stairwell.

"What do they say?" she asked.

Helena smiled.

"It's from your Mr. Austin," said Helena seriously.

"What does he say?" smiled Janet.

"He says the sex was great and wants to know if you're ready for more," snickered Helena.

Janet closed her eyes and slowly shook her head.

"Really? You think this is a good time for that sort of thing?" said Janet.

"Actually, it's the perfect time," smiled Helena.

"Two blocks away from one of the blackest pits of terror in the world and you're giving me shit about Thomas," sighed Janet.

"What's a sister for?" smiled Helena.

"Enough," said Janet. "What does our message actually say?"

Helena handed her notebook to Janet. She read the message over a few times, then handed it back.

TARGET REMAINS SUB-LEVEL THREE. CELL 313. PRIMARY FLIGHT ARRIVES AT 0200. GOOD LUCK.

Helena ripped the original coded message, the plain text and the cypher key pages out of her book. Reaching into her backpack, she pulled out a book of matches. In a flash, the paper went up in a puff of smoke. Janet looked at her watch.

"Okay, we've got a little over two hours to collect Mr. Nikolov and get to the airport," she said.

"Let's set the Psychedelics and get going," said Helena.

Janet gripped her hands into fists to warm them up. Then she picked up the slingshot and arranged the Psychedelics in a line. Janet quickly looked over the edge of the stairwell to make sure she was clear. Helena looked at her watch.

"I'm guessing we have about 5 more minutes before the short fuses begin exploding," said Helena.

Janet looked at Helena.

"Now or never?" she said.

"Now or never," repeated Helena.

Janet stood up and quickly looked around again. No one seemed interested in the two cold women in the stone stairwell. She dropped down on one knee, picked up the first clay Psychedelic and aimed it right at Iron Felix's nose. In less than a minute, she covered the statue's face, shoulders and chest. The last two, larger Psychedelics were aimed just above a corner office of The Lubyanka and just above the main door.

"That's it," said Janet.

Helena stood up, slipped on her backpack and held her hand out. Janet quickly rolled the sleeve down over her bare arm and quickly pulled on her jacket. She rubbed her nearly frozen arm a few times before taking Helena's outstretched hand and stood up.

"Now or never?" she smiled.

"Now or never," repeated Helena.

The square was packed with people slowing Janet and Helena down as they made their way toward the imposing building. Janet stole a glance at her watch.

"I'm guessing we only have a few minutes before the first Psychedelics go off," she said.

Helena stopped and pushed herself as high on her toes as she could go. Looking around, she pointed off to the far side of the square. She looked back toward the imposing iron statue.

"Most of the people seem to crowded around old Felix. Let's go that way," she said.

"These people will start running away once the Psychedelics begin firing off," said Janet

Suddenly, Helena looked in the opposite direction.

"What is that?" she asked.

Janet looked and saw several heavy duty cranes slowly driving into the square. They were heading toward the famous statue.

"Don't know, don't care. Let's get to that side entrance before the Psychedelics start up," said Janet.

Helena and Janet continued pushing their way through the crowd. The arrival of the cranes helped a bit. They were clearly making their way toward the statue. Janet looked at her watch.

"I think we're getting down to about a minute before the first Psychedelics go off," she said.

"Almost there," said Helena.

As they stepped up on the sidewalk, Janet and Helena noticed several guards blocking the side entrance they hoped to use. Helena thought fast and quickly turned to Janet.

"Remember all those times you wanted to hit me when we were kids?" she asked.

The question took Janet completely by surprise. Helena smiled at her sister.

"We're going to need a distraction. I figure a bloody nose might do the trick," she said.

Janet looked over her shoulder. The cranes were still inching their way to the statue. The crowd was getting louder and rowdy.

"You sure?" asked Janet.

Even though her back was turned, she could hear Helena take a deep breath.

"Yeah. Let's go," said Helena.

"I don't like this," said Janet quietly.

"It's okay," said Helena.

Without looking at her sister, Janet twisted halfway around and looked at the guards. They were watching the crowd and the cranes. In a flash, Janet landed a solid punch on her sister's nose. Blood immediately began flowing.

"Remind me to never make you really mad at me," Helena choked through the blood.

"You shouldn't have reminded me about all the times I wanted to punch you," said Janet.

Janet looked at her sister and the blood gushing out of her nose. A small tear formed on a corner of her right eye and dropped down to her cheek.

"I'm not going to like some of this spy shit," she said.

Helena was wiping her nose with the back of her hand, then smearing the blood on her shirt. She looked up at Janet.

"It's gonna be okay. Let's get this guy and go home," said Helena.

Another tear leaked out of Janet's eyes and fell on her cheek. She moved her hand up to wipe the tears away when Helena grabbed it.

"Leave them. It'll make it more realistic," said said.

Janet shook her head once, then squared her shoulders and put her arm around Helena. They both started walking toward the side entrance when one of the guards noticed them and pointed his rifle in their direction. Helena pointed to her nose and to a corner just inside the doorway.

"Pozhaluysta. Vannaya," said Helena.

The guard looked at Janet and Helena, then back at the crowd. The cranes were getting closer to the statue. The crowd was getting noisier. He looked back at Janet and Helena. Apparently their act worked, because he dropped his rifle and waved them into the building.

"Spasibo," said Helena.

As they walked past the guards, one of them pointed to a door. He said something Janet and Helena couldn't understand. So they walked down the short hall and into the unmarked door. It was a small restroom. They closed the door behind them.

"When did you learn how to speak Russian?" asked Janet.

"Just learned a few words on the plane. It's amazing how far you can go with please, thank you and bathroom," said Helena.

She walked over to the sink and started washing away the blood. Janet stood by the door listening. When she was sure no one was on the other side of the door, she slowly opened it.

As the door opened, Janet and Helena heard a small explosion from outside the building. It was followed by another three explosions and the sounds of voices shouting.

"There go the first Psychedelics," said Janet.

Helena grabbed a few paper towels and joined Janet at the door.

"Come on. Let's get going while everyone is watching the show," she said.

Janet opened the door wider and checked the hallway. It was clear. Helena was still dabbing her nose as they silently took off down the hall.

Most of the doors were closed. But a few were open. No one was at their desks. Everyone was standing at the windows watching the drama in the square unfold before them. Janet and Helena walked by the open doors as quietly as they could.

Suddenly, they heard a lot of footsteps on the parquet floor from a ways down the hall. Looking up, all Janet and Helena saw was closed doors and pale green walls. But the footsteps were getting closer.

Janet and Helena looked at each other for just a moment. They knew they had to get out of that hallway immediately. Looking up and down the hall, Helena pointed to an open door and they ducked inside. Janet closed the door as Helena looked around.

It was a large office with several desks. The desk tops were bare except for a a phone. A few had a coffee mug and there was an ash tray on every desk. The room smelled like old, cheap tobacco smoke.

Chalkboards lined the walls. They were covered with pictures and names. Along with the names and photographs, each chalkboard had a paper flag taped to the top. Several chalkboards had American flags, a few had the Union Jack of the United Kingdom. One blackboard had a German flag, another had the Honiara, the circle of the sun flag of Japan.

And one blackboard had the Jolly Roger or pirate's flag. Helena walked over to that one. As she got closer, the color drained out of her face as she recognized the pictures taped next to the names written in white chalk

The pictures were old, taken when the subjects were a lot younger. But the picture at the top was definitely Alan Dennis. Nancy and David McNally had pictures on the board. Helena recognized about half the people. Near the bottom was a new, color picture of Janet's new love. The name Thomas Austin was scrawled next to his picture.

Helena stole a glance at her sister. Janet was still listening through the door. Unslinging her backpack, Helena gently pulled out the small Minox camera Alan Dennis tossed at her just as she was leaving his office. Checking the lens setting on the front of the camera, she began snapping pictures of the black boards.

As Helena slowly made her way around the room, she decided not to tell Janet what she found until after they were safely back at The Castle. She was snapping pictures of British spies when she noticed five pictures in the lower right corner. Helena tiled her head slightly and laughed once through her nose. She didn't think Russian spies had a sense of humor.

"What's so funny?" whispered Janet.

"Tell you later," whispered Helena.

Bending both her knees, she took an extra picture and turned to join Janet at the door. Janet was listening carefully, but smiled at Helena.

"I think they're almost gone," she said.

They waited a few more minutes before Janet carefully opened the door. She looked up and down the hall.

"All clear," she said.

Janet opened the door and walked out of the room. As she left, Helena took one look back at the chalkboard with the Jolly Roger. She liked the fact that the feared KGB used a pirate flag to identify The Castle's agents. But it bugged her to see how much the KGB knew about the organization she'd just joined.

Before she turned the corner, Helena stole one more glance at the chalkboard with spies from MI6. Sean Connery and the other movie stars who played the famous, fictional secret agent smiled back at her.

Helena smiled as she winked at James Bond.

24 CELL 313

Moscow, The Lubyanka, Sub Level 3

~ ~ ~

PLAYLIST:
"Jupiter" - Voices in My Head - Celldweller
~ ~ ~

It took only a few minutes for Janet and Helena to find the stairway leading down to the old prison. Taking the steps two and three at a time, they quickly found themselves at bottom and in front of a locked door. Janet looked at Helena as she slung her backpack around, unzipped a pocket and pulled out her set of lock picks.

Kneeling down by the door handle, she examined the lock. Without looking, she unzipped the small leather pouch of picks and pulled out the tension wrench. After silently inserting it into the lock, Helena briefly looked at the other picks, selected a basic rake and gently began running it over the pins.

As Helena worked the lock, a door at the top of the stairs opened and the sound of several pairs of boots began stomping down the stairs. Helena kept working the lock. The boots turned a corner and kept getting closer.

Janet looked up as the boots approached. She heard what sounded like someone jingling a set of keys as they walked. And they kept getting closer.

Helena kept working the lock. But she was finding it harder and harder to concentrate on gently running the rake over the lock's pins. Her brain was getting a bit fuzzy when she felt Janet's lips close to her ear.

"Take a breath Luv," whispered Janet.

Helena couldn't believe her ears. Why would Janet want her to take a breath. Someone was coming down the stairs and they were seconds away from being found out. They would be arrested at any moment, then probably shot as spies. And Janet wanted her to take a breath? Then Helena opened her mouth and clean, cool air filled her lungs. She'd been holding her breath.

"Thanks," whispered Helena.

She continued running the rake over the pins and the boots kept getting closer. Just as they were about to start down the last steps leading to Janet and Helena, the keys jingled again. A door opened and the boots disappeared on the level above.

Janet and Helena looked at each other. They both took a deep breath. Helena went back to work on the lock. This time, she took regular breaths and after a few more passes with the rake, the tension wrench turned. Helena gently turned the door knob and pushed.

The first thing Helena saw beyond the door was a glassed in guard station. There were several guards behind the glass, but they weren't looking at the stairway door. Their attention was focused on TV coverage of the crowd outside KGB Headquarters. As Helena and Janet scooted by, they stole a glance into the guard room and at the TV.

The crowd outside had grown in the past few minutes. The cranes were getting closer to statue. The guards were watching the drama unfold before them with little thought about what was happening on the other side of the glass. Janet and Helena looked at each other once, inched away from the guard station and silently made their way down the dark, cold cell block.

As they walked, Janet pointed to the cell doors. Each was heavy metal with a small eye hole. A pair of ragged electrical wires lead from the top of the door to a bunch of other wires running the length of the cell block.

"Door alarms?" speculated Helena.

"That's what I'm betting," said Janet.

She unslung her backpack and pulled out a small, black zipper pouch. After a few moments of sorting through odds and ends, Janet pulled out a short wire with alligator clips at each end. She also pulled out a small knife before zipping up her pack and slinging around her back.

About halfway down the cell block, they came to number 313. Janet looked up at the wires coming out of the door, then back at Helena.

"I'll need a boost," she said.

Helena dropped down on one knee and Janet climbed onto her shoulders. Helena had to steady herself as she slowly stood up. As soon as Janet could reach the wires, she stripped away some of the old shielding with the knife and quickly attached the jumper wire. Then she tapped Helena on the head.

As Janet hoped off Helena's shoulders, she held out a hand to help her sister stand back up.

"So far, so good," said Janet.

Helena huffed a few times and rubbed her shoulders.

"So far, so good," she said.

"So, what if our guy isn't in this cell?" asked Janet.

Helena looked at the door, then up at the eye hole.

"Easy way to tell," she said.

Helena walked to the door, stood on her toes and peered through the hole.

"There's one guy doing sit ups on the floor. Medium size, salt and pepper hair. I can't see his face," said Helena.

"Sounds like Nikolov," said Janet.

Helena looked at the lock, selected a different pick and went to work. It didn't take as long as the first lock. The pins lined up and Helena twisted the heavy dead bolt open. Grasping the heavy metal handle, she looked up at the wire as she swung the door open.

No alarm sounded.

Helena and Janet looked into the dark, stone cell. A wood bench was shoved up against a wall. Several blankets and a few towels were folded at one end. Two small buckets were on the floor at the foot of the bed.

A medium sized, middle aged man sat in the middle of the floor with his back to the door. He was doing sit ups.

"Just twenty more and I'll be right with you," he said.

Janet and Helena looked at each other, then back at the prisoner. He continued doing sit ups. Janet looked at Helena who was slowly shaking her head.

"Um, we really don't have time for you to finish your workout," said Helena impatiently.

The prisoner continued with his sit ups. Janet didn't have to look at Helena to know her reservoir of patience was about to run dry. Janet was about to say something, when Helena cut her off.

"Listen Jackass. I know you've been locked up a long time and you might not know a prison break when you see one. But that's why we're here. So I suggest you get off your butt right now," said Helena.

The prisoner did one more sit up, wiped the sweat off his face and turned around. Yuri Nikolov's file said he was 55 years old. Even though he appeared to be in good shape, the gray hair and lines in his face made him look more like 70.

The prisoner stared at Janet for a few moments, looking up and down at her. Then he turned his attention to Helena. He was clearly checking them out. Helena looked impatiently over her shoulder, then down at the prisoner.

"You can enjoy the view when we got on the plane. But we need to leave right now," she said.

The prisoner nodded a few times and smiled.

"A prison break huh. You two?" he said.

"My file on you says you've been here just over three years. I'm leaving in 10 seconds. So if you want to stay a little longer, be my guest," said Helena.

"How do I know this isn't another nasty little KGB trick?" said Yuri.

Helena was about to answer him when Janet cut him off.

"Fair question. Commander Dennis wondered if you'd join him for a pint," said Helena.

Yuri looked up and down at Janet and Helena again.

"A pint with Alan Dennis sounds good. Where?" asked the old prisoner.

"Deep in the Cliffs Pub," said Helena.

The old man looked around his cell once. After a few moments he nodded and jumped to his feet.

"So, the old man is still alive? Alright then. If old Alan Dennis wants to share a pint, we shouldn't keep him waiting," said Yuri.

Helena looked over her shoulder.

"Coast is still clear," she said.

As they stepped out of the cell, Yuri looked up and down the cell block. All the doors were closed. All the guards were gone. Janet quietly closed the door. When she heard the snap of the lock, she gave the door a tug then pointed up at the wire jumper.

"You're taller. Can you get that?" she asked.

Yuri unhooked the small alligator clips. After examining it for a few moments, he handed it to Janet.

"How did you manage to get rid of the guards?" he asked.

"They're still here. But they're a bit distracted right now," said Janet.

"Distracted?" asked Yuri.

"It's chaos in Moscow. There's been a coup and things out on the streets are getting a little out of control," said Helena.

"Well, to be fair, we've added to the chaos," said Janet.

"Just a bit," said Helena.

"How?" asked Yuri.

But before he could get his answer, they arrived at the guard station. Janet and Helena flattened themselves against the wall under the station's glass window. Yuri watched at they glanced at each other for just a moment.

A second later, they unslung their backpacks. Helena pulled out her lock pick set. Janet pulled out a small, black 9mm handgun. They looked at each other once more and nodded.

Helena crouched down with her head just next to the guard station's glass window. She took a quick breath. In a flash, she moved her head just enough to see what was going on in the guard station, then leaned back against the wall. Helena took another breath, then stole one more look. After checking things out, she whispered something to Janet, then crawled under the window and began working the lock with her pick. Janet turned to Yuri.

"There's just a few guards and their attention is on the TV coverage of the crowd outside. We'll wait here until Helena gets the door open. Then you sneak under the window and out into the stairway. I'll bring up the rear," said Janet.

As Yuri inched past Janet, he nodded to the gun in her hand.

"Any chance you brought a few more of those?" he asked.

"Get going," said Janet urgently.

Yuri took several deep breaths as he waited for Helena to unlock the door. He looked up nervously at the guard station's windows, then down at the ground. Still breathing deeply, he closed his eyes. After a few moments, he felt Janet put her hand on his shoulder.

"You okay?" she said.

Yuri looked at the young woman. But this time, it wasn't an old man checking out a young woman. Even though his face was lined with the years he spent as a prisoner, his grey-blue eyes were clear and sharp. For a moment, Janet felt as if he were looking into her soul. But instead of blinking her eyes or looking away, Janet stared back.

It only took a moment for Janet and Yuri to realize they could trust each other. Then the old man smiled.

"I've been dreaming of this moment for years," he said.

Yuri looked back over his shoulder down the cold, stone cellblock. His eyes stopped on Cell 313, the cage he'd been locked up in for the past three years.

"It's exciting to finally be on my way. But terrifying that I might find myself back down that hallway," he said.

Janet thought for a moment. She thought back to the conversation she had with David McNally just before leaving him in Helsinki. She made a quick decision and reached into her backpack.

David told both Janet and Helena what to expect when they came face to face with Yuri Nikolov. He warned them about what years in a prison cell could do to a spy. Then David handed a small box to Janet.

"Once you decide you can trust him, give him this with my complements," David had said.

Janet pulled a small handgun out of her backpack. It was older than the one she held in her hand. She looked up at Yuri and handed it to him.

"David McNally said you preferred this old thing," whispered Janet.

The old man weighed the gun in his hand. Then he silently checked the clip of ammunition and chambered a bullet. Yuri looked up at Janet and smiled.

"This old thing got James Bond out of many a fix. I think it'll help us out too," he said.

Janet looked down at the gun. Sure enough. It was the famous Walther PPK. She smiled up at the old man.

"They do love their spy stories at The Castle, don't they?" she said.

"What's not to love?" said Yuri.

He looked over at Helena as she continued to work the lock. Janet looked at her watch. The second round of Psychedelics would begin exploding in about ten minutes. Everything seemed to be going according to their plan. Just as she was about to whisper something else to Yuri, Janet heard the lock open. Looking around Yuri, she saw Helena smiling and waving.

"Okay. Get going as quietly as you can. Stay low," she said.

Yuri looked up once, took a deep breath and crawled past the window, through the open door and out into the stairway. Janet cinched the straps of her backpack tight, inched past the guard station and through the door. Seconds later, Helena quietly let the door close until she heard the lock snap into place.

"So far, so good," said Helena.

"So far, so good," said Janet.

"Now what?" asked Yuri.

"Up the stairs and out the door," said Helena.

"Not the same door we came in," said Janet.

"Why?" asked Yuri.

"Too many guards," said Janet.

"They might let us out, but not our guest," said Helena.

"Let's get out of this stairwell first," said Janet.

She looked at her watch.

"Looks like about five minutes before the Psychedelics go off," she said.

"Psychedelics?" asked Yuri.

"A new toy from The Castle," said Janet.

"Psychedelics," repeated Yuri. "Can't wait to see what they do."

Helena looked at her watch, then gave Yuri a gentle push.

"Then we need to pick it up just a bit," said Helena.

It didn't take long before the three made it to the ground floor. Janet peered around the corner, then looked back at Helena and Yuri.

"Coast is clear," she said.

"Let's try to find another empty office where we can figure out our next move," said Helena.

"If we've got less than five minutes before your distractions go off, then we don't have time for a pit stop," said Yuri.

Helena and Janet looked at each other for a moment. It only took a few moments of non-verbal communication to decide to listen to the old prisoner.

"What do you have in mind?" asked Helena.

Yuri only had to think about it for a few moments.

"Based on what I've heard so far, you've got some kind of diversion set to go off in less than five minutes. You also don't think we can all get out the door you came in. Am I right so far?" he said.

"On the button," said Helena.

"I'm guessing you came in the east entrance. All of the entrances and exits are guarded. But there's a hidden exit on the north-west end of the building," said Yuri.

"Sounds perfect. What's the fastest way there?" asked Helena.

"Across the courtyard," said Yuri.

"Sounds a little too open for me," said Janet.

"The Psychedelics could help with that," suggested Helena.

"If we're going to use them as cover, then we need to get across the hall and down about ten doors," said Yuri.

Janet checked out the hall once more.

"Let's go then," she said.

A second later, the three were heading down the deserted hallway. Janet led the way, followed by Yuri and Helena. As they walked Helena pulled out the walkman, slipped the headphones over one ear and gently pressed the on button. Through the static, she was just able to make out a short stream of numbers.

"1. 2. 1. 7. 3," the far away voice repeated.

Helena pressed the power button again and slipped the headphones down around her neck. She didn't need her codebook to decipher the message. On the flight out from Stromness, David McNally made her memorize several different codes.

"Our ride outta here is running a little late," said Helena quietly.

"How late?" asked Janet.

"About fifteen minutes," said Helena.

"Good to know," said Janet.

They moved quickly down the green hallway, walking as softly as they could on the parquet floor. Janet was counting doors. As they approached the tenth door, Yuri pointed down the hall.

"Sorry. Twelve doors down," he said.

The door to the courtyard looked like all the other doors that lined the green hallway. It opened to a much shorter hall and another door. Janet pressed her ear against the door.

"Don't hear anything," she said.

Helena looked at her watch.

"The Psychedelics should start firing off any minute now," she said.

Almost immediately, they could hear muffled explosions coming from outside the building. Helena nodded over her shoulder.

"That's it," she said.

"Come on," said Yuri.

He took off out the door, but didn't walk straight across the courtyard. Instead, he skirted one wall. Looking up, he could see what looked like the occasional flash of fireworks. He looked back at Janet and Helena.

"That's them," said Helena.

"Brilliant," he said.

As they continued making their way around the courtyard, Yuri paused by a wall that appeared to be riddled with bullet holes. He slowly ran his hand over a few of the holes, then looked down.

"What are you doing?" hissed Helena.

The older man didn't look up. He closed his eyes for a moment, then spoke quietly.

"Paying my respects," he said.

He looked up, nodded to Janet and Helena and started walking toward a old wood shed in the corner of the courtyard. As he pulled the shed's old door open, he looked at Janet.

"To who?" she asked gently.

"A lot of brave people died there," he said.

The shed was filled with what appeared to be garden tools, dirt and bags of seeds. A dirty workbench sat next to the courtyard's stone wall. Yuri dropped down on his knees and pushed some old burlap sacks aside. They covered some wood planks which Yuri pushed away revealing a hole in the stone floor.

"This is a small tunnel that leads to a drain outside the building. Once we're through, we'll be on the sidewalk outside. Where do we go from there?" he said.

"We've got a plane on the way to Vnukovo Airport in about," began Janet.

She looked at her watch.

"A little more than an hour," she said.

"Vnukovo is about forty miles away. Do you have a car?" asked Yuri.

"Not yet," said Helena.

"Okay, Once we're on the sidewalk, let's head west down Nikol'skaya. We'll walk across the square, say hi to Vladimir Ilyich, turn south and cross the river," said Yuri.

"Square?" asked Janet.

"Red Square," said Yuri.

"Vladimir Ilyich?" asked Helena.

"Lenin's tomb," said Yuri.

"Once we get across the river, we should be able to find a car," said Yuri.

"Then it's a quick drive to the airport," said Helena.

Yuri swung his feet into the open hole and disappeared. Helena quickly sat down beside the hole. Before she disappeared, she looked up at Janet.

"Now or never?" she asked.

"Now or never," said Janet.

25 ESCAPE FROM MOSCOW

Moscow, Near Red Square

~ ~ ~

PLAYLIST:
"Fearless" - Sun - Thomas Bergersen

~ ~ ~

After emerging from the drain outside The Lubyanka, Janet, Helena and Yuri made their way across Red Square. It was packed with people and sticking together was becoming difficult. After what seemed like hours of pushing and shoving, they finally emerged from the crowd.

The Moscow River lay before them. Janet and Helena looked right and left. Both bridges across the river were hopelessly jammed with people.

"Let's head east for a while," suggested Helena.

After another fifteen minutes of pushing and shoving, the crowd began to thin out a bit. Still hugging the Moscow River, they noticed more and more cars had been simply abandoned by people wanting to be a part of the day's historic protests.

The river began turning south. As the three spies continued weaving in and out of abandoned cars, Janet began tugging on a few door handles. Most were locked, but a few of the car doors opened.

"What are you doing?" asked Helena quietly.

Janet pointed to her watch.

"We've got to find some transportation soon or we'll miss our flight," she said.

"Right," said Helena.

As the continued walking south, the white posts of the Crimean Suspension Bridge appeared. Janet was walking faster, but continued tugging on car door handles. One popped open and three small dogs jumped out. After barking at Janet a few times, they took off, enjoying their new found freedom. Janet peered into the car, but Helena tugged on her elbow.

"This one's totally blocked in. We can do better," said Helena.

As they passed the bridge, Helena looked back at Yuri.

"Still with us?" she asked.

"Still with you," smiled Yuri.

"You've been pretty quiet," said Helena.

"I've been in a stone cage the past three years. It's nice to be outside again," said Yuri.

Helena nodded. Janet looked over her shoulder at Yuri and smiled. The older man was having no trouble at all keeping up with the younger women. But ever since they left the prison, Yuri was looking at the world around him with the wonder of a child. The old man they found in that dark prison cell was now visibly years younger.

As they continued south, the number of abandoned cars began to thin out. Janet was still tugging on door handles and a growing number of cars were locked. She walked up to a small, green four-door sedan and gave the handle a tug. It was a small, Moskvitch 408. Rust lined the wheel wells and the interior was a dusty, dirty mess. But the door opened. The best part was finding the keys still in the ignition.

"This might be our ride outta here," said Janet.

Helena and Yuri looked in the car, then at each other.

"It's a wreck," said Helena.

Janet slid into the drivers seat and twisted the key. The four cylinder engine sputtered to life. Then it backfired once and stopped as quickly as it started. Janet pumped the gas pedal a few times and twisted the key again. The motor started again and backfired again. But this time, it kept running.

"Come on. I'm tired of walking and we really don't want to miss our plane," said Janet.

"Yeah. I guess," sighed Helena.

As Helena sat down in the front passenger seat, the rusty bolts holding it to the floorboard came loose. She grabbed the handle on the dashboard, but it came off in her hands. The dirty seat fell backward leaving Helena staring up at the rusty roof. Janet looked over as Helena was falling backward and laughed.

"You think that's funny, don't you?" said Helena.

"Yeah," snickered Janet.

Yuri opened the back door and slid in behind Janet. He shoved his hand under Helena's back and pushed her and the seat upright.

"Let's get going," he said.

"Buckle your seatbelt," said Janet.

She pressed the clutch, shifted the small car into gear and the rusty old car began rolling down the road. Janet was in a hurry and had to constantly change lanes, weaving around slower traffic on the E-101 heading south out of downtown Moscow. She quickly looked at her watch as she weaved right, then left around a slower car. As she passed the other car, she punched the accelerator and the engine almost stalled.

"Careful," said Helena.

"Piece of shit," mumbled Janet as she dodged another slow car.

Half an hour later, Helena pointed toward an off ramp.

"There's the exit to the airport," said Yuri.

"We want the second one. Right?" said Janet.

Helena had her small notebook out. She flipped a page and nodded.

"Right. That's the passenger terminal. The next exit takes us to the general aviation ramps," she said.

Janet nodded as she pulled off the highway and slowly drove past the long row hangers of Vnukovo International Airport. A quickly improvised guard post blocked the way into the first entrance to the general aviation ramp. Continuing on, they found all the entrances were blocked by armed guards.

"That's going to be a problem," observed Janet.

Helena looked at her watch.

"We'd better figure something out in the next ten minutes or we'll miss our flight," she said.

Helena pulled the Walkman's headphones over one ear and gently pressed the on button. Outside the prison, the voice from The Castle's numbers station was coming in much clearer. But the news wasn't so good. Helena looked over at Janet.

"Not ten minutes. Looks like they made up for lost time. We now have less then five minutes before the plane lands," she said.

"Shit," said Janet quietly.

The small car silently drove past the blocked entrances to the airport. No one said anything. Finally Janet looked at Yuri in the rear view mirror.

"What do you think?" she asked.

Yuri was looking out the window as airplanes continued landing and taking off. He looked over his shoulder at the last guarded entrance to the airport, then up at the fence guarding the north end of the runway.

"What kind of a plane are we looking for?" he asked.

"A Cessna Citation private jet," said Helena.

"Okay. That means they'll have to land and then taxi back for take off. Do you have any way to talk to the pilot?" asked Yuri.

Helena pulled out a flip phone and showed it to Yuri.

"Once they're on the ground, they'll give us a call," she said.

As the rusty car slowly rolled away from the general aviation hangers, Yuri looked at the fence that circled the airport. He looked back over his shoulder at the last guarded entrance. There were two big trucks, a few jeeps and about ten guards. He shook his head.

"This car will never be able to break through that fence. So we're going to have to crash one of those guard stations," said Yuri.

Helena held up her small handgun.

"We're no match for those guards," she said.

Yuri reached forward, grabbed Helena's wrist and pulled it up so he could see her watch. They had about a minute before the plane was scheduled to land. He looked out the front window. A small, grey business jet was just touching down. The phone in Helena's other hand began ringing.

"Hey," she said flipping the phone open.

She listened for a few moments, then began explaining their situation. Yuri listened to Helena's side of the conversation for a few moments before tapping her on the shoulder.

"Is that David McNally?" he asked.

"Yes," said Helena over her shoulder.

Yuri released Helena's other hand and motioned for her to give him the phone. Helena handed the phone back.

"Hey Mac. You still loosing money betting on football teams?" said Yuri.

He laughed a few times, exchanged a few more pleasantries and then began explaining their situation. After a few minutes a plan began to emerge. Janet looked at Helena as Yuri spelled out what he had in mind. Helena looked at Janet and slowly shook her head.

"He's gonna get us killed," she said quietly.

Janet nodded in agreement.

"All righty then Mate. You just have a double poured for me when we get to your toy airplane," said Yuri.

He snapped the phone closed and tossed it up to Helena. Reaching for his own gun, Yuri dropped the magazine, cleared the chamber and dry fired it. Replacing the bullet in the clip, he then slapped it back into the pistol grip, pulled the slide back and released it.

The small grey jet had just turned off the runway and was slowly heading toward the ramp. The airport was clogged with airplanes and before long, it had mixed in with the other jets lined up for take off. Yuri nodded back over his shoulder.

"Okay then. Let's start heading back to that last entrance," he said.

Janet looked at Helena once and quickly turned the car around. Helena was looking down at the gun in her hand. After taking a breath, she checked out her gun the same way Yuri had checked his. After a few moments, Janet handed Helena her gun.

"Do mine," she said.

As Helena worked the action on Janet's gun, Yuri was looking out the window. He briefly looked up at Janet.

"Slow it down. We're going to have time this out a bit," he said.

Janet shook her head slightly, but eased up on the gas. Other cars were now passing the rusty, green Moskvitch. A few honked their horns as they darted around Janet.

"Why don't you pull off for a second," said Yuri.

Janet smoothly pulled the car out of traffic and onto the gravel shoulder of the road. She sat with both of her hands tightly gripping the steering wheel. Helena finished checking the gun and gently placed it back on Janet's lap. Yuri kept looking out the window, watching the small grey jet slowly inch toward the runway.

Janet kept looking straight ahead trying not to think about what they were about to do. She almost hit her head on the rusty roof of the car as she jumped in fear. Yuri had leaned forward and gently placed his hand on her white knuckles gripping the steering wheel. Helena jumped too

"You two need to relax just a bit," said Yuri softly.

Helena and Janet looked at each other. They took a deep breath, then looked back at the old man. Yuri smiled back.

"I know you're scared. I was terrified the first time I tried something as crazy as this," he said.

Yuri looked over at the grey business jet as Helena asked about his first time doing something as crazy as this. He nodded up toward Janet.

"The best thing I had going for me back then is the same thing that's going for us today. We'll catch them completely by surprise," he said.

Another big jet took off and the small grey jet moved closer to the end of the runway. It was now third in line. Janet looked down at the gun resting in her lap, then over at the gear shift.

"I'm not going to be much help with the shooting," she said.

"Just concentrate on the driving. All you need to do is get this car next to that airplane," said Yuri.

Janet kept looking straight ahead. She took a deep breath and relaxed her grip on the steering wheel.

"It's just that I'm a much better shot than Helena," said Janet.

"Bull shit," said Helena.

Everyone in the car laughed a bit.

"We're going to be fine," said Yuri.

Another big plane took to the sky and the small jet moved up another spot. Yuri tapped Janet on the shoulder.

"Okay. Slow and steady until the shooting starts. Then pedal to the metal until we get to the jet. Get going," said Yuri.

Janet nodded once, glanced at Helena and took another deep breath. Helena smiled back as the small green car pulled out into traffic.

A black, government limousine pulled into the airport driveway in front of Janet. A second one tried to cut in front of Janet, but wasn't quick enough. Yuri looked over his shoulder, then back up as the first black car was waved past the guards. The driver in the car behind Janet began honking the horn impatiently.

"Perfect. Just what we needed. Quick, hide your guns and start smiling," Yuri said urgently.

He rolled down his window as they pulled up to the guard. Before the guard could say a word, Yuri began speaking urgently in Russian. The only word Janet and Helena could make out was 'commissar'. When Yuri stopped speaking, the guard started laughing. The other guards looked at Janet and Helena and started laughing too. Yuri laughed too and waved pleasantly to the guards as they were waved through the checkpoint.

"What did you tell them?" asked Helena suspiciously.

"I told them you were the commissar's mistresses," smirked Yuri.

"Excuse me?" said Helena.

"Really?" huffed Janet in disbelief.

"Hey. It worked," said Yuri.

Helena looked at her clothes, then at Janet. After a few moments, she over her shoulder at Yuri.

"Do we look like a couple of Russian hookers or something?" asked Helena.

She gave Yuri a slightly amused look, then looked past him out the back window. In a flash, the expression on her face turned from slightly amused to genuinely concerned. The guards had suddenly turned, were looking in their direction and started shouting. Even though the car windows were closed, they could hear the sound of machine guns being readied to fire.

"Maybe not enough. Get going," said Helena.

As he turned to look out the back window, a bullet smashed through the window hitting Yuri in the shoulder. Blood sprayed the back seats, the back of Janet's head and Helena's face. As Helena wiped the blood from her eyes, a second bullet passed so close to her, that it whipped the long black hair out from behind her ear.

"Go, go, go," shouted Yuri.

Helena grabbed her gun and fired three shots out the back window. Yuri turned just as three guards fell like dominos. Three more guards took their place and began shooting at the small car. But all they hit was a tail light, the driver's side mirror and the pavement near the back tires. Yuri watched in amazement as Helena squeezed off three more shots and three more guards fell to the ground.

"Damn you're good," said Yuri.

"She's the expert," said Helena nodding to Janet.

Helena smiled and began sighting in her next three targets. But before any more shots could be fired, Janet spun the wheel and the rusty, green car disappeared behind a large hanger.

Yuri fell on his badly injured shoulder as Janet took the turn fast. But as Yuri cried out in pain, he also pushed himself back up so he could look out the front window. Another large jet rumbled off the runway and the small grey airplane slowly inched out on the runway.

"We're out of time. Take that first taxiway on your left, then straight down the middle of the runway," yelled Yuri.

Janet swerved to the left sending Yuri flying to the other side of the car. He landed on his good shoulder as another bullet flew through the shattered rear window and took out the front window. Cold air began blowing through the car, but Janet kept speeding down the runway.

Helena fired out the back window at the truck that suddenly appeared behind them. She shot directly at the windshield in front of the driver, but the bullets just ricocheted off.

"They must have bullet proof windows," she yelled over the rush of air.

The small gray business jet was just beginning it's final turn to line up on the runway when Janet saw the aircraft door open. A man appeared in the doorway holding a long, black tube. He waved at the car once, then pointed the tube right at Janet.

"Oh no he's not," said Janet.

"Oh yes he is," said Helena.

Janet swerved the car to very edge of the runway as fire spat from the black tube. Less than a second later, the truck behind the rusty green car exploded.

Seconds later, Janet let off the gas and swung the car behind the jet as the pilot lined up on the runway. She swerved around the left wing of plane and punched the brake. Leaving the car on the runway, Janet and Helena grabbed their backpacks and jumped out of the car.

Helena opened the back door with so much force that the rusty hinges snapped. Standing on the runway with a car door in her hand, Helena looked at the door, then up at Janet.

"Get a move on you two," yelled David McNally from the plane's open door.

Janet reached in and dragged Yuri out of the car and onto the runway. As Helena reached down to pick up Yuri's good shoulder, more bullets began whizzing by. Before she could think about the bullets, she and Janet dragged Yuri to the open plane door.

"Time to go," yelled David as he stepped half out of the plane.

The jet's engines began spooling up as Janet jumped into the open door, dragging Yuri behind her. David helped Yuri up the last step and reached around for Helena. As she stepped into the airplane, she felt something brush past her right shoulder. A coffee pot in the small galley in front of her exploded as David slammed the door shut.

The jet suddenly accelerated forward throwing Helena into the seat in front of her. Just before her face hit the seat, she blocked her fall with one hand, spun around on one foot and smoothly sat down. Helena quickly buckled her seatbelt and looked out the window. She looked back over the wing just as the thrust from the small jet flipped their rusty, green car and sent it rolling across the empty field. Helena looked forward as the jet picked up speed.

Looking down, Helena was surprised to see she was still tightly clutching her gun in her right hand. Her eyes ran up her arm to her right shoulder. They stopped on the small, black hole in her jacket. Without moving her right hand or arm, she felt her shoulder with her left hand. Everything seemed to be okay.

She stuck her finger into the hole in her jacket. There were actually two holes. One where a bullet went into her jacket, one where it went out. Helena felt her shoulder again. The bullet that made the holes never touched her shoulder.

Janet helped Yuri toward the back of the plane where David had an open first aid kit. After a few minutes, she decided she didn't need to help out and fell into the seat next to Helena. Looking over at her sister, Janet watched as Helena wiggled the finger stuck in the jacket's bullet holes. Janet slowly shook her head.

"That was too close," said Janet.

Helena closed her eyes and nodded.

The noise in the cabin decreased significantly as the pilot raised the landing gear. The plane was climbing fast and made a quick turn toward the west. Looking back out the window at the lights of Moscow, Helena continued to hold her gun with her right hand and her shoulder with her left hand. The airplane started climbing through some clouds and the lights of Moscow began to dim.

Helena gave Russia one last look, then closed her eyes again. A cold shiver ran up and down her spine. Looking out the window, she saw her face faintly reflected in the window by her seat. Helena felt her blood run cold, In that moment, she knew fate would be catching up to her some cold Russian winter.

"*That country will be the death of me,*" she thought to herself.

PART 3: THE COLD TRAIL

26 THAT PING

The Castle, The Pit

Janet and Thomas stood in silence, watching Léa and Tara sleep. Janet was a million miles away, thinking back to her first days at The Castle when her adopted sister and best friend Helena was still alive. She remembered a movie night just like the one Léa and Tara had been enjoying.

Thomas had seen that far away look in his wife's eyes before. He knew she was in pain, But Thomas also knew all he could do was hold Janet tight and never let go.

Léa slowly rolled over from one shoulder to the other. As soon as she moved, Tara moved a bit too. But they both appeared to be sleeping soundly.

Janet reached for the hand Thomas had wrapped around her waist. She squeezed his hand, looked into his dark blue eyes and smiled. Thomas smiled back.

They were a bit of an odd couple. They were both tall and slim. But any similarity ended there. Thomas was a blonde-gray haired, blue eyed product of middle America. Janet was found wandering the streets of Tokyo, an abandoned child of a mixed race, one night stand.

Janet smiled again at Thomas, then looked back at Léa and Tara. Thomas whispered in Janet's ear.

"Suppose this is what it would be like if we decided we wanted kids?" he asked.

"They'd be way too mental," whispered Janet.

Thomas quietly laughed once through his nose. They stood there looking at Léa and Tara a few more moments before Janet patted Thomas' hand again and shook her head.

"Come on, this is beginning to get a little creepy," said Janet.

"Ya think?" said Léa and Tara together.

Janet and Thomas jumped a bit as Léa and Tara pushed themselves up, resting on their elbows. They looked at each other, then smiled up at their visitors.

"How long have you two been awake?" asked Janet.

"Since we heard you come in," said Léa.

"If someone walked into my room like this, I don't think I would have just played possum," said Janet.

"We know we're among friends," said Tara.

Janet and Thomas looked at each other, then back at Léa and Tara.

"I'm guessing we got a ping?" said Tara.

She sat up and inched to the end of the bed. Léa started moving to the end of the bed too.

"How did you know that?" asked Janet.

"If we didn't have a ping, then you two being here would be truly creepy," said Tara.

"And we don't think you're creepy," said Léa.

"Nice to know we're not creepy," said Thomas.

Tara started walking toward the bathroom, but Léa moved faster. She got to the door first, turned and smiled sweetly at Tara.

"Won't be a minute," said Léa.

As soon as Léa closed the door, Tara turned to Janet.

"You were thinking about Helena, weren't you?" she asked.

Janet looked up at Thomas. He held Janet a bit closer, but noticed his wife didn't tense up like she usually did when Helena's name popped up. That was unusual. No one, it seemed, could mention Helena's name without it effecting Janet badly. Thomas could hardly believe his eyes when he looked at his wife. She was actually smiling.

"Just remembering a movie night like this," smiled Janet.

"Oh yeah? What movie were you two watching?" asked Tara.

"Silence of the Lambs," said Janet.

Thomas let go of Janet's waist. He looked at her with mock concern.

"Now that is creepy," he said.

"Not as creepy as some of the movies you worked on," said Janet.

"What movies were those?" asked Tara.

Janet started to name a few names before Thomas cut her off.

"Never mind. Those will have to remain a closely guarded secret," he said.

"What's a closely guarded secret?" asked Léa as she emerged from the bathroom.

"My sordid past," said Thomas.

"More like your kinky past," smirked Janet.

"Hey now. I didn't write those scripts. I just came up with some special effects and stunts," protested Thomas.

"Yeah. Whatever you say honey," said Janet.

"Can we go. We do have a ping," said Thomas.

Janet, Tara and Thomas started walking toward the door. But Léa didn't move. As the door opened, everyone looked back.

"I want to hear about your kinky past," she said.

"I've already seen his personnel file. It's not that exciting," said Tara.

"What are you doing reading his personnel file?" asked Janet.

"I've read everybody's personnel file," said Tara as she walked past Janet and Thomas.

Thomas smiled at Janet.

"See. It's okay. She's read everyone's file," he said.

A few minutes later, Léa, Tara, Janet and Thomas arrived in Tara's workshop. Thomas' assistant, Toby Barnes was already tapping away on Tara's computer.

"Uh, oh. This could be trouble," said Léa quietly to Janet.

"Yep," Janet whispered back.

Toby looked up at Tara. Fear washed over his face and he quickly moved away from the computer. Tara sat down and quickly tapped a few keys. She was closely examining the screen when she started talking.

"Don't worry. I can't wait to see where our ping came from too. So you're not in trouble. Just check with me next time. Okay?" said Tara.

"Yes ma'am," said Toby nervously.

Tara stopped typing just long enough to look up at Toby.

"Now you definitely are in trouble. Don't ever call me 'ma'am' again," she said.

"Yes ma," he said quickly cutting off the last word.

Tara nodded to one of the big monitors that lined the walls of her workshop. It had just changed to a world map and started zooming in.

A big red dot appeared in London. Then the map zoomed over to Italy. A red dot appeared in Rome. Then the map zoomed to Cairo. Then to the island of Sri Lanka. And it didn't stop there. Every few seconds, the map zoomed to another location. Tara started tapping furiously on the keyboard.

"The little shit is bouncing off servers all around the world," she said.

The map kept zooming all across the globe. Tara slouched back in her chair.

"This is going to take for fucking ever," she huffed.

"But eventually it's got to come to the end of the line. Right?" ventured Léa.

"We can only hope," sighed Janet.

Thomas was looking closely at the map. The dots remained mostly in Europe and part of Asia. Each of the dots were connected by a slightly transparent, red line tracing the computer packet's journey from server to server. Suddenly, the map stopped zooming.

"Bloody hell," said Thomas under his breath.

He turned and looked at Janet, then at Tara.

"Zoom the map all the way out," he said nervously.

Tara tapped a few buttons and the map zoomed out. Léa looked down at her friend as Tara calmly looked up at the big screen. Léa was expecting an explosion of curse words from her best friend. But Tara just sat there. Even though she didn't say a word, you could feel the tension in the room building.

The red lines connecting the dots spelled out three simple words ...

FUCK YOU GOTH

Tara tapped a few more keys and the screen flashed. She had just taken a screen shot of the map and Perry Drilling's taunting message.

Thomas looked from Tara to his wife. Janet was barely breathing. She was looking down and off to one side. Her head was tilted slightly and her lips were pressed tightly together. Her fists were tightly clinched by her side. One fist was moving ever so slightly as she slowly hit her left thigh.

No one spoke for a few minutes. Thomas watched as Janet kept slowly hitting her thigh. Finally, she looked up at the map with fierce determination in her eyes. Léa looked from Janet to Tara and back. The same look of fierce determination appeared in Tara's eyes too.

Janet finally stopped pounding her thigh and nodded a few times. She looked at Tara, then at Thomas.

"Transfer all of this shit to your operations center. We brief Commander Dennis and the department heads in fifteen minutes." she said.

Janet gave the map one final look of determined anger, then turned and left the room. As the door closed behind her, everyone looked toward Thomas. He looked at the empty door, then down at Tara.

"I've only seen that look on my wife's face once before," he said.

"When she found the scum who killed Helena?" guessed Tara.

Thomas nodded once, then looked back up at the map.

Léa walked over and sat next to Tara on one of the metal stools scattered around the room. The mood had changed in so many ways. It had started with fear. But the fear was slowly being replaced with anger. Léa was good at picking up on the mood around her and this mood made her nervous.

"Who was Helena?" she asked.

"Her sister," said Tara.

"Her best friend," said Thomas.

"My aunt," said Tara.

"Your aunt?" asked Léa.

"Grandma and Grandpa Wells also raised a few of The Castle's orphans," said Tara.

"Wow," said Léa.

"Lots of families are connected like that here on The Island," said Thomas.

"Family ends up being one of the few bonds of trust a spy can count on," suggested Léa.

"Family and life long best friends. It's one of few bits of normal stability spies have," said Thomas.

"Until one of us gets killed," said Tara.

"Until one of us gets killed," agreed Thomas.

Léa nodded slowly. No one said a word for the next few minutes. Finally, Thomas snapped out of it, He looked down at Tara.

"I assume you know the i.p. address for mission operations?" he asked.

Tara started typing. After less than two seconds, she punched the enter key.

"Yeah. Of course you do," said Thomas with a weak smile.

"All my stuff should be there now," said Tara.

"Okay. I want everyone here to take a short walk. We all need to shake this mood so we can focus. We need to find a way cut through all of Perry Drilling's shit and find him," said Thomas.

Léa started to say something, but Thomas cut her off.

"Not here. Not now. Get out of this room. Take a walk, clear your head. Then be in Mission Ops in the next ten minutes with some suggestions," he said.

Thomas started walking toward the door. As he walked past Toby, he snagged the kid's elbow and began pulling him along. The door closed behind them. Léa looked at Tara.

"I don't like it that he can play with us like this. That he can see everything we can see," she said.

Tara looked at Léa.

"He was diddling with us on the train to Stockholm too. But don't worry. Remember, we've got all the really sensitive stuff off the internal network," she said.

Léa nodded.

"What about all that stuff you just sent to that Mission Ops thing?" she asked.

"I really didn't send out anything he doesn't know about," said Tara.

Léa looked up at the map.

"How are we going to find him?" she asked.

"Don't know," said Tara.

She stood up and started walking toward the door. As it opened, Tara looked back at Léa. She nodded toward the hallway.

"But we will find him. Come on. Let's take a walk like the man said. We've got to start brainstorming in about ten minutes," said Tara.

As she left the room, Léa took one more glance up at the map. The red letters of the three, short words popped off the map. She looked at the map long enough to burn the image into her memory.

"Fuck you too Perry," said Léa under her breath.

27 MOVIE NIGHT

The Castle, Main Auditorium

~ ~ ~

PLAYLIST:
"Piano Prelude" - The Spy Who Came In from the Cold - Sol Kaplan

~ ~ ~

Léa and Tara edged closer together and looked around The Castle's amazing auditorium. The A/C was cranked a bit high that night and they were both freezing. But it wasn't just the temperature.

The two best friends had the ability to pick up on the mood of a room and the mood in that room was cold, grey and ruthless. Just like the movie everyone was watching. It wasn't a happy movie and no one in the room was happy either.

It had been three days since the ping came in from Perry Drilling's computer. Immediately after the map with the nasty message appeared on Tara's big screen, the trial went cold. No one was happy and no one felt like going to Movie Night. But Alan Dennis insisted that everyone needed a break, so Léa, Tara, Janet and Thomas found themselves all sitting together near the back of the auditorium.

Léa looked up at the screen and thought back to one of her first classes in Spy School. She remembered Janet Austin saying this was one of her favorite movies. But this movie was just too depressing to be her favorite.

Léa and Tara yawned at the same time.

The movie started out with a spy being killed at Berlin's infamous Checkpoint Charlie at the height of the Cold War. It was quickly followed by pouring tea and a meeting.

Léa fidgeted in her seat.

The movie continued with the star wandering the streets of London, getting a job at a library and drinking a lot.

"What's next? Grocery shopping?" whispered Léa in Tara's ear.

Tara nodded up to the screen as the star, Richard Burton, walked into a grocery store. Léa shook her head, then leaned forward to look at Janet. Tara looked at Janet too.

"Riveting grocery story action," said Léa.

"I was hoping for another meeting scene," said Tara.

"Maybe some more smoking and drinking?" suggested Léa.

"And another trip to the grocery store," said Tara.

"You two are worse than the gang from Mystery Science Theater 3000," said Thomas.

"They'd have a lot to work with on this film," said Tara.

She looked over as Janet continued to watch the movie. Leaning back, Tara looked at the screen again. The story had moved back to another library scene. Tara felt she was missing something. This slow speed movie clearly had Janet's attention.

"Hey, don't we know that guy?" asked Léa.

The star spy was back in the grocery store and had just started punching the store owner.

"That's Bernard Lee. He'll go on to play 'M', James Bond's boss," said Thomas.

The movie slowly moved from lunch, to the main character riding busses, to buying cigarettes, then to taking a cab ride. Tara looked over at Janet who's eyes hadn't wavered from the screen. Clearly something was going on and Tara was determined to figure out what it was.

The main character was wandering around town. He was drinking. He got into a fight, then went to jail. Now another meeting had begun. Then the main character said four words and everything made sense to Tara.

"So I'm to defect," said Richard Burton.

That was it. Tara nodded in satisfaction.

"He's been building a legend," she said.

Janet smiled and nodded back to the screen.

"It's rather good tradecraft for a movie from the 60s," said Janet.

A few minutes after the plot for the spy's defection was revealed, Léa and Tara's attention was pulled away from the screen as someone on the other side of the theater got up and began inching his way toward the aisle. Once free from the seats and the people sitting in them, the short man stood as tall as he could, squared his shoulders and began marching up the aisle toward the exit.

"Looks like Little Dick doesn't like the movie," observed Léa.

As he walked past, Dick Boxx glanced down at Janet and Thomas. As his eyes returned to the path ahead, he also stole a glance at Tara and Léa. It was the look in his eyes that sent a shiver down Léa and Tara's spine.

Janet looked away from the screen as Léa and Tara were engaged in some of their non-verbal, best friend communication. It was clear they had picked up on Dick's hostile glance. She leaned over and whispered to Léa and Tara.

"Dick Boxx has always been an angry, resentful little man. Don't let him bug you," she said.

Tara looked over at Janet, then back at Léa. Janet watched as the best friend's silent communication continued. She remembered communicating the same way with Helena. Without looking away from Tara, Léa whispered back.

"We're not so sure," she said.

Tara turned to Janet.

"He may be an angry, bitter little man. But there was something more. We think he's going to do something about it," said Tara.

Janet took a few moments to look the two young spies directly in their eyes. The look on her face was deadly serious as she examined Tara's face, then Léa's. It was a long stare, the kind meant to discover lies, prejudices and subterfuge. But all she saw were two observant, smart and capable young women. Janet nodded once. She was satisfied.

"That's what Tommy and I think too," said Janet.

Tara looked back at Léa for a moment, then back at Janet.

"So what do we do about it?" asked Tara.

Janet smiled and turned her attention back to the movie. After a few moments, Léa and Tara got the message. There was nothing to do just then. They would keep their eyes and ears open.

As Léa and Tara turned their attention back to the screen, an old jetliner pulled up and stopped. The camera focused on the airplane's door which opened. It remained focused on the door as the old style air-stairs emerged from the airplane and locked themselves into place.

"Damn. We missed the seatbelt and oxygen announcement scene," whispered Léa.

"I'm guessing we'll be treated to a few moments of tense, yet exciting passport control action next," groused Tara.

Janet closed her eyes, shook her head slightly from side to side. But she also smiled.

About an hour later, the crowd at Deep in the Cliff's Pub was beginning to clear out for the night. It had been a quiet night at the pub. Usually the crowd was a lot louder after a movie. But the grey mood of the movie along with the frustration of the cold trail of Perry Drilling hung in the air like a thick, chilly London fog.

Léa leaned back in her chair and sipped her amber ale. She was looking around the room watching people finish their brew and leave. Tara's eyes were also roaming around the room as the un-fun evening was coming to a close.

Thomas Austin was sitting with them, but his attention was on his iPad. Every few minutes, he would look up at a booth in the corner. Janet had been asked to join Commander Dennis and Dick Boxx. They had been talking for almost an hour. Every so often, Janet would glance over at her husband with what he called her 'just shoot me now' look. Their eyes briefly met and it was clear her mood hadn't improved.

Tara was watching Janet and Thomas. She caught Janet's look of desperation too. Looking back at the booth in the corner, she could see Alan Dennis clearly wasn't happy either. The third person at the table was sitting with his back to the room, so Tara couldn't read his expression. But she guessed he was cause of Janet and Alan's looks of discomfort.

"What's going on over there?" asked Tara.

"It's pretty obvious that no one at that table is full of joy and happiness,' said Léa.

Thomas looked up from his iPad and laughed. He looked over at the booth just as the short man stood up and gave Alan a crisp, military salute before turning and quickly leaving the pub.

"Clown," said Thomas quietly to himself.

Léa and Tara looked at each other, then back at Thomas. It was the first time either of them heard anyone at The Castle make a less than respectful comment about someone else. It was even more surprising coming from someone as high in the chain of command as Thomas Austin.

He looked back at Léa and Tara and smiled. Thomas didn't need any special mind reading skills to figure out what Léa and Tara were thinking.

"Yes, we're all one big happy family here. But that doesn't mean we don't have a few crazy aunts and uncles," he smiled.

Janet and Alan were slowly walking over to the bar. They talked quietly until David McNally appeared. Looking over her shoulder, Janet held up three fingers. Thomas nodded back. After pouring four fresh pints, David, Alan and Janet continued their quiet conversation. Finally, Alan patted Janet's hand, turned and left the pub.

Janet watched the old man leave, then looked around the room. More than a few people were looking her way hoping for some answers. But all Janet could manage was a look of mild irritation and fatigue. She gathered up the four pints and carefully made her way to the table. Before she had a chance to sit down, Tara started talking.

"Are you okay? Whatever that was all about, it looks like it left you and the old man beat to shit," she observed.

"Pretty much," sighed Janet.

"What was that all about?" asked Léa.

No one said anything as Janet sat down. She took a long sip of her ale and leaned back in her chair. Léa suddenly felt like the person who said what everyone was thinking, but really shouldn't have brought it up.

"If I'm allowed to ask," Léa quickly added.

Janet looked up at Thomas. Her amused, smirky smile appeared on the right corner of her mouth.

"Actually, it's all your damn fault," she said.

"Me? Don't drag me into that lunatic's delusions," said Thomas.

"Who chose the movie tonight?" asked Janet.

Thomas didn't say anything. Léa and Tara both watched as the mood at the table lightened up. It was one of Janet's many gifts. She was one of those special people who was able to put people at ease and make every's day better.

"I thought it was one of your favorites," said Thomas.

"It is. But some movies give stupid people stupid ideas," said Janet.

"Really?" said Thomas.

"Really," said Janet.

Then the conversation stopped. Léa and Tara looked at Janet, then Thomas, then at each other. After a few moments of silent communication, Léa looked at Janet and smiled. Tara just looked at Janet.

"So do we get to guess what's going on?" asked Léa.

Janet and Thomas didn't say anything.

"I think that's the general idea," said Tara.

"Great," said Léa.

Tara leaned back in her chair. She pulled her glass of ale closer and began running her finger around the rim. Léa was learning forward with her elbows on the table and her chin in her cupped hands. They were both looking around the room, clearly thinking. After a few moments, Léa broke the silence.

"Dick got up and left the movie just as your boyfriend, Richard Burton, was told he was to stage a fake defection," she said.

"Apparently, that genius thinks if he tries the same thing, he'll smoke out Perry Drilling," said Tara.

Everyone looked at Tara when she called Dick a genius. It clearly wasn't meant as a complement. Janet and Thomas looked at Tara with mild amusement. Léa seemed surprised that Tara was so openly criticizing someone that high up in the chain of command. Tara looked over at Léa.

"The guy is okay when it comes to teaching basic self defense and physical training. Beyond that, he's not the sharpest knife in the drawer," said Tara.

"Wait a minute. It looked to me like you guys gave his plan your blessing and sent him on his merry way. But now you're telling us he's not capable of pulling it off. What's with that?" asked Léa.

Janet sighed and shook her head. Thomas looked at his wife, then at Tara and Léa.

"You got it. Nailed it on the head. This is way beyond what he's shown he's capable of," said Janet.

"So he's either had an unusual flash of brilliance," began Léa.

"Or he's got someone coaching him," said Tara.

"What if that someone is Perry Drilling?" asked Léa.

Janet looked at Tara and Léa and smiled. Thomas sat back in his chair and smiled too.

"Like you said, nail on the head," he said.

"But if he's in league with Drilling, why let him go?" asked Léa.

"Because the trail has gone cold," said Tara.

"But if he gives us the slip, the trail stays cold," said Léa.

"We're right back where we started from," said Léa.

"Only Boxx gets away with updated information about where we are," said Tara.

"What can he tell Drilling that he doesn't already know? That we're stuck at the beginning of a cold trail," said Janet.

Léa slumped back in her chair. She looked at Tara.

"I hate this waiting around," she said.

"Me too," said Tara.

Janet looked at Thomas. Her half, slightly sarcastic smile reappeared.

"Our two young spies appear a bit restless," said Janet.

"They clearly need to blow off some steam," said Thomas.

"Maybe a few extra hours of physical training," suggested Janet.

"We could volunteer them to clean out David's beer lines," said Thomas.

Janet and Thomas stopped and looked at Léa and Tara. Thomas' smile was one of genuine amusement. Janet's typical, slightly sarcastic smile covered half of her face. Léa and Tara looked at each other.

"They think they're funny, don't they?" said Léa.

"Not funny," said Tara.

The conversation paused again. A slight stare-down began between the two sides of the table. It wasn't a hostile stare-down. But no one blinked. Finally, Janet broke the silence.

"Maybe, tonight would be a good time to show them your latest creation," she said.

"You think they're ready?" asked Thomas.

"Probably not. They're still pretty soft," said Janet

"They'll probably get hurt," said Thomas.

"Stub their toes," said Janet.

"Go home crying," said Thomas.

Janet and Thomas kept looking at Léa and Tara. Both had wicked smiles on their faces. Even though Léa was still relatively new, she wasn't about to fall for whatever Janet and Thomas had in mind. Tara nudged Léa.

"They still think they're funny," said Tara.

"Even less funny," said Léa.

"They think they're tough," said Janet.

"Not tough," said Thomas.

No one said anything for a few minutes. The polite stare-down continued. Every now and then, someone would take a sip of their drink. After about five minutes, Tara broke the silence.

"I'm getting tired. Let's either do this or I'm going to bed," she said.

Janet looked at Léa.

"Sounds like we've got one victim. You game?" she asked.

Léa glanced at Tara, then back at Janet.

"I'm with her," said Léa.

Janet and Thomas stood up.

"Great. We'll meet you in the atrium in ten minutes. Get suited out in full tactical gear," said Janet.

"That includes live ammo," said Thomas.

Janet and Thomas turned and left Léa and Tara sitting alone at the table. Léa reached for her half full ale glass. Tara slapped her hand away.

"We're done drinking," said Tara.

"Live ammo?" asked Léa.

"We've got this," said Tara.

The two best friends sat at the table for another minute, then got up and left the pub.

28 GEAR UP

The Castle, Sub-Level 2

Léa and Tara sat on a hardwood bench outside a large, heavy metal sliding door. The stone hallway was painted black with low level soft light. A small digital timer across the narrow hallway was counting down minutes and seconds.

2:32

Léa fidgeted in her new black tactical gear as she watched the seconds tick by. Despite the total badass look, the gear was tight and uncomfortable. She wiggled her toes in the heavy new boots, took a deep breath and sighed.

"This waiting sucks," said Léa.

"It's meant to fuck with your head. Real tactical operations never start when you're ready. This teaches you to be ready at any time," said Tara.

"That holster is definitely fucking with my leg. It's so tight, it's cutting off my circulation," said Léa.

Tara was leaning her head against the wall with her eyes closed. She smiled when Léa tossed out the 'f' word, opened her eyes and rolled her head looking at her friend. Reaching down, she wedged her fingers between the holster and Léa's leg.

"Yep. It's a bit tight. But you don't want it flopping around either," said Tara.

Léa looked at the clock. They had just over a minute to go, so she carefully drew the pistol out of the holster and handed it to Tara. Pushing the hard plastic clips, the holster popped off her thigh. Léa rubbed her leg, loosened the strap, snapped the clips back in place and tapped the holster. Tara slid the gun back in place.

"Better?" asked Tara.

"Much," said Léa.

She tugged at vest, then re-adjusted the chest rig. A flashlight was attached to her left shoulder. Four spare ammunition clips were attached to the chest rig and an additional four clips were grouped together on the left side of her belt.

As she was gearing up, Léa had wanted to use her smaller 9mm gun instead of it's larger brother. Léa had been training with the smaller gun most of her life, but the range director insisted she use the larger weapon.

Léa reached her right hand around the vest and spare clips and touched the smaller gun nestled under her left armpit. When the range director was inspecting Tara's rig, Léa edged over to the equipment rack and snagged a shoulder holster and stuffed it between her vest and black t'shirt. She was also able to slip her smaller gun into a pocket of the stiff, new tactical pants.

Once the range director left Léa and Tara to wait outside the door, Léa pulled the shoulder holster from it's hiding place and looked at Tara.

"Help me with this?" she asked.

Tara shook her head and smiled.

"You and your small gun," said Tara.

Within a few moments, Tara had the holster securely attached to the chest rig. Léa checked her ammo clip once, then secured the gun under her arm. She reached around and gripped the pistol without pulling it from the holster a few times. When she was satisfied she could reach it, Léa looked up at Tara.

"Better?" asked Tara.

"Better," said Léa.

Half an hour later, Léa leaned back against the wall, fidgeted a few more times and closed her eyes. Tara's eyes were closed too. But just a few seconds later, they both opened their eyes and looked at the clock.

0:47

Tara leaned forward, took a deep breath and stretched her arms above her head. She checked to make sure the bluetooth earbud was securely stuffed in her right ear, then picked up the combat helmet and carefully placed it on her head. She looked over at Léa as she snapped the chin strap into place.

"Gear up," said Tara.

As they stood, Léa and Tara picked up the tactical rifles resting on the floor next to them. Checking the ammo clip, they checked to make sure the safeties were on and slung the rifles over their shoulders.

A few seconds later, Léa and Tara were standing on the two yellow X's painted on either side of the black, steel door. Léa glanced over at the clock.

0:23

"Hey," said Tara.

Léa looked back. The look on Tara's face startled her. There was a look of intense determination in Tara's eyes. Her nose flared a bit as she took several deep breaths.

"Remember the drill. We make our way down the street to the airport. Board the plane and rescue four hostages," said Tara.

Léa took a deep breath, closed her eyes for a moment, then nodded at Tara. She looked back at the clock.

0:01

The heavy metal door slid open. Léa peered around the door, then looked back at Tara.

"Remember what Thomas said. We can get seriously hurt or even killed in there. So be super fucking careful," said Tara.

"Super fucking careful," repeated Léa.

They both pulled the safety goggles down over their eyes and took one more deep breath. Looking back at each other, they both nodded once and disappeared into the darkness.

29 THE MAZE

The Castle, Maze Stage 1

~ ~ ~

PLAYLIST:
"Aura" - Illusions - Thomas Bergersen

~ ~ ~

Near total darkness enveloped Léa and Tara as the door closed. It took just a few moments for their eyes to adjust. Soon, a series of lighted dots stuck to the floor emerged from the darkness over Léa's left shoulder.

One of the lights on the floor seemed to be flashing. As Léa's eyes continued to adjust to the darkness, she saw it wasn't the light that was flashing. It was the gun in Tara's outstretched hands in front of one of the lights. Her gun was moving up and down slightly with Tara's breath. Léa reached for the smaller gun under her left arm.

"Save it for when you need it," Tara said quietly.

Léa's right hand moved away from the smaller gun and down to the larger weapon that was strapped securely to her right leg. She had to give it an extra tug to pull it out of the new holster. After pulling the slide back to chamber a bullet, Léa rested her finger just outside the trigger guard and took a deep breath.

"Now what?" she quietly asked.

Tara nodded down to the glow in the dark dots on the floor. They seemed to lead in a straight line down a dark hallway to their left.

"Follow the dots," said Tara.

As they took one step forward, they immediately stopped.

"Hear that?" whispered Léa.

"Up ahead and to the right," said Tara.

Without making a sound, Léa and Tara inched forward. Then they stopped and listened. After a few moments, the muzzle of Tara's gun slightly moved to the right. Léa nodded. Whoever or whatever was making the noise was ahead and to their right.

They silently took one more step forward. Then two more steps. Whatever was ahead had stopped making noise.

By now, Léa and Tara's eyes were fully adjusted to the darkness and they could see they were in a long hallway. Looking down, Léa saw the floor lights were angled off to the left. Looking up, Léa saw the hallway would eventually split. If they followed the lights and gone down the left hallway, they would have come to a dead end. The hallway to the right appeared to continue past the dead end.

"Sneaky," Léa whispered to Tara.

"There's gonna be a lot more sneaky shit ahead," whispered Tara.

The sound ahead briefly reappeared. Léa quickly closed her eyes and turned her head, listening very carefully. Tara glanced at Léa as she opened her eyes. Using their best friends, non-verbal communication, Tara was able to tell there was something about the sound that had Léa thinking. Léa smiled and nodded off to the right. Tara smiled and nodded in agreement.

"Ready, set, go?" said Léa.

As soon as she began speaking, the sound returned. Léa looked at Tara.

"Just what I thought. That's a recording of the same sound," she said.

Once again, the sound returned as soon as Léa began talking. A big smile of satisfied success spread across her face. Looking down, Léa saw a slight smile appear on one corner of Tara's mouth. At the same time, they gave themselves permission to briefly forget where they were and what they were doing to bask in the warmth of their friendship and share the moment of success.

They released their left hands from supporting their guns. Léa and Tara's gloved fingers reached out as their hands came together. After a moment, Léa's satisfied smile slowly transformed to one of adventure and confident determination. She nodded toward the left hallway.

Looking into each other's eyes, they both saw the same thing. Confident determination with a touch of excitement for the adventure to come. Léa and Tara realized they were not just the best of friends, but they were becoming a great tactical team.

"Let's go kick their ass," said Tara.

"Asses, prepare to meet our boots," said Léa.

Tara couldn't help herself. Before she could stop it, a single laugh erupted through her nose. There were times when her best friend could be funny as hell.

They gave each other's gloved hands one last squeeze as the sound activated recording was once again triggered by Tara's laugh.

It took less than ten steps before they were at the end of the hall. Tara tapped her boot against the ground triggering the automated sound. It was just around the corner and to their right.

With her back to the wall, Tara dropped her left hand to her side. Her right hand held her gun just below her shoulder level, pointed straight up. Léa silently crouched down and scooted past Tara's legs right up the edge of the wall. Tara silently tapped Léa's shoulder once.

Léa was now close to the ground, down on her hands and knees looking at the corner. Tara lifted her gun above her head and tapped the muzzle against the wall. As the automated sound triggered, Léa quickly poked her head around the corner then stood up.

"Another empty hallway," Léa whispered.

Tara quickly looked around the corner.

"Looks like it. Let's go," she said.

In a single, fluid motion, Léa and Tara quickly stepped around the corner. Looking up, Léa nodded toward the ceiling. Tara tapped her boot against the floor and the black grilled speaker sprang to life with the same recorded sound they heard when the first entered The Maze. Looking back down the hallway, Léa noticed it seemed even darker than the first.

"Talk about the black hallway to nowhere," observed Léa. "Flashlights?"

"No. We still don't know what's down there and this is a hostage situation," said Tara.

"Flashlights could give us away," said Léa.

"But I've got an idea," said Tara.

She quickly holstered her gun and reached behind her back. Looking down, Léa saw Tara had pulled out what looked like a long, thin flashlight. As Tara snapped her hand forward and down, the flashlight tripled in length. It made one loud click which activated what was becoming an annoying sound effect of The Maze.

"It's a special nightstick," said Tara.

Holding it out in front of her, she began slowing walking forward. Each step Tara took, Léa matched almost immediately. After each step, Tara would lean forward slightly, probing the darkness ahead. After less than ten steps, the edge of the stick clanked against metal. The sound fired off another automated sound effect behind them.

"I'm about the shoot out that speaker," whispered Léa.

Tara looked at her friend. Normally, nothing irritated Léa. But from the tone of her voice, it was clear that sound effect was clearly getting under Léa's skin. Within seconds, Tara figured out what was going on. They were in a tactical situation. Léa's adrenaline was working overtime and that wasn't good. Tara leaned back against the wall. Léa quickly followed. Tara took a deep breath. She turned to Léa.

"Remember how you felt back in that alley in Uppsala?" asked Tara.

"What do you mean?" Léa whispered back.

"You were calm, cool Léa," said Tara.

"Okay," said Léa slowly.

Tara smiled.

"Listen to your body. Your heart is pumping a hundred miles an hour. Adrenaline has you so pumped up right now that you probably couldn't hit that annoying speaker even if you really wanted to," said Tara.

Looking straight ahead, Léa couldn't believe her ears. What the fuck was Tara talking about, Léa thought to herself. Then she felt sweat break out over her whole body. She noticed her heart really was racing. Still staring ahead, Léa snapped her head from side to side, clearing the cobwebs. She took slower breaths and felt her heart rate start to settle down.

Tara smiled as Léa shook her head.

"So predictable," whispered Tara.

Léa took a few more breaths. Her heart stopped pounding. Reaching up, she ran the gloved back of her hand over her forehead. Lifting up the safety goggles, Léa wiped the sweat off her eyebrows. After a few moments, she looked at Tara.

"Um. Wow. That got out of hand a little too fast," she observed.

"It happens. Don't worry," smiled Tara.

Léa looked straight ahead. A wave of self doubt washed over her as she realized she got so caught up in the moment, that she was about to loose control.

"This isn't good," said Léa.

"Of course it is," said Tara.

Léa looked at her best friend.

"Think back to that alley in Uppsala. I was in trouble, you came in, figured things out and saved me," said Tara.

"Maybe that was just a fluke. Maybe I'm not ready for this," said Léa.

Tara turned toward Léa. Their faces were inches apart. Léa could tell Tara's volatile temper was inches from a massive eruption. Her eyes were blazing.

"Don't even fucking think of going there," Tara hissed.

Léa was shocked by her best friend and took a step back against the wall. But Tara took a step closer. Leaning off to one side, Tara's lips were inches from Léa's ear. She could hear her best friend take a deep breath.

"Nothing is wrong here. This is your first tactical exercise and you've gotten a massive adrenaline rush. Nothing more, nothing less. But if you start going down the road of self doubt, then we're both in very big trouble," hissed Tara.

Even though it was pitch black in the hallway, Léa could see the fury burning in her best friend's eyes. But Léa wasn't afraid. This was her best friend and Tara wouldn't talk to her like this without a very good reason.

Léa looked back over her shoulder back the way they came. She thought back to that alleyway in Uppsala when an evil man was holding a gun to her best friend's head. Léa quickly understood what Tara meant. Taking a deep breath, Léa turned back to see Tara's expression hadn't changed.

"You know, you're really hot when you get mad," smiled Léa.

A single laugh bubbled up through Tara's nose. One side of her mouth ever so slightly turned up into a smile. It was about as much as Tara ever smiled, but it was enough for Léa to know everything was okay.

As Tara turned and leaned back against the wall, Léa leaned over to Tara's ear.

"Sorry," she said.

Tara looked down for a moment, then leaned over to Léa's ear.

"No need to be sorry. That adrenaline rush happens to everyone. Part of training drills like this is learning how to control that rush. What scared me was how fast I heard you begin to doubt yourself," said Tara.

Léa looked straight ahead. She realized that self doubt had no place in the spy world.

"Got it," said Léa.

"Back to the chase?" asked Tara.

"Back to the chase," said Léa.

Turning to the path ahead, Tara reached out with her gloved hand and began feeling the wall in front of them. Léa joined her and they quickly figured out it was a solid wall. As Tara moved along the wall, her gloved hand ran over what appeared to be a metal pipe. Feeling above and below, she felt more pipes and figured out that they formed a ladder they would have to climb.

"Guess we climb," said Tara.

She collapsed the baton she was using to probe the darkness and slipped it into its holster behind her back. Léa kept her gun out as Tara began climbing. After a few moments, Léa heard Tara's soft voice in the small earbud.

"It's about fifteen steps up. There's a small air duct up here," Tara whispered.

Léa holstered her gun and began climbing up into the darkness. She counted rungs as she climbed. After a few more rungs, she felt the wall in front of her disappear. Tara had crawled into the duct and was waiting for her.

"It was seventeen rungs," said Léa.

Léa could hear another shot of air blowing through Tara's nose. It was as close to a laugh as her friend could usually manage, but it was all Léa needed to hear to know everything was okay. Tara scooted around and began crawling through the narrow air duct.

"I don't like having to keep my gun in it's holster," whispered Léa after a few moments on crawling.

As they inched forward, the muzzle of Léa's rifle clanked against the top of the duct.

"I also don't like this rifle on my back," she said.

"We may need it later," whispered Tara.

They continued crawling along narrow air duct. The muzzle of Léa's rifle bumped the metal top a few more times. I was also getting hot and stuffy. After a few minutes of crawling, Tara whispered back.

"I think we're slowly heading up hill again," she said.

Léa thought a moment.

"What goes up, probably will go down again," she whispered.

"Yeah," whispered Tara.

They continued to crawl into the darkness. As they went along, the slope of the duct continued to slope upward. They were also turning right and left which quickly left them disoriented. The air in the duct was getting hotter and stuffier by the minute. Turning right, then left, Léa and Tara crawled into the darkness. Suddenly, Tara seemed to fall on her face. Léa reached out and grabbed Tara's boots.

"Fuck me," hissed Tara.

"What's up?" whispered Léa.

"The duct just ended. There's nothing in front of me but a steep slope," said Tara.

"How can you tell?" asked Léa.

"There's a faint, red glow ahead. It's a long way down," said Tara.

"So what do we do?" asked Léa.

"Back up a bit," said Tara.

As Léa inched back, Tara began trying to turn herself around, feet first. It wasn't easy with all the tactical gear she was carrying. As Léa watched Tara struggle to get turned around, she realized she'd never be able to do the same thing.

"I'm not as small as you," observed Léa.

"We'll figure something out," said Tara.

Once Tara got her feet in front of her, she inched forward, letting her boots and legs hang over the edge of the duct. Sitting still for a few moments, Tara's eyes continued to adjust to the low, red light ahead. The shaft angled down steeply, but every two feet, there was a joint that Tara guessed was just big enough to use as steps.

"I'm going to start down. You follow me. When you get to the edge you'll have to grab on to my shoulders and I'll walk us down," said Tara.

"You sure?" asked Léa.

"Pretty sure," said Tara.

She began inching down the shaft. The first few steps were easy, but then Léa began inching over the edge and after a few more steps, Tara felt Léa's full weight on her shoulders. As Tara kept stepping down the shaft, Léa knew she was nothing more than useless weight on her friends shoulders. Tara's breathing had quickly picked up. But she kept stepping down the steep shaft.

"It's a good thing you're stronger than you look," said Léa.

"Yeah," said Tara through clenched teeth.

She kept working her way down the shaft. The red glow was getting brighter. As Tara looked down, she knew they were in trouble.

"The shaft is widening out," said Tara.

Tara's boots were getting further and further apart. But she kept stepping down. Looking over Tara's shoulder, Léa could see it wouldn't be long before the shaft would become wider than Tara's legs could manage.

Léa knew she had to do something.

"Stop a second," said Léa.

As Tara stopped, Lea looked right and left.

"Brace yourself," said Léa.

Before Tara could say anything, Léa pushed herself off Tara's shoulders. Her hands quickly reached for each side of the shaft. With her hands and arms supporting her weight, Léa's heart rate and breathing took off.

"Get down fast and keep me from falling on my head," hissed Léa through clinched teeth.

It took Tara only a few moments to realize what was going on. She pushed her feet off the sides of the shaft and quickly slid to the bottom. The fall knocked the wind out of her, but Tara quickly looked up and reached out to catch Léa.

Léa looked at each of her gloved hands as they supported her body in the air shaft. It took plenty of effort to hold her body, upside down. But Léa was pleasantly surprised that she wasn't struggling to support her weight. Her years of first thing in the morning workouts were paying off. Looking down, she smiled at Tara.

"Come on. I've got you," said Tara.

Léa waited just a few more moments, feeling the strength in her arms. She looked down at Tara, but didn't move. Léa smiled as she felt her strong arms and shoulders easily support her weight.

"Any time," said Tara.

Léa took a deep breath then pushed off from the sides of the shaft. She slid downhill fast. Tara reached for her friend's shoulders to slow her descent.

"Gotcha," said Tara.

But Léa fell with enough force to knock Tara to the ground. They lay in a heap of boots, holstered guns and black tactical clothes at the bottom of the shaft for a few minutes catching their breath. Sitting up, Tara rotated her sore arms around a few times.

"It's a good thing you're stronger than you look," repeated Léa.

"Back at you," said Tara.

The red glow was a lot brighter at the bottom of the shaft. As Léa and Tara started to stand up, Léa felt something breeze past her face. A small explosion erupted from the wall behind her. They both immediately hit the ground. Once on the ground, they looked up. Léa drew her gun.

"Those fuckers are shooting at us," hissed Tara.

"Let's get outta here," said Léa.

Tara began crawling to one side of the hallway. Léa followed. As they crawled, a few more bullets hit the wall behind them. The end of the hallway was bright red. Léa and Tara were now clearly visible to whoever was shooting down the hallway. But the bullets only continued to fly over their heads.

At the end of the hallway, Tara looked down, took a deep breath and peered around the corner. She looked back at Léa.

"You're not going to fucking believe this," said Tara.

30 MAIN STREET AT THE CASTLE

The Castle, Maze Stage 2

~ ~ ~

PLAYLIST:
"The Ascent " - Pulse of Life - Futureworld Music

~ ~ ~

Léa inched past Tara and peeked around the corner. After once glance, she looked back at Tara.

"Okay then," said Léa.

She crouched lower to the ground and took a longer look. As she took in the view, Léa had to remind herself she wasn't in a big city, but deep in the cliffs under a medieval castle on the small island of Orkney.

Another few bullets exploded on the wall behind her. Léa looked over her shoulder, then back around the corner.

"I think those are just squibs," she said.

"Squibs?" asked Tara.

"A small explosive special effects guys use to simulate bullet hits," said Léa.

"Special effects guys like Thomas Austin," said Tara.

"The same," said Léa.

To test her theory, Léa stood up. Her back was flat against the wall. A few more bullets appeared to hit the wall back in the tunnel. She turned her head left and right a few more times. A few more bullets hit the wall. Satisfied, Léa nodded once in determination and stepped away from the wall. More bullets appeared to hit the wall, magically passing through Léa's body.

She turned and looked at Tara.

"Just like I thought," said Léa.

"So what whizzed past your face back there?" asked Tara.

"I'm guessing some kind of compressed air jet to complete the effect," said Léa.

"So the bullets aren't real," ventured Tara.

"It's just an exercise, so I guess the bullets aren't real and the coast is clear," said Léa.

"So why give us real ammo?" asked Tara.

"Good question," said Léa.

"So we're still gonna be super fucking careful," said Tara.

"Super fucking careful," repeated Léa.

She looked at her best friend and smiled. Tara half-smiled back. They nodded once, stepped away from the wall they'd been hiding behind and walked around the corner. The scene before the was an urban nightmare. With their guns at the ready, Léa and Tara stood side by side studying the bizarre view before them.

London, Paris, Chicago or Moscow. The city block before them could have come from any of those big cities. What appeared to be skyscrapers lined the street. But dense smoke obscured everything above the second floor.

Abandoned cars, trucks and even an attenuated commuter bus blocked the three lane city road. Most of the cars were on fire. Trash littered the street along with what appeared to be a few dead bodies. More simulated bullet hits appeared all up and down the street.

After a few moments, Léa and Tara holstered their handguns, then swung the tactical rifles off their shoulders. After releasing the safeties, they looked at each other and realized they decided to change weapons at the same time.

"We really do think alike," observed Léa.

"Watch out bad guys," said Tara.

They both looked back down the street. Signs in various languages lined the road. But one clearly said: Airport. An arrow pointed directly ahead. Léa pointed her gun at the sign.

"I guess that's where we're going," she said.

"Let's do it," said Tara.

They both took one step forward. More simulated bullets appeared to explode on either side of the street. They took a second step. A car exploded down the block. As they took a third step, Léa felt something breeze past her face. Looking at Tara, she saw the fabric of the t'shirt next to her left arm suddenly tear and disappear. A small trickle of blood appeared on her pale skin. They both dove behind the nearest burning car.

"What the fuck was that?" yelled Tara.

Léa looked down at Tara's shoulder. A small patch of skin had been shot away along with part of her t'shirt.

"That was a real bullet," said Léa.

"They're shooting real fucking bullets at us?" said Tara.

"Are you okay?" asked Léa.

Tara rotated her arm. She reached her gloved hand up and wiped the blood away from her shoulder. It took only a second before more blood oozed from the small wound.

Reaching into one of the many pockets on her black tactical pants, Tara pulled out a small pouch. Laying her gun on her lap, she sorted through the pouch for a few seconds before pulling out a two inch square bandage. Tara handed it to Léa.

"Stick this on my shoulder," said Tara.

It took Léa only a few seconds to tear open the bandage and carefully place it over the inch line of blood just below Tara's shoulder. She gently patted it once.

"It's gonna leave a scar," she said.

"No doubt the first of many," said Tara.

Léa looked back at the bandage. Tara looked at her friend. In less than five seconds, she saw a whole range of emotions wash over her best friend's face. What started as pain and concern quickly transformed into anger and rage. But just as soon as Tara saw the flames of rage in Léa's eyes, they quickly vanished and were replaced with icy determination.

Léa stuffed the bandage wrapper in an empty pocket and picked up her gun. Tara watched as her best friend momentarily closed her eyes and snapped her head once to each side.

Opening her eyes, Léa set her rifle down and drew the small gun from her shoulder holster. She quickly pulled the slide on her gun back. A single bullet popped from the chamber which Léa caught in her free hand. She thumbed the magazine release, quickly reloaded the bullet she caught and slapped it back in place. With the bullet chambered and the gun cocked, Léa returned the smaller pistol to it's holster, picked up the rifle and rested her right finger just outside the trigger guard. Then Léa took a long, deep breath.

"Spy lesson number one. Never assume the coast is clear," said Léa.

"Spy lesson number one. Never assume the coast is clear," repeated Tara.

They looked at each other. Léa and Tara nodded once, then peeked around the side of the burning car. After a few moments, they leaned back against the car.

"Both sides of the street are just as trashed," observed Léa.

"The sidewalks are fairly clear," said Tara.

"We need to get from here to the end of the street," said Léa.

She took one more glance around her side of the car, then leaned over Tara and looked at the other street. Leaning back, she looked at Tara.

"Yeah. They're both about the same," said Léa.

Tara reached up and grabbed one of the smoke grenades hanging from her tactical vest. It took Léa only a second to grab one from her vest. Tara flipped the plastic lid offer her grenade and gently placed her thumb on the firing button.

"See you at the end of the street?" said Tara.

Léa nodded as they pressed their grenade's firing buttons at the same time. Rising up a bit, Léa and Tara turned. Resting on one knee, they kept their heads low behind the burning car. A second later they lobbed their grenades over the car. Dense white smoke quickly filled the street on each side of the burning car.

"Ready," said Tara.

"Set," said Léa.

"Go!" said Tara.

In an explosion of controlled energy, Léa and Tara took off in separate directions. Running as fast as they could, they emerged from the smoke. Dodging debris and burning vehicles, Léa and Tara quickly made it halfway down the city block.

Pausing for a few moments to catch their breath, Léa and Tara looked at each other across the city street. It only took a second for them to know they were both okay. Looking down the road, they both noticed more trash and debris on the sidewalk ahead.

More fake bullets began exploding around them. They ducked down lower to the ground as Léa and Tara looked back at each other. Glass from the shops exploded above them. It was time to go, but it was time to change direction.

Léa and Tara examined the situation and came to the same solution. Without saying a word, they agreed on a change in tactics. Simultaneously, they took a deep breath and took off running.

Instead of running down separate sides of the urban chaos, they met in the center of the street and ran side by side. More bullets exploded on each side of the street. A few cars ahead exploded. But Léa and Tara continued running down the street. In less that half a minute they ran the length of the street.

As they ran, a small hill with trees appeared on the horizon. What appeared to be the tail of a large airliner appeared through the trees.

"I think that's were were going," huffed Léa.

As they emerged from the street, Tara and Léa were still looking up at the hill, the trees and the tail of the massive jetliner. Then Tara looked down.

"Whoa! What the fuck is that?" yelled Tara.

Léa looked down and saw the pavement of the street was about to abruptly end. Looking quickly to both sides, she saw there didn't appear to be a way around the quickly approaching pit. Léa looked at the approaching edge, then to the other side and quickly made a decision.

"Jump," she yelled.

Keeping up with her best friend, Tara was also looking at the pit but came to a different conclusion.

"I'm too short. I'll never make it," huffed Tara.

"Keep going. You'll make it," yelled Léa.

There were less than five steps before the pavement ended. As the edge approached, Léa tried to run just a little faster. Four steps to go. Léa took deeper breaths as she poured on the speed. Three steps. She could hear Tara running faster to keep up. Two steps. Léa was able to see into the approaching pit. One step. She never took her eyes off the opposite edge of the pit.

Both Léa and Tara launched themselves into empty space as the pavement ended. Flying through the air, they quickly glanced down. The sides of the pit disappeared into nothing. It was clearly a long way down. As fast as Léa and Tara looked down, they looked back up again as the edge approached.

The other side of the pit was coming up fast. Léa looked down just as her black boots touched the ground. As she landed, Léa transferred the gun from her right hand to her left and reached out for Tara. But her friend's hand wasn't there. Léa rolled once, then quickly spun around to see Tara's terrified face disappear below the edge of the pit.

Dropping her gun by her side, Léa reached for a medium sized pouch hanging on her belt behind the gun's holster. As she continued to run for the edge, Léa pulled a bright orange bag out of the pouch. It had two loops of rope coming out of each end. Looking down at the approaching edge, Léa looped one end of the rope around a pipe sticking out of the ground. A second later she launched herself over the edge.

Tara had fallen just a few inches short of the ledge. As she fell, Tara noticed branches and pipes sticking out of the side of the pit. She grabbed a pipe with her left hand, stopping her fall. Her entire body snapped as her momentum stopped and the gun bounced out of her right hand.

Her whole fall was going in slow motion as adrenaline surged through her body. Tara saw the gun bounce out of her hand, but caught it as it began falling. She quickly slung the gun over one shoulder just in time to see Léa falling past her. Tara reached out into open space and caught Léa's tactical vest. But the force of Léa's fall was too much for Tara and she lost her grip on the pipe.

Yellow rope continue to play out from the bag in Léa's hand as they both fell. Tara reached her other gloved hand and tried to grab one of the passing pipes and hunks of wood sticking out of the pit's walls. After a few unsuccessful attempts, she firmly grasped one pipe. Once Tara realized she had the pipe, she gripped Léa's vest as tight as she could, took a deep breath and braced herself.

As the fall broke, Léa looked up just as Tara looked down. Even as their bodies snapped from the sudden stop in momentum, the two best friends never let go of each other's eyes. Looking up, Léa saw Tara's gloved hand never let go of the pipe or her vest. But she also saw it had come at a cost. Even though they never closed, Léa could see the wave of pain that washed over Tara's eyes as she broke their fall.

It only took a moment for Léa to give the yellow line a gentle tug to make sure it was secure before she looped it around her foot and stood up.

As she stood, Léa could visibly see the relief in Tara's eyes. Léa then reached out and grabbed Tara's vest as her grip loosened and she began to fall.

"Gotcha," said Léa.

Hanging by her vest, Tara looked down and took a few deep breaths. After flexing her hand a few times, she reached out and grabbed the rope.

"I told you I was too fucking short," wheezed Tara.

Léa looked down and smiled.

"We made it. And you're not too fucking short," she said.

A single snort-type laugh erupted from Tara's nose. She looked up at her friend.

"Thanks," said Tara.

"What's a best friend for?" said Léa.

After making sure Tara had a good grip on the rope, Léa looked up and started climbing. Tara looked down, but couldn't see the bottom of the pit. After a few moments, she closed her eyes and quickly snapped her head from side to side once. Then another snort-type laugh popped out of her nose. Léa looked down as she climbed and smiled.

"What's so funny?" she asked.

"Just pulled a Léa," said Tara.

"A what?" asked Léa and she continued to climb.

"Had to clear the cobwebs," said Tara.

"You laugh at me, but it really helps," said Léa.

"True that," said Tara.

After a minute or so of climbing, Léa reached the top of the pit and crawled over the side. A moment later, she looked over the side at Tara.

"Your turn," said Léa.

Tara looked at her skinny arms, then up then up to the top of the pit. She wasn't nearly as strong as Léa and didn't want her best friend to have haul her sorry ass up the side of the pit.

Looking down, Tara quickly formulated a plan. She reached down and gathered up the rope below her hand, then held both ends above her head. Tara then slipped her boot into the loop and stood up. Transferring her weight back to her hands, she pulled the rope up again and slowly 'walked' her way up the side of the pit. It didn't take long before her head popped up above the edge to see her friend's smiling face.

Léa had retrieved her gun from the dirt and was working the action to make sure it was clean enough to fire. As Tara crawled over the edge of the pit, she lay on her back taking deep breaths.

"I wish I was as tall and strong as you," wheezed Tara.

"I wish I was as small and tough as you," smiled Léa.

Tara rolled over and reached out her gloved hand. Léa smiled and reached for Tara. As their hands connected, Tara looked down as another of her snort-type laughs popped out of her nose. Léa smiled, but tiled her head off to one side.

"What?" smiled Léa.

Tara looked up. Her half-smile appeared on one corner of her mouth.

"I'm always happy to share a best friends moment, but I was actually going to check your gun," she said.

Léa looked down and smiled.

"Best friend moments are the best moments," she said.

Léa held out her gun, but Tara held onto Léa's hand for a few more seconds.

"They are," agreed Tara.

Pushing herself up on her elbows, Tara worked the action on Léa's gun. After it was unloaded, she blew through the empty barrel and stuck her small, gloved finger into the chamber. A second later, she reloaded the gun, spun it around in her hand and handed it back.

"It should be okay," said Tara.

"I'd rather use my Shield," said Léa referring to her smaller gun.

Tara hopped up on her feet and held her hand out to Léa.

"It's always there when you'll need it," said Tara.

Léa let Tara pull her to her feet. She dusted herself off and patted the smaller gun hanging just under her left arm. It was the gun her father had given her. It was the gun she practiced with every day for years. It was the gun that had already saved Tara's life. Looking down, Léa transferred the bigger gun to her right hand and looked up at Tara.

"Ready to finish this thing?" asked Léa.

Tara rotated her left arm, then her right arm. She was clearly sore, but everything seemed to be working. Tara unslung the rifle off her shoulder and looked up the hill to the line of trees.

"Let's go," said Tara.

The two best friends began slowly climbing the small hill. As they neared the top, they heard the sounds of jet airplane engines. When Léa and Tara reached the top of the hill, they could see the huge jet airliner tail emerge from behind what appeared to be a small airport terminal.

Crouching down behind a tree, Léa and Tara scoped out their next challenge. After a few moments, they turned and leaned back against the tree.

"That's a whole Boeing 757, passenger terminal and jetway," said Léa.

"How the fuck did they get all that down here?" asked Tara.

Tara took a deep breath, turned and knelt behind the tree. She looked down at the ground for a few moments, then over at Léa.

"I think we need a better tactical layout of all this," she said.

As Léa turned to kneel next to Tara, she looked at her friend's shoulder. Part of the bandage covering the bullet graze had come loose and a small trickle of blood was running down Tara's arm. Léa gently pushed the bandage back into place and lightly ran her finger around the adhesive edge.

Tara looked at Léa as her friend fixed her bandage. For just a moment, Tara saw a wave of pain and concern wash over Léa's face. In that moment, Léa's lips pressed together as the sides of her mouth tightened. The pupils of Léa's emerald green eyes contracted for just a moment.

Growing up together, Tara knew all of Léa's moods, personality tics and expressions. Her best friend was capable of a wide range of emotions, but she rarely allowed them to get out of control.

To the world, Léa seemed to be a wide open book who always seemed to be in a pleasant mood. But Tara knew Léa could go from pleasantly personable to deadly serious in no time at all. It was a side not many people saw.

And while both Léa and Tara were the best of friends, they were almost polar opposites. Tara was perceived as mostly moody bordering on almost always angry. She never wore anything that wasn't a deep, dark, forbidding black.

Unlike Tara's always black, nearly goth look, Léa almost always wore bright colored workout clothes, except, of course, when she was home. Léa's clothing optional zone was clearly her happy place, but it was also the cause of more than a few uncomfortable incidents with family and friends.

Tara didn't mind any of Léa's personality quirks. In fact, Léa's eccentricities were her most endearing qualities. Her best friend was her best friend and that was that.

"Say that again?" said Tara.

Léa smiled. Clearly, Tara had taken a quick mental vacation from the mission. Anyone else would have been concerned, but not Léa. Tara's vacation lasted less than a second or two. Léa smiled.

"I said, I'll go right, you go left," said Léa

"Right. See you back here in a five minutes?" said Tara.

"Five minutes," said Léa.

31 THE CONTROL ROOM BY THE HILL

The Castle, Maze Control

As Léa and Tara went their separate ways, Thomas Austin pressed a few buttons and looked up at the wall of monitors in front of him. He was in a small control room on the other side of a wall from the hill Léa and Tara were checking out. He was setting up some options for the third phase of the simulation when a door opened behind him.

"I'd hate to be you when Tara finds out who was shooting live ammunition at her," said Thomas.

Janet walked up and put her hand on Thomas' shoulder. Leaning over, she gave him a quick peck on the cheek and whispered in his ear.

"She doesn't really need to know, does she?" she said.

Thomas reached up and put his hand on Janet's hand.

"Your secret is safe with me. But that won't stop Tara from finding out," said Thomas.

Janet stood up and looked at the monitors. Léa and Tara were both hugging the tree line just below the ridge of the hill. Thomas looked back at Janet.

"Anything she wants to know, she'll know," he said.

"Then she'll understand why," said Janet.

Janet leaned down and punched a few buttons on the computer in front of her husband. As she punched buttons, Thomas leaned forward a few inches, kissed her cheek and started sneaking his hand under Janet's bullet proof vest. He felt Janet's shoulder blades tighten as his hand inched further up her back. Janet looked over her shoulder.

"I'm trying to finish setting up the simulation," she said.

Thomas began running his fingers around in a circle in the middle of Janet's back. That caused Janet's back muscles to tighten even more. As she looked back at the wall of monitors, she felt the fingers of Thomas' other hand begin lightly moving up and down her inner thighs. A moment later, Janet felt the sides of her nose flare as she take a deep breath. Her heart rate began to pick up. As her skin began to tingle, Janet took another deep breath and shook her head.

"We don't have time for this," she said between slightly clinched teeth.

Thomas leaned closer. His mouth was just inches from Janet's ear.

"They're taking five minutes to scope things out. Then they have to get down the hill to the terminal. You know we have plenty of time," he whispered.

Janet smiled. She turned to another control computer, punched in her access code and shut down the control room cameras. Thomas leaned closer to Janet's ear.

"The guys in security will never forgive you," he said.

"The guys in security can get over it," said Janet.

She punched a few more buttons on the console, then looked over her shoulder at Thomas. A slightly wicked smile appeared on one corner of her mouth.

"I think this is our first time down here," she said.

"No time like the first time," said Thomas.

Janet stood up slightly, spun around and sat down facing Thomas. She started tugging at his knit shirt as he began unbuckling her bullet proof vest. It only took a few moments of un-buttoning, un-clipping and un-zipping before their clothes were scattered around the control room chair.

The only item they handled with care was the black 9mm handgun tightly strapped to Janet's right thigh. Thomas unsnapped the holster, but waited for Janet to draw the weapon. Even in moments of heated passion, Thomas never forgot that his wife was a highly skilled assassin. It wasn't fear, but respect for his wife and her deadly skills that kept him from ever touching her weapon.

Janet looked away from Thomas as she drew the gun. They both looked down at the dull, black metal. Janet's nose flared again as she caught a whiff of gunpowder. She only took one shot, the shot that grazed Tara. But the smell lingered. Thomas smelled the gunpowder too. He looked up from the gun, but Janet's eyes were still looking down. For a moment, she was a thousand miles away. Even the slightest scent could trigger powerful memories.

Thomas knew where Janet had gone. It was that terrible day back in Moscow when Janet's skills were put to the most extreme test ever. Faced with three killers and with only two bullets left in her clip, Janet made the most famous kill in The Castle's history. But it was a day no one ever talked about, because moments later, Janet watched her best friend die in her arms.

Never looking away, Thomas watched as his wife relieved that awful day. A tear began to form at the corner of one of Janet's eyes. Thomas knew their moment of passion was about to fade away.

It had happened more than a few times before. But Thomas wasn't disappointed or even irritated. Ghosts from the past were just a part of everyday life when you were in love with a spy. Thomas' hands were resting on Janet's hips. He slowly reached his right hand up her left arm, then around her back. Janet looked at the gun a few more moments, then turned slightly and gently placed it on console behind her.

As she turned back, her head and eyes continued to look down. She took several deep breaths then reached for the hand Thomas left resting on her right thigh. After a few moments, she slowly looked up. Thomas was still smiling at her. Shifting slightly from side to side, she could still feel him between her legs.

Janet shook her head slowly from side to side. A small, sad smile appeared on one side of her face. But it wasn't all sadness. It was also a smile of knowledge, wonder and gratitude. She leaned down and kissed Thomas gently.

"No man on this earth would still be here with me," she said quietly.

Their bodies began slowly rocking back and fourth. Their breath was getting deeper and deeper. Their eyes never closed or looked away.

"Here with you is the only place I could ever be," said Thomas between deepening breaths.

Moving together, their breathing slowly fell together in perfect synchronization. Moments later, Janet and Thomas cried out together as a fiery lightning bolt of white hot passion surged through their bodies. As their breathing slowed, Janet leaned over. Her head fell on Thomas' shoulder.

As their breath returned to normal, Janet sat up and pushed her long, black hair over her shoulders. Looking into each other's eyes, they didn't have to say a word. But the feelings they communicated was clear.

Love. Respect. Gratitude.

After a few moments, Thomas reached up for the hand Janet was resting on his shoulder. Their fingers fell together, tightly interlaced as they felt each other's breathing. Janet finally broke the silence.

"So. I guess we have another spot we get to cross off our list," she said quietly.

"Not too many spots left," said Thomas.

"Where else do we need to do it?" smiled Janet.

"The McNally's apartment," said Thomas.

A single snort of laughter erupted from Janet's nose.

"Okay, that's just sick," she said.

They both laughed together.

After a few minutes, Janet leaned back and looked at Thomas. They continued to hold each other's eyes for a few more minutes.

Then Janet turned and looked up at the wall of monitors. Léa and Tara were back together behind the big tree at the top of the hill. Their heads were close together. After a few moments, they split up and disappeared over the top of the hill.

"I think they've figured out their plan," said Janet.

32 THE 757

The Castle, Maze Stage 3

~ ~ ~

PLAYLIST:

"From Zero to Galactic Hero" - Other Worlds - Really Slow Motion &
Instrumental Core

~ ~ ~

Running down a steep hill is not a good idea.

Running down a steep hill at full speed is less of a good idea. It's an even worse idea when you're carrying about twenty pounds of tactical gear.

Léa and Tara's mad dash down the hill was even more treacherous because the hill was made up of loose gravel. Every few steps, there was another stick of wood, another hunk of concrete or another big rock in just the right spot to trip someone running down the hill.

After scoping out the situation, Léa and Tara decided there simply was no way to sneak down to the airport terminal unobserved. The best thing to do was get down the hill as fast as they could, then find cover by the airport's main door. The side of the hill was littered with debris they'd have to dodge, but that could be a good thing. Weaving around the sticks, rocks and pipes would probably help them avoid snipers.

As she ran, Tara quickly glanced to her right. Léa was running along side, but Tara knew her best friend could easily run down the hill a lot faster. The best friends had a lot in common, but they were clearly not sisters. Tara was short and skinny. Léa was taller and a lot stronger.

What Tara didn't have in physical strength, she more than made up for with determination and intelligence. Along with a deep, lifelong emotional bond, Léa and Tara were kindred spirits because they had more brain power than anyone they'd ever met. Sometimes being the smartest kid in class is great. But sometimes it's not easy at all. Luckily for Léa and Tara, it was easy because the best friends had each other.

Suddenly, Tara felt something tug at her left boot. She felt herself beginning to fall. Tara glanced down and saw the ground was coming up fast. Rocks, sticks and gravel were getting closer to her face. In a split second, Tara knew she was falling and about to do a massive face plant into the gravel. In that split second, Tara knew she had to act fast.

Léa sensed that something was wrong. She looked to her left just as Tara tucked her chin down to her chest, hunched her shoulders and rolled onto the ground. As momentum carrier her forward, Tara was back on her feet, running alongside Léa.

"You okay?" Léa huffed.

"Yeah. Fine," Tara huffed back.

"Nice move," huffed Léa.

She stole another glance at her best friend as the small, half smile appeared on one side of Tara's mouth. Before Léa turned her attention back to running down the hill, she glanced at Tara's shoulder. The bandage was gone and blood oozed down Tara's arm.

Then the hill abruptly ended and Léa and Tara were running across a small parking lot. There were junked cars to dodge and a few deep potholes too. Running between the cars, Léa and Tara saw the front end of a small yellow VW Bug sticking up out of the ground. And it was coming up fast.

"Split up," huffed Tara.

After running around the sunken VW Bug, Léa and Tara hopped the curb and ended up on either side of the main terminal entrance. With their backs to the brick wall, it only took Léa a few moments to recover her breath after the high speed run down the hill and across the parking lot. Tara huffed a few more times before she looked at Léa and nodded.

"So far, so good," said Léa.

"So far," agreed Tara.

As they stood with their backs to the airport brick wall, Léa tilted her head to one side and listened. Whoever designed the terminal had an eye and an ear for detail.

"The white zone is for immediate loading and unloading of passengers only. There is no stopping in the red zone," said a male announcer.

The same message was repeated by a female announcer. Then the male announcer. Then the female announcer. Suddenly, Tara let out a single half snort, half laugh. Léa looked at her best friend.

"What's so funny?" asked Léa.

Tara's half smile remained on her face as she shook her head and closed her eyes.

"Wait for it," said Tara.

The announcements continued a few more times. Léa didn't hear anything different. Then the message completely changed.

"Listen Betty, don't start up with your white zone shit again," said the male announcer.

Tara laughed out loud again. Léa smiled. It was rare to see Tara actually laughing.

"I've heard that before," said Léa.

"It's from the movie Airplane," laughed Tara.

"Thomas Austin is having way too much fun," smiled Léa.

Suddenly, Tara stopped laughing. The smile disappeared from her face. Léa gripped her gun tighter as she saw Tara's expression completely change.

"What?" said Léa quietly.

"Shit doesn't happen around here without a reason," said Tara.

"So that's not just there for fun?" said Léa nodding to the speakers.

"Right," said Tara.

"But they like to have fun around here," said Léa.

"There's a time for fun and there's a time for serious shit," said Tara.

Léa surveyed the scene before her. She saw the burning cars, the debris scattered around the front of the terminal, the bullet holes in the wall. Then she looked at Tara's bloody shoulder. She nodded to the speaker that was still broadcasting the loading zone messages.

"He's not having fun at all. That's a distraction. He's messing with us," said Léa.

"Giving us a false sense of security," added Tara.

Léa looked forward, her eyes stopping on the yellow VW bug sticking out of the ground. Someone even thought to put a cute, customized license plate on the wrecked car. Léa looked back at Tara's bloody shoulder. She nodded a few times, then looked straight ahead.

"Worked on me," she said.

"Me too," said Tara.

Léa started to say something, but Tara cut her off.

"Let's get through this thing. We can analyze the lessons we need to learn later," said Tara.

Léa cleared the cobwebs, looked at Tara and nodded.

"Ready?" said Tara.

"Set," Léa nodded.

"Go," said Tara.

In a split second, Léa and Tara turned, took two steps sideways and stood shoulder to shoulder as the glass doors to the terminal slid open. With their guns pointing directly ahead, they took four steps forward and two steps to each side. Within seconds, they were standing with their backs against the exact opposite side of the brick wall.

The inside of the terminal was absolute chaos. Small fires were burning. Waiting room chairs were upside down and scattered around the floor. Computer terminals were shattered. Every so often, a small explosion erupted on a wall or counter simulating gunfire. Léa looked at Tara's bloody shoulder.

"Those may be more fake bullets, but we shouldn't be fooled," she said.

Tara looked down at her shoulder, then up at Léa. She could tell Léa was feeling guilty about calling the coast clear back at the entrance to the street. Tara rotated her shoulder a few times. It oozed a little more blood, but Tara smiled.

"It's just a scratch. Doesn't even hurt," she said.

Léa nodded, then looked straight ahead. She scanned the lobby, looking for a way up to the departure gates. The signs were in multiple languages, just like at any real international airport. Looking to her right, Léa finally found the sign she was looking for.

"I think we're going that way," she said pointing with her gun.

"Let's do it," said Tara.

Walking side by side, they slowly made their way around the broken chairs, fires and trash that littered the simulated airport lobby. Whoever constructed the airport and roadway did an amazing job. Every so often, Léa had to remind herself she was deep in the cliffs under the haunted castle north of her hometown.

As they turned the corner, they saw a long flight of stairs that followed the wall, then turned to the left. A sign above the stairway said: To All Planes.

The airports' security checkpoint stood between the stairs and Léa and Tara. There was a metal detector and a carry-on scanner. Aside from several piles of burning trash, it was almost like a real security area. Almost. The big difference was the absence of all the security people.

"This will be the first time I've ever gone through security and not had to wait an hour," groused Tara.

"I guess I can leave my laptop in my backpack this time," said Léa.

"I am not taking off my fucking shoes," quipped Tara.

Léa smiled as Tara started walking through the metal detector. As she stepped through, alarm bells sounded. Startled, Tara jumped away from the metal detector and almost tripped over some grey security scanner trays. Léa let out a a long, loud laugh.

"Fuck me," said Tara.

"Nothing wrong with your cat-like reflexes," observed Léa.

Tara eyed the metal detector as Léa walked through. The bells sounded once more. Léa patted the small gun holstered under her arm and smiled up at Tara. But Tara wasn't smiling.

"Whoever put this place together is a real fucking comedian," she groused.

"I'm guessing that would be your pal Thomas Austin," smiled Léa.

"He's not my pal," said Tara.

Léa nodded in the direction of the stairs.

"Ready?" she asked.

"Lead on," said Tara.

As they took off, Tara glanced over her shoulder back at the metal detector.

"Fucking comedian," said muttered under her breath.

Walking up the stairs, Léa and Tara had to dodge more debris and a few more fires. As they walked past one fire, Léa paused to examine it more closely. What appeared to be a pile of burning trash was really a ceramic model with several small jets of flames.

"Propane," sniffed Léa.

"Pretty realistic," agreed Tara.

"More special effects from Thomas?" Léa speculated.

"He's a fucking genius," groused Tara.

"Was he in on your your little show back at Deep in the Cliffs?" asked Léa.

When Tara didn't say anything, Léa looked over her shoulder. She saw the ever so slight smile appear on the corner of her best friends mouth.

"I'll never tell," said Tara.

"Yeah, your cover is blown on that one," said Léa.

Léa got to the top of the stairs first. Tara was a step or two behind. Standing shoulder to shoulder, Léa and Tara scanned the passenger boarding area. Only a few overhead lights worked. It was dark with long, grey shadows. Most of the light came from the propane fires burning around them.

Without saying a word, they started walking toward an open door that lead to the jetway. As they got closer to the door, small explosions from bullets began erupting on the opposite wall. Someone must be in the Jetway shooting.

Léa and Tara moved closer to the wall farthest from the bullet hits. After a few more steps, the brick wall ended and was replaced by shattered glass windows. Looking to their right, they saw a full sized Boeing 757 parked at the gate. A small baggage truck burned near the right wing. As they looked over the jet, Léa and Tara noticed shadows moving behind the passenger windows. They watched the scene before them for a few minutes.

"I think I counted four different shadows moving inside the plane," said Léa.

"I don't see anyone on the tarmac," said Tara.

"Let's check the Jetway," said Léa.

As they stepped out from behind the brick wall, a wave of heat from the fires burning near the airplane blew into the terminal. A few more bullet holes appeared on the opposite wall. Léa and Tara immediately dove for the floor.

"Think those are real?" asked Léa.

"Don't know, don't care," said Tara.

With her gun cradled in her arms, Tara began inching across the floor toward the door to the Jetway. Léa followed closely behind. More small explosions from bullets erupted on the terminal wall. Suddenly, a larger explosion, strong enough to shake the terminal, blew flames and debris over Léa and Tara. They crouched lower to the ground, but kept moving toward the door.

"Hang back," said Tara over her shoulder.

She looked down and closed her eyes for a second, then looked up and peered around the corner and down the Jetway. A few more simulated bullets exploded on the opposite wall. But Tara didn't see anyone shooting.

"No one in the Jetway," said Tara over her shoulder.

Léa inched up beside Tara and quickly poked her head around the corner. Then, staying very close to the ground, she inched past Tara to the other side of the door. Shuffling around so she faced Tara, Léa peered around the Jetway door again, then looked out the shattered glass window down at the airplane.

Several fires burned around the airplane. Baggage was scattered near one of the cargo doors. A truck with a silver tank was overturned near the right wing of the airplane. A pool of nasty looking blue liquid had spread out around the truck. Clearly, that area needed to be avoided all costs. She looked back at Tara.

"We need to steer clear of the right wing of the airplane," she said.

"Why?" asked Tara.

"The, uh, bathroom truck rolled and spilled," said Léa.

"No shit?" smirked Tara.

"A lot of shit, actually," smiled Léa.

Tara's half smile briefly appeared as she looked at her best friend. But her smile quickly disappeared as more gunshots appeared to come from the Jetway. Tara stole another glance around the corner.

"I can't see anyone in the Jetway and those may be fake bullets. But I think we need to figure out another way onto the plane," said Tara.

Léa peeked around the corner down the Jetway. Looking back outside the window at the airplane, Léa agreed that going down the Jetway wasn't a good idea. Looking at the tarmac, she saw the path seemed fairly clear. But a Boeing 757 sits fairly high off the ground making getting aboard the aircraft from the ground nearly impossible. Then Léa looked up at the Jetway.

"How about up there?" she said.

Tara looked down the Jetway, then out the shattered glass window at the left wing of the big jet. Looking up, she saw the path to the plane appeared to be completely clear.

"Looks good," she said.

Placing her gun on the floor in front of her, Léa did a quick pushup. She kept her upward motion going as she kicked her feet forward bringing her knees to her chest. She only paused a moment, looking around to make sure she was clear to stand. In the next second, Léa pushed her hands off the floor, grabbed her gun and was standing with her back to the wall by the door.

"Your turn," she said looking down at Tara.

As Tara stood, Léa clipped the rifle to her tactical vest. Reaching into the thigh pocket in her tactical pants, Léa pulled out a tightly coiled black rope. Reaching behind her, Léa pulled a heavy metal hook from a pocket attached to her belt.

"I hate climbing up ropes," said Tara.

Léa looked over as Tara attached the heavy metal hook to her own rope. She was flexing her hands and fingers as she uncoiled the rope. Tara was also breathing deeply, building up oxygen in her blood.

"It's not that far up," said Léa.

With her back to the wall, Tara looked out the shattered window and up to the top of the Jetway.

"I'll make it," she said.

Once the ropes were uncoiled, Tara took a few more deep breaths, adjusted the half finger gloves she was wearing and looked at Léa. They nodded at the same time, turned and tossed their ropes. Both hooks caught the top of the Jetway and Léa and Tara were out the window and on top within seconds. Crouching close to the top of the Jetway, they surveyed the scene around them.

"No one seems to be shooting at us here," observed Tara.

"For now," said Léa.

As they looked down the Jetway, Léa and Tara were carefully coiling up their ropes. Léa looked over the edge. Her eyes grew in size as she realized how high up they were. She closed her eyes as her head snapped slightly from side to side.

Tara caught Léa clearing the cobwebs and the small, half smile briefly appeared. She'd watched her best friend's personality tic for years. It was just one of the things that made Léa uniquely Léa. There was no one else like her and Tara found that comforting.

"What?" said Tara warmly.

Léa looked over at her best friend and realized Tara had once again caught her clearing the cobwebs. Most people found Léa's many personality tics annoying. But Léa knew her cobweb clearing tic was something Tara actually appreciated.

"Long way down," said Léa.

Tara looked over the side of the Jetway. It really was a long way down. Looking down the Jetway, Tara saw the rain shroud was pressed firmly against the big jet.

"How are we going to get into the airplane?" she asked.

"One of the pilot's windows has been shot out. We can get in there," said Léa.

"We'll only need one of the ropes to crawl down," said Tara.

She removed the heavy metal hook, stuffed it back in it's belt pocket and began carefully coiling up her rope. Léa removed her rope hook and put it away too. Unlike the spies in the movies, they learned it was best not to leave equipment behind. You never knew when you might need it again.

Léa stuffed her coiled rope under one of her tactical belt's suspenders, unclipped her gun and shuffled her feet. Tara unclipped her gun, then looked at Léa.

"Ready?" said Tara.

"Set," said Léa.

"Go," said Tara.

Running side by side, Lea and Tara quickly made their way down the top of the Jetway and onto the top of the jetliner. Once on slightly curved top of the airplane, they crouched low in case anyone decided to start shooting. Tara kept watch as Léa pulled the rope from under her suspenders, looped it over one of the jet's radio antennas and threw the end over the nose.

"Think that antenna strong enough to hold us?" asked Tara.

Léa nudged the antenna and gave the rope a firm tug.

"Looks like it," she said.

"Off you go then. I'll cover you up here," said Tara.

Léa gave the ropes another firm tug, then started inching toward the front of the airplane. As the fuselage began dropping toward the nose, Léa swung her boots around.

"Good thing these boots have rubber soles," she said.

Tara looked back as Léa began to disappear down the nose of the plane. She was careful to stay in the middle of the airplane so she wouldn't slip off the side. Léa inched forward and down until her boots touched the edge of the shot out windshield.

"Careful around the window," said Tara.

Léa looked up and smiled as she lowered herself into the cockpit. Just before she crawled through the window, Tara noticed a look of pain suddenly appear in Léa eyes. But before Tara could ask, Léa disappeared into the big jet. A second later, Tara saw the rope bounce twice.

"Your turn," said Léa from inside the airplane.

Tara quickly clipped her gun to her vest, picked up the rope and started inching forward. As she swung her legs over the front of the airplane, her feet quickly found the edge of the shattered windshield. Gripping the ropes tightly, she inched into the cockpit.

Cockpit windows are the biggest windows in a jetliner, but it was still a tight fit for Tara. She wiggled over the dashboard, then rolled on to her back just before neatly sliding into the pilot's seat.

The control panel in front of her was a mass of broken glass, tangled wires and red flashing lights. The air was thick with electrical smoke. Tara looked at the overhead panel and saw the jet's auxiliary power unit appeared to be running. She tapped a few gauges, then pressed a button labeled recirculating fans and the smoke quickly cleared.

"I didn't know you spoke airplane," said Léa behind her.

"There are several classes on airplanes in Spy School," said Tara over her shoulder.

She tapped a few more gauges on the upper panel, then spun two dials.

A few seconds later, cooler air began blowing through the vents in the cockpit. As she pressed a few more buttons, the lights flickered, then got brighter.

"Any chance you can fire this thing up and fly us to our hotel pool on Mykonos?" asked Léa.

Tara pointed to a small digital readout in the center of the upper panel.

"Afraid not. We don't have much fuel," said Tara.

"Plus there's the minor detail of several tons of rock, a castle and a small pub between us and the sky," said Léa.

Mentioning the pub brought the slight, half smile to back to Tara's face. But it quickly disappeared as Tara turned to look at Léa.

"Fuck! What happened to you?" exclaimed Tara.

Léa was leaning against the door to the cockpit. One hand was tightly gripping her shoulder. Dark, red blood was flowing between her fingers.

"It's nothing. I got a little too close to the broken glass when I was crawling through the window," she said.

Tara practically jumped out of the pilot's seat. After taking a quick look at Léa's shoulder, she reached into the thigh pocket of her black tactical pants and pulled out the small first aid kit. Léa looked at her best friend as Tara went to work cleaning out the deep cut. Lines of tense concern appeared around Tara's eyes and mouth.

"It's just a cut. I'll be fine," said Léa.

Tara continued gently cleaning out the cut. The flow of blood had slowed. But there were still a few chunks of glass Tara was trying to dig out. She put the first aid kit in Léa's good hand.

"Hold this," said Tara.

She sorted through a few of the bandages and wipes until she found some small tweezers. After wiping the tweezers off, Tara examined the cut closer. She took a deep breath, then gently pushed the tweezers into Léa's shoulder. Tara tried to be careful, but she could tell she was hurting Léa.

"Sorry," said Tara.

"At least now we match," said Léa.

"Match?" asked Tara.

"Our shoulders," smiled Léa.

"Huh?" said Tara.

She was concentrating on digging the last hunk of glass out of Léa's shoulder. It was wedged in deep, but Tara eventually wiggled it free. A fresh river of blood started flowing from Léa's shoulder as Tara dropped the glass on the floor.

"Gimme that," said Tara.

Léa held the first aid kit just out of Tara's reach.

"Gimme that, please," smiled Léa.

Tara closed her eyes. Even though she was sadly shaking her head from side to side, the small half smile appeared on her face. She could always count on Léa to lighten the mood.

"So what's this about us matching?" asked Tara.

"We're both going to have matching shoulder scars," said Léa proudly.

Tara looked down at her own shoulder, then over at Léa's shoulder. Both shoulders were still bleeding. Tara pulled two square bandages out of her thigh pocket. Ripping it open, she gently covered Léa's shoulder.

"Gimme that," repeated Tara.

Before Léa could admonish Tara for forgetting the 'p' word, Tara quickly said it.

"That's better," said Léa as she handed Tara the first aid kit.

With matching bandages on their shoulders and the first aid kit stuffed back in it's pocket, Léa and Tara unslung their tactical rifles and looked over the cockpit door. They stood on either side of the narrow door. After taking a few deep breaths, they nodded to each other. Léa reached out and gently turned the knob. The door easily swung open.

But Léa and Tara didn't immediately look around corner to check out the cabin. Without moving a muscle, they kept their backs flat against the cockpit bulkhead, waiting.

When nothing happened for a few moments, Tara and Léa looked at each other. At the same time, they both turned to face each other, then dropped down on one knee. Tara reached into a vest pocket and pulled out a small mirror. It was lined with heavy, black plastic.

After one more deep breath and a nod from Léa, Tara slowly inched the mirror into the cockpit doorway. Moving it slightly up and down and from side to side, Tara checked out the galley and first class cabin. She looked up at Léa.

"Nothing much there. Just an airline cabin," said Tara.

"They've probably got the hostages in the back of the plane," said Léa.

They both stood up at the same time. Tara stuffed the mirror back into it's pocket. Léa slung her rifle over her shoulder, then pulled the larger handgun from the thigh holster. Tara looked at her and started to speak. But Léa cut her off.

"Airline cabins aren't that big. This'll be easier to use, if we need it," she said.

Tara thought about it for a few moments, then nodded. She slung her own rifle and pulled her handgun. After checking it over, she looked up and nodded to Léa.

"I've done more of this shit, so I'll go first," said Tara.

"Speaking of shit, don't forget what's spilled all over the tarmac on the right side of the plane," said Léa.

"No matter what, we leave on the left side," agreed Tara.

Léa pulled the slide on her gun back, then let it snap forward. Placing her left hand under her right, she moved the gun around. Léa stretched her shoulders and arms, testing her limit of motion with the tactical suspenders, rifle sling and thick tactical belt. Then she quickly cleared the cobwebs and looked at Tara.

"Ready?" said Léa.

"Set," said Tara.

"Go," said Léa.

Tara led the way out of the cockpit, past the galley and into the first class section of the big jet. Lights were flickering and a few seats were broken and blocked the aisle. Even though a few fires were burning, the cabin was surprisingly clear of smoke.

Following close behind Tara, Léa was barely a step behind. She paused at the first class lavatories to make sure no one was hiding, ready to surprise them from behind. The front of the airplane appeared to be deserted.

As they reached the mid-cabin passenger doorway, Tara stopped and held up her right hand. She clinched her fist, then pointed to the door that lead to the Jetway. Léa transferred the gun to her left hand and tapped Tara's shoulder. She got the message. With her free right hand, Léa snagged her smaller gun and took a half step to her right. With guns pointed fore and aft, she could deal with any threat from any direction.

Tara quickly stepped into the door, then briefly disappeared down the jetway. It only took a few moments for Tara to return.

"No one home," said Tara.

Léa waved the gun in her left hand.

"Onward then?" she asked.

"Onward," said Tara.

Léa stuffed the smaller gun back in it's holster as Tara took up point and began making her way through the business class cabin. A curtain hung in the aisle in front of them.

Just three more steps to the curtain. Léa and Tara knew The Maze's ultimate challenge would be on the other side of that curtain.

Two more steps to the curtain. Both Léa and Tara felt their pulse rates begin to pick up. It was the anticipation building. Both felt a surge of excited adrenaline.

One more step. The surge of excitement quickly changed to a surge of dread. Tara looked back at Léa. Their expressions were the same.

Fear of what they would find on the other side of the curtain.

Tara turned and stepped to one side of the curtain. Léa took the other side. Tara dropped to one knee. Léa quickly followed. They looked at each other once more.

The fear in their eyes would be completely justified once Tara opened the curtain.

33 HARD LESSONS

The Castle, Maze Stage 4

"Mom? Dad?" said Léa and Tara at the same time.

Tara hadn't seen her parents for quite a while. An icy chill had descended on the Wells home since Tara found herself in The Castle's infamous Dungeon Test. While Tara was cold and distant in the year since she arrived at The Castle, her parents understood and kept their distance. A lot of people came out of The Castle's dungeon feeling angry and betrayed.

It was different for Léa. She had always known there was something different about the Taylor family and couldn't wait to talk things over now that she was in on the family secret. But Léa was told the reunion would have to wait until after Spy School. After her first mission to Sweden, Léa had been going full speed and simply hadn't had time to miss her parents.

Now, Léa and Tara stood in stunned silence as they tried to make sense of what their eyes were seeing. Their parents were seated near the back of the airplane. A thick piece of silver tape covered their mouths. They were leaning forward in their seats, probably because their hands were tied behind their backs. There was fear in their eyes and for good reason.

Four heavily armed terrorists were standing behind them holding guns to their parent's heads. Three of the terrorists wore masks. One didn't.

"Janet?" said Tara.

"Game's up kids. Drop your guns," said Janet calmly.

Léa and Tara couldn't move a muscle.

"I said, drop your fucking guns, now." said Janet.

That was enough to snap Tara out of her stunned trance. She slowly lowered her gun. Léa took a second longer. Before she lowered her gun, she closed her eyes and slightly snapped her head from side to side. Léa's eyes opened just before she finished clearing the cobwebs. As her head turned, she caught a glance of the passenger window next to her Dad.

Something wasn't right.

She stole another glance off to the side. The passenger seats were reflected in cabin windows. But she couldn't see any people. Léa looked the other way. There were seats reflected in the windows, but no people.

"This isn't real," said Léa quietly to herself.

Tara was slowly lowering her gun to the ground. But Léa hadn't moved.

Her brain was still kicked into high gear when Janet broke the silence.

"Hey Stripper. I said, drop your fucking gun," said Janet.

A slight smile appeared on one corner of Léa's mouth. She slowly transferred the larger gun to her left hand and began slowly lowering it to the ground.

"I prefer clothing optional," smiled Léa.

As she lowered the gun to the ground, Léa turned slightly to her left and edged toward the passenger seat next to her.

"I don't give a fuck what you prefer," said Janet.

Tara had just gently laid her gun on the ground and was starting to stand up. Léa continued to turn slightly as she lowered her gun to the ground. As she gently placed the larger gun on the ground, Léa reached under her left shoulder and pulled her smaller gun from it's holster.

"Sorry about this," said Léa quietly to Tara.

In a blur of motion, Léa stood up, pushed Tara off her feet behind some passenger seats and opened fire.

Four bad guys.

Four shots.

But Léa didn't shoot to kill. Instead, she aimed at the shoulders of of the bad guys, just in case she was wrong. But Léa wasn't wrong. As she fired, a plate of glass in the back of the cabin shattered. Léa dropped to one knee and hid behind the passenger seat.

Tara was just sitting up after being roughly pushed over by Léa. She peeked around the passenger seats in time to see shattered glass falling to the ground. She looked at Léa.

"How did you know?" asked Tara.

Léa smiled at Tara and nodded toward the passenger windows. But she didn't have time to reply. As soon as the glass stopped falling, an explosion rocked the whole jet. Peeking around the seats, Léa saw the back of the cabin was engulfed in flames.

"We gotta get outta here," said Léa.

They were crouched down next to the twin window exits over the wings. Remembering what was just outside the right exits, Léa and Tara looked up at the left side exits. Another explosion rocked the big jet. It was just outside the left windows. Léa and Tara looked at each other for just a moment, then over at the right side of the airplane.

"Oh fuck me," said Tara.

"Me too," said Léa.

After quickly moving across the aisle, Tara quickly opened the over-wing exit and tossed it outside the airplane. As she stepped out on the wing, Tara stole a quick glance back where Janet was standing. The tail of the airplane appeared to be falling off.

Léa quickly joined Tara standing on the wing. Looking around, Tara realized she had left her gun inside the airplane. As she turned to go back to get it, Léa touched her shoulder. Tara saw her best friend was smiling. Looking down, she saw why.

"Forget something," smiled Léa.

"Thanks," said Tara.

As Léa handed the gun to Tara, she looked over the edge of the wing. Blue goo with what looked like nasty, brown clumps was slowly oozing away from the punctured lavatory truck.

"I am not jumping into that shit," said Tara.

"Me either," said Léa.

Tara looked down the wing.

"It's dry further down," she said.

The big jet's wing bounced at bit as Léa and Tara carefully made their way towards the tip. Walking closer to the back of the wing, they'd glance down looking for a dry spot to jump off. Suddenly, the airliner's speed brakes popped up. Léa was able to quickly side-step the metal plate as it rose. But Tara wasn't quick enough and it knocked her off her feet.

Tara fell on her side, knocking her gun out of her hands. As it slid off the wing, Tara began sliding too. Moving fast, Léa jumped over the speed brake and dove for Tara's outstretched hands. One hand gripped Tara's hand. She had just enough time to holster her gun and grab the slot in the wing just below the speed brake.

"Gotcha," said Léa.

Tara was hanging mostly off the wing. Looking down, she saw her gun sitting in the ooze. Before Tara could say anything, Léa spoke up.

"Are we far enough down that I can swing you clear?" she asked.

"Just barely," said Tara.

"On three?" asked Léa.

Tara looked down at her gun, the ooze and the dry spot she hoped to land in. Looking back up at Léa, she nodded and began swinging her legs.

"One," said Tara.

"Two," said Léa.

"Three," said Tara.

Léa released Tara's hand on three, then crawled a bit further down the wing. After she was sure she'd clear the ooze on the ground, Léa swung her legs over the wing and inched over the edge. Halfway off the wing, she rolled over and continued inching down until she was holding on to the edge. She looked down, saw her feet and dry concrete. It was a long way down. Looking up, she hoped she wouldn't break anything and let go.

The fall knocked the wind out of her, but Léa appeared to be in one piece. After catching her breath, Léa slowly got to her feet. Tara was just standing up. She was holding her gun as far away from her nose as possible. Blue ooze dripped from the barrel.

"Eeew," said Léa.

"Fuck me," said Tara under her breath.

Suddenly, Léa and Tara were plunged into darkness. Even the fires burning around them disappeared. Then a soft, blue light began to emerge around the airplane. Brighter blue lights appeared just off the right wingtip. The light grew in intensity. It was dead quite. Then a calm voice filled the room.

"Okay you two. The exercise is now over. Secure all weapons. Stand down," said Janet.

Tara held her dripping gun at arm's length. Léa had drawn her gun as soon as the lights went out and continued to hold it ready. The two best friends looked at each other and nodded at the same time. Léa lowered her gun. Tara continued holding her gun at arm's length.

A door slid open near the big jet's wing tip. Léa and Tara glanced at each other briefly and began walking toward the door. It was wide enough for them to walk through together.

"Hey kids," said Léa's Mom.

Léa and Tara's parents were just standing up from behind a single aisle of airline seats. Tara's Dad was peeling the strip of duct tape off his mouth. Janet was holstering her gun. Bright stage lights were slowly dimming. A single broadcast quality TV camera was on a tripod in the middle of the room. The far wall was painted electric green.

A door opened behind Léa and Tara.

"What did you think?" asked Thomas Austin.

Tara looked from Thomas, to her parents, then to Janet. In just a few moments, she felt a whole range of emotions. Seeing her parents held hostage was a bit of a shock. But seeing Janet holding a gun to her parent's heads was even more unsettling. She looked down and mumbled something no one could hear.

"Amazing," said Léa.

Stepping around the camera, Léa ran over and gave each of her parents a big hug.

"That's my girl," said her father.

Tara hadn't moved. She could only continue staring at the ground. After a few moments, she looked up at Janet.

As she hugged her mom, Léa looked back at Tara. Then she felt her mom tap her shoulder. She looked back.

"She needs you," said her mom.

Léa rushed back to her friend as Tara fell to her knees, her whole body was shaking. Léa knelt in front of her friend and reached for her hands. Tara was still holding the gun dripping with blue ooze. Léa gently took it from her and laid it on the ground.

"What?" said Léa.

Tara didn't respond. She was still looking at the ground when Léa gently placed her hand under Tara's chin and pushed her head up. Immediately, she could tell that Tara was not in good shape. The look in her eyes was the look of pain, anger and confusion.

Léa looked over Tara's shoulder at Thomas Austin. It only took one look for her to convey her message. Thomas motioned to Janet and started for the door. Léa and Tara's parents quietly followed leaving the best friends alone.

Léa patiently waited with her friend. Growing up together, she's witnessed Tara's volatile temper on more than one occasion. When confusing, conflicting emotions bubbled to the surface, Tara would often respond with anger.

Léa had seen her best friend cry only once. Now, a single tear had fallen from one eye onto Tara's smudged cheek. Tara looked over her shoulder at the door her parents, Janet and Thomas had just walked through. After a few moments, Tara stopped shaking and turned back toward Léa.

"It's just," began Tara.

But she never finished the sentence. Léa smiled and started cleaning the smudge marks from Tara's face.

"I think I understand," said Léa.

"I don't," said Tara.

Léa looked at her watch.

"That was nearly an hour of intense, tactical, dangerous," began Léa.

She paused a bit, searching for the right word. After a few moments, she found one. The word she used brought a very slight smile to Tara's face. So Léa repeated herself.

"Shit," said Léa again.

She nodded back toward the doorway leading to the chaos of the jetliner, the cliff and the city block.

"It may have been simulated, but it was well simulated. It seemed so very real and we were totally immersed. We were also getting tired and then what happens? We come face to face with our parents and the one person we both think we can completely trust," said Léa.

She paused to let that sink in. Tara nodded once and looked at Léa. Her face was smudged with dirt too. Tara reached into a vest pocket and pulled out some wipes and started cleaning off Léa's face.

"Yeah," nodded Tara.

"Add to all that, I suspect you and your parents haven't been getting along so well since you got here. So it was probably even more upsetting to see them," said Léa.

Tara nodded as she tore open a new wipe pack and started cleaning Léa's shoulder wound. Léa looked down at her shoulder, then back up at Tara.

"Add to all that, you see one of the few people in the world that you trust holding a gun on your parents and I'm guessing that slammed you into maximum emotional overload," said Léa.

Tara's nostrils flared as she took a very deep breath. Looking down, she sat back on her feet. Léa sat back on her new combat boots. The new heels dug uncomfortably into her butt muscles. Tara nodded again.

"Yeah. Sounds about right," said Tara.

Léa looked back at the door leading to the chaos, then back at Tara.

"It didn't just test our tactical skills. The Maze put us in extreme emotional distress," said Léa.

"Something that sure as shit will happen out in the real world," said Tara.

"Sure as shit," smiled Léa.

That brought another half smile to Tara's semi dirty face. The two friends sat together, thinking back over the past hour. The distractions, the danger, the smoke and then the shock. As they sat in silence, Léa looked at Tara's shoulder and reached for a wipe. Tara pulled a few more bandages from her pants pocket. Léa and Tara bandaged each other's shoulders in silence.

After a few more minutes, Léa stood up. Looking down at Tara, she reached her hand out to help her up. Tara stood, but never let go of Léa's hand.

"Sorry to break the mood, but the heels of those new boots were digging into my butt," smiled Léa.

Tara had to think about that for a few moments. Once it registered, a single, sort-type laugh erupted through Tara's nose. Then something happened that Léa didn't see very often. Both sides of Tara's mouth turned up in a smile.

"Damn you have a devastating smile," said Léa.

Tara looked down as the smile disappeared. After a few moments, she looked back up at Léa.

"That's what Janet says," said Tara.

"She's right," said Léa.

After a few more moments of silence, Léa moved her shoulders under the tight straps of the tactical suspenders. She nodded toward the other door in the room.

"Come on, these clothes are killing me," said Léa.

"I'm ready for a long, hot shower," said Tara.

As the two friends turned and walked toward the door, Tara stopped, knelt down and picked up her smelly gun. She closed her eyes and turned her head away as it's nasty aroma reached her nose.

"Ugh. This is not going to be fun to clean," said Tara.

"We'll just drown it in some Hoppe's," said Léa.

As they made their way to the door, Léa reached out for Tara's hand. They walked slowly and silently across the floor. When the reached the exit, they turned and looked back at the small studio. Then they looked back toward the door leading to the chaos.

"We need a way to remember the lessons we learned today," said Tara.

"We do," said Léa.

Still holding hands, they stood in the doorway. Both were lost in thought about the last hour of their lives. The lessons they learned in the simulation were important. Lessons that they were sure would one day save their lives.

"I've got it. We just need to remember Daphne," said Léa.

"Who's Daphne?" asked Tara.

"Back in the parking lot," began Léa. "It was the customized license plate on that yellow bug sticking up out of the ground. It was just one of the many distractions."

"I lost count," said Tara.

"Me too," said Léa.

They continued to stand in silence. Their minds wandered back through The Maze. Once again, down the city street and through the airport terminal. There was so much to remember.

"I just can't nail it all down," said Tara.

"Me either," said Léa.

"That's why you shouldn't try right now," said a voice behind them.

The voice was calm and reassuring. Léa and Tara turned slowly and saw Alan Dennis. He was smiling proudly at his two newest spies.

"There's a reason why we always de-brief an exercise like this the next day," he began.

Léa and Tara stood in silence. They had to let go of each other's hands to turn around. But after a few moments, their hands quickly re-joined.

"You were right about those intense, conflicting emotions Miss Taylor. You're both exhausted, physically and emotionally. That's one of the goal's of this exercise. So we'll sort it all out tomorrow," smiled Alan.

The smile disappeared as quickly as it appeared. Alan's nose twitched.

"Right now, you two need those hot showers," said Alan.

He turned to leave.

"And you should do something about that nasty smelling gun," he said over his shoulder.

Léa and Tara looked at each other. It only took a second of their best friends, non-verbal communication before they slowly followed Alan out of the room.

34 OUT IN THE COLD

The Castle, Dick Boxx's Dorm Room

Dick Boxx looked around the empty room that had been his home for the past fifteen years. No, it was almost twenty years. As a professional soldier, home for Dick was where ever he went to sleep that night. Since he didn't really have any friends at The Castle, he certainly wasn't nostalgic about leaving this stone dorm room.

Reaching down, Dick picked up a garment bag and slung it over his shoulder. With his other hand, he grabbed the small duffel bag and quickly left the room.

The hallway outside his door was empty. Dick slowly walked down toward the main atrium of The Castle. It was early in the morning and everyone was asleep. Only the creaky rumbling of the old Paternoster lift broke the silence.

Dick looked over the railing. A slight ripple of water lapped up against the hulls of the two submarines tied up to the docks. The old German U-Boat was a lot smaller than than the newer, nuclear sub. Dick looked up toward the roof of the atrium. The lights had been dimmed during the night time hours. He looked over at the old lift.

Turning, he started walking up the stairs. It would be quite a climb, but Dick was in excellent shape. Toward the end of the climb, he began taking the steps two at a time. Dick Boxx didn't want to be in The Castle complex a second longer than he had to.

At the top of the stairs, you could turn left or right. Either way led to the circular walkway that ringed each level of The Castle's atrium. Several hallways branched out in different directions from the central hub. Directly ahead was a sliding metal door. Several cameras covered the area in front of the door.

An old fashioned, phone hung from a box next to the door. As Dick reached for the phone, the metal doorway silently slid open. Dick looked up at the camera, then back over his shoulder. He was completely alone.

He was sure word had spread quickly about his departure from The Castle. Once Commander Dennis approved his plan, all that was left to do was pick up a few things in his office, pack his few personal items from his dorm room and leave.

The official reason for his departure was that Commander Dennis felt he had outlived his usefulness and it was time for him to retire. The rumor mill reported that Dick had been given the choice to retire or be fired.

That was the rumor.

The scheme Dick sold to Commander Dennis was that he was involuntarily being put out to pasture. Since he didn't have any friends at The Castle, Dick hoped Perry Drilling might try to turn him, just like what happened in the movie.

Alan Dennis thought it was a stupid idea. So did Janet and Thomas Austin. Even the McNallys thought it was ridicules. But Dick insisted it could work. As word of Dick's idea spread, no one in The Castle believed the plan would work. After the meeting in Deep in the Cliff's Pub, Thomas suggested to Janet that Dick might have some other motive.

"You mean that little shit may be working with Drilling?" exclaimed Janet.

"Not saying that. But something's fishy for sure," said Thomas.

It took less than a second for Alan Dennis to agree with Thomas. Since there was no way to be sure what Dick Boxx was up to, Alan granted his request.

Four hours later, Dick stood at the entrance to The Castle Complex and no one showed up to wish him well. Even the faceless security people who controlled the main doorway didn't want to talk to him.

Seventeen years ago, Dick had been hired away from the Royal Marines as essentially The Castle's P.T. Instructor. As a Royal Marine, Sgt-Major Boxx was their top drill instructor. Yelling at people on the verge of exhaustion was a largely thankless job. But long after the training sessions had ended, Dick remained aloof, distant and just a bit snotty.

The empty corridor outside the main doorway was just one more confirmation that Dick didn't have any friends. Without looking back at the camera, Dick squared his shoulders and walked out the door. He didn't have to look to know it quickly closed behind him.

Without breaking his military stride, Dick marched up the circular, stone stairway and emerged next to the stone fireplace in The Castle's old main hall. Never looking back, Dick walked outside, then down the goat path that lead to the road.

An hour later, Dick Boxx stood on the deck of the ferry boat that would take him to the dock at Scrabster, Scotland. From there he would catch a train to a cottage rented for him in Glasgow where he would appear to retire into obscurity.

Dick watched as the small island town of Stromness disappeared behind the ferryboat. As the ever present light rain and fog enveloped the boat, Dick put the second part of his plan into action. He walked across the deck and into the boat's bar to begin getting as piss drunk as he could.

35 ANOTHER PING

The Castle, Central Park

"I can't decided. Shower first or food," said Léa.

"Food," said Tara.

The Maze was on the level just above the submarine docks. When Léa and Tara emerged from the long, stone hallway into The Castle's atrium, they looked at the old Paternoster lift and then began climbing the stairs. Léa looked at her watch.

"Where are we going to find food at this hour?" she asked.

"Food here is 24-7," said Tara.

Léa looked up the stairs. They would have to climb almost to the top of The Castle Complex and they were still carrying all of their tactical gear. The long climb after the intense workout of The Maze had both Léa and Tara's heart rates soaring.

"Why didn't we take the lift?" wheezed Tara.

"Because we're such bad-asses?" huffed Léa.

Halfway up, Tara stopped. Léa took several more steps, then stopped and looked back at her best friend. Tara was hunched over with her hands on her knees, trying to catch her breath. She turned her head to look at Léa through sweaty strands of her long, black hair.

Léa's breathing had almost returned to normal. She was standing straight up. After shifting the tactical rifle to her other shoulder, Léa looked down at Tara.

"You need to work out more," said Léa.

"I work out each morning, just like you do," said Tara.

"Getting your heart rate up for a few minutes each morning isn't enough," said Léa.

Tara took one more deep breath, stood up, shook the matted hair out of her face and frowned at Léa.

"I work out enough," said Tara.

"Yeah. Whatever you say skinny girl. You need more muscles and a lot better cardio. Come on. I'm starving," said Léa.

Without waiting for Tara, Léa began walking toward The Castle's cafeteria. It took a few steps for Tara to catch up. The two best friends walked in silence. Inside the cafeteria, they walked past the steam tables, picked up their food and sat down in silence.

"Hang on a sec," said Léa.

She got up and disappeared into the kitchen. When she emerged, Léa was carrying several hot, steaming towels. Back at the table, she tossed half of them at Tara and began scrubbing her face and hands. Ignoring the towels, Tara grabbed her fork. Léa spoke up just as Tara took her first bite.

"Your hands are filthy," said Léa.

"I'm hungry," said Tara with her mouth full of food.

Léa finished up with her towel and reached for her own fork.

"We just got through climbing through a nasty old jetliner including whatever was leaking from the toilet truck," said Léa.

Tara shoveled another fork full of food into her mouth. She was tried, hungry and her shoulder was hurting more than thought it would. But the image of what was oozing out of the truck by the airplane stopped Tara from chewing. After thinking about it a few moments, Tara swallowed with a big gulp and reached for the pitcher of water. Her pale white skin appeared to turn a shade of green.

"Sorry about that," said Léa.

Tara gulped down a glass of water, closed her eyes and took several deep breaths. She filled the water glass and gulped half of it down. After a few more deep breaths, she looked at Léa.

"Thank you so much for that mental image," scowled Tara.

"Not to mention the memory of The Maze's wonderful aroma," smiled Léa.

Tara closed her eyes as the green tint returned to her skin. After holding her head in her hands for a few moments, she reached out one hand.

"Okay. Fine. You win. Gimme one of those towels," said Tara.

Léa briefly thought of holding the towel just outside of Tara's reach, but changed her mind. She'd had enough fun at Tara's expense. Best friends only messed with each other a little bit.

After holding the towel against her face for a while, Tara began rubbing her eyes. Then she ran it over her forehead, nose and chin. She opened her eyes and finished by cleaning her hands. As she wadded up the towel, she looked at Léa.

"That's got to feel better," smiled Léa.

Tara looked down at the towel and began twisting it into a rat tail. As she continued twisting the towel, she looked at her best friend. Léa smiled for a few moments, then her expression turned serious.

"Don't even think about it," cautioned Léa.

"Think about what?" said Tara.

She continued rolling the towel.

"Remember our first towel fight?" asked Tara.

"I remember the big red welts I snapped onto your hip, stomach and back," smiled Léa.

Tara continued twisting the towel.

Léa looked over Tara's shoulder.

"Uh oh," said Léa.

"Nice try, but I am not going to fall for that old trick," said Tara.

Léa looked at Tara. The expression on her face was serious, but with just a tinge of amusement. One eyebrow tilted up slightly.

"Fine then. Don't," said Léa.

Tara closed her eyes for a few moments. She slowly shook her head from side to side before turning to look over her shoulder. Janet and Thomas Austin stood in the cafeteria doorway.

"Sometimes I just don't know if you're messing with me," sighed Tara.

She looked back her childhood friend. Léa smiled, then her expression turned deadly serious.

"I'd never mess with you when we're in trouble," she said.

"I know that," said Tara.

A few moments later, Janet and Thomas sat down next to Léa and Tara. Janet's expression was serious, but Thomas was smiling.

"What?" asked Léa and Tara at the same time.

Janet looked at Tara, then at Léa, then at her husband. Thomas continued smiling.

"We got another ping," exclaimed Léa.

"Yep," said Janet.

"A good one?" asked Tara cautiously.

"We think so," said Thomas.

"Most of Perry Drilling's web traffic has been bouncing from one server to another. But eventually all the little bits and bytes come to a stop," said Janet.

"And they're all stopping in the same place," said Thomas.

"Looks like we're hitting the road again," said Léa looking at Tara.

"Where?" asked Tara.

Janet took a breath, but Thomas cut her off.

"It's a famous castle near a small town in Austria called, Werfen," he smiled.

Tara looked from Thomas to Janet.

"What's he so happy about?" she asked,

"It's a famous movie castle," said Janet direly.

"Of course," sighed Tara.

"Are we sure it's not a false trail of bread crumbs like Uppsala?" asked Léa.

"No way to be sure,' said Janet.

"What we are sure about is most all of the web traffic stops at that castle," said Thomas.

Léa looked at Tara. A few moments of the best friends non-verbal, instant messaging passed over the table. Without looking away from Tara,

Léa spoke up.

"Sounds a little too good to be true," she said quietly.

"Just like what we're hoping to find," said Tara.

They both looked at Janet who nodded toward her husband.

"Wow. You two are good. That's what we think too," she said.

"But the traffic is so deeply encrypted that there's no way to know for sure," said Thomas.

"I guess we'll find out when we get there," said Léa.

"Can we finish our dinner and grab a shower?" asked Tara.

"You'll be leaving tomorrow afternoon," smiled Janet.

"Why not first thing in the morning" asked Léa.

"Because you're both exhausted," said Janet.

"We think giving you two a few extra hours of sleep will make big difference," said Thomas.

"Go home, take a long shower and we'll see you in Mission Ops after breakfast," said Janet.

"Sounds good," said Léa.

Tara reached for her fork and was about to begin eating when she looked up. Janet and Thomas hadn't moved.

"Something else?" said Tara, her fork halfway to her mouth.

Janet rolled her eyes and nodded toward her husband. Thomas was smiling again as he laid a USB jump drive on the table.

"What's that?" asked Léa.

"This won't be on your mission briefing tomorrow. Just a little something to help you pass the time on your trip to Werfen," smiled Thomas.

Léa and Tara looked at the jump drive, then up at Janet.

"So you two really think the cold trail just got hot again?" said Tara.

"Could be," said Janet.

"But it could be another fake trail just like Uppsala," said Léa.

"Yep," said Janet.

"Guess we'll find out," said Tara as she shoveled another fork full of food into her mouth.

PART 4: CASTLE IN AUSTRIA

36 STUCK ON A TRAIN

Seat 211-A & B, The Next Day

"Okay. For an old movie, that wasn't so bad," said Léa.

She reached for the sky as she sat straight up and stretched. Tara gently closed the laptop lid and twisted her shoulders from side to side.

"It might have been better if these seats weren't so fucking hard," groused Tara.

Léa looked out the window of stationary train. Heavy snow had been falling for the past several hours. She looked back into crowded coach. The train hadn't moved for quite a while and everyone was getting restless.

The journey from Stromness to London and under the Channel was effortless and snag free. But once they boarded the train out of Paris, things began to go wrong. The train broke down just as it was crossing into Switzerland from France. It limped into Zurich almost ten hours late. Then, an intense early season snowstorm stopped the train, along with Léa, Tara and the rest of the passengers, dead in their tracks.

To kill time during the delay, Léa and Tara decided to go over the mission files again. They'd already read over everything several times. After analyzing several gigabytes of data from the bug Tara snuck into Perry Drilling's laptop, they were able to triangulate a possible location for the rogue I.T. guy's hide-out.

Most of the web traffic just bounced from server to server. But eventually, it stopped just outside the small town of Werfen, Austria. It was a location that brought a huge smile to Thomas Austin's face. After watching the movie he handed over as Léa and Tara were were chowing down in The Castle's café, Thomas' amusement was easy to figure out.

After a few minutes of stretching and flexing muscles to work out the kinks from spending too much time sitting on uncomfortable train seats, Tara reached for the laptop and her iPhone. Léa watched as Tara set up a hot spot through the phone and opened a web browser. After a quick web search, she had several pages of data and a few movies open on her desktop.

"I get why you are using the phone instead of the train's WiFi," began Léa. "But why are you researching that old movie?"

"We just spent the last few hours watching a movie about the place we're going. Time to separate fact from fiction" said Tara.

Léa looked down at the laptop as Tara started the YouTube video she saved. It showed a series of still pictures from the movie, cut with recent photos taken from same locations. Léa looked up at Tara.

"Wow! Things really do look different in the movies," she observed.

A small, half smiled appeared on Tara's face as she nodded down at the screen. She scrubbed the video back a few seconds, made sure Léa was watching, then hit play.

A still picture of Richard Burton and Clint Eastwood dressed as German soldiers filled the screen. They were standing by some stairs and a door marked Funkraum. The next scene showed the same stairs were now blocked by a locked, iron barrier and the Funkraum appeared in reality to be a public bathroom.

The video played on showing the courtyard of the castle from the movie and then from recent day. Instead of having enough room to land a helicopter, the modern day courtyard was filled with picnic tables. Each table had a big umbrella and most had several people sitting around enjoying some food and conversation. A few people had laptops open. A few others appeared to be tapping away on their phones.

"There's no way Drilling set up a network at that old castle because they have free WiFi." speculated Léa.

"He moves far too much data around for a public hot spot," agreed Tara.

"Suppose he's tapped into their main service with a Cat 5 line?" asked Léa.

"He'd still need a lot more bandwidth than you get with normal internet service," said Tara.

She moved the mouse pointer back to the video timeline and scrubbed back and fourth examining pictures of the present day castle. One picture showed the front and side of the castle. Tara spotted what appeared to be utility lines. She grabbed a still picture from the video and opened it in Photoshop.

Léa looked on as Tara zoomed into the power lines, sharpened the photo and tweaked the contrast. After less than a minute of adjusting sliders, the grainy photo gave up what might be an important clue.

"There," said Tara pointing to the screen. "They don't just have regular internet. That's a high capacity fiber line."

"So they have more than enough bandwidth for Drilling to push around all of his data," said Léa.

Tara zoomed the picture back out. After examining the postcard picture of the famous old castle, she tapped the video window and began looking at the pictures of happy tourists. After a few moments, she looked at Léa.

"We're not going to find shit here," said Tara.

"Because it's too public a place for Perry Drilling to be basing his operations." added Léa.

"All we're going to find a junction between two hubs in a closet," said Tara.

"Maybe more than just a junction box," speculated Léa.

"What else?" asked Tara.

Léa looked at the pictures that covered Tara's desktop. She looked out the window for a few moments, then back at Tara.

"I'll bet he's also got some kind of intruder alarm to let him know of someone like us discovers his hub," said Léa.

"Maybe more than just an alarm," said Tara.

"Maybe some sunglasses people?" suggested Léa.

Tara gave her a rare smile back. Sunglasses people was the name Léa came up with for the thugs chasing them back in Uppsala.

"So maybe it's more than just a data junction. Maybe it's a spy trap," said Tara.

She reached for her now cold cup of coffee. Just as she was about to take a sip, the train lurched forward sloshing the coffee into Tara's face and down her black leather jacket.

"Fuck me!" exclaimed Tara loudly.

Several people turned to give the small, foul mouthed girl dressed in black looks of disapproval. In turn, Tara stared each one down until they broke eye contract.

37 WERFEN

Austria, Outside a Famous Castle

~ ~ ~

PLAYLIST:
"Checking On Smith / Names In Notebook" - Where Eagles Dare
Soundtrack - Ron Goodwin

~ ~ ~

Almost four inches of fresh snow covered the path up to the castle. Tara checked the time on her phone. It was just a few minutes before ten in the morning and it had been slow going from the train station, through the town and up the path.

Almost all of the castle's visitors were waiting in line for the small tram that ran from the base of the mountain up to Hoenwerfen Castle. But the line of tourists meant nearly an hour wait and Léa and Tara wanted to get up to the castle before noon.

As they climbed the hill to the castle, the snow was clearly getting deeper. The early season storm was dumping several feet of snow in the higher mountains. What had been a manageable four inches of snow in town was approaching ten inches on the pathway to the castle.

Tara was wearing her customary black tactical pants, boots and leather motorcycle jacket. Before leaving the train, she took one look out the window at the snow covered platform and stuffed her pant legs into the tops of her boots. Tara had no trouble with the deep snow on the hill.

But Léa wasn't doing so well. While her extra long, cobalt blue sweater, yoga leggings and casual loafers fit in well with everyone else on the train, her traveling gear wasn't much help on the cold, snow covered path up to the castle. Her grey and blue ski jacket was keeping the top half of her body warm. But the bottom half was soaked through and Léa's toes were going numb.

As soon as they started up the trail, Léa fell in behind Tara and tried to step in the deep footprints Tara's combat boots left in the snow. As they neared the end of the path, Tara looked over her shoulder.

"Almost there," she said helpfully.

"I'll make is," said Léa.

A few minutes later, they walked through the entrance to Hoenwerfen Castle. As they emerged into the open courtyard, a few rays of sunshine broke through the clouds. Most of the people sitting outside looked up and quietly applauded the arrival of the sunshine. Walking past Tara, Léa had obviously spotted the public bathrooms and was clearly heading in that direction.

Just a few steps behind Léa, Tara looked around as she entered the public restroom. She hesitated at the door just a moment as she recognized it as the same one she was looking at in the before and after video. The locked, iron barricade and the stairway Clint Eastwood and Richard Burton were standing by was off to the right. The doorway marked Funkraum in the movie now had the international symbol for a public restroom off to her left. One of Tara's slightly sarcastic smiles appeared as she thought about the movie people using that bathroom door as the radio room.

"Welcome to the Funkraum," said Tara.

Léa only looked at Tara and shivered with cold. She was at the sink, stripping off her cold shoes, socks and leggings. The hot water in the sink was flowing as fast as the old faucet would allow. Léa gently climbed up and sat on the side of the next sink and stuck her frozen toes into the stream of slowly warming water. She shivered once again, then closed her eyes as her feet and legs began thawing out.

"Finally," she breathed.

Tara started digging through Léa's overnight bag, found some dry socks and a pair of sneakers. Léa opened one eye and looked over as Tara pulled out dry clothes.

"Clearly my current travel clothing isn't working out for our new spy life," she said.

"Actually, you are fitting in with the traveling public a lot better than I am," said Tara.

"Yeah, but once we get off the train, there's no way to know where we'll find ourselves. So clearly, more field functional gear might be a good change for me," said Léa.

"We can't both be walking around in tactical gear. In fact, you may remember that my biker girl look may have tipped off the bad guys back in Uppsala," said Tara.

"But you're handling the snow and cold like a total, bad-ass commando," smiled Léa.

That brought the half smile back to Tara's face. She nodded toward Léa's legs. The cobalt blue sweater had slowly been inching up Léa's waist as she soaked her feet in the hot water.

"I'd say you're doing just fine with your own commando look," smirked Tara.

"Funny," said Léa dryly.

She scooped up the wet leggings and tossed them at Tara, then nodded toward the hot air hand drier by the door.

"See if that thing will dry this out," she said.

Tara snatched the wad of wet leggings as they sailed through the air as she turned to the hot air dryer. A quick punch of the large, stainless steel button produced a torrent of hot air. Tara shook out the soaked leggings and held them under the drier.

A few minutes later, Léa finally felt the circulation return to her frozen toes. She gently lowered her wet feet to the tile floor and stood up. Looking down, she realized the floor was filthy.

"Eeew," she said.

Tara looked over at Léa, then down at her wet feet. The floor really was a bit on the nasty side. While one hand continued to turn the wet leggings under the blast of hot air, Tara reached over and grabbed a wad of paper towels from the dispenser and tossed them at Léa.

"Try these," she said.

Léa soaked a few of the paper towels in the hot stream of water, then washed off a small area of the floor in front of the sink. After carefully balancing on one foot, she re-washed off the other foot in the hot stream of water.

"Wish I were tall enough to do that," said Tara.

Léa carefully placed the clean, wet foot on the clean spot on the floor, then moved the other foot up into the sink.

"It's not so much height as it's balance and flexibility," she observed.

Tara checked the leggings, decided they were dry enough and walked back over to the sinks. The drier cut off just as she arrived at the sink. With one foot on the floor and the other one stuck in the sink, Léa wobbled a bit. Tara reached out and grabbed Léa elbow.

"Thanks," said Léa.

She looked over Tara's shoulder at the closed door. Tara saw a look of surprise on Léa's face, but didn't hear anything behind her. Tara shook her head.

"Not going to get me to fall for it," she said dryly.

Léa shrugged.

"I had to try," she said.

Léa pulled her foot out of the sink and stood straight up on the small, clean patch of bathroom floor. After drying off her feet, she pulled on clean, dry socks and reached for the leggings. After slipping into her shoes, she pulled the cobalt blue sweater down and stood up.

"Much better," she said.

Tara reached down and picked up Léa's backpack. She tested the weight a few times, then looked at her friend.

"Doesn't feel as heavy," observed Tara.

"Decided to leave the DSLR and lenses at home," said Léa.

A few moments, later, the overnight bag was zipped up and Léa and

Tara walked out of the bathroom.

"Now what?" asked Léa.

Tara nodded toward the small, outdoor food and beverage counter.

"Let's get something warm to drink, then get our bearings," she said.

Léa ordered two cups of coffee and a croissant while Tara slid her iPhone out of the black leather jacket pocket. She was sliding and pinching a map on the phone as Léa handed her the coffee.

"What are you looking at?" asked Léa and she munched on half the croissant.

"Map of the castle," said Tara.

After a few more minutes of sliding the map around, Tara took a few sips of the coffee and nodded toward a stone hallway.

"That's where the fiber internet line comes into the castle," she said.

Léa offered up half of the croissant, but Tara shook her head. Léa shoved the croissant closer.

"Come on, you have to have something more than just coffee and, well, coffee," she said.

"I'm fine," said Tara.

"You're 90 pounds of skin and bones," began Léa. "Come on, we might be scaling down the side of this castle before the end of the day."

"I'm 98 pounds of skin and bones," corrected Tara.

"Whatever," said Léa.

Tara took a few more sips of her coffee. She was looking up at the ceiling of the hallway ahead. It only took a few moments before she found what she was looking for.

"See that painted bunch of wires along the ceiling?" asked Tara.

"Yeah," said Léa.

As they started walking down the cold, stone hallway, following the wires, Tara began explaining what they were looking at.

"They started building Hoenwerfen Castle back in 1075, long before the need for electrical cable runs. Rather than chip into the stonework, electricians ran cables along the wall where it met the ceiling. They pounded an iron spike into the wall to support the cables. Then the whole bundle is painted grey to match the stone work," explained Tara.

They slowly walked side by side down the long, cold hallway. Tara would look up every so often, then look over her shoulder to make sure no one was following them.

"So what's the big deal with those cables?" asked Léa.

"Those old electrical lines were installed about a hundred years ago. But the fiber cable was probably put in within the past year," said Tara.

"So we're looking for newer cables," said Léa.

Tara looked up and stopped.

"And there it is," she said.

Looking up, Léa saw the newer fiber optic cable running along side the older, painted wires. Looking back down the hallway, it was easy to see the black cable dipping out of the cable bundle and into the wood frame of a door. Léa and Tara looked up and down the hall, then walked up to the door.

"Suppose it's booby trapped?" asked Léa.

"No way to know. But I'd count on it," said Tara.

They both looked up and down the hallway again. Léa and Tara were alone. Léa looked around the door, then down at the lock. It appeared to be a simple deadbolt.

"I can unlock this, but then what?" asked Léa.

Tara unslung her backpack. After digging around in one of the side pockets, she pulled out two USB drives and held them up.

"This is a USB type one and this is a type three," she said.

The small plugs had clearly been split open and glued back together. Tara held them both up so Léa could examine them closely.

"I need to get these plugged into whatever is in there as fast as possible. So once you get the door open, let me go in first," said Tara.

"You're gonna just shove those in the first open sockets you can find?" asked Léa.

"Yep. Once it gets power, these little puppies begin copying everything they can see. They'll also map the entire network. So with any luck, we'll get a complete picture of whatever is going on in there before any burglar alarm goes off," said Tara.

"Then we get out before trouble arrives," suggested Léa.

"That's the plan," said Tara.

Léa fished out her lock pick set, looked at Tara and nodded. Once Tara nodded back, Léa went to work on the lock. It only took a few seconds before Léa had the door open and she stepped aside.

Tara quickly brushed past, found two open USB ports and jammed the drives in as fast as she could.

Nothing happened.

Léa peered around the door and looked into the room. There were three racks bolted to the stone floor. A pile of old computer gear was shoved into the far corner of the room. And that was it. No cameras. No alarms. Just the quiet hum of computer fans. Tara looked over her shoulder at Léa.

"No alarms," said Tara.

"Unless they're silent," suggested Léa.

Tara turned at looked at the racks of equipment. Everything looked like it was operating normally. Green lights flashed on the network's Cat-5 plug board. But that was it. Léa continued to look into the room, but didn't step inside. Tara walked around the back of the computer racks. After a few moments of examining the racks, she poked her head out and nodded to Léa.

"Looks like your basic network hub," said Tara.

"Hooked into a mega-high speed fiber optic line," said Léa.

"Yep. Just what you need for high speed, mega data relay junction," said Tara.

Léa remained cautiously outside the door as Tara continued to examine the various computer components stacked in the racks. As she walked around the opposite side of the rack, Tara noticed a hinged, open window. She stuck her head outside the window, then quickly pulled it back in again.

"Long way down," she said.

Tara finished walking around the computer racks, then pulled out her iPhone. She tapped on the touch screen for a moments, then looked up at Léa.

"It's almost finished copying. The network has already been completely mapped," she said.

"Good. Let's get it done and get outta here," said Léa.

Tara looked at her best friend. Léa was clearly nervous about something. That made Tara nervous because the only time Léa became nervous was when something really was wrong. She looked over the computer racks again. Nothing seemed out of place. Suddenly, Tara's iPhone beeped. Both Léa and Tara jumped at the sound.

"Done," announced Tara.

"Good. Something just doesn't feel right here," said Léa.

"Yeah," agreed Tara.

"We need to get going," said Léa.

"Yeah," said Tara again.

She punched two spots on her iPhone and reached for the two USB drives she plugged into the castle's computer system. As the first one slid out of it's slot, an alarm from deep in the castle sounded.

In less than a second, Léa swung her backpack off one shoulder, unzipped the hidden compartment and drew her small gun. She slung the pack back around her shoulder, grabbed the overnight bags and took a few steps inside the room for cover. She checked the hallway, then quickly glanced at Tara.

"What are you waiting for?" she asked.

"The second drive won't eject," said Tara.

"So?" said Léa.

"We might not get all the files," said Tara.

Léa looked up and down the hallway. It remained empty. Suddenly, the distant alarm shut off. Léa expected to hear the sound of footsteps coming down the hall any second. But the hallway remained empty.

"We're not going to stay lucky much longer," said Léa.

Tara looked down at her iPhone. It showed the stubborn drive was still trying to disconnect. She looked up at Léa standing guard by the door. Both overnight bags and Léa's backpack were slung over her shoulders. Léa stood with her back to the heavy, wood door. The gun, held at the ready in Léa's hands was all it took for Tara to make a quick decision. She snatched the USB drive from the rack and tucked it into the top zipper pocket of her black leather biker jacket.

"G.T.F.O.H.?" said Léa over her shoulder.

"G.T.F.O.H.," said Tara.

38 OUT THE WINDOW

Austria, Castle Hoenwerfen's Court Yard

~ ~ ~

PLAYLIST:
"Journey Through the Castle Part 1" - Where Eagles Dare Soundtrack -
Ron Goodwin

~ ~ ~

"Let's see if we can blend in with those tourists over there," said Tara.

"Brilliant," said Léa.

Returning to the courtyard, Léa and Tara were a bit surprised to see nothing much had changed. It was almost like that alarm had never sounded. People were still seated at the picnic tables enjoying the morning sunshine.

But the pleasant scene before them didn't last long. As Léa and Tara approached the picnic tables, the happy, peaceful mood began to change. When they got halfway across the courtyard, most everyone stopped what they were doing, turned and glared at Léa and Tara.

"So much for blending in," muttered Léa under her breath.

"Looks like we ran into a pack of sunglasses people," said Tara.

Tara suddenly turned, tugged Léa's arm and began walking toward the bathrooms. After a few steps, Tara nodded toward the locked iron barrier and the stairs beyond.

"Think you can pick that lock?" whispered Tara.

"Easy peasy," said Léa.

As they approached the old, iron barrier, Léa fished her lock pick set out of her jacket pocket. Then she held her right jacket pocket flap open and nudged Tara.

"Get my gun," she said.

Tara looked over her shoulder. Everyone was still looking at Tara and Léa. But no one was getting up to follow them. Tara guessed that would probably change once they saw Léa go to work on the lock. She took a step behind Léa so no one would see her reach into the jacket pocket and pull out the gun.

"Get ready," said Léa.

At the bathroom door, Léa took a sudden step to her right and stopped in front of the old iron barrier. She took one look up the dusty stone steps, then went to work on the rusty padlock.

Standing directly behind Léa, Tara glanced over her shoulder. It was worse than she expected.

"Oh fuck me," hissed Tara.

"Bad?" asked Léa.

"Half the fucking room is heading our way," said Tara.

"No pressure then," said Léa.

She continued gently running the lock pick over the pins in the padlock. Even though the lock appeared to be old and rusty, Léa could feel the pins sliding easily up and down as she pushed and pulled the rake. She felt Tara take a step closer, then heard the unmistakable sound of her small gun being readied to fire.

"Almost done," whispered Léa.

"Good," whispered Tara.

A second later, the old padlock sprang open. Léa carefully slid the rake and tension bar back into her leather lock pick set and zipped it into one of the many pockets of her ski jacket. Then she gave the old, iron barrier a firm tug. It barely moved.

"Really?" Léa said quietly.

She shuffled her feet, gripped the barrier handle firmer and gave it a much harder tug. The iron squeaked loudly as it slid a quarter of the way open. One more tug was all it took and Léa stepped through and onto the first of the stone steps.

Tara took three careful steps backwards past the iron barrier. She handed the smaller gun to Léa, then took hold of the iron barrier. With just one tug, Tara slammed the heavy, rusty, iron barrier closed.

"Not bad for 90 pounds of skin and bones," said Léa.

"98," said Tara as she snapped the padlock.

About half the people in the courtyard had gotten up from the tables and were slowly walking toward Léa and Tara. A few had guns of their own out. But as soon as Tara locked the barrier, they hid their guns and returned to the picnic tables.

"That's probably not a good sign," said Tara.

"Definitely not," said Léa.

They both turned and hurried up the old, stone stairs.

At the top of the stairs, Léa and Tara carefully peered around the stone corner into the long hallway. It was completely empty. They took a step back, looked at each other, looked down the stairs, then back up at the empty hallway.

"Suppose no one followed us because that's the only way down?" asked Léa.

"Either that or they have all the other ways down guarded," said Tara.

Léa looked around the corner again. The hallway remained deserted.

"Let's check this floor out. Maybe we'll find another way," she said.

Stepping around the corner and into the hallway, Léa and Tara stood back to back waiting for something to happen. Both ends of the long, stone corridor remained empty. After a few more moments of nothing happening, Léa nudged Tara's back with her elbow.

"Which way?" she asked.

"Let's try this way," said Tara.

Léa turned as Tara started walking down the hallway. Whenever she came to a door, Tara tried the handle. Most of the doors were locked, but a few opened. Tara glanced inside each room. A few were completely empty, one was a small bathroom and one was filled with junk no one had time to throw out.

As Léa and Tara stepped out of the junk room and back into the hall, a door suddenly opened and five very large and heavily armed guys appeared in the corridor. They immediately began shouting orders at Léa and Tara to drop their guns.

"Fuck that," said Tara.

They slowly began backing away from the guards when Léa heard something over her shoulder. She glanced over her shoulder just as five more guards stepped off the stone stairway and into the hallway.

"Fuck that too," said Léa.

Hearing her best friend throw out the 'f' word brought a brief, half smile to Tara's face. But it quickly disappeared as the guards at the other end of the hallway continued ordering them to drop their guns.

There were now guards at both ends of the hallway. Even the stone stairway exit was now cut off. At the same time, Léa and Tara nudged each other and nodded toward the junk room. They took two steps toward the door and disappeared inside.

"There's no lock," said Tara as the door slammed shut.

"Look up," said Léa.

The medieval version of a dead bolt was attached near the top of the door. As Tara reached up to slide the heavy, iron bolt into place, she saw why it was higher on the door than expected.

"Looks like someone else was trapped in this room before," said Tara.

Several large chunks of stone were missing from lower down on the door frame. But it was the four empty bolt holes on the door that left the best clue where the old dead bolt originally was.

"Wonder how long it took those old bad guys to break through this door?" asked Tara.

"We won't be here long enough to find out," said Léa.

She was over at the small window across from the door trying to get the old, rusty latches to open. After tugging on it unsuccessfully, she turned and began scanning the pile of junk in the middle of the room.

"What are your looking for?" asked Tara.

"Anything I can use to knock that latch open," said Léa.

Tara rummaged through the pile. She pulled a book end out, weighed in her hands, then tossed it back on the pile. Léa found an old hammer, but the wood handle snapped as she tapped it on the floor. Then Tara pulled a black iron fireplace poker from the pile.

"Try this," she said.

Léa jammed the poker under the latch and into the wood frame around the window. All it took was one tug and the rusty window latch snapped open.

"Perfect," said Léa.

She pushed the window open and carefully leaned outside. Looking down, Léa realized they were more than three floors up from the base of the castle. The rescue rope she pulled from her backpack wouldn't reach to the ground.

"Got your throw rope?" asked Léa.

When Tara didn't say anything, Léa looked over her shoulder. Her best friend was already holding out the small blue bag that held her rescue rope. Léa smiled.

"You did the math?" she asked.

"Yep. We're over three stories up. Too far for just one rope," said Tara.

Léa tied one end of her rope to the iron window and gave it several firm tugs. Tara attached the other end of Léa's rope to her's, then tossed them both out the window. Seconds later, Léa slung her overnight bag over her backpack and crawled through the window. Tara leaned out as Léa's smiling face inched below the edge of the window.

"What was that you were saying earlier about crawling down the side of the castle?" quipped Tara.

Léa looked up as Tara crawled out the window and began inching down the rope.

"I think that's the same window the two movie stars climbed through in the movie Thomas gave us," observed Léa.

"Easier going down, than climbing up," said Tara.

"Too bad we don't have time to take a selfie for Thomas," said Léa.

Léa continued inching down the rope. Tara stopped and began fidgeting with one of the inside pockets in her black leather jacket. A few moments later, she twisted halfway around and looked down.

"How about a big, cheesy smile?" said Tara.

Tara had pulled out her iPhone and was pointing it's camera down at Léa. Tara snapped a picture as Léa looked up in total disbelief.

"Now give us your killer smile that melts all the guy's hearts," said Tara.

"We really don't have time for this," said Léa.

"Sure we do," said Tara.

"They could be breaking that door down right now," said Léa.

"That iron latch will hold them back until next Tuesday. Now smile," ordered Tara.

The smile she got was a mix of sarcasm and impatience.

"And they call me the cranky one," said Tara.

She twisted around even more, held the camera out at arm's length and snapped a selfie with the castle window over her shoulder. Then, as fast as her iPhone appeared, it was safely zipped up in Tara's jacket.

About a minute later, Léa and Tara's feet touched the rocky base of the old castle. They paused to look up the side of the castle they had just repelled down. The two friends looked at each other, smiled, then disappeared into the woods.

39 FALSE TRAIL

Werfen, Austria

Several hours later and several miles down the road from Burg Hoenwerfen, Léa and Tara found a nearly deserted coffee shop. The fresh snow made the hike down the side of the hill from the castle to the roadway slow going. Just like the trip up the hill, the trip down left Léa soaking wet and chilled to the bone.

Léa and Tara passed up several coffee shops and other places they could stop, dry off and warm up. Even with the cold, soaking wet leggings, Léa would always press on, wanting to get as far away from the castle as possible. As she was about to pass on another shop, Tara grabbed her elbow and steered her inside.

"We're far enough for now and you're freezing," said Tara.

After picking up coffee and food, Léa and Tara slid into a booth near the shop's back door. But it wasn't just a good strategic spot. The booth was also next to a small electric space heater. Léa slid in closest to the wall, looked up to see if anyone was watching, then began stripping off her wet shoes, socks and leggings.

"When we get back to Stromness, you're going to help me choose better mission clothes," said Léa.

Tara just shook her head as she pulled the two jump drives she jammed into in the old castle's computer hub out of her pocket. After pulling her laptop out of her backpack, Tara dug around in one of the side pockets until she pulled out a small black box. It only had a few LED lights and several USB sockets. One socket was green, the rest were red.

"What's that?" asked Léa.

Tara held up the small box and plugged one of the jump drives into a red USB socket. Then she pulled a small USB cable out of her backpack and plugged it into the green socket. As the laptop powered up, she plugged everything into one of the Mac's USB ports. The small LED lights on the box immediately began flashing green, then slowly started flashing red.

"This is a bug trap. It lets us look at what's on the drive, but won't let anything get out," explained Tara.

"And those red lights?" asked Léa.

"That just confirms that there are bugs trying to get out," said Tara.

"Bugs? You mean viruses?" asked Léa.

"Not necessarily. Probably more like bots programmed to 'phone home' with their location if they've been lifted from the mainframe," said Tara.

"Oh," said Léa quietly.

She took a drink of her coffee and looked at the flashing lights. After a few moments, she reached for the wet leggings hanging by the heater. The spot near the hot air was nearly dry. As Léa shuffled the leggings around so more spots would get dry, she looked back at the red flashing lights on Tara's bug trap. Then Léa looked up at Tara as her best friend continued tapping away on her Mac. The small half smile appeared on Tara's face.

"Don't worry, I built the trap myself. None of those bugs will get out into the wild unless I release them," she said.

"That's amazing," said Léa.

As she moved the leggings around in front of the heater again, Léa's phone buzzed. She looked down at the caller ID.

"Janet," she said to Tara.

"Go ahead. This will take a while," said Tara.

"Hey," said Léa.

She listened for a few moments, then quietly recounted the events of the past few hours. Tara's half smile briefly re-appeared as Léa began whining about her wet leggings and soaking wet socks. But the smile quickly disappeared as she hacked deeper into the data she lifted from the old castle's servers.

"Well, it may sound like a dead end for now, but there may be a way to find our next step," said Léa.

She listened a bit more, then rang off and set her phone next to her coffee. Léa checked the leggings, shuffled them around again, then reached for her coffee.

"Well. You called it, right down to the hub jump and intruder alarm. Janet agrees," said Léa.

"Yeah, fucking great," mumbled Tara.

"Okay, I love it when you talk dirty," began Léa.

"This is really scary shit," Tara interrupted.

Léa blinked, looked down at the computer, then up at Tara.

"Okay. But looks like simple computer code," said Léa.

"Yeah, it's code alright. But this is super sophisticated," said Tara.

"Well, this is a first," smiled Léa.

"What?" asked Tara.

"I don't recall ever seeing you this impressed with anything before," said Léa.

Tara shook her head and pointed to her laptop screen.

"I'm not impressed. I'm scared. This is really advanced stuff. Half of it is shit I've never seen before. It's like I just downloaded computer code from the Starship Enterprise," said Tara.

"Okay, so what does that mean?" asked Léa.

Tara thought a moment.

"I don't think this is the work of just one guy. Even a brilliant coder like Perry Drilling couldn't come up with all this on his own," said Tara.

"So you're suggesting we're not dealing with just one or two rogue coders," speculated Léa.

"More like a team of the most elite coders ever assembled," said Tara.

The conversation stopped as Léa and Tara took in everything they'd just learned about the guy they were chasing. It wasn't just one angry guy with a grudge anymore. The two best friends both reached for their coffee at the same time. They briefly looked at each other, then Tara looked back down at her computer.

Léa took another sip of her coffee, then looked over Tara's shoulder at the nearly deserted coffee shop. The storm that dumped the snow on the Austrian mountains had moved on and brilliant sunshine began streaming through the shop's front windows.

Her nose twitched as she picked up the scent of something burning. Without looking, she reached over and snatched the dry and slightly smoky leggings from in front of the heater.

As she examined the leggings for burn holes, Léa's mind ran over the day's events and what they'd learned so far. They had a lot of data to sift through, some angry computer bots trying to escape from Tara's trap and a cold trail.

Léa looked over Tara's shoulder again. No one was looking their way. Léa pulled the leggings on each foot, stood up, hitched the long, cobalt blue sweater up over her hips and pulled the leggings into place. As she stood, she caught Tara briefly look up.

"Okay. Go ahead and make your commando comment again," sighed Léa.

Tara opened her mouth, but Léa cut her off.

"Never mind. We've got a cold trail that we have to pick up again," she said.

"Yeah. I know," said Tara quietly.

Léa sat down. After thinking things over for a while, she reached for her overnight bag and pulled out another pair of dry socks. Her sneakers and the small loafers she wore on the train were still soaked. Léa decided the loafers would dry faster and leaned them up near the heater. As she zipped her sneakers into the overnight bag, Léa decided the plan that popped into her head when Tara first told her about the angry bots trying to escape seemed to be the only way to get back on the trail.

"So, I have an idea. But I don't like it and you won't either," said Léa.

"Let's hear it," said Tara.

"Release a few of those bots, but modify one or two of them with your pinger," said Léa.

"You're right. I don't like it because Perry Drilling and what's beginning to look like a nest of angry coders will know where we are," said Tara.

"Sounds like a fair trade to me. If you attach your pinger to a few of the bots, then we'll know where they are," said Léa.

Tara looked at the data streaming by on her Mac, then down at the little black box with the flashing red lights. The idea was a good one, but something about the plan made Tara nervous. Still, it was they only plan that made sense.

"Okay. Why don't you run it by Janet and I'll start re-programming a few bots," said Tara.

Léa reached for her phone as Tara began tapping on her Mac's keyboard. The call didn't take long.

"Janet doesn't like it either. But she agrees that it's the only way to get this show back on the road," said Léa.

Tara nodded as her fingers flew over the keyboard. Léa took a few more sips of her coffee and looked out the coffee shop's window. More sunshine was streaming in through the quickly clearing clouds. It looked like it was going to be a very nice afternoon and Léa found herself wishing she could check into some alpine hotel. She wanted to spend the day in a hot tub, drinking coffee and Bailey's. Instead, she was on a dangerous trail that she knew was about to get even nastier.

"Okay, I think I've got it," said Tara.

She spun the laptop around so Léa could see the screen. Several windows were open including a map of the world. A few text apps were open beside the map.

"Last chance to figure something else out," said Tara.

"We could sit here for hours and probably not come up with a better plan," said Léa.

Tara nodded, then clicked a few of the apps behind the map. The red lights on her bot trap stopped flashing. Then several lines began painting on the map.

"Each line represents one of the bots I re-programmed with my pinger," explained Tara.

The lines bounced from Moscow, to London, to Washington, to Paris. A few went across the Pacific to Tokyo. One went all the way down to New Zealand. But in less than two seconds, they all came to a rest.

Léa and Tara looked at the map for a few moments, then looked up at each other.

"Montana?" they both said together.

Léa and Tara stared at the map in total disbelief. After a few moments, they both nodded and looked at each other.

"Montana," they said again.

Tara's hands began flying over her keyboard. After a few moments she looked up and the half smile appeared on her face.

"Fastest way to get there is take the train to Vienna, then fly to Paris, then Chicago. We take a train from there," she said.

Léa looked at Tara who was still smiling. But it wasn't Tara's sarcastic, smirky smile. It was big and genuine.

"What are you so happy about" asked Léa.

Even Tara's sky blue eyes seemed to twinkle a bit. One of her black eyebrows moved slightly up.

"I think we may have just enough time to stop for something I've always wanted to try," said Tara.

PART 5: A LODGE IN MONTANA

40 FIRST PRIORITY, PIZZA

Chicago, USA

The small pizzeria was packed and Léa and Tara were lucky to get a small table near the back by the bar. Always the observer, Tara quickly scanned the room. It appeared to be a mix of tourists and locals. Several people in business suits were already at the bar getting an early start on their daily buzz.

"Welcome to Lou Mal's. Can I get you something from the bar?" said the waiter who magically appeared.

Lou Mal's was Chicago's famous Lou Malnati's Pizzeria on North State Street. After their flight from Europe landed at Chicago O'Hare, Léa and Tara hopped on a few trains and eventually arrived at the historic, downtown Union Train Station. The double decker Amtrak train that would take them west wouldn't leave for four hours. So they stashed their overnight bags into a locker, slung their backpacks over their shoulders and went out hunting for some of Chicago's famous deep dish pizza.

Léa flipped the drink menu over from mixed drinks to beer and ale, then back again. Tara appeared to be casually looking at her own drink menu. But she already knew what she wanted and was really watching the waiter, trying to predict what he would do. Watching and predicting was a game the two best friends played for years.

If things went along like they always did, the waiter would continue smiling at Léa. And why not? Léa was just genuinely fun to be around. Not bubbly, just genuine and fun. She also had what more than a few of the guys back at school called a killer body with just the right touch of magnetic, sexual attraction.

"Irish coffee for me," smiled Léa.

"Awesome," said the waiter.

"*Here it comes,*" thought Tara to herself.

She looked up just as the waiter turned his attention to her. The smile on the waiter's face didn't waiver as he looked at Tara. She didn't expect that part of the waiter's expression to change. The best waiters had the ability to make everyone feel welcome, like they were all best friends. It increased the chances of getting fatter tips.

But Tara wasn't watching the waiter's smile. Her small, sky blue eyes were focused like lasers on the waiter's eyes. Just as she predicted, Tara saw the slight sparkly flame of interest the waiter showed Léa disappear as fast as you could blow out a candle. It was the way it always went.

Unlike Léa, there was nothing magnetic about Tara. She rarely smiled, hardly ever laughed and her angular, small, thin body was what most men considered a zero on the attraction factor scale.

Tara wasn't shy, she just didn't like wasting time making small talk with people who would be in her life for less than five minutes. That made Tara come off as arrogant, condescending and aloof. A former boyfriend said she had all the warmth of a pissed off badger.

"Look in the dictionary for 'resting bitch face' and you'll see Tara's picture," another former boyfriend once observed.

Years before, Léa found Tara at home crying. It was right after the 'bitch face' comment. It was also Tara's Sweet Sixteenth birthday and the only time Léa could remember seeing Tara cry. Léa sat on the bed, holding her friend as Tara's body convulsed with deep, emotional pain. Tears appeared at the corner's of Léa's eyes too.

Even at that early age, the two best friends could have entire conversations without having to utter a word. Léa hated the fact that people treated her best friend so badly. Tara knew that too. She looked at Léa with watery, red eyes and smiled. They both understood what was going on. It wasn't fair, but it was the way things were. From that day on, Tara resolved to never let anyone hurt her again.

Tara looked away from the waiter and into Léa's eyes.

"Brindle Amber Ale," said Tara.

"Excellent choice. Be right back," said the waiter as he turned to leave.

"Brindle?" asked Léa.

"It's a local brew. Supposed to be toasty, malty and bitter. Most important, it's just over five percent alcohol. So I won't get too plowed," said Tara.

"I think we're done getting smashed for a while," said Léa.

"Not like that night back at The Castle," said Tara.

"Yeah," said Léa.

The drinks arrived. The waiter smiled at Léa and asked if they were ready for pizza. She picked up the menu and began studying the pizza choices.

"We'll do your Chicago Classic," said Tara.

Once again, the smile didn't waiver as the waiter's attention turned to Tara. But the disinterest washed over his eyes as fast someone turning out a light.

"Any appetizers?" asked the waiter.

"Just the pizza," said Tara.

"Outstanding," said the water as he left the table.

"What's their classic?" asked Léa.

"Deep dish sausage, extra cheese and tomato sauce," said Tara.

"Mmmmm. Sounds perfect," said Léa.

It took almost an hour for the pizza to arrive at Léa and Tara's table. They were sitting in an out of the way table, just behind the bar where they could keep an eye out for trouble.

Léa and Tara sat in silence, sipping their drinks while letting their eyes slowly scan the room. Their eyes would stop at each table as they quickly evaluated the people sitting there. It took less than five minutes before Léa and Tara looked back at each other. Léa took a sip of her Irish Coffee, slightly shook her head and laughed.

"Think there will ever be a day when we don't check out every person in every place we go?" she asked.

"Probably a good thing to do now that we're at The Castle," said Tara.

Léa thought for a few minutes.

"Suppose it's something our parent's started us on to make us better spies?" she asked.

"Absolutely," said Tara.

The minutes waiting for the pizza ticked by. They both nursed along their second pint of amber ale and Irish Coffee. Léa called Janet. Nothing new to report. Just as they were about the examine the Chicago Transit Authority map a third time, the pizza magically appeared.

"Can I get you anything else?" asked their waiter.

Léa and Tara could only shake their head 'no' as they quickly realized just how big their pizza was.

"Enjoy," said the waiter as he left.

Tara shoved the small, white plate aside and picked up her fork. It only took a glance between the best friends for Léa to understand why. Getting a slice of the deep dish pizza from the still, sizzling hot pan to the plate would only result in most of what was piled high on the pizza to fall off. The plate was pointless.

Léa picked up her fork, then closed her eyes as she took her first bite of the steaming, deep dish pizza. It was so hot, it burned the top of Léa's mouth. But the pizza tasted so good.

After using the fork for the first few bites, the slice was now a more manageable size. Tara carefully picked it up off the still piping hot pan. Léa took one more bite before setting her fork aside too.

"This is amazing," she said through a mouth full of pizza.

Tara only nodded in agreement. It took her no time at all to polish off one big slice of pizza before Tara started on her second. But Léa wasn't far behind and it didn't take long before they began cutting into their third slices of pizza.

Léa looked up as Tara took another bite. Her best friend looked completely at ease which was rare. Tara wasn't high strung, she just never seemed happy and content. Tara looked over at Léa and smiled. Just as Léa felt another warm, best friend moment bubbling up, her blood suddenly turned cold.

While smiling at her best friend, Tara leaned slightly to her left, looked over Léa's shoulder. The warmth from Tara's sky blue eyes disappeared as her small, black pupils sharply focused on the pizzeria's door.

"Fuck me," said Tara under her breath.

Without looking over her shoulder, Léa knew exactly what was happening. She, in turn, looked over Tara's shoulder toward the entrance to the kitchen.

"There's gotta be a back door in the kitchen," said Léa quietly.

"I'll go to the bar and order another round of drinks. You make like you're heading for the restrooms, then we meet in the kitchen," said Tara.

Léa took another few bites of her pizza as Tara watched the people who just came through the front door. They were still scanning the crowd, but apparently hadn't spotted Léa and Tara. Léa took another bite of her pizza.

"They could have at least waited until we finished," groused Léa.

"Doesn't look like they've spotted us yet," said Tara.

"Then finish up," said Léa through a mouth full of pizza.

Tara's half smiled appeared as she picked up another slice of deep dish pizza. The two best friends managed to polish off about half the pizza before Tara looked toward the door. There was genuine surprise on her face. Enough surprise, that Léa turned to look over her shoulder. She looked back at Tara.

"They're gone?" she asked.

Tara looked off to the side, her head tilted just slightly as she tried to figure out what happened. She began to shake her head slowly from side to side.

"There's no way they could have missed us," said Tara.

"Maybe they were looking for someone else?" ventured Léa.

"Nope. I recognized one of them from Uppsala," said Tara.

Léa thought about that a few moments.

"Maybe they just really suck at being secret agents?" smiled Léa.

Tara's half smile appeared as she took another bite of pizza.

"It might appear that we've been pretty lucky so far. But I'm not so sure we're really all that lucky," she said.

Tara was about to take another bite, when the slice of pizza stopped halfway to her mouth. She set the slice back down on the still hot pizza pan.

"What now?" asked Léa quietly.

"Yeah. We're not that lucky," said Tara.

Léa put her slice of pizza down too. After thinking about it for a few moments, the two best friends began talking.

"They did spot us," said Léa.

"They're out there waiting for us now," said Tara.

"Think we can get out the back way?" asked Léa.

"They probably have that covered too," said Tara.

"Then we're gonna need some kind of distraction to get out of here," said Léa.

Tara looked around the packed pizzeria. She looked back at the door, then at the hallway that lead to the bathrooms. A door behind the bar led to the kitchen.

"One distraction coming up," said Tara.

She reached for her backpack, pulled out her laptop and began tapping away on the keys. Léa watched as her friend's fingers flew across the keyboard. A few minutes later, Tara shut the lid, stuffed her Mac back in the backpack and picked up her next slice of pizza.

"We've got about five minutes before our distraction arrives," said Tara.

"What did you do?" asked Léa.

Tara smiled and took another bite of pizza.

41 ON THE RUN

Table 16, Lou Malnati's Pizza, Chicago

After a few more minutes of eating pizza, Tara got up and went to the bar with two empty drink glasses. Looking over her shoulder, she scanned to room looking for 'sunglasses people'. To her amazement, she didn't spot anyone suspicious in the pizzeria and returned to the table with two fresh drinks.

A few minutes later, grey smoke began wafting through the open kitchen door. The fire alarms sharply cut through noisy pizzeria. As everyone frantically made for the main door, Léa and Tara calmly enjoyed a few last bites of the amazing pizza. Then they scooped up their backpacks and calmly made for the exit. Standing with the other customers on the other side of the street, Léa nudged Tara.

"How did you manage that?" she quietly asked.

"Modern industrial kitchen vents are on-line so a computer can maintain temperature control. I just closed them down," said Tara.

Fire trucks began arriving on the scene. Léa and Tara scanned the crowd hoping to spot the bad guys. It didn't take long.

"Sunglasses people at nine o'clock," whispered Léa.

Tara casually glanced over Léa's shoulder. Sure enough, a group on-lookers who didn't look like locals or tourists were scanning the crowd. There were five of them and had clearly spotted Léa and Tara. They were slowly pushing their way through the crowd, getting closer and closer.

A few more police cars arrived and the cops began pushing everyone down the street and away from the pizzeria. That slowed things down for the 'sunglasses people', but not much. Léa looked over her shoulder as one of Chicago's famous 'L' Trains rumbled by a few blocks away.

"Coast is clear behind us. Mad dash or discreet exit?" she asked.

Tara slipped her other arm through the backpack strap and cinched it down tight against her back.

"I'd say discreet exit. For now," said Tara.

Léa tightened her own backpack straps. As the police slowly pushed the crowd down the block, Léa and Tara moved casually along until they reached the corner. Traffic on State Street was blocked off because of the fire trucks, but it was bumper to bumper on Elm. Léa and Tara turned the corner and started heading west.

As they crossed Dearborn Street, Léa casually looked over her shoulder. The busy downtown Chicago sidewalk was jammed with people, but it didn't take Léa long to spot what she was looking for.

"Looks like three 'sunglasses people' are still behind us." she said.

"Just three?" asked Tara.

"Yep," said Léa.

"There were at least five back at Lou Mal's," said Tara.

"So they've spit up and may be trying to get in front of us," said Léa.

Tara scanned the crowd as they passed Beakman Place. A couple of tourist busses were blocking the road and traffic was at a standstill. Tara glanced over her shoulder.

"Our train outta here is to the south and I'm guessing the 'sunglasses people' know that. So how about if we change things up and turn north?" said Tara.

"Think maybe we can duck in between those busses and shake these guys?" asked Léa.

"Yeah. As soon as we get between the busses, make a mad dash for the next block and head north," said Tara.

"Sounds good," said Léa.

It only took about five more steps before Léa and Tara suddenly stepped off the curb and in between the two tourist busses. Walking between the busses was a tight fit. The first thing Léa noticed was the roar and heat of the diesel engine idling just inches from her right shoulder. Almost immediately, Léa and Tara started coughing as their lungs filled with diesel exhaust.

Looking to her left, Léa looked up as the expression on the second bus driver's face turned from surprise to seeing two young women trying to squeeze in between two monster sized busses, to annoyance that anyone would be that stupid. He was about to lean on his horn, when Tara looked up and gave him one of her rare, full, devastating smiles. That stopped the driver from blasting his horn, A few steps later, and still coughing from the exhaust fumes, Léa and Tara stepped on the opposite curb. It took a few moments to clear the smoke out of their lungs. Tara shook her head as she coughed.

"This is no good," she wheezed.

"But we've gotta get moving," said Léa.

Still coughing, they forced themselves to continue walking west. It didn't take long before they came to the corner of Elm and Beakman Place. Without saying a word, Léa and Tara suddenly made a hard right turn and began jogging north. They coughed a few more times as they exhaled the last of the diesel fumes.

"Let's never get that close to the back side of a bus again," suggested Léa.

Tara just nodded in agreement as she scanned the road ahead. Traffic seemed heavier on the road they were approaching. As they emerged from the shadow of the two buildings that lined Beakman Place, Tara looked left and Léa looked right. Léa nudged Tara's shoulder and pointed down the block. A small sign with the green mermaid that was instantly recognizable around the world stuck out between a sandwich sign and a hot wings sign.

"Let's hide out in 'The Empire' for a while," suggested Lea.

"Yeah," said Tara.

The south side of the block of West Division street was lined with outdoor seating and umbrellas. Light jazz music greeted Léa and Tara as they stepped inside. It only took a few minutes before they made it through the line, got their drinks and snagged a few seats back in the corner.

"How long should we hang out here?" asked Léa.

Tara thumbed the home button on her iPhone.

"We've got a few hours before the train leaves. So I think we could give it at least twenty minutes," suggested Tara.

"Sounds good," said Léa.

Sitting in silence, Léa and Tara sipped their drinks as they watched people come and go from the corner coffee shop. Every few minutes, they would scan the people passing by, heading east and west on the busy street.

Léa took another sip of her coffee, then reached for one of the hidden pockets on her backpack. After fidgeting with the zipper, she let it go and wrapped her fingers around the paper cup. Tara sipped her own coffee while keeping an eye on the crowd passing by the window. Out of the corner of her eye, she caught Léa reaching for the zipper.

"Outta Bailey's?" asked Tara.

"No. Just don't want any right now. Not while we're being chased by sunglasses people," said Léa.

"You're not worried about this are you?" asked Tara.

"A little," said Léa.

"We'll be fine," said Tara.

"I'm beginning to think all this is a lot bigger than just pissed off little Perry and a few bad guys," said Léa.

"What are you thinking?" asked Tara.

Léa paused a moment and looked down at the black cup of coffee she cradled in her hands. She glanced at Tara, then looked out the window into the street.

The slight, half smile briefly appeared on Tara's face as she took a sip of her own cup of deep, black coffee. Léa was collecting her thoughts. It only took a few seconds, but Tara knew when her best friend paused to carefully consider her next words, Léa would invariably come up with something brilliant, concise or funny. Usually, it was all three.

"First off, where did little Perry get the kind of money for a state of the art hacking operation, sophisticated mirror computer sites around the world and fairly well equipped, multiple goon squads?" ventured Léa.

The half smile briefly appeared again on Tara's face. Léa's question was brilliant, concise and funny. But it wasn't just the words. Léa's cool voice and slightly upper class accent common in south England gave her best friend's words the kind of urgency and credibility as only the accent of the U.K. could.

"Yeah. I'm thinking the same thing," said Tara.

Like her best friend, when Tara spoke, her voice and accent commanded attention too. But any similarity stopped there. Tara's voice was unusually deep and smokey for such a small woman. To outsiders, her British accent sounded like every other accent of the U.K.

But there were differences. Léa's accent was sometimes referred to as BBC English while Tara's was more Multicultural London English. But it wasn't just the quality of the voice or the accent. When Léa and Tara had something to say, their words commanded attention.

"Second, why is all this happening? I understand Perry is pissed at The Castle, but this is starting to look like more than just one guy's temper tantrum," said Léa.

"Castle's been around for a lot of years. I'm pretty sure they've left a trail of angry, busted up bad guys looking for some payback," agreed Tara.

"Suppose Perry stumbled on a nest of angry, wanna-be dictators?" asked Léa.

"More like the 'sunglasses people' found Perry and are letting him be their public face," said Tara.

"Um. Speaking of sunglasses people," said Léa.

Tara followed Léa's gaze out the window as two people started walking toward the front entrance to the coffee shop. Tara looked at Léa and nodded to the door behind the coffee shop's counter. They casually slipped off the coffee bar stools, scooped up their backpacks and quietly walked behind the counter and into the back storeroom.

"Hey! You two can't be back here," said a stern voice.

A younger man and a middle aged woman stopped stocking shelves and stood between Léa, Tara and the back door. Tara was about the say something, but Léa cut her off.

"Sorry. But her ex-boyfriend just came in the front door. He's really bad news," Léa said.

The woman and man briefly looked at each other, then over Tara and Léa's shoulders into the shop. It wasn't hard to spot a big, bad guy wearing sunglasses who'd just entered. The man and woman looked at each other again, nodded and went back to stocking shelves.

"Be our guest," said the woman pointing to the back exit.

"Thanks," smiled Léa.

As the back door to the coffee shop closed behind them, Léa and Tara found themselves in a narrow alley lined with dumpsters and very big bags full of smelly trash. Léa looked down at her half full cup of coffee and scrunched up her nose. The coffee went into a half open dumpster as she turned and started picking her way through the alley clogged with trash.

The narrow alley opened up into a slightly larger alley, big enough to drive a small truck through. Léa and Tara briefly looked to their right and busy Division Street.

"That takes us back to the front door of the coffee shop and probably more sunglasses people," said Léa.

"Time we started heading south anyway," said Tara.

A few minutes later, they emerged onto Elm Street. A tan high-rise apartment building was directly across the street. Looking east, Tara and Léa were a bit startled to see what was coming their way.

"How many 'sunglasses people' are there in Chicago?" asked Léa.

"Too fucking many," groused Tara.

They immediately turned right and began heading west. After walking a few blocks, they came to Chicago's famous La Salle Street. A small church and a tree lined courtyard with a winding path lay before them.

"Let's see if we can loose them on that path," suggested Léa.

After crossing the busy four lane city street, Léa and Tara walked past the church, around a tree and down another path. For a few moments, they were out of sight of the two guys following them.

"Maybe we can loose them around the back of the church," said Léa.

As they turned the corner behind the church, a small road with cars parked along each side lay before them. Realizing they were still out of sight of their perusers, Léa and Tara took off down the small side street. But they didn't get very far. A large man in a black suit and wearing mirrored sunglasses suddenly emerged from between two buildings and grabbed one of Léa's arms.

"Got one of 'em! Over here," shouted the man.

Léa cried out in pain as the man's vice like fingers tightened around her arm. She struggled to get free, but the big guy's fingers only held on tighter. She tried to reach for one of the pockets on her backpack, but there was no way Léa could get to her hidden gun. Then, like magic, the man's fingers loosened and he staggered away from Léa.

With lightning speed, Tara stepped around her friend, stood directly in front of the man and delivered two brutally accurate punches to his face. Then, Tara turned her back on the man and looked over her shoulder. As blood poured from the man's mouth and nose, She glanced at her best friend, her eyes blazing with a calm, but savage force that startled even Léa. Turning slightly to one side and leaning back on one foot, Tara delivered a side kick to the man's abdomen that sent him sprawling back into the alley he had suddenly appeared from.

"You can clear the cobwebs later. We gotta get going," smiled Tara.

She grabbed Léa's hand and they took off running down the small side street and disappeared into the tree lined pathways of a large apartment complex.

Léa's brain was still trying to process the events of the last few seconds. Despite Tara's small, skinny appearance, Léa knew her best friend was a lot stronger than she looked. But the lightning speed and savagery of Tara's attack left Léa's head spinning.

"I've had some self defense training over the past year," said Tara sensing Léa's confusion.

"Yeah. I guess," said Léa.

They made their way through the apartment complex, passing several people on the pathways. None of them appeared threatening, until the path ended at the apartment's parking lot. Three big guys stepped out of a black Mercedes and looked directly at Léa and Tara.

"Whoa! More 'sunglasses people," said Tara.

"They're making it harder for us to make our discreet exit," observed Léa.

"Fuck the discreet exit. It's time for a mad dash," said Tara.

She took off running full speed, heading directly toward the black car and big guys wearing sunglasses. Not sure what to do, Léa quickly took off, closely following her friend. As they approached the car, Tara turned her head slightly and spoke softly over her shoulder.

"Small hole in the fence to the left," she said.

"Got it," said Léa.

The 'sunglasses people' were clearly caught off guard as the two young women they were supposed to capture suddenly charged directly at them. At the last moment, Léa and Tara side-stepped around the three guys and their big, black car. The three men turned in time to see Léa and Tara run around a small, blue car heading directly toward a high chain-link fence.

"We got 'em now," said one of the men as they took off running toward the fence.

But they stopped a few steps later as they watched the smaller girl, the one dressed in black from head to toe, suddenly drop down to the ground and crawl through the hole in the fence. The second girl quickly followed, but she wasn't as quick as her cobalt blue sweater-dress got temporarily snagged on the fence.

Léa and Tara took off running along the fence to the south, but stopped running as they realized another fence would soon block their way. The three men wearing sunglasses arrived at the fence and quickly realized they were too big to fit through the hole. Tara and Léa looked from side to side and saw the only way out was to climb the high fence. Looking back over their shoulders, they realized the bad guys had them trapped.

"We still got 'em," said one of the men.

Two of them started walking toward the end of the fence. The third remained behind to guard the hole.

As Léa and Tara searched for a way out, a sharp, metallic whine appeared in the distance behind them. Looking back over their shoulders, Léa smiled, nudged Tara and pointed to the sky. Looking up, they realized they were standing directly below one of Chicago's famous "L" train routes.

"Remember that movie you like so much?" asked Léa.

"Oh yes I do," smiled Tara.

"Let's go," said Léa.

Léa walked over to one of the heavy metal posts that supported the elevated train tracks and began climbing.

42 HOPPING THE "L"

Chicago's Brown/Purple Line

~ ~ ~

PLAYLIST:
"Run Boy Run (Instrumental)" - Run Boy Run - EP - Woodkid

~ ~ ~

The rumble of one of Chicago's famous "L" trains off in the distance was getting louder. Halfway up to the track, Tara stopped to look down. Three more 'sunglasses people' had arrived bringing their number to seven. But none of them were making any effort follow Léa and Tara up to the tracks.

"The 'sunglasses people' aren't following us up," said Tara.

"Probably because they don't think we have any place to go," said Léa.

As she neared the tracks, Tara looked back down at the 'sunglasses people'. A few of them had their hands stuffed in their jackets, probably reaching for their guns. The rest appeared to be angrily ordering them to leave their guns out of sight.

"Anytime now," said Léa.

Tara looked up and saw Léa smiling down from the tracks. She took a deep breath and in no time at all, was standing next to her best friend looking down at the dirty track bed.

"Wow," said Tara under her breath.

"What?" asked Léa.

Tara was looking at the oily, dirty tracks. She nodded toward the third rail in the middle.

"You can almost feel the electricity in the track," she observed.

"Six hundred volts," said Léa.

Tara's eyes ran up and down the third rail, then she looked off in the distance. The line appeared to make a small 's' turn before straightening out and heading south. Looking over her shoulder, Tara heard the sound of the approaching train getting louder. She looked down at the tracks again and realized hopping on the 'L' wasn't going to be as easy as she first thought.

"There's not gonna be a lot of room up here when the train arrives," observed Tara.

"Yeah. Let's try over there," said Léa.

She carefully stepped over the electric third rail and started walking down the tracks. After walking half a block, they came to a large, metal box mounted just off to the side of the tracks. The box hummed with electricity making it sound like a hive of angry bees.

"Come on around here," said Léa.

She walked around the box and crouched down, hiding her from the view of the oncoming train's operator. Tara quickly followed. As Tara knelt by her friend, the cuff of her black tactical pants rose slightly above her black tactical boots. Léa caught the glint of metal resting just above the boot.

"That's new," said Léa.

Tara looked down at her boot and adjusted the small ankle holster from side to side. Then she tugged the pant cuff down and looked up at Léa.

"I got it from Janet after what happened in the alley back in Uppsala," said Tara.

"Isn't an ankle holster a little awkward?" asked Léa.

"Just an extra surprise for anyone who tries to knock me down," said Tara.

"What did you get?" asked Léa.

"A 9mm Shield," said Tara.

"Just like mine," smiled Léa.

"I learn from the best," said Tara.

"That holster doesn't look like it's very comfortable," said Léa.

"It's always digging into my fucking ankle," growled Tara.

"Might throw you off balance when you're running too," said Léa.

After a few moments of silence, the squeal of train wheels on tracks sounded loudly on the other side of the box. Léa shifted from one knee to the other as she cautiously glanced around the metal corner. The train had just cleared Sedgwick Station and was turning south. Tara looked around the other side of the box.

"It's not going very fast," said Tara.

"Here in the city, they only go about five to ten miles an hour around those hairpin turns. But they'll get up to sixty-five heading out of town," said Léa.

Tara's half smile appeared on one corner of her mouth as Léa continued to recite more train trivia. Just like their first mission to Sweden, Léa put their travel time to good use studying everything she could about the town there were heading to.

After observing the approaching train for a few minutes, Tara looked off to the side of the tracks. It was a long way down. Tara looked back the way they came, but didn't see any of the 'sunglasses people' who were following them. She looked back toward the tracks and was able to see down to the ground in a few spots.

"No sign of our shadows," said Tara.

"They're there," said Léa drily.

As the train slowly approached the box, Léa and Tara began inching closer to the edge of the platform. Léa snuck another look around the corner of the box. Sure enough, the train operator was keeping a close eye on the tracks ahead looking for anything unusual, like two spies about to hop aboard his train.

"We've got to move around this box fast so we don't get spotted," said Léa.

"It would be nice to avoid falling too," said Tara.

The train was almost at the box. Léa looked over her shoulder at Tara, smiled once, then began edging around the box. Everything was going smoothly until the edge of Léa's long, cobalt blue outfit snagged on the corner of the box. Just in time, Tara spotted the snag and gave the dress a tug in the right direction.

The train rumbled by as Léa and Tara edged around the box. As soon as the operator's window passed, Léa stood up and looked for a hand hold on the passing train. The first car was almost passed, but there simply wasn't anything to grab hold of. Then Léa spotted what she was looking for. It was a hand-hold and step next the the coupling between the cars.

"Next car. Two hand-holds over the coupling," said Léa.

Tara had stood up and was standing directly behind Léa. She saw the rough, metal hand-hold too.

"We can hide in between the cars too," said Tara.

The train continued rumbling past. It wasn't going very fast, but it would still take precise timing to grab the hand-hold. Léa took a deep breath and tightened the straps on her backpack. Tara tugged on her backpack shoulder straps too.

"Ready" said Léa.

"Set," said Tara.

The second car of the commuter train was almost past. Léa looked up as she took a step toward the train and stopped in her tracks.

"Whoa! No go," she said.

The two hand-holds she had been expecting between the train's second and third car were nowhere to be seen. Léa looked over her shoulder at Tara and nodded back to the train.

"We still have two more chances to catch this ride," she said.

"Here comes the next one," said Tara.

Just like the second car of the train, the hand-holds and step between the third and fourth car were missing. Tara looked down and spotted one of the 'sunglasses' people looking up at her.

"One of our shadows has returned," whispered Tara.

"Let's hope this is our ride," said Léa.

The train seemed to slow down a bit as the fourth car inched past Léa and Tara. After what seemed like an eternity, the coupling between the cars appeared along with two solid metal hand-holds. Léa took three steps toward the train, reached for the hand-hold and stepped onto the metal step just above the third, electric rail.

Tara need just one extra step to follow Léa. She looked down just in time to see the guy in a black suit and sunglasses talking into his sleeve. She turned to Léa.

"One of the 'sunglasses people' spotted us getting on the train," she said.

"Nothing we can do about it now," sighed Léa.

The train continued slowly around another small 's' curve, then actually seemed to pick up a little speed. Tara leaned out a bit to look at the side of the train. A passenger door was so close, she could have easily swung around and stepped into the cabin if only she could open it. Tara leaned back and looked at Léa.

"How am I supposed to do my "Dauntless" train hop if I can't open the doors and jump inside?" she complained.

"If only real life were just a little more like the movies," her best friend smiled.

Léa was holding tightly to the metal grip, while trying to thumb past a few screens on her iPhone. Suddenly, the train hit a bump in the tracks. In a flash, one of Léa's flat shoes slipped off the oily platform and she began to fall. Then everything went into slow motion as Léa's adrenaline took over.

She watched as the small shoe slipped off her stocking foot and landed on the third, electric rail. Léa's hand tightly gripped the hand-hold and she only fell a few inches. But the fall was enough to send the iPhone in her other hand flying straight up before it began falling down to the tracks.

Léa saw the phone falling, but her other hand was now also gripping the hand-hold as she pulled herself back up the few inches she had fallen. Her brain told her this was the last she'd see of her iPhone until she saw Tara's hand reach out and catch it. Léa looked up to see her best friend begin to smile.

"How many times have I told you that texting and train hopping are dangerous?" said Tara.

"Funny," said Léa.

Tara looked down at the phone and saw that Léa had been looking at a transit map. It showed their present location and that a station was coming up. Tara stuffed the phone in one of thigh pockets on her black tactical pants. She looked down at Léa's shoe-less foot.

"This is the second time that this outfit has caused a problem on this mission," complained Léa.

"But no one would ever suspect you of being a super secret agent," smirked Tara.

Léa switched hands, balanced on the foot that still had a shoe and leaned out to view the track ahead. A speed limit sign whizzed past her head and she quickly ducked back into the gap between the train cars.

"We're coming up on a station," she said.

"As soon as this thing stops and people start getting off the train, we need to step onto the platform and blend in," said Tara.

"Question is, do we get on the train or head back to street level?" asked Léa.

"Let's stay on the train at least until we get across the river," suggested Tara.

The train jogged slightly to the left and then to the right before coming to a stop at the Chicago Avenue and Franklin Street Station. As the doors opened and passengers began filling the station, Léa and Tara casually stepped onto the blue edge of the platform. No one seemed to notice that Léa was wearing only one shoe as they ducked into the train and sat down.

Staring straight ahead, Léa and Tara both took a deep breath, then slowly exhaled. After a few moments of staring straight ahead, Tara felt a nudge. Léa tapped the pocket her phone was stuffed in. Tara handed Léa's phone over, then pulled out her own phone and ear buds. After a quick search through her music, Tara found the song she was looking for and hit play. After a few moments, the small, half smile appeared on one corner of her mouth.

Léa pinched and dragged the map on her phone around a few times. It only took a few seconds for her to figure out exactly where they were, where they wanted to go and the best way to get there. She was about to show Tara when she heard the beat of Woodkid's "Run Boy Run" pulsing from her friend's earbuds.

Looking over at Tara, Léa expected to see her best friend's eyes closed as the music from her favorite movie played. But Tara's eyes were open and she was scanning the crowd boarding the train. Léa began scanning the boarding passengers too. Then, as the doors closed and the train slowly pulled out of the station, the short song came to an end and Tara pulled the ear buds out and stuffed them into her pocket.

"I figured you'd be lost in a movie moment," said Léa quietly.

"I was. But there's still a swarm of 'sunglasses people' out there, so I didn't want to get too lost," said Tara.

The train slowly picked up speed and continued south. Less than ten minutes later, it came to a stop at the Merchandise Mart Station. Léa and Tara kept careful watch, but it didn't look like any of the 'sunglasses people' got on the train. After a quick glance and some non-verbal communication, the best friends kept scanning the crowd. The silent question that passed between Léa and Tara was simple.

"*Where were the bad guys?*" they both silently wondered.

The doors closed and the train slowly pulled out of the station and crossed the Chicago River. Léa and Tara continued to scan the passengers. No one appeared to be keeping an eye on the two spies sitting by the door.

"Think we gave them the slip?" asked Léa.

"Only temporarily. They're probably stuck in traffic, trying to get across the river," speculated Tara.

"Or they have people waiting at all the stations along the route," suggested Léa.

"That's a possibility," said Tara.

"But not too realistic," said Léa.

"They'd have to have fifty people on the ground just to track us. I only counted seven," said Tara.

"So they're probably stuck in traffic," said Léa.

"So we should get off this train and get as far away from the 'L' as possible," said Tara.

Léa thumbed the home button on her iPhone to check the time. Then she looked at her map. They had a little more than an hour before the train that would take them west would leave Chicago. The question was where would be the best place to hide. The train rumbled to a stop at the Washington and Wells station. Léa looked down at her one shoe. As the doors opened, she flexed her shoe-less foot, then stood up.

"I do not want to spend the next hour hiding out in a fucking shoe store," groused Tara.

"Can you think of a better place to hide?" asked Léa.

Tara didn't say anything as they left the train. As they walked toward the stairs down to Wells Street, Tara looked back toward the train. The small half smile appeared on one corner of her mouth.

"When Janet finds out we hopped the 'L', she's gonna split wide open," said Tara.

43 THE TRAIN WEST

Coach Car 2, The Amtrak Empire Builder

~ ~ ~

PLAYLIST:
"Overnight Sleeper" - Natural Elements - Acoustic Alchemy

~ ~ ~

Léa and Tara were asleep before the train emerged from the underground boarding area beneath Union Station. The game of cat and mouse they played with the 'sunglasses people' around Chicago's famous Loop only lasted a few hours. But the chase and climb up to the tracks of an 'L' train left them exhausted.

Their only break was the half hour in Chicago's massive REI Outdoor store. After crossing the south branch of the Chicago River, Léa and Tara walked a few blocks past the train station and picked up the Halstead bus north. It only took Léa a few seconds of tapping away on her iPhone to find the perfect place to replace the shoe she lost back on the 'L'.

But instead of just picking out some new replacement shoes, Léa decided on a complete transformation from the cobalt blue knit dress and leggings to brown and green hiking gear. The remaining shoe and badly shredded leggings went into the trashcan located just outside the store doors. The southbound number 8 bus left them at Chicago's famous Union Station with less than ten minutes to catch the Empire Builder train that would take them north and west.

Almost six hours after boarding the train, Léa and Tara felt it coast to a stop. Léa inched up in the coach seat and looked through the extra large window of the double-decker train. The sign on the side of the station read: La Crosse, WI. Léa silently did the math and realized they had slept through the train's first six stops. They had just over twenty-four hours left before they'd arrive in the small Montana town of Whitefish.

"Where are we?" asked Tara quietly.

She was slouched half-way down in the aisle seat, her head rested on Léa's shoulder. Tara kicked off her boots as soon as she sat down, then pulled her knees up to her chest and wrapped her arms around her legs. Just before she went to sleep, Tara untied her shoulder length, black hair and let it fall over her eyes.

"Just pulling out of La Crosse," said Léa.

Tara fidgeted in her seat and scrunched down even more. As she settled deeper into her seat, the cuffs of her black, tactical pants inched up above her small ankles revealing the muzzle of the gun Tara had started carrying.

Léa caught the glint of black metal just below the nylon holster. She nudged Tara who fidgeted a bit, but didn't respond. Léa nudged Tara harder.

"What?' whined Tara.

"Pull your pant leg down a bit," said Léa.

"What for?" asked Tara.

"You're showing a bit too much gun," smiled Léa.

It took a few moments for Léa's comment to register. Tara's eyes popped open as she reached up and brushed her hair away from her face. Looking down, she saw the problem. After a few moments of pulling and tugging at her pants, the gun was hidden again.

"Better?" asked Tara.

"Better," said Léa.

Within minutes, they were both asleep again as the train picked up speed. Heading north-west, the Empire Builder followed the meandering Mississippi River through Wisconsin. As the train crossed into Minnesota, it stoped briefly in small town of Winona. A family of four boarded the train. As they walked to their seats, Tara opened one eye and looked them over through her tangled, black hair. The family sat down a few seats away from Léa and Tara.

About an hour later, the train lurched to a stop, shaking Léa and Tara out of their nap. The sign on the fully restored, vintage train station read, Red Wing, MN. About ten more passengers boarded the train. The new passengers included another large family and two overweight guys who appeared to have already spent too much time at some local bar.

As the train pulled out of the station, a few of the kids began playing hide and seek. The two drunk guys started arguing about politics. The general noise level in the cabin increased to the point that sleep would now be impossible.

The train picked up speed. Léa and Tara inched up in their seats and tried to enjoy the view of the passing Minnesota countryside. But the noise in the cabin kept getting louder as the argument between two drunk guys grew more heated. Léa and Tara looked at each other, sadly shook their heads and rolled their eyes at the same time.

"Perhaps now would be a good time for you to announce that you're starving," said Tara.

"Actually, I'm still kinda full from all that pizza. But a quiet snack might be nice," said Léa.

"Good news is, there's a snack bar a few cars behind us. Bad news is we have to walk past Drunk and Obnoxious back there," sighed Tara.

"I think we can handle those two," said Léa as she stood up.

As it turned out, 'Drunk and Obnoxious' as Tara named them, never looked up as Léa and Tara walked by. The snack bar was three coach cars away on the lower level of the long train's lounge car. Settling down in a corner booth, Léa began sipping her coffee and stared out the window at the passing country side. After a few more sips of coffee, she looked at Tara.

"Have you noticed how the 'sunglasses people' always seem to know where we are?" asked Léa quietly.

"Way too many times for it just being a coincidence," observed Tara.

"And no one is as lucky as they are," said Léa.

Léa turned back to the window. Tara pulled out her laptop, tapped a few buttons and began slowly scrolling through pages of data. After a few minutes, Léa looked over Tara's shoulder, then reached for her backpack.

"Finally," she said under her breath.

"Been waiting for the snack bar lady to look away?" asked Tara without looking up from her computer.

"Took her long enough," said Léa.

In less than five seconds, Léa's hand disappeared into one her backpack's secret compartments and emerged with a mini bottle of Bailey's. The bottle was quickly opened and emptied into the coffee cup before it sailed through the air and landed noiselessly in a nearby trash can. Tara glanced over her shoulder at the trashcan. As she turned back to the computer screen, the small, half smile appeared on one corner of her mouth as she briefly held up eight fingers.

"Only an eight? That was a perfect ten," whined Léa.

Tara's half smile briefly appeared again as she continued scrolling through pages and pages of data. Léa turned back to the window. She briefly closed her eyes and enjoyed a long whiff of her now fully loaded coffee's aroma. She glanced at the time on her iPhone as farmland was slowly being replaced with homes and shopping centers of St. Paul's suburbs.

"I don't think it's us," said Tara.

"Not us?" said Léa.

"Nothing like a pinger appears to be attached to our Macs or phones," said Tara.

She closed the lid of her laptop and reached for the black coffee sitting in the middle of the table. After taking a sip of the not-so-hot coffee, Tara nodded toward the window.

"Where are we?" she asked.

"Coming into St. Paul," said Léa.

"Great," sighed Tara. "Another twenty hours."

"It's not so bad," said Léa.

"It's just getting too crowded and too noisy back in our coach," complained Tara.

The train began slowing more as it rounded the last turn before sliding into the St. Paul train station. The platform was packed with more passengers waiting to head west. Tara and Léa scanned the crowd as the train silently rolled to a stop.

They were only able to scan the crowd for about a minute before two big guys wearing black suits stood directly in front of their window. They stood back to back, clearly keeping a eye on the train's exit doors. As the men scanned the crowd, the muzzle of a very large gun appeared just under his black suit jacket.

"I think now would be a great time for one of your classic 'fuck me' comments," said Léa as she quickly turned her back to the window.

"You said it," said Tara.

She began stuffing her laptop into her backpack as she started sliding out of the booth. Léa gently pulled her backpack over her shoulders and she slid away from the window.

"We need a place to hide right now," said Léa.

"We've got two bathrooms down here," observed Tara.

"First place they'll look," said Léa.

"But that one is out of order," said Tara.

"Okay, that one has possibilities," said Léa.

They were met by a locked door, but Léa picked the lock in less than thirty seconds. The handicapped accessible toilet was big enough for Léa, Tara and their bags.

"This won't hold them for long," said Léa as she locked the door.

Tara moved quickly to the sink. As she dropped to her knees by the toilet, Tara pulled her double edged knife out of her boot and began prying a lower panel off the wall.

Just as Léa stepped away from the door, someone on the other side tried the handle. Then they shoved the door a few times. After a few moments of silence, Léa silently walked back and gently put her ear up against the door. After a few moments, she looked back at Tara and nodded. It took only a few more minutes, before Tara had the panel off. After quietly setting the panel aside, Tara peered through the hole.

The first thing Tara saw was a very large, shiny train wheel. It was attached to the forward truck of the double decker train car and surrounded by black, greasy springs and supports. With a small jolt, the big wheel began slowly moving.

Looking down, Tara expected to see the train bed slowly moving by. Instead, there was a small two foot platform bolted to the train car, just in front of the wheels. Looking to her left, Tara saw another small platform just ahead of the other, slowly moving train wheel. Several unconnected hoses were coiled on the two empty platforms. Tara guessed the platforms held fresh water and sewage tanks.

While Tara scoped out the greasy world beyond the bathroom wall, Léa kept her ear pressed against the locked door. She guessed there were at least three 'sunglasses people' in the snack bar area. It sounded like they were in the booth Léa and Tara were sitting in just a few minutes before. After discussing the progress on their search, they changed the subject.

"You know boss," began one of the 'sunglasses people'. "Those two girls may have given us the slip back down the line and may not even be aboard."

"Naw. Our intel is they're staying on the train all the way into Montana," said another voice.

"Well, they're not in this car and the coffee sucks," said a third voice.

One of Léa's eyebrows twitched up slightly at the comment about the bad coffee. But she couldn't help wonder how they had 'intel' about Montana. She was about to turn away from the door when one of the 'sunglasses people' called out to the others.

"Hey guys. One of them carries a stash of Bailey's mini bottles, right?" said one of the bad guys.

"Yeah," said another.

"Look what I found. And I don't think they sell mini bottles like this on the train," said the sunglasses guy.

"At least one of them was here," said another sunglasses guy.

"Well they're not here now," said the first bad guy.

"Yeah? Let's see if they're behind that locked door," said another voice.

Léa quickly turned just as one of Tara's black tactical boots disappeared into small opening beside the toilet. As she crouched down by the toilet, Léa tightened both straps on her backpack and she began crawling through the dark, greasy hole in the wall.

"Careful, there's not much wiggle room in here," said Tara.

"They're coming through the door any minute now," said Léa.

Tara had crawled across the gap between the platforms as Léa inched through the hole. As she turned around, one of Léa's new hiking boots slipped off the small platform and came a little too close to the slowly turning train wheel. Grabbing the side of the platform, Léa quickly pulled her foot away from the tracks as she reached back in the hole for the panel Tara removed just a few minutes before. The door to the bathroom swung open, just as Léa gently snapped the panel in place.

"That was way too close," whispered Léa after a few moments to catch her breath.

As Léa's eyes adjusted to the dim light, she noticed the train wheels seemed to be picking up speed. She fidgeted a bit on the small platform and looked over at Tara. She wanted to tell her about the 'intel' the sunglasses people had on their destination, but now clearly wasn't the time.

"I don't think we can stay here all the way to Whitefish," said Tara.

"Me either," said Léa.

Tara rolled over on her stomach and inched over the three foot gap between platforms. Bracing herself on Léa's platform, Tara inched her head down closer to the track trying to get a look at what was coming their way. After a few moments, she pushed herself back up on her platform.

"Can't see a thing," she said.

Léa looked down at the rolling wheel, then up at the dirty side of the train car. There was a metal bracket that looked strong enough to hold her. So Léa traded places with her overnight bag, grabbed the bracket and inched her head closer to the rolling wheel.

They had clearly left the station in St. Paul as the train twisted and turned through the downtown area of Minneapolis. Suddenly, the train's brakes screeched loudly as it began making a sharp turn to the left. After the turn, the big steel wheels began turning faster. Léa pulled herself back up on her platform.

"We passed a small lake just before the the turn," said Léa.

"I'll bet we're halfway through the city. Once we're out of Minneapolis, the train will really pick up speed and it'll get very uncomfortable down here," said Tara.

Léa pulled out her iPhone and was pinching and dragging her map app. Tara traded places with her overnight bag, found a hand hold and took a look out her side of the train. It was definitely picking up speed and Tara didn't waste time sightseeing.

"We just passed a couple of sports stadiums," said Tara.

"I think we're gonna catch a break here," said Léa.

Tara traded places with her overnight bag and leaned over the gap between the platforms to look at Léa's phone.

"We're coming up on a junction where a commuter line joins this main track. Just beyond that junction is what looks like one of those trenches where technicians can work under the train," said Léa.

"Looks like our best bet," said Tara.

"It's not very long," said Léa.

"So once we see it, we jump," said Tara.

"And make sure none of our jackets or backpack straps gets snagged on these platforms," said Léa.

"That would be bad," agreed Tara.

Léa and Tara both reached for their overnight bags and patiently waited for the trench to appear. As the minutes ticked by, it appeared that the train was beginning to pick up speed. That meant they'd have even less time to jump.

Then, without warning the train's brakes screeched and the train began to slow. Looking down, Léa and Tara saw the spot where the other line joined the main line. A few seconds later, the trench appeared.

Without saying a word, the two overnight backs were tossed into the trench. Léa and Tara swung their legs off the platform. Tara nodded to Léa who jumped. Then Tara jumped. It was only a four to five foot fall, but it was enough to knock the wind out of them both.

The train rumbled overhead as Léa and Tara crawled back toward their overnight bags. Suddenly, they were plunged into bright sun light as the train cleared the trench.

"Let's just wait here until the train is a long way down the tracks," wheezed Léa.

"Yeah," was all Tara could say.

After about fifteen minutes, Léa and Tara managed to catch their breath and decide it was okay to take a look around. The train line ran along an alley way between several buildings. No one was around, so Léa and Tara crawled out of the trench and walked to the nearest road.

Looking both ways, they decided to head north-west to a larger road with more traffic. When they rounded the corner, they found themselves in a busy part of town, that appeared to be mostly warehouses. But something was different about the red brick warehouse on Broadway. The black and white painted sign that wrapped around the building brought the slight, sarcastic half-smile to Tara's face.

"Oh perfect," said Léa.

Turned out, the warehouse was a big coffee shop. Léa and Tara crossed the busy street and walked through the door to be greeted by a smiling barista and the scent of freshly roasted coffee. The sign above the bar read: Spyhouse Coffee.

"I think we just found our perfect home away from home," smiled Léa.

44 COFFEE AT THE SPYHOUSE

Minneapolis, MN

~ ~ ~

PLAYLIST:
"Warning Sign" - Scars On 45 - Scars On 45

~ ~ ~

Light rain and snow began to fall as Léa and Tara made their way to one of the tables by a big window. Normally, the two young spies wanted a table near the back and away from windows. But the coffee shop was clearly a popular place in town and most of the tables were taken.

After a few moments of listening to the various conversations around them, Léa reached for her backpack and the zipper holding her stash of Bailey's mini bottles. After a few moments, she withdrew her hand and looked down at her black cup of coffee.

"Back on the train, if I hadn't tossed my empty into the trash, the 'sunglasses people' probably would have never come through that door," she said.

Tara took a sip of her own cup of black coffee and looked at her best friend closely. It wasn't like Léa to second guess herself. A wave of self doubt showed its angry head back in The Castle's Maze and that worried Tara. She sat in silence until her best friend looked up from her cup of coffee.

"Don't even fucking think about starting to second guess yourself. You didn't blow our cover by tossing an empty in the trash," said Tara.

"But how did they even know I like Bailey's?" asked Léa.

"Look. We know Perry Drilling has The Castle completely wired. Chances are he read your file months ago and made sure all of his goons know you like Bailey's and I like dark beer," said Tara.

Léa nodded, sipped some coffee and turned to look out the window. She sipped her coffee a few more times before turning back to Tara.

"Here it comes," said Tara under her breath.

Léa closed here eyes as her head slightly snapped from side to side. When she opened her eyes, she was smiling. The same look of confidence that Tara recognized had returned to her friends eyes.

"So predictable," said Tara.

"Hopefully not too predictable," smiled Léa.

"Just to me," said Tara.

"You're right. People toss away empties hundreds of thousands of times each day. And you're right about second guessing. It's probably fatal in this business. Thanks," said Léa.

"Any time," said Tara.

"That being said. None of this feels right," said Léa.

"Yeah. It feels pretty weird. But this is not a perfect business. Things hardly ever go smooth and by the numbers," said Tara.

"They seem to know what we're going to do, long before we do it," said Léa.

"One of the things they teach in Spy School is to trust how things feel. If things don't feel right, chances are they're not and you're in serious trouble," said Tara.

"When things don't feel right, they probably aren't," said Léa.

"It's a warning sign," said Tara.

"Well things certainly don't feel right to me," said Léa.

"Me too," said Tara.

"So how do we beat bad guys who seem to know your every move, long before you make it?" asked Léa.

"They do seem to know way to fucking much about us, what we're doing and where we're going," agreed Tara.

Léa turned away from Tara and stared out the window. Without looking, she reached into her backpack and pulled out a mini bottle of Bailey's. She smiled at Tara as she dumped it into her coffee.

"One thing's for sure. Second guessing will get us killed for sure," said Léa.

"That it will," said Tara.

"But still, and I'm not being a 'Debbie Downer' here, something really feels wrong. Like we're being pulled and pushed in the direction Perry Drilling wants us going in," said Léa.

"It does feel like that," agreed Tara.

"It feels like we're heading into real trouble. Fatal trouble," said Léa.

After a few moments, Tara spoke up.

"You hear the song that's playing?" she asked.

Léa listened carefully for a few minutes.

"*I never knew a warning sign could hide and fade.*" sang Aimee Driver from Scars on 45.

"Warning Signs. How appropriate," said Léa.

"Listen a bit more," smiled Tara.

Léa looked up to see the warmth her best friend hardly ever showed. Tara's normally hard, sky blue eyes were warm. Her full smile was genuine. It was the best friend no one ever saw.

"*I will rescue you, if you rescue me,*" sang Danny Bemrose.

"No matter what happens, you and I will be there for each other. It could get ugly for us. But that's the risk we take," said Tara.

"We've got that best friends advantage," said Léa.

The song continued playing on the coffee shop's speakers as Léa and Tara silently drank their coffee. Outside, the rain had changed to snow and the sidewalks were getting icy. Léa and Tara looked back at each other as the song's chorus began again.

"*I will rescue you if you rescue me,*" sang Scars on 45.

"Yeah," said Léa.

"Yeah." said Tara.

"It's our lucky number," said Léa.

"Drink up. We've gotta get tickets for the next train west," said Tara.

On her way out the door, Léa suddenly turned back to the table, grabbed the empty mini bottle and stuffed it into her backpack. Tara looked at her best friend.

"I'm not second guessing. But I don't want to make it any easier for them either," smiled Léa.

45 DINNER AND DRINKS

24 Hours Later, Whitefish, MT

"Okay. Now we're talking craft brew," said Tara

The train was just pulling out of the station in Whitefish, Montana as Tara pointed down the street. Off to the right and down a block was the clear focus of her attention. Lights blazed brightly from a three story, glass brew-pub. At least five, two story, shiny brewing vats lined the north side of the pub. A brightly painted delivery van sat in front of the brewery proudly advertising Going to the Sun Pale Ale.

"Have we had any of that back at The Castle?" asked Léa.

"Yeah. It's pretty good for an I.P.A. But I like something with a bit more bite," said Tara.

"Okay. I'll bite. What do they have that has more bite," smiled Léa.

"Funny," began Tara. "The Big Frog Amber is pretty good."

The Great Northern Brewery Draught House was packed with people. It was only nine o'clock and more people were filtering in. Léa looked up and down the three floors of the glassed in brew pub. Each floor was standing room only. Even the outside deck was jammed. Léa was just taking a breath to speak, but Tara beat her to it.

"Yeah. I want to give it a try too. But tonight's not the night. We've got about four blocks to our hotel and there might be 'sunglasses people' hanging around," she said.

Another pub greeted Léa and Tara on the next block. It appeared to be doing about as much business as Great Northern. Léa and Tara glanced in the window as they passed and there still appeared to be a few tables open. Without saying a word, they both stopped, turned around and walked in.

As it turned out, Léa and Tara were able to snag the last available table at Casey's. Clearly, downtown Whitefish was the place to be on a Thursday night. Léa and Tara glanced at each other as they scanned the room. The non-verbal communication was pretty clear.

"*It must be twice as insane on a Friday night,*" they both thought.

The drinks arrived after about about ten minutes of scanning the crowd. It didn't look like any of the 'sunglasses people' were lurking around the bar. After another few minutes of sipping their drinks, Léa and Tara decided they could relax a bit and figure out where to go next.

"So, here we are in Whitefish," said Léa.

Tara tapped her backpack near the laptop compartment zipper. On the second train out west, she spent several hours scouring the internet logs she was able to download from the server in Austria. She had managed to snag most of the internet traffic going in and out of Castle Hohenwerfen. Her initial analysis showed almost all the data packets were directed to this small, Montana community at the base of Glacier National Park.

But Tara's data download was interrupted by the urgent need to get away from 'sunglasses people', so she didn't have a complete picture of exactly what data was coming and going and the exact destination. The best Tara could do was narrow the search to about 75 miles.

Ten minutes later, two massive Montana burgers arrived at the table. Léa got the Railway with bacon strips and cheddar. Tara ordered the Wildfire with jalapeños and pepper jack. A haystack of fries arrived in a separate bowl with several cups of dipping sauce.

Léa and Tara ate in silence. It had been a long few days, starting with being chased through a old castle in Austria, to being chased around the loop in Chicago, to being chased off the train in Minneapolis. And it wasn't over yet. Léa and Tara knew they'd probably get chased out of several more places before returning to their warm, safe dorm rooms carved into the cliffs below the old, haunted castle in Stromness.

About halfway through her burger, Léa pulled out her iPhone and began tapping around the internet. Tara kept scanning the room for sunglasses people. The two best friends continued to eat in silence. A second round of drinks arrived at the table. Léa barely looked up from her iPhone.

"What's snagged your undivided attention?" asked Tara.

"I'm looking for local ghost stories," said Léa.

"That could get us going in the right direction," nodded Tara.

"I'm not so sure. Hohenwerfen back in Austria isn't really known for it's ghost stories. So Perry and Company may be breaking away from the smoke and mirrors of a haunted castle," said Léa.

Using local ghost stories was a long tradition at The Castle stretching back to the 1940s. It had been one of Sir Richard's first ideas for protecting the secret work of his dream to build an international intelligence organization. The whole idea was to use local ghost stories to keep the number of curious explorers to a minimum and the scheme worked over ninety percent of the time. It was an idea Perry Drilling took with him when he abandoned The Castle and began his life on the run.

"Find anything?" asked Tara.

"Yes actually. Seems there are a lot of ghosts rushing about here in Montana. There are a few haunted spots in Missoula and Kalispell. There are a few ghosts right up the road at Glacier too," said Léa.

"Now that's gives me something to work with," said Tara. "Maybe I can help narrow the field a bit."

She pulled her laptop out of her backpack and began sifting through the data she collected in Austria. It took only a few seconds for Tara to set up a search for the heaviest data traffic in a 100 mile area around Whitefish. A few minutes later, she had a few answers.

"Of the haunted sites around Whitefish, most have next to no data usage at all," said Tara.

"Not surprising," said Léa.

"Except one," said Tara.

"Really?" said Léa. "Which one?"

"A hotel called Lake McDonald Lodge," said Tara.

"Enough to account for all the giga bytes Perry must be shoving around?" asked Léa.

"Only about five times the data that was coming in and out of the hub at Hohenwerfen," said Tara.

"Five times?" said Léa.

"Five," said Tara.

"Okay then. Time to book a few rooms at Lake McDonald Lodge," said Léa.

"I'm on it," said Tara.

Léa smiled and turned her attention back to her iPhone and began researching ghost stories at Lake McDonald Lodge. Tara tapped on her computer for a few minutes. After a few searches, Léa found an old story in The Flathead Beacon about the ghosts up at Glacier National Park. Stories included invisible couples arguing and a woman dressed in old-time clothes looking through windows.

"We're good," announced Tara. "Snagged two rooms up at Lake McDonald Lodge for the weekend and I got us a 4x4 Jeep rental to get us there."

"Great," said Léa.

She shut off her phone and finished off the last of her burger. Tara stuffed her laptop into her backpack and began picking at the fries. Léa looked up and saw Tara had barely touched her food.

"Something wrong with your burger?" asked Léa.

"Not really. Just not hungry, I guess," said Tara.

"You better eat something after those three pints of brew," said Léa.

"I know," said Tara.

Léa watched as Tara played with a few fries and the dipping sauce. It wasn't like Tara not to eat. Even though she was small and skinny, Tara usually polished off a large plate of food and went back for seconds. Now Léa was getting concerned. When Tara didn't eat, she was either sick or worried.

"You don't look sick to me. So what's bothering you?" asked Léa.

"I don't know. Just a scary feeling that something bad is about to happen," said Tara.

Léa munched on the last few bites of her burger. Thinking back over the past few months, she wondered if Tara's experience in the alley back in Uppsala was still bugging her. Léa didn't think so, especially after learning Tara had started carrying the small gun hidden in an ankle holster. Léa reached for a few fries.

"I know what you're thinking. But it's not about what happened back in Sweden," said Tara.

"What then?" asked Léa.

"Just a bad feeling about," Tara's voice trailed off.

"We are in a dangerous line of work," began Léa.

"I know all that. Maybe all I need is a good night's sleep," said Tara.

"Let's find our hotel then," said Léa.

As they left the bar, Tara looked back at their empty table. A shiver ran up and down her spine as a wave of fear washed over her. Léa quickly picked up on her best friend's change of mood.

"You okay?" Léa asked.

Tara looked at her friend, back at the table, then again at Léa. She was only able to shake her head, no.

"Well then, we need to be extra careful," said Léa.

Tara tried to smile, but couldn't. She knew something bad was on the horizon.

46 GLACIER GHOSTS

Lake MacDonald Lodge, Glacier National Park, USA

~ ~ ~
PLAYLIST:
"Corso" - The Ninth Gate (Soundtrack) - Wojceich Kilar
~ ~ ~

"I think that mountain goat is staring at me," said Léa.

"Huh? What?" said Tara.

Léa and Tara were up with the sun after their burgers and brews the night before at Casey's. After picking up a nearly new Nissan xTerra from the car rental next to the train station, Léa and Tara hit the the road. It took a several hours to drive from the small Montana town of Whitefish up to Glacier National Park's Lake McDonald Lodge. The parking lot was almost full, but Tara snagged a spot near the entrance.

The three and a half story mountain lodge sat facing Lake McDonald. The ten mile long lake fills a valley carved out by glaciers. It's chilly water is mostly melted ice and snow. Built back in 1913, the first floor of the lodge is stone, while the second and third levels are wood-framed. Several cabins and a campground were located around the parking lot. A large, white stucco chimney dominated the lodge's lines as it rose out the roof.

The three story lobby was lined with guest room doors, bear skins, paintings and antlers. Just like anyone entering the lodge for the first time, Léa and Tara paused for a moment and looked straight up at the ceiling, then down to the massive fireplace. Along with more than a few deer trophies, there were quite a few stuffed animals. One of those animals, a white mountain goat, caught Léa's attention.

"I swear that goat's eyes moved as we walked in," Léa whispered.

"Which one?" asked Tara.

"The white one off to the left," said Léa.

Tara looked up at the goat, then down at the check in desk. It was in the perfect spot to scope out anyone entering the lodge and heading over to the main desk. Tara nodded toward the smiling clerk at the desk.

"Come on. I'll get us checked in. You be sure to keep an eye on your goat," said Tara.

"It's not my goat," said Léa.

"Definitely your goat," said Tara.

The best friends arrived at the check in desk before Léa could continue the goat debate. Tara had one of her passports and a credit card ready to go. But she had to nudge Léa to draw her attention away from the goat.

"Come on then. Passport," said Tara.

As was becoming a bit of an annoyance, the first thing the clerk at the desk noticed was Tara's accent. From the moment Léa and Tara arrived at O'Hare back in Chicago, nearly everyone they spoke to said the same thing.

"Oh. You're British," said the clerk at the desk.

"Yeah. But don't worry. We don't bite," said Tara dryly.

"Well. She does. Sometimes," said Léa.

After some more banter about how intelligent Léa and Tara sounded and a few complements about how funny they were, Léa and Tara finally got their room keys and started for the stairs. But they stopped just as they picked up their bags.

"Did you remember your bear spray?" called the desk clerk.

"Bear spray?" asked Léa.

"Thought so," said the clerk.

He reached under the desk and pulled up two black cans with red spray nozzles. They were both wrapped in a vinyl holster with a big belt loop. The lodge's name was embroidered on each side of the holster.

"You're not in the big city anymore and we have about three hundred hungry bears roaming around the park," said the clerk.

Léa and Tara looked at each other, thinking the same thing. They both had guns and could probably handle any wildlife that crossed their path. But admitting they were packing probably wasn't the best idea. They looked back at the clerk.

"Whatever pea shooters you two may be carrying won't be nearly as effective as this if you've got a bear sizing you up for an afternoon snack," said the clerk.

Léa and Tara slung their backpacks over their shoulders and walked back to the desk. The clerk held a can of bear spray out to Léa's outstretched hand. But he held on to Tara's can.

"If you run into a bear, chances are they'll run away from you. But if one comes at you, wait until they're about fifteen to twenty feet away, then spray them, sweeping back and fourth like this," demonstrated the clerk.

The clerk swept the can from side to side, drawing an imaginary 'z' in the air in front of Tara. After a few moments of looking at both the visitors, the clerk handed the other can to Tara.

"Chances are you won't need them. So be sure to return those cans when you check out," said the clerk.

"Yeah. Okay," said Tara.

"Thanks," said Léa.

Up in her room, Léa set the can of bear spray on the small table by the door. It was early in the afternoon and she had a few hours before meeting Tara back in the lobby. Léa walked to the window.

She was in a third floor room on the north side of the hotel. Tara was in a second floor room on the south side. The idea was, they could observe more of the hotel if they had rooms at opposite ends. After looking out at the lake, she decided a quick nap might be the best use of her time.

Tara decided on a nap too. After a few hours, the two spies met in the lobby and headed over to the restaurant. After dinner choices were made and drinks arrived, Tara pulled out a hand drawn sketch of the hotel and the surrounding cabins.

"I don't think there's anything fishy going on here in this building," she said.

"Because this place is so old that there can't be any secret hiding places," suggested Léa.

"Actually, there's a lot of hiding places. I was able to download the floor plans. While there are a lot of nooks and crannies, there's nothing big enough to house the kind of internet operation I think they're running," said Tara.

"Maybe one of those cabins?" suggested Léa.

"That's what I'm thinking," said Tara.

"Any of the cabins closed for repairs?" asked Léa.

The slight, half smile appeared on one corner of Tara's mouth. It never ceased to amaze her how fast the two friends figured things out together.

"As a matter of fact, there are three cabins closed for repairs," she said.

"Which one has been closed the longest?" asked Léa.

"The one on the north side of the hotel. It just happens to be closest to the buried utility lines too,' said Tara.

"Our next stop then," said Léa.

Two steaming plates of food arrived and Léa and Tara ate in silence. The dining room was beginning to fill up. It was during the dinner hour that Léa and Tara decided would be the best time to sneak around looking for what they hoped would be Perry Drilling's computer center.

After dinner, Léa and Tara stopped by their rooms to pick up the cans of bear spray and their backpacks. Back in the lobby, Léa looked over her shoulder as they walked through the hotel's main doors toward the lake. She was sure that stuffed, white mountain goat was looking at her again.

Walking north, they passed several cabins. The first was clearly the scene of a party that was getting a bit out of hand. The next cabin was closed for repairs. It was small and the window curtains were open. Léa peered inside, but didn't see anything but dust, a ladder and paint cans.

Continuing down the path, they passed several more cabins. An older couple sat in front of one cabin and pleasantly greeted Léa and Tara. After a few minutes of polite conversation, they continued down the path, passing a few more cabins.

The last cabin was off by itself and just visible through some trees and bushes. The windows were covered with dirty blinds. But unlike the other empty cabins, this one had caution signs on the front and back doors. Walking around the cabin, Tara was first to notice another difference.

"Hello there. This cabin appears to have a basement," she said.

"I don't remember a stairwell like this at any of the other cabins," said Léa.

Looking around, they decided they were alone and quickly walked down the stairs. The locked door was easy to pick and they were inside within a minute.

Just inside the door was a long bench with coat hooks and a heavy duty grill covering the concrete floor. Several drains were spaced under the grill. Clearly, this was where you stopped to knock snow off your boots during the winter months.

Several doors lined the other side of the concrete room. A set of double doors was at the far end. Léa and Tara decided to check that one out first. It wasn't locked and as it turned out, their instinct was right. One wall of the room was lined with computer gear, the other with several work stations.

"Whew," breathed Léa.

"Yeah," said Tara.

"Think they're all out to lunch?" asked Léa.

"Hopefully," said Tara.

Tara pulled a few jump drives from her back pack and began plugging them into servers. Léa examined a few of the work stations. But the one closest to the door caught her attention. The other desks were clearly for operators running the vast network. The desk Léa walked up to appeared to be a security station.

After looking at the the big screen monitors, Léa counted at least twenty cameras scattered around the lodge complex. Each camera was labeled, one brought a smile to her face as she laughed out loud.

"I was right. That goat really was looking at me," she exclaimed.

Tara came over and looked at the camera feed Léa was pointing to. It was clearly labeled: Lobby Goat Cam. That brought the half smile to Tara's face, but it quickly disappeared. Another monitor had about ten camera feeds routed in. One was labeled: Cabin Cam. But the one labeled: Cabin Path got Tara's attention.

"Fuck me," she hissed.

Five sunglasses people were walking down the path. Léa looked at the camera, then over at the five jump drives Tara had plugged into the servers. She looked back at the camera and did some quick math in her head.

"How long do you need to copy all this?" asked Léa.

"Too long. Let's take what we can get and scram," said Tara.

She raced back to the servers, pulled the jump drives and they both raced up the stairs. The nice, older couple they had just been politely talking too was walking hand and hand down the path. Once they spotted Léa and Tara, the man reached for a gun and the woman began talking into her sleeve.

"Really?" said Tara in disbelief.

"Run," yelled Léa.

47 RIPPED APART

Lake MacDonald Trail

~ ~ ~

PLAYLIST:
"No Light, No Light" - Ceremonials - Florence + The Machine

~ ~ ~

The path ended just north of the short driveway that lead to Glacier National Park's famous Going to the Sun Road. There were several hiking trails around Lake McDonald. Léa and Tara continued to try to make their way north. They could hear traffic from the road, but they also heard voices behind them.

The further they got away from the lodge, the thicker the trees and brush. It was getting harder to move as quickly as they wanted to, but Léa and Tara continued their jog north. The sounds of the 'sunglasses people' behind them remained at a steady level, which didn't seem right to Léa.

"They're a little noisy aren't they?" she asked.

"Yeah. I'm starting to think they're herding us into a trap," said Tara.

Léa reached for her phone and thumbed the map app. But the cell service wasn't that great at the park and she wasn't able to get a signal.

They continued running north, over a few small hills. The sound of the 'sunglasses people' began to grow faint and Léa and Tara began to think they might have lost them.

Suddenly, the trees cleared and they found themselves stopped at wide creek spilling into the lake. There was a small beach on the other side of the creek, but it looked too deep to walk across. Léa and Tara turned to their right and jogged up the creek. It narrowed a bit and they found a spot where someone had arranged large rocks in the water to form a bridge for hikers to cross.

On the other side, noise from the road grew louder, so Léa and Tara turned back toward the lake. When they arrived on the small beach, they were stopped in their tracks. At least five 'sunglasses people' were waiting for them with guns drawn. Several more suddenly appeared from behind, cutting off their only escape.

No one said a word. Everyone stood still for a few moments, then one of the 'sunglasses people' stepped forward. With his outstretched gun, he dipped the muzzle toward the ground a few times. Léa and Tara gently slipped their backpacks off their shoulders and let them fall at their feet.

Then the man tipped the muzzle of his gun up a few times. Léa and Tara slowly raised their hands. The man and the other 'sunglasses people' started slowly walking backwards. The leader motioned with his gun for Léa and Tara to walk forward too. The backpacks were scooped up by the 'sunglasses people' behind them. Soon, everyone was standing on the sandy beach. Léa and Tara were now completely surrounded. The leader began speaking into the cuff of his black suit jacket. A few minutes later, a powerful helicopter appeared on the horizon and landed on the beach. The passenger door opened and Perry Drilling stepped out.

He never said a word as he walked up to Léa and Tara. Perry carefully looked them both over, then motioned for two of the 'sunglasses people' to join him. Perry held out his hand and was given a small handgun. He continued to examine Léa and Tara closely and silently for a few minutes. Then he nodded toward Léa.

As two of the 'sunglasses people' roughly grabbed Léa's arms, Tara dropped to one knee and reached for the gun holstered around her left ankle. But she never even touched her gun as Perry pointed his own gun at Tara's right leg and pulled the trigger. Perry nodded toward the helicopter as Tara fell to the ground. Léa began calling out to Tara as she was dragged away.

The minute Léa saw one of the 'sunglasses people' produce a set of high security, black handcuffs, she began to struggle violently. Even with two goons twice her size it was difficult for the third goon to secure Léa's hands behind her back. She continued to struggle violently until a single gunshot rang out. Everyone stopped and looked in the direction of the noise. Perry Drilling's gun was pointed at Tara's right leg. She never made a sound, but writhed on the ground in pain with another bullet in her already wounded leg.

"Enough," yelled Perry.

He walked over to Léa and put his face inches from her's. She was breathing quickly, her eyes darting from Tara writhing on the ground to Perry's dull brown eyes. Strangely, the one thing Léa noticed was Perry's yellow teeth and his evil breath.

"You've lost. Stop it now, or my next shot goes right between your besties eyes," sneered Perry.

Léa stopped struggling. She looked over at Tara as her friend's painful convulsions began to subside. The second shot had clearly done a lot more damage as blood spilled from the hole in Tara's already darkly stained black tactical pants. Léa's mind raced as the sight of the blood pulsing from the new bullet hole made her realize Tara might die from blood loss.

The next thing Léa heard was the sound of the handcuffs ratcheting closed behind her back. Léa's eyes winced as the black steel closed tightly around her wrists, pinching her skin. The high security handcuffs limited movement more than everyday cuffs. Then she felt a hand grab the cuffs between her wrists as she was dragged backwards toward the waiting helicopter.

Perry walked over to Tara. He pointed his gun directly at her head. After a few seconds, he looked off to the side of the gun and smiled.

"Bang," he said loudly.

Tara jumped a bit as she realized the brilliant, but evil little man was just fucking with her. She mentally went through the small arsenal she carried in her pockets for anything she might use to defend herself. The small gun was still holstered around her left ankle. But with both hands pressing tightly against the two bullet holes in her leg, she didn't have many options. Suddenly, Perry reached down and snatched Tara's gun from it's holster, then tossed it into the sand near the water. He looked back at the helicopter, then down at Tara.

"The good news is, you aren't going to die today. Unless a bear comes after we leave. But I wouldn't worry about that 'cause you're too fucking small and skinny to even make a good snack," sneered Perry.

Tara's eyes glared back at Perry like daggers. She heard Léa yell something in anger, but Tara couldn't make it out over the noise from the helicopter.

"Worried about your little friend? Well you should be. She'd going to pay for those kills she made back in Uppsala and I can assure you, it'll be long and painful," said Perry.

The taunting and pure evil of the man in front of her was bad enough. Hearing Léa would be made to suffer made something snap as Tara lunged at Perry's throat. But her badly injured leg prevented her from getting within grabbing distance. As the broken bones in Tara's leg ground into each other, she collapsed in pain.

"You really do need to get that temper of your's under control," taunted Perry.

"Fuck you, you miserable piece of shit," growled Tara.

"Language my dear. You know how the old man feels about those four letter words," sneered Perry.

She looked up at Perry as he smiled down at her. Just like Léa, one of the first things she noticed was his yellow teeth. The small, sarcastic half smile appeared on one corner of her mouth.

"*He's totally pathetic,*" she thought to herself.

She looked toward the helicopter. Both passenger doors were open and Tara saw that Léa had been shoved into a seat on the far side of the aircraft. One of the 'sunglasses people' had just snapped her seatbelt into place and tightened it so hard, it jerked Léa back in the seat a few inches. Perry started talking again, but Tara continued to look at Léa.

"So like I said, I'm not killing you today because I need you to do me a favor," she said.

"What?" asked Tara through gritted teeth.

"Simple. Deliver a message to my old friend Alan Dennis," he said.

Tara was still looking at Léa when Perry kicked her blood soaked leg. Tara looked at Perry as the pain from the kick subsided. She was determined to not cry out, but it took every ounce of strength she had.

"Do I have your attention now?" asked Perry.

He lifted his foot like he was going to kick Tara again. Her eyes blazed in anger. She glanced once toward the helicopter, then back at Perry. After a few seconds, she gave him a single, violent nod.

"Good. Here's the message. It's simple. Stand down," said Perry.

He looked down at Tara. Her eyes still blazed with more fury than pain. But a slight look of disbelief also appeared.

"What's the fuck is that supposed to mean?" she hissed.

"It means you all are way out of your league. You have no idea what you're up against. Remember, I read everything everyone writes back at that fucking castle. You are all completely clueless. Stand down now and maybe I'll let a few of you live," he said.

He knelt down by Tara and pulled out his iPhone. After tapping a few buttons, he showed her the screen. It had one button labeled: CASTLE KILL.

"Here's a demonstration to make sure you, that stupid old man and all those other fossils get the message," sneered Perry.

He hit the button, stood up and kicked Tara's wounded leg again. Blinding pain shot through her body. Tara clenched her jaw, not allowing herself to make a sound. Her eyes never blinked and remained focused on Perry like lasers.

"As of right now, your Castle is completely dark. You are all completely shut down. Tell Alan Dennis that the next time our paths cross, more than one of his junior agents will die," said Perry.

With that, he turned and walked back to the helicopter. Perry slid into the seat next to Léa and slammed the door. He looked over at Tara, then shouted something to the pilot.

The helicopter slowly rose a few feet off the ground, then rotated so Léa's side of the aircraft was closest to Tara. Their eyes met.

It only took a few seconds for the two best friends to communicate the love of their long friendship and the pain they felt knowing they were being torn apart.

The tear that formed on the side of one of Léa's emerald green eyes and the nod toward Tara's blood soaked leg made it clear she was worried about her friends wounds. The angry fire of determination that burned in Tara's sky blue eyes was all Léa needed to know her best friend wouldn't rest until she was home safe.

As the helicopter began to slowly rise in the sky, Léa briefly turned away. Not able to believe how fast and how badly their situation had changed, her brain went into overdrive looking for a solution. But it only took a few seconds to realize the truth.

The situation was hopeless.

The only thing she could do was briefly close her eyes as her head slightly snapped from side to side. Léa looked back at Tara as the helicopter rose higher. The last thing she saw, was Tara's mouth form two words.

"So predictable," said Tara.

Within seconds, the helicopter was gone and silence returned to the lake. Tara stared in the direction the helicopter had departed, breathing heavily. She could feel her pulse racing. Looking down at her blood soaked hands, she felt her skin going cold and clammy. Tara knew she was going into shock.

Looking up, Tara had to remain in control and conscious as long as possible. She scanned the sandy beach in front of her and saw where Perry had tossed her gun. Léa's can of bear spray was somehow standing upright near the spot where the helicopter had landed.

Tara slowly rolled over and, using her good leg and both arms, she crawled over to her gun. It was slow going as Tara's useless leg left a trail of blood behind her. After what seemed like an eternity of painful crawling, Tara finally reached the gun. A wave of fatigue washed over her. Tara checked off another symptom and knew the shock of being shot twice was setting in. Keeping her mind busy, she examined the gun.

It was dirty after being tossed onto the sandy beach. Tara cleaned it as best she could and stuffed it back into the ankle holster still strapped to her good leg.

Looking around, Tara thought she heard the sound of police sirens off in the distance. A low flying helicopter and gunshots may have caught someone's attention and Tara cautiously hoped that help might be on the way.

A wave of dizziness washed over Tara. Checking off another symptom of shock, Tara also suspected she had been loosing a lot of blood. As she reached down to undo her black web belt, something caught her eye near the shoreline. Someone had left a new pair of hiking boots in the sand.

Crawling over, Tara realized they were the new boots Léa picked up in Chicago. The 'sunglasses people' probably stripped them off her feet making it harder for Léa to make a run for it if an opportunity presented itself.

"Fuckers," said Tara under her breath.

Another wave of dizziness, followed by a wave of nausea hit her like a powerful ocean wave. She quickly pulled the laces from a boot and tied it around her leg to hopefully slow her blood loss.

After tying the shoelace as tight as she could, Tara inched over to a rock.

Slowly pushing herself around, she tried to sit up as straight as she could. The sound of those police sirens were definitely getting closer.

A grey fog began to form around the sides of Tara's eyes. She knew she was close to loosing consciousness. Snapping her head from side to side, Tara tried to shake the grey fog away. It worked for a second. Then Tara did something she hardly ever did. She laughed out loud as she realized she had just cleared the cobwebs.

Just like Léa always did.

Tara looked in the direction of the empty sky where she last saw her best friend. It had only been a few minutes, but Tara felt herself desperately missing Léa. She looked down at her blood soaked, wounded leg and felt her pulse begin to pick up. But this time, it wasn't from the shock.

It was an emotion she kept deeply buried and tightly under control. It was a white hot, raging anger that had scared her so bad as a child, Tara kept it tightly locked away. But there were times she couldn't control it.

Times like right now.

Her pulse continued to quicken along with her breathing. She felt her normally cool and in control heart begin blazing with raging heat. When the buildup inside finally reached it's breaking point, Tara threw back her head an opened her mouth. The sound that came from the small, wounded spy on the beach was long and loud.

"Léa," cried Tara.

But what started as her best friend's name, slowly transformed into a howl of pain.

Then it transformed again, into a growl of white-hot rage.

Unconsciousness mercifully washed over Tara.

48 JUST A LITTLE SCREWED

A Hospital Room, Seattle, WA

"She's lost a lot of blood," said one voice.

"Will she be able to walk again?" asked another, vaguely familiar voice.

"There are two fractures, one is serious, the other's not so bad. So yes, she will walk again, but not without a lot of therapy," said a third voice.

"If she survives the blood loss," said the first voice.

"She'll make it," said a fourth voice.

"It's not a sure thing. Even though she's not underweight for her size, she's still not much more than skin and bones," said the first voice.

"Appearances are deceiving. Tara's not just skin and bones. If she wasn't in that hospital bed, she'd probably be up kicking your fat ass just for saying that," said the fourth voice.

The voices Tara was hearing sounded fuzzy. She couldn't feel much either. But Tara did feel one side of her mouth twitch up in her slight, sarcastic smile.

Even though she wasn't sure who the first three voices were, Tara was nearly 100 percent sure the fourth voice belonged to Janet Austin. She couldn't be sure, because all Tara could see was a dark, gray fog. She tried to move, but only felt the side of her mouth twitch up.

"Did you see that?" said the voice that sounded like Janet.

"What?" asked the first voice.

"It's that little smile that sometimes cracks through her R.B.F.," said the second, slightly familiar voice.

"R.B.F.?" asked one of the other voices.

"Resting Bitch Face," laughed the voice that sounded like Janet.

Now she was certain the female voice was Janet Austin's. She was also practically certain one of the other male voices belonged to Thomas Austin. She felt half of her mouth twitch up in her half smile again. After that awful day the bullies in school made her cry, Tara never minded being known for her R.B.F. In fact, she was proud of it.

"Great," sighed the tired, unfamiliar voice. "Another pouty little bitch. Anyway, as far as her leg is concerned, the lower fracture should knit fairly normally. The bullet only cut through the fibula. The second fracture is a bit more complicated. It completely shattered the upper femur. But we were able to 3-D print a bone wrap and it should knit in time. Here are my notes on the wrap and some therapy recommendations. Any questions?

No one said a word.

"None? Out-freaking-standing. Then I'm officially done with you spooks and your little miss R.B.F.," said the tired, unfamiliar voice.

Tara thought she head a door open and close. No one said anything for a while. The silence gave Tara time to take stock of the current situation. Apparently, her leg was broken in two places and she'd lost a lot of blood. But she couldn't remember how all of this could have happened. It took Tara's brain a few minutes of swimming around in the dark, grey fog before her memory cleared.

The image of her best friend, handcuffed and being taken away in a helicopter by the man who left two hot slugs of lead in her leg slapped her out of the fog and into a hospital room. Tara's eyes popped open. The first person she saw was Janet. Her eyes darted around the room before returning to Janet.

"Léa?" was all Tara could say.

Janet looked at Thomas, then nodded toward the two strangers in medical coats. It only took a few moments before Tara and Janet were left alone in the room. Janet walked over to the hospital bed, sat down and took Tara's hand.

"We don't know," said Janet.

"Helicopter?" whispered Tara.

"They found it abandoned at the airport down in Missoula," said Janet.

"Where," began Tara.

"Where are you?" smiled Janet.

Tara nodded.

"You're in Seattle. It's been four days since you were shot. And no, we haven't been contacted by Perry to ransom Léa," said Janet.

"Said he's going to kill her," whispered Tara.

"Do you know why?" asked Janet.

"Pissed about the goons she killed in Sweden," said Tara.

"Oh," was all Janet could say.

Tara looked down at the tent that covered her right leg. She couldn't feel anything, but realized that was because she was on fairly strong pain killers. She looked at the tubes feeding saline and drugs into her right arm and remembered a similar day over a year ago. The day she woke up and saw Janet smiling down at her the first time. At least this time, Tara wasn't chained to her hospital bed. She looked up at Janet.

"Been here before," whispered Tara nodding up to the I.V.

Janet smiled down at Tara as she remembered the young spy's first days at The Castle. Stories of Tara putting several security guards in the hospital the minute she was freed from her Dungeon Test handcuffs had become a

Castle legend.

"Your tough as nails legend just got reinforced with those two slugs in your leg," smiled Janet.

"Léa," said Tara quietly.

She looked away from Janet and over to the big, glass windows of her hospital room. She was clearly in a high rise because all she could see from her bed was the tops of other high rise buildings. Big, fat Seattle raindrops ran down the glass as a jet airliner passed overhead on the way to SeaTac.

"I know. I'm worried about Léa too. But we've got another, bigger problem," said Janet.

Tara looked back at Janet, but didn't say anything. Suddenly, the door opened as two big guys in suits and sunglasses burst into the room closely followed by Thomas Austin. Tara immediately felt adrenalin surge through her body as two big guys with sunglasses walked from the door to her bed. Janet was still holding Tara's hand as she felt the young spy's grip suddenly tighten. Janet patted Tara's hand.

"It's alright. They're not 'sunglasses people'. Just a couple of American spooks who don't know when to stay the fuck away," said Janet.

Tara looked up at Janet with genuine surprise in her eyes. Of all the people in The Castle, Tara was one of the few who ever tossed out the 'f' word. She'd never heard it from Janet before. Tara used the 'f' word because it was her favorite word. It appeared that Janet held it back for the few times she needed something more than a please and thank you.

"You know what little lady? You're not over in your little castle in Scotland. You're here in the U.S. of A. and you're here without our invitation or even our knowledge," said the first spook.

"It's only because the Director of Intelligence at C.I.A. is personal friends with your boss that I'm not tossing every one of you into a super max prison cell. So all attitudes will be shoved up your free-lance asses from here on out," said the second federal agent.

"I'd do what he says since we hear your whole operation is now completely off-line and shut down," said the first federal agent.

"Shut down," whispered Tara.

"We've had a few technical difficulties," said Janet.

"Technical difficulties my ass. We've got reports that your whole network is totally hacked and the only power you've got back on that island of yours is from flashlight batteries," said the federal agent.

"That's not your problem. Your problem is to arrange immediate transportation for the three of us ASAP," said Janet.

"Not until you tell us exactly what your agent was doing here to get herself shot not once, but twice," said the federal agent.

"That's also not your problem," said Janet.

But before the federal agent could fire back, Thomas broke his silence.

"Before this goes too many more rounds, it might be good for me to introduce everyone. That's Janet Austin, second in command of The Castle. She's right up there directly under Alan Dennis. She has the internationally accepted diplomatic rank of a head of state. She's also my wife and the young woman with two bullet holes in her leg, is like a daughter to both of us," said Thomas.

Tara looked from Thomas to Janet. She knew her friend was high up in The Castle's chain of command. But she never knew how important Janet was.

"Nice to meet you both," smiled Janet.

"So before everyone starts bugging our very important and very powerful bosses, why don't you two get on the phone and get us a plane back home," said Thomas.

"Now please," smiled Janet.

Thomas casually walked to the door and opened it. Janet turned her back on the federal agents and smiled down at Tara. After a few moments, the feds turned and walked out of the room.

"Shut down?" asked Tara quietly.

Janet nodded.

"Totally screwed?" asked Tara.

Janet laughed and nodded again as Thomas walked up to the bed.

"My shadow net?" asked Tara.

Thomas looked at Janet who nodded once.

"Can you keep a secret?" smiled Thomas.

Tara nodded.

"Up and running. Just like you planned it," smiled Janet.

"So, not totally screwed," said Tara.

"Just a little screwed," said Janet.

49 MOVIE FILES

The Castle on the Island, Stromness

~ ~ ~

PLAYLIST:
"Into Darkness" - Into Darkness - Single - Thomas Bergersen

~ ~ ~

A week later, Tara was back at The Castle and was actually getting around fairly well for someone with two leg fractures. A pair of rigid, carbon fiber splints were held tightly to the sides of her leg with several, thick Velcro wraps. She would be in this contraption for at least a month. Depending on her progress, the medical people at The Castle told her to expect at least a month of intense physical therapy before she'd be able to put any weight on her leg and three to six months before she'd be fully healed. Tara vowed to be back to 'normal' in half the time.

Getting around was hard enough with the cast and crutches. But Tara, Janet and Thomas were worried that it would be even harder with power systems completely fried. The kill command Perry sent on his iPhone caused anything that relied on electricity to instantly destroy itself.

First to go were hundreds of desktop computers. The air and water systems fried next. Finally, the electrical distribution system overloaded itself plunging the entire castle complex into darkness.

Command and control of The Castle's world-wide operations immediately transferred to one of the nuclear submarines on patrol in the North Atlantic. It was a nostalgic moment as Alan Dennis made his way down the tight crew hatch of the old World War II era German uBoat that originally brought him to The Castle almost half a decade ago. The 90 year old commander made it through the hatch and down the ladder like he was still 30.

Rather than wait for a more modern command post to arrive back in Stromness, the old diesel sub would transport Alan and a few other department heads to a rendezvous point near Iceland where he would direct The Castle's recovery and outside communication with the rest of the intelligence world.

Once Alan was aboard the old submarine, he established contact with a few of the more friendly intelligence services around the world. The picture he painted was one of total chaos.

The British Prime Minister immediately offered the services of the U.K.'s military and M.I. 5 and 6. Alan's long time friend and head of the C.I.A. also offered assistance. Offers of help came in from France, Germany and even the head of the the Russian F.S.B. offered help. All messages received a sincere reply of gratitude before Alan politely declined each and every one.

Communications with the outside world were handled by secure text messages because secure voice communications were down.

At least that's what Alan wanted the rest of the world to think.

A plan for dealing with outside communications in case of a disaster at The Castle had been decided upon long ago. That plan was to paint a picture of total chaos no matter what the actual situation was.

There was one phone call Alan did take. It was a simple cell phone call that came in just as the old uBoat was about to dive off the Scottish coast. It was the good news, bad news call from Janet. The good news, Tara would be okay. The bad news, Léa had been taken.

"Okay. You all get home as quick as possible," said Alan after a few moments of silence.

"How are things at home?" asked Janet.

"Not great. But not nearly as bad as you might hear," said Alan.

"Roger that. On our way," said Janet.

By the time Tara, Janet and Thomas arrived back at The Castle, the chaos was about over. You could still smell the scent of fried electrical components, but the air was mostly clear. The Castle's L.E.D. lights burned brightly. Even the old Paternoster lift was rumbling along with its usual groans and squeaks.

The only real difference Tara, Janet and Thomas could see was the increased presence of armed security teams. After an attack of this magnitude, and with the world believing The Castle was hopelessly crippled, there was a real concern that some outside force might attempt to permanently shut the whole thing down.

"Welcome back Ma'am," said the heavily armed security supervisor.

Tara, Janet and Thomas had been stopped just inside the door beside the old fireplace in The Castle's great hall. The dusty old spiral staircase was brightly lit as they were escorted down to The Castle's real main entrance.

It took longer to get to the bottom of the staircase because Tara was still learning how to use her crutches and wouldn't accept any assistance. Once at the bottom of the stairs, they made quick time down the now brightly lit stone corridor. As they approached the entrance to The Castle's infamous dungeon, the hidden stone doorway slid open and they entered the main atrium. Except for all the security, things looked almost normal. As they made their way deeper into the atrium, Tara tried to break away and head to her room.

"Sorry, miss. You all are needed for debriefing. If you'll just follow me," said their armed escort.

Tara looked tiredly at Janet, but kept on limping along with the group. She only had to manage one flight of stairs before they started down one of the carpeted, stone corridors that lead to the command offices of The Castle. Tara slowed as they approached the door to a main conference room, but their escort continued down the hallway. She was a bit surprised as they were herded into the wood panel lined office at the end of the corridor. She was even more surprised when she saw Alan Dennis sitting at his large desk.

"I head you were out on a cruise," she said.

"Several of our designated decoys are enjoying the frigid waters off the coast of Iceland. Meantime, it's business as usual here," said Alan.

"So as far as the world is concerned, we're still in chaos and helpless mode?" asked Janet.

"For a little longer," said Alan.

He motioned to the over-stuffed, leather couches that lined his office's wall as he got up and walked over to Tara. He never said a word, but gently placed one of his steady hands on her shoulder. Looking each other directly in their eyes, words were not necessary. Tara knew the old man felt her loss as deeply as she did. She also knew Alan Dennis would stop at nothing to get Léa back.

Watching Tara and Alan, Janet remembered her own day, standing almost where Tara was standing right now. It was the day when the old man walked around his desk and put his hand on her shoulder. Her loss was permanent and Tara might have to face the same thing too. Janet hoped the outcome would be different.

"Let me bring you up to speed," said Alan after a few more moments of silence.

After everyone was seated, Alan pushed a button on the table next to his overstuffed leather chair. A few minutes later, a tray of coffee, water and light snacks arrived. Alan passed out coffee and sandwiches, then leaned back in his chair.

"Everyone all set?" he asked.

Janet and Thomas were able to fit polite replies in between bites of sandwich and gulps of coffee. Tara said something through a mouth full of sandwich that sounded like she was happy too. Alan smiled briefly, then began the briefing.

Everything at The Castle was mostly back to normal. The shadow network Tara and Thomas had set up was working perfectly. A completely independent hookup to the internet was supplying data outside of The Castle's usual channels giving the false appearance that Alan Dennis' intelligence agency remained in the dark. Air, water and power had been restored within hours thanks to years of pre-planning for just such an attack.

"So far, there hasn't been any kind of assault on any of our overseas assets or any hint of unusual activity near The Castle," said Alan.

"So we're mostly secure, up and running?" asked Janet.

"Totally secure, up and running," said Alan.

"Any news about Léa?" asked Tara after a few moments of silence.

Alan looked at Tara, then over at Janet and Thomas. This was the moment he'd been dreading since early that morning. There was news and it wasn't good. He looked back at Tara.

"Early this morning, a kid on a bike threw a package at the door of our safe house in Bucharest. It contained instructions for accessing a secure F.T.P. site. When we checked it out, it contained just one file. A movie file," said Alan.

Everyone's blood ran cold. Tara, Janet and Thomas's faces even turned a few shades of grey. But Alan quickly spoke up.

"It's not an execution," he said.

Everyone in the room began breathing again. But the tension remained high. Janet and Thomas were tightly holding each other's hands. Tara was gripping her mug of coffee so tightly that you could see slight ripples in the liquid. Everyone looked at Tara, who was looking at the ground.

"Okay. What?" she said after a few more excruciating moments of silence.

"It's CCTV video of what appears to be a old, stone prison cell. Léa is in that cell," said Alan.

"So she's okay?" asked Janet.

"It appears so," said Alan.

"Can I see it?" asked Tara.

Alan reached for a remote, punched a button and one of the big screen TVs bolted to the wall sprang to life. He hit one more button and a computer movie file began to play.

The camera was bolted high up on the wall opposite what looked like a steel, prison door. It's fish-eye lens showed everything in the cell except the wall it was bolted to. There was a single window in the door. A stainless steel, prison style sink and toilet was bolted to the stone wall next to the door. A thin mattress was on the floor next to the opposite wall.

Léa sat on the mattress. She was still wearing the forest green t'shirt she bought back in Chicago. Her legs and feet were bare. Tara knew they'd removed her new hiking boots back by the lake in Montana. They'd also taken her pants, coat, socks and the tan hiking shirt.

Léa's wrists and ankles were secured with old fashioned, large, heavy duty cuffs and shackles. Tara stood up and walked over to the monitor. Léa sat on the mattress with her arms wrapped around her bare knees. Dark, red marks appeared to ring her wrists and ankles. Her hair was matted and there were several bruises on her arms, legs and face.

The movie file had a time code stamp in the upper right corner. Part of the stamp read: DAY 1. The other part showed time and the numbers were flying by fast. The movie covered what appeared to be a whole day. But it was time compressed, making the day fit into a ten minute movie.

Léa hardly moved all day. No guards ever appeared at the door or entered her cell. Léa made several trips over the the prison sink for a drink of water. At one point, she appeared to fall asleep for a few hours. And that was all. Just a prison cell and Léa hardly moving.

"I guess there's no way to know where this is," stated Tara.

"No. It's just a movie file. We can't see anything that gives us even a hint of where she might be," said Alan.

"No one gave her any food," observed Tara.

"We noticed that too. Maybe they cut that out so we couldn't identify her guards," said Thomas.

"We haven't seen cuffs and shackles like those in a long time," observed Alan.

Tara and Thomas looked over at Janet as she instinctively began rubbing the scars that ringed her own wrists. A far-away look washed over Janet's eyes as long forgotten memories, bubbled up to the present.

"They're called Darby style cuffs," she began. "The modern ones are made of smooth stainless steel. But those are antiques and the metal is obviously very rough."

"Looks like they've already started tearing up the skin around her wrists and ankles," observed Thomas.

"At least they locked her hands in front of her and not behind her back," said Tara.

"They're not there for security," said Thomas.

"Agreed," said Janet. "That cell is plenty secure and it's obvious she's been throughly searched. There's nothing she could have hidden in that t'shirt either."

Tara briefly looked back at Janet. She glanced down at her scarred wrists, then back up. Their eyes met. Janet glanced down at her own wrists.

"Take it from me," said Janet. "Darby cuffs are heavy and painful."

Emotions of hopeless sadness and despair washed over Janet's face. Tara looked at Alan, then to Thomas.

"Those cuffs are just there to make Léa more miserable," said Thomas.

Tara took a step closer to the monitor. She examined her best friend's face as carefully as she could through the CCTV camera. Léa never looked up. She just stared off into the space.

"They've succeeded," said Tara.

"We'll need to examine every frame of the movie. There might be some clues we're not seeing during the replay," said Janet.

"I'll do that," said Tara.

"Maybe you should let someone else take care of it," suggested Janet.

"I can do it. I need to do it," said Tara.

The next morning, Tara walked to her workshop. People passing her in the corridors of The Castle noticed she walked as straight as she could with her crutches and splints. Only a few stopped her to ask how she was and if there was any news about Léa. After a few of those pointless conversations, Tara politely acknowledged people, but didn't stop to talk.

She was getting good with her crutches and easily managed the stairs to her workshop and quickly entered the pass code. The door slid silently open. After pouring a cup of coffee, Tara logged on to her computer and began carefully examining the movie file she saw the day before.

Half an hour later, a notification window popped up on one of the screens in front of Tara. She quickly ran it through her bug scanner. When she was sure it was clean, she opened it and found it was a new CCTV file from Léa's prison cell.

Just like the day before, Léa sat in the corner of her cell and hardly moved. She sat very still, hugging her knees. But the circles under her eyes appeared to be getting deeper as she stared off into the distance.

Tara only took a moment to look at her friend in the video before she began analyzing every frame of the new file.

TARA'S PLAYLIST

Music is almost always playing whenever I'm writing. Here is the complete playlist for Castle in the Mountains. Most every track is available on iTunes or as a CD on Amazon.

"Waking UP" - Oblivion - M83
"Choosing Dauntless" - Divergent - Junkie XL (feat. Ellie Goulding)
"Science" - Miracles - Two Steps From Hell
"Sun Gazer" - Miracles - Two Steps From Hell
"Rain" - Reach for Glory - Blackmill
"Blizzard" - Skyworld - Two Steps From Hell
"Jupiter" - Voices in My Head - Celldweller
"Fearless" - Sun - Thomas Bergersen
"Piano Prelude" - The Spy Who Came In from the Cold - Sol Kaplan
"Aura" - Illusions - Thomas Bergersen
"The Ascent " - Pulse of Life - Futureworld Music
"From Zero to Galactic Hero" - Other Worlds - Really Slow Motion & Instrumental Core
"Checking On Smith / Names In Notebook" - Where Eagles Dare Soundtrack - Ron Goodwin
"Journey Through the Castle Part 1" - Where Eagles Dare Soundtrack - Ron Goodwin
"Run Boy Run (Instrumental)" - Run Boy Run - EP - Woodkid
"Overnight Sleeper" - Natural Elements - Acoustic Alchemy
"Warning Sign" - Scars On 45 - Scars On 45
"Corso" - The Ninth Gate (Soundtrack) - Wojceich Kilar
"No Light, No Light" - Ceremonials - Florence + The Machine
"Into Darkness" - Into Darkness - Single- Thomas Bergersen
"Scars" - Allegiant Soundtrack- Tove Lo

LÉA'S LINKS

The Paternoster Lift - https://en.wikipedia.org/wiki/Paternoster

Hohenwerfen Castle - http://en.wikipedia.org/wiki/Hohenwerfen_Castle

Where Eagles Dare: Then and Now - https://www.youtube.com/watch?v=4i2qIXCNaVk

Spyhouse Coffee: https://spyhousecoffee.com

Flathead Beacon - Many Glacier Hotel Haunted: http://flatheadbeacon.com/2016/10/25/glaciers-haunted-history/

Mykonos Theoxenia - Léa and Tara's favorite hotel in The Aegean: https://mykonostheoxenia.com/en/

Léa and Tara on Facebook - www.facebook.com/TheCastleEbooks

Léa and Tara on Twitter - www.twitter.com/TDsSpyStory

Léa and Tara's webpage - www.fstopespresso.com

EPILOGUE: AN UNUSUAL MEETING

The Castle

~ ~ ~

PLAYLIST:
"Scars" - Allegiant Soundtrack- Tove Lo
~ ~ ~

Days stretched into a week. After examining each frame of the video that arrived daily, Tara got herself down to the fifth level of The Castle and checked in with the doctors. Her leg was healing fast and they told her to begin preparing for the intense and painful therapy that would begin sooner rather than later.

After her doctor visit, Tara made her way down the stairs to her room at the end of the long corridor. She tried to ignore the door to Léa's room. But it was a twice daily, painful reminder that her friend was gone and in trouble.

Once in her room, Tara began gently working her hip, knee and ankle of her broken leg hoping to get the jump on her therapy. Pain shot through her leg and her whole body would be covered in sweat from the small movements she tried to make. But she was resolved to work her leg joints an hour every day.

Careful not to put any weight on her broken leg, Tara would then hobble into the shower. After a long hot soak, she would crawl into bed. Ever since returning to The Castle, Tara was sleeping a lot longer than normal.

Tara closed her eyes. When she opened them, the bright sunlight of the Aegean replaced the black walls of her dorm room. She had been hoping her dreams would take her to the warm Greek island where she might catch a glimpse of her friend. But that night, she didn't find Léa. Instead, she found someone she had begun to hate.

Tara looked down and saw one of her long throwing knives had appeared in her hand. Looking up, she calmly walked around the pool and up to a table in the shade. A Mac laptop, a pitcher of water and a snack tray was neatly placed around the table. The author sat with his back to Tara, typing away.

In a sudden, violent motion, Tara kicked the chair out from under the author sending him sprawling to the ground. The next thing she knew, Tara saw her knee pressed against the author's chest and her knife was pressed against his throat. But the author smiled up at Tara.

"Can't kill me," he said.

"Why the fuck not," snarled Tara.

"First, this is only a dream. Second, if it's not a dream and you do kill me, you'll never be able to save your friend," he said.

After a few moments, Tara growled in frustration. She withdrew the knife from the author's throat and sat down next to him. The author sat up. A single tear had formed on one corner of one eye on Tara's face.

"You don't make people life long best friends, then fucking tear them apart like this," said Tara.

"Actually, us writers do this all the time. But I do have some good news for you," said the author.

Tara looked up angrily at the author. Her knife was still tightly clutched in her right hand. After a few moments of silence, she put the knife back into the sheath stuffed into her tactical boot.

"Okay fine. I'll bite. What's the good news?" said Tara.

"These are fun spy stories, not dystopian nightmares. Plus, I really like all of the characters in this story. Well, most them. So things will definitely turn out well for you, Léa and all the other good guys," said the author.

Tara thought a few moments. She looked up across the blue water of the pool at Léa's favorite resort. Bright Aegean sunlight twinkled in the waves in the water. Other guests were looking at her. Once they saw the fight was over, they turned back to their suntans and drinks. Tara looked longingly at the two empty beach chairs she and Léa shared at the end of their first adventure.

"You think you're pretty smart, don't you?" said Tara.

"Not really. You and Léa are about ten times smarter than I'll ever be," confessed the author.

"But it takes you so fucking long to write these things. I just can't wait over a year for my best friend to come back." said Tara.

"Then don't wait," said a voice behind Tara.

Tara suddenly turned. Kneeling beside her was her best friend. Tara's body convulsed in emotional pain as big tears appeared on her face. Léa sat down as Tara hurled herself at her best friend. Holding each other tightly, Léa felt tears forming around her own eyes. After a few minutes, Tara pulled back from her tight embrace so she could look at Léa.

"I can't stand this," said Tara.

"Me too. Maybe you should kill him after all. Then we can commandeer his computer and finish the story the way we want it to end," said Léa.

"Who said anything about ending the story?" asked the author.

Léa and Tara both looked at the author. He stood up, then picked up his chair. Reaching out with both hands, he offered to help Léa and Tara up. After a few moments of non-verbal conversation, they took his hands. A few moments after that, everyone was sitting around the table.

The author ordered a round of drinks. Léa had her usual Bailey's and coffee. Tara got a new amber ale imported from a distant corner of the world. The author got a frosty Moscow Mule. After a few moments of polite conversation about the food and brews Tara got right to the point.

"So. Dude. What the fuck?" she said.

"Yeah," said Léa.

"By now, I'm sure you both know how important you are to the story and to me. So you've gotta know things will work out," said the author.

"Important to you?" repeated Léa.

"You two have been a part of my life for more than a few years now. You're as close to me as my real world best friends are," said the author.

"Nice. But we've got to live in this world and this world isn't all that nice for us now," said Tara.

"You can't take as long to write the next story as you took on this one," said Léa.

"Sorry about that. Real world, annoying, crazy things always seem to keep popping up. But I'll be getting right to work on the next adventure," said the author.

"Just don't split us up ever again," said Tara.

"No promises," said the author.

"But our story isn't ending anytime soon?" asked Léa.

"I'm hoping for at least four more adventures right now," smiled the author.

"Any idea how we're going to rescue Léa?" asked Tara.

"Oh yeah. I've got it all worked out," said the author.

"Great. Tell me about it," said Tara.

"Okay, we're cutting you off," smiled the author.

Léa reached for Tara's glass of ale and started to slide it away. Tara grabbed it and a small game of tug a war over the beer glass began. Tara then made a grab for Léa's mug of Bailey's and coffee ending the battle over the brews.

"See how fun and amazing you two are," smiled the author.

Léa and Tara smiled at each other, then back at the author. After everything that happened, they knew this was the kind of adventure where most everything would eventually turn out okay.

"So can you at least give us some idea about what's happening next?" asked Tara.

"Well. We still have to rescue you," said the author looking at Léa. "Then, you two have to stop those nasty bad guys who want to rule the world."

"How are we going to do that?" asked Tara.

Just like at the end of their first adventure, the author reached for his laptop and typed out a few lines. He smiled at his two best friends and spun the computer around. Léa and Tara looked at the screen, then at each other.

Léa and Tara will return in …

CASTLE IN THE DESERT

"Can we at least all stay here together until you're finished writing?" asked Tara.

The author smiled and looked at Léa. She turned to her best friend and took her hand.

"Of course we can. It's your dream," said Léa.

www.ingramcontent.com/pod-product-compliance
Lightning Source LLC
Chambersburg PA
CBHW070839250626
47159CB00003B/840